the Devil's Bible

A Novel

DANA CHAMBLEE CARPENTER

PEGASUS BOOKS
NEW YORK LONDON

THE DEVIL'S BIBLE

Pegasus Books Ltd.
148 W 37th Street, 13th Floor
New York, NY 10018

Copyright © 2017 Dana Chamblee Carpenter

First Pegasus Books edition March 2017

Interior design by Maria Fernandez

Library of Congress Cataloging-in-Publication Data is available.

ISBN: 978-1-68177-337-7

10 9 8 7 6 5 4 3 2 1

Printed in the United States of America
Distributed by W. W. Norton & Company

For Jim, Shane, and Beth:
anchors in the tempests,
wings to help me soar.

Part One

The strongest and the fiercest spirit

That fought in heaven, now fiercer by despair.

—*Paradise Lost*, Book II, Lines 44–45

PROLOGUE

AVIGNON, 1236

It happened like the others, sweat and blood, screaming, and then—disappointment.

"I am very sorry," the doctor mumbled as he wiped his hands on the sheets between the woman's legs.

The father thought about snapping the doctor's neck. He had done that once before. But the sting of failure cooled his rage. He had no one to blame but himself and the woman, and she would be dead soon anyway. Now it was just a matter of ridding himself of the unfortunate outcome. He had no need of a girl.

He watched as the nurse lowered the baby into the arms of the woman lying twisted among bedcoverings soaked with blood and afterbirth. She lifted her breast and teased the infant's lips with her nipple until, mewling with hunger, it opened its mouth and latched on to suck. The mother whispered a lullaby: *"On t'aime, ma petite. On t'aime. Le bon Dieu, au ciel, t'aime. On t'aime, ma petite. On t'aime. Ta mère, à jamais, t'aime."*

The father cocked his head in confusion at the tender moment. Compelled by a craving to understand this intimacy that was so alien to him, he took a step toward the bed.

"Like the others, my lord," the doctor interrupted. "A girl. But this one is alive. Shall I dispose of it?" He smirked with self-importance.

The father turned swiftly, his arm snaking from underneath the cloak and closing around the doctor's neck. His claws sank into the doctor's flesh. When he snatched his arm back, he held the doctor's ragged and bloody throat in his hand. He flung the bits of shattered cartilage as he pivoted back toward the bed.

The mother lay dead.

The nurse and the infant were gone.

The father moved to the open door and listened for the sounds that would expose them; he heard nothing but a peal of thunder as it found its way down the alley. He sniffed the air to catch their scent, but the rain muted everything and mingled smells together like soup. He knew he would not be able to track them.

"Unexpected," he whispered.

This girl—this disappointment—would live. For now. He needed to turn his thoughts toward his next conquest—the one that would profit him a son. He took the edge of his cloak and pulled it over his shoulder, folding himself into the blackness of the night.

Cowering in the deeper dark of a bend in the alley not far past the still gaping door, the nurse laid her face gently against the baby's head, silently pleading: *Don't make a sound. Be quiet. Quiet as a little mouse.*

CHAPTER ONE

The cicadas were singing in the early afternoon. Their rhythmic ditty mingled with the soft sweetness of the just-blooming magnolias and the warm sunshine. Mouse breathed in air that was full of the promise of the coming summer.

She'd just turned in final grades, and, starting tomorrow, the days would be hers to do with as she pleased. Mouse started to smile at the thought but caught herself. A smile opened the door for happiness, for joy, and she wasn't quite ready for that. Not yet. She sighed instead as she turned down the sidewalk toward the student center and her last task of the semester: the history department's end-of-year lecture and reception.

Typically she found some excuse to get out of such public and social gatherings, but the chair of the department, Dr. Williams, had stopped by Mouse's office that morning and made it clear that attendance was mandatory for anyone who wanted to keep her job. And Mouse very much wanted to keep teaching. She struggled with one-on-one interactions with students and colleagues, but, in the classroom, she felt almost normal.

She yanked at the outer door of the student center, shivering at the blast of too-cold, air-conditioned air as she stepped into the crowded lobby. Offering the curt nods of necessary acknowledgement, she made her way to the table lined with name tags and programs. She grabbed hers and headed to the auditorium where there would be a little more breathing room. Mouse didn't do close spaces and crowds. The onslaught of perfumes and colognes, the hundreds of disparate chatters and bodies pressing past triggered her claustrophobia.

Even as a child, Mouse had never liked small spaces, though once upon a time she had enjoyed being among people, especially at parties where she could listen to the music and dance. But not anymore. Now, even at a professional gathering like this one, the pats on the back and the casual hugs, the bits of gossip shared, people saving seats for each other—it all reminded Mouse of how isolated she really was. How different. And how dangerous.

Mouse kept to the back of the auditorium, leaning against the wall near the doors. She kept her eyes on the speckled carpet at her feet and counted the ratio of black specks to white to gray. It was a trick Father Lucas, her childhood mentor, had taught her when she needed to control her emotions—filling her mind with something monotonous and mundane worked like a sedative. Mostly it was her temper she wrestled with back in those days, but now she counted to shut out the world. All of it, all the time. No joy; no despair. No love; no anger. Feel nothing. It was safer that way—safer for her and for everyone else.

The houselights dimmed, tossing a blanket of darkness on everyone in the auditorium, and the people grew quiet.

"I'd like to welcome you all to this year's Burns History Lecture." As Dr. Williams meandered through the obligatory flattery of deans and other administrators, Mouse realized she had no idea who this year's guest lecturer was. She looked down at the program, but it was too dark to read. As Dr. Williams rattled off the highlights of the yet-unnamed lecturer's resume, degrees, and publications, Mouse could hear a hint of disapproval in his voice. Something pinged in the back of her mind, a quiet early warning.

"Please join me in welcoming our distinguished guest, Dr. Jack Gray." The crowd offered polite applause.

Mouse looked up sharply and then her shoulders sagged. She knew the young man who stepped out onto the stage, but the last thing she needed was to deal with a complication from her past.

She could tell Jack Gray was fighting back a chuckle as he leaned into the microphone. "Thank you for that *warm* welcome, Dr. Williams." He shoved a hand into his jeans pocket and ran the other through his hair. Mouse pressed herself against the brick wall at her back. Jack hadn't changed much since she'd last seen him.

Mouse had occasionally run into former students at conferences over the years, but after the initial awkwardness—"Oh my, you haven't changed a bit. I'm sure you don't remember me, but I was in your class"— Mouse had simply avoided more contact by shunning the conference dinners and receptions, slipping in late to panels and leaving early. She would secretly give herself a moment of pleasure to hear that her students were doing well and remembered her fondly, but she couldn't afford long-term relationships and so kept her distance.

Jack Gray was different though. She'd made a mistake with him.

"I'm beginning to question the sincerity of your Southern hospitality," he said to the audience. "Because despite the very polite smiles and kind inquiries about my flight, I have the impression that some of my fellow historians may have invited me here under duress." He let the chuckle bubble out this time. Jack Gray had always been very sure of himself. He threw his hands up in mock surrender. "But that's okay. Believe me, I understand. My academic pedigree isn't nearly as long or prestigious as most of yours, and, of course, there's the issue of my subject matter."

The title slide of his presentation flared to life on the screen behind him. It was a picture of his just-published book: *Who Wrote the Devil's Bible?* Mouse pressed harder against the back wall of the auditorium and dug her fingers into the spaces between the bricks, the rough edges of the stone cutting into her cuticles.

She thought she had left Jack Gray several states and thirteen years away. Maybe his coming here was coincidence. Maybe he didn't even know she was here. It was certainly not surprising that he'd been researching the Devil's Bible; he'd been doing the same when she saw him last. It was why she had left. She'd hoped that her absence would cause him to lose interest, but clearly he had continued his work. She wondered how much he had learned since then. How dangerous was he?

"We scholars like to call it the Codex Gigas—literally, 'giant book,'" he said as he flicked the slide to show the cover of the ancient text. "A nice, safe, and scientific title based on what we think we know about it. It was the biggest book of the Middle Ages and compiled the most important historical and religious documents of its time. It was once considered an eighth wonder of the world. Giant, indeed. Monumental, even. There is simply no other book like it in the world—not then, not now." Mouse could hear the fervor in his voice, and she didn't like it.

"And yet we know so little about it. Where was it scripted? What happened to the legendary missing pages? Who took them? And why? We haven't even answered the most basic mystery of all: Who wrote it?" He paced as he spoke, then stopped, center stage, and clicked the projector remote. A distorted, horned beast, clothed only in an ermine loincloth, split-tongue flickering and clawed hands raised, now loomed on the screen.

"Was it *the* Devil, as legend claims?" Jack Gray spoke in a mock horror movie voice, and his audience laughed with him. "Did poor Herman the monk, walled up in his cell, eventually admit the impossibility of his penitent task—to write a single book containing all the world's knowledge—and call on Satan to rescue him?"

Mouse could feel the anxiety building, like bugs crawling in her chest, and her mouth had gone dry. But she couldn't leave until she knew what Jack knew.

"Of course, it wasn't some demonic conspiracy any more than it was ancient aliens," Jack Gray scoffed. "But we've let the myths work their magic on us all the same. Like some bogeyman, they've scared us off of doing real, academic study of this magnificent medieval manuscript. Surely it's not the *Devil's* Bible, but in order to put that ridiculousness to rest, we must answer the question—who really wrote the Codex Gigas?"

Dr. Gray clicked the slide again, revealing a series of ampersands and minims that Mouse recognized all too well. The graphs of the handwriting samples, all measured and ruled, were a stark contrast to the previous portrait of Satan, and the stuffy room sighed with relief to be returned to the mundane and knowable facts of their field. Even Mouse felt her tension uncoil a little. This wasn't about her. This was simple, academic inquiry, an extension of the project he'd started in her class at Chapel Hill thirteen years ago. He probably didn't even remember their conversation.

But Mouse remembered. He had come to talk to her about the paper he was writing for her class, a paper about the Devil's Bible.

"It's called the Codex Gigas, Jack. And it's not worth your time," she had answered.

"I know *you're* not interested in it. You didn't even talk about it in class. But I'm fascinated with it."

"Why?"

"It's shrouded in mystery. No one knows who wrote it or even where it was written."

"It was written at Podlažice monastery."

He cocked his head. "Nobody believes that. All the sources I've read say that monastery was way too small to be able to make a book like the Devil's Bible."

"That's just academic prejudice, Jack. They take what they know about other ancient books and assume that a small, insignificant monastery like Podlažice wouldn't have monks with the education or the ambition to script a book like the Codex Gigas, much less have access to high quality parchment or inks or gold leaf." Mouse sighed. "So because it doesn't fit their expectations, scholars can't accept the fact that it was written at Podlažice."

"The *fact* that it was written at Podlažice?" He leaned forward onto her desk. "How can you be so sure?"

Mouse had replayed this scenario in her head a hundred times in thirteen years, not because she could undo it, but to remind herself that, despite her discipline, she could still screw up. If she had just swallowed her ego and brushed him off, claiming that it was only her opinion and that she was probably wrong, Jack might have forgotten all about it. But she had lied instead. "I read something about it by another scholar, a specialist in ancient books, if I remember correctly," she said. "He believed the book was written at Podlažice."

Jack Gray's follow-up was predictable, something she should have easily anticipated. "Oh, what was his name? I'd like to take a look at the article."

And so she had to lie again. "I don't remember."

Mouse never forgot anything. It was one of the "gifts" inherited from her father—abilities that she considered curses, abilities that made her anything but normal. She remembered everything: what she and Jack had been wearing that day, what music had been playing on her laptop, the exact order of the books on the shelves against the wall of her office behind Jack's head. And she remembered the arrogant surety in her voice when she told him the Devil's Bible had been written at Podlažice. She had left no room for doubt.

But though she might remember it all, she doubted that Jack did. He had pestered her for the rest of the semester to give him the name of the article she'd read. He was clearly hooked by the mysteries of the Devil's Bible, but she had dismissed his persistence as the act of a student trying to prove himself. She'd left Chapel Hill because she thought it was the safest way to avoid more contact with him, not because she thought she was in any real danger. That's what she did anytime there was a hint of trouble or inconvenience—she ran.

Not far enough, she thought now, as Jack Gray's voice brought her attention back to the stage.

"The distinctive script marks on the screen are unique to this writer, like a thumbprint. We know the writer scripts differently than a typical scribe of the time, and yet, we've always insisted that he must be a monk."

Mouse wondered where he was going with this.

"But my study of these marks leads me to believe that we've been very wrong in our assumptions. I don't think he was a monk at all. Clearly the writer had an uncommon education and was quite an artist—which is even more rare for the time and place. So I think it's fair to conclude that we're talking about someone of worth, perhaps a member of the nobility."

Mouse couldn't help but smile a little. Jack was so close yet so wrong.

"As a scholar, I wasn't satisfied with what we thought we knew, and, thanks to a generous grant from a patron who wishes to remain anonymous, I was able to obtain access to the Codex with a team of specialists and their cutting-edge technology. Our analysis of script style, size, and, most significantly, measurements of the pressure of the writer's hand on the page based on the depth of indentation in the parchment, suggests that our writer is . . . a woman."

The joy Jack Gray took in the communal gasp from the audience played on his face. In the back of the room, Mouse had gone completely still.

"Now, before I walk you through the basics of the study, I want to take a moment to thank a mentor. Had it not been for her wisdom in challenging me to think outside the box of conventional medieval scholarship, I wouldn't be here today." Jack smiled. "She's actually now one of your own, and I'm pretty sure I saw her in the audience earlier. Please join me in thanking Dr. Emma Nicholas." He pointed toward the back of the room and began clapping. Everyone turned, squinting against the projector light into the darkness of the back wall, staring at Mouse.

She had spent her life trying to be invisible and now hundreds of people were staring at her, waiting. She couldn't breathe, and the reflection of the stage lights started to pulse at the edges of her vision. As Mouse lowered her head, she saw the lanyard hanging around her neck: EMMA NICHOLAS. All these people were staring at Emma Nicholas, she reminded herself, not at her. Not at Mouse. She had held plenty of titles over the years—most recently Assistant Professor—but in her mind, she was always just Mouse. No one had ever given her a proper name. But society seemed to demand something more substantial than "small rodent" for applications to graduate school, passports, and name tags, so she had invented "Emma Nicholas"—a name borrowed from people she had once belonged to, who had once belonged to her.

That had been a long time ago. Now, no one knew her as Mouse. No one knew her at all. And it had to stay that way.

She cut her eyes up to Jack Gray, who was no longer clapping. He leaned against the podium, smirking, and Mouse understood that he meant this as his first salvo.

Well, she'd done battle before and with far more dangerous opponents.

She pulled her head up, smiled, gave a quick nod, and raised her hand to acknowledge the still-applauding audience. She waited until they turned their attention back to Jack, who had begun to explain the science behind the technology used in his research. Then Mouse slipped quickly and silently out the door.

○—┼—○

Mouse bounced her leg against the stool as she sat with her back to the door of the pub. She had already counted the pavers in the student center lobby and then her steps up to the third floor, but nothing was working to slip her back into that impassive state she needed. Her heart was still thumping, and she could feel the heat of embarrassment in her face, fueled by a growing anger.

THE DEVIL'S BIBLE

"Know the score?" Jack Gray asked as he leaned into her, tossing her the note she'd left for him with the attendant at the book-signing table.

Mouse turned and saw the disappointment in his face. He'd thought he'd get the jump on her, slipping up from behind, but she wouldn't be caught unaware again. She had smelled him as soon as he walked in the door. Heightened senses were another gift from her father, and for once she was appreciative of the advantage they offered. She meant to put an end to whatever game Jack was playing.

He sat on the stool next to hers and nodded to the television over the bar. "Who's winning?"

"It's top of the seventh. Sox down three to two. Yanks with two in scoring position. One out. Three-one count on the hitter," she said.

"You a fan?"

"No."

In addition to the announcer's play-by-play, Mouse could have repeated the healthcare stats one of the talking heads had just rattled off on the flat screen at the back of the pub. She could have also told him that two professors from the art department sitting at the table behind her were refinancing their house. Mouse knew the names of the loan officers they were considering, the appraisals they'd gotten, the interest rates, the mortgage payments—everything. She hadn't meant to eavesdrop; her brain just worked that way. She heard everything, saw everything.

It was exhausting, but Mouse had no control over most of her inherited abilities—the perfect memory, heightened senses, and acute perception were just part of her, like the color of her eyes. She couldn't turn them off any more than she could tell her heart to stop beating. But Mouse had other, darker powers, too, that were part of her father's legacy. Powers that scared her. Powers she lulled to sleep by keeping herself emotionally flat, like a self-inflicted lobotomy. The counting usually helped. But not tonight.

Jack pulled his stool closer to hers and gave her an appreciative once-over. "My God, you haven't changed a bit."

"You neither." Mouse didn't like the awe she heard in his voice or the flare of temper it evoked in her.

"No, I've got a bit of gray coming up in the stubble now, but you, my God . . ." He whistled, soft and low. "Did you know I had a massive crush on you back then?" He laughed. "It wasn't just me. All the guys, even some of the girls, thought you were—"

"What do you want, Jack?"

"Still as cold as ever, I see." He took a long swig from his beer. "Maybe I want you to go back to my hotel with me."

Mouse listened for a lie, some skip of his heart or catch in his breath, but she heard none. "You came all the way to Nashville to get me in bed?" she scoffed.

"God, no. I came to sell books." This time, Mouse heard something— not quite a lie, but certainly not the whole truth. "Did you read it?" He nodded at Mouse's copy of *Who Wrote the Devil's Bible?* on the bar.

"Of course." Mouse had read the book while she waited out the lecture and reception; three hundred pages in an hour came easily to her. His ideas were sound, but the computer process he used on the script was too theoretical, and his other research was surprisingly shoddy. No one would take him seriously. And he'd made no mention of her. Mouse had nothing to worry about from his book. Jack himself was a different matter, however. Something wasn't right with him.

"What'd you think?" he asked, his words starting to slur. He'd clearly had plenty to drink at the post-lecture reception.

"Too much conjecture," Mouse answered.

"Glad Cambridge Press didn't agree with you." His voice dripped with booze and disdain.

"How'd you manage to convince them to give you a book deal?" Mouse kept her question casual, biting back an urge she hadn't felt for a long time—the desire to *make* him tell her what she wanted to know.

She could do it. She had compelled people before—another "gift" from her father. The first time had been when she was just a girl and a local boy had tried to force himself on her. She'd screamed at him to go away. He had turned on his heel, his pants still unfastened, and walked out of town. He never came back. Compelling someone like that tapped into Mouse's darker powers, which she swore she would never use again, not on purpose. All the discipline she relentlessly practiced—the counting, the isolation, never letting herself feel anything—were her safeguards against accidentally using that power.

Mouse ran her finger through the water rings on the bar, trying to quench her emotions, and asked again, "So how'd you do it?"

"Friends in high places," Jack said.

"We should all be so lucky." She took a slow drink. "Want to introduce us?"

"Actually, I think he might like that."

Mouse put the glass on the bar and swallowed the sense of urgency that was now running through her. "He?"

Clearly, Jack Gray had come with an agenda—but maybe it was not his own. Getting Jack access to the Devil's Bible, encouraging his theories, convincing the oldest publishing house in the world to print his sham of a book, sending him to the most prestigious history lectureship—it was the sort of game her father might play, toying with his prey from a safe distance before swooping in to make the kill. Had he sent Jack to draw her out?

Mouse spun to look out over the rest of the room, scanning the growing crowd of patrons. If her father was Jack's benefactor, then he knew where she was. And it was time to get out. Now.

"So what's the name of your friend in high places?" she asked quietly as her eyes darted from face to face, looking for signs of her father.

"I don't think you'd know him."

"Come on, Jack. Tell me who he is."

She realized her mistake instantly—she hadn't asked Jack a question. She'd told him what to do. Her hand shot up to her mouth, but it was too late. Jack Gray's eyes went blank, as if he'd stepped away from his body.

Mouse hadn't meant to lace the words with power; she hadn't meant to make them a command. But it wasn't the first time the power had snaked through her lips of its own will and beyond her control. It's what happened when she allowed herself any real emotion—joy, despair, anger, fear. The power woke and broke free of her. She watched in horror as Jack's mouth worked to answer her like a puppet obeying its master, and she thought bitterly about the last time she'd lost control.

In her mind, she could hear the remembered sounds of battle—screaming horses and squealing swords. She sat in the midst of it all as war raged like violent eddies swirling around her. She was back at the battle of Marchfeld, seven hundred years ago. And in her blood-soaked lap lay Ottakar, the only man she had ever loved, the father of her child. His face was shiny with sweat and dirty from the battlefield. Mouse stroked the hair curling across his forehead and moved her other hand toward his chest in a vain attempt to staunch the blood gurgling out with the slowing rhythm of his heartbeat. There were too many wounds, too much blood. She had saved the lives of hundreds in the march to war, but she could do nothing to save him. This one. Hers. He was beyond even the healing she could do. The pain of letting him go scorched her throat, and she wept as she bent down to kiss him. This was God's choice, not hers, but she did not have to let Ottakar suffer.

"Go now," she had told him. "Die," she said, the command meant as an act of mercy for him alone.

But they all had. Every soldier on that battlefield, dead. Ten thousand souls.

In her grief, she had lost control and her power had spilled out, killing every living thing around her. She'd lost everything that day. Ottakar. Her son. Her humanity.

Every day since, for seven hundred years, Mouse had paid penance for that moment. She supposed some would envy her immortality, but to Mouse it was the worst of her father's inheritance. To be forever alone.

To forever bear the guilt of what she'd done. She'd sworn then that she would never use her power again, that she would never kill again.

Despite that vow, Mouse knew there would be no reconciliation for her. She'd gone looking for it once after Marchfeld—at Podlažice monastery seven centuries ago.

But Mouse hadn't found reconciliation. She had found her father instead.

Podlažice Monastery,
Bohemia
1278

"In the beginning."

They were her father's first words to her. They dropped like stones into the silence of Mouse's tiny cell in the monastery just outside Podlažice.

The monks had found her at the monastery pond. She had been dressed in a habit, her head shaved and her breasts wrapped, so they had thought her one of them and took her in. So weak she could barely move, her bones jutting under paper-thin skin, the monks had also thought she would be dead by morning. They were wrong.

Mouse knew that death would not come for her. She had tried to kill herself several times after the battle at Marchfeld but to no avail. The sweet sleep of death would claim her only for a little while and then she would wake again. And so she learned about the last of her father's gifts: immortality. It had driven her to the monastery where she hoped to pose as a monk and claim the rights of *inclusus*—to be walled up in a cell where she could not hurt anyone else and where she might eventually waste away to nothing. It was the only hope left to her.

The Brothers had asked for her name when they performed last rites. She told them to call her Herman—a German word for soldier. She thought it fit, as she now carried the guilt for each of the thousands of soldiers she'd killed at Marchfeld.

When she was still alive the next morning, the Brothers called it a miracle. Mouse leveraged their awe to demand an audience with the abbot, Bishop Andreas, and she bartered with him to grant her *inclusus*. She promised she would script a book in exchange for being closed up and left alone. She promised the book would be a wonder, full of the world's knowledge. Bishop Andreas thought it an act of penitence. But Mouse did not seek to be shut away from the world in hope of the forgiveness of her sins. Mouse could never be forgiven for what she'd done or for what she was. She just didn't want to hurt anyone else.

As the last stone slid into place, squealing against the mortar and shutting out the light, Mouse pulled the candlestick closer and bent over the blank parchment on the floor. The sooner she finished the book, the sooner Bishop Andreas would leave her alone. Mouse had just pinched her fingers around the quill when she heard someone behind her.

"In the beginning." The voice was light, teasing.

Mouse spun around. "Who is there?"

There was no place in the bare cell for a man to hide himself, and no way in or out. Even in the dim candlelight, Mouse could see that she was indeed alone, and yet it was a man's voice she heard inside the closed-in space with her.

"Greetings, daughter. I thought it was time we met."

Sudden rage erupted in Mouse. She had never met her father, but she had cause to hate him anyway. He was the root of all the evil in her life—the source of all the uncanny power that had marked her as different and made her an outcast. Everyone she had ever loved had been hurt because of her connection to him, because of the taint of her father's blood. And Marchfeld had proven that she was more monster than human—all because of him.

Her father laughed softly as he leaned forward through the wall; such a wall was no boundary to one like him. He took a single cautious step beyond the dark to make himself seen.

That was a mistake.

Mouse threw herself at him with such quick, animal-like abandon that he barely had time to pull himself back into the shadows. Her fingers raked his cheek. But despite her violent intentions, only the soft rounds of her fingers slid gently along his face as he drew back—a caress whether she meant it to be or not. He could not remember the last time someone had touched him gently.

He heard her screams as she beat against the wall where he had disappeared, but he could make no sense of her garbled words. He lifted his hand to his cheek and slipped farther back into the darkness to think about his next move.

He contemplated killing her. It was what he meant to do all those years ago at her birth. But then he had forgotten about her. Well, not really forgotten because he never forgot anything, but he considered her to be of no value and so never gave her another thought. Until Marchfeld. The strength of her power had called to him, and he'd come in time to see the men and horses drop where they stood but too late to see how she had accomplished it.

It was unexpected. He lifted his hand to his cheek once more; there was much he hadn't expected.

He had followed her all those long days after Marchfeld as she wandered the countryside. He had watched her kill herself over and over again. The first had happened too quickly for him to intervene as she

20

ran the sword across her throat on the battlefield, surrounded by the death she had caused. He had thought her gone and screamed in rage at his unanswered questions. The devastation at Marchfeld had shocked even him, and knowing that the scope of it was beyond his own unsettled him. He could whisper his wishes in the ear of a man and make it so, but how had this girl worked the strings of two armies and silenced a horde at her whim? He wanted answers.

For hours he had knelt beside her body in the bloody mud, shooing away scavengers. And when he saw the sliced skin at her neck knit itself closed and heard her first, raspy breath, relief settled on him. It gave way quickly to fear and desire. Desire he wore comfortably as he toyed with all he might do with her, but the fear pricked at him and made him slip back into the mist at the edge of the battlefield. Unsure of himself for the first time in a very long while, he had followed her at a distance, followed her to this monastery.

He tethered himself now in patience. He could wait for the answers he wanted.

❦

"Brother Herman!" the man yelled outside Mouse's cell. "It is Bishop Andreas! Answer me!"

Reluctantly, Mouse looked up from the page. Her vision was blurry. Her eyes had grown so accustomed to staring at letters just inches away that they couldn't focus on anything at a distance. She caught a glint of gold at the small opening in the wall along the floor in the far corner. For the first time, she noticed the cups of wine and bowls of soured stew jumbled around the opening. The rats were at them. How many days had she been walled up? Had it been weeks? She only counted the passing of time by burned-out candles and finished pages. The work was everything. It was all she had to keep the grief at bay and to keep the claustrophobic panic from consuming her.

"Brother Herman! Tell me you are working on my book!"

Mouse's sight cleared, and she saw the bishop's gold embroidered robes and his wiry chin pressed close to the floor on the other side of the bowls and cups.

"I swear to you that if you give me no answer, I will tear down this wall brick by brick and expose whatever sins you are trying to hide."

"I am here." Her voice cracked with disuse.

The bishop sighed. "You are still alive then. You are working on my book?"

"Yes."

"Good. But you must eat. You must live long enough to give me my book." The rats scattered as his hand snaked through the slot and pulled out the old food and drink and shoved fresh ones in their place. "Eat," he commanded again as he left. "Drink."

Mouse felt empty—her body sore and limp, her mind and spirit drained. She had no will of her own and so she did as she was told. She dragged herself to the bowl and took up handfuls of food and crammed them in her mouth.

She did not see her father watching from the darkness in the corner behind her—watching as she took a swig of wine, watching as she wiped her soiled fingers on her habit, watching as she inched back toward the parchment that lay in neat stacks beside a row of ink jars against the far wall.

Even the momentary distraction, just a few minutes' break from the work, ran like fissures in Mouse's dam against the grief and panic. She grabbed at the small knife she used to sharpen the goose-feather quills when they dulled, and she sliced it savagely down one side of the quill and then the other. She dropped the knife to the floor and dipped the sharp quill into the ink and set to work again, but her hand was shaking and the tears made it difficult to see.

She was scripting one of the alphabets in the old style she had learned from Father Lucas at Teplá Abbey when she was a girl. As her hand formed the letters, her mind flooded with memories of the two of them reading together. She closed her eyes at the remembered smells of him—a mustiness like earth, the sharp scent of ink, and the softness of incense that lingered in his hair—and then grief washed over her. Father Lucas had raised her, protected her. He had loved her. And he had died a violent death, tortured—by whom she did not know—for keeping her secrets. His was another name to add to the list of victims who had suffered because of her.

Mouse bent down, weeping, her head resting against the parchment.

In the shadows at her back, her father cocked his head, studying her.

Mouse sat up again and looked down at the ruined parchment, the letters badly made in her shaky hand, the ink smeared where she had rested her head. Shame and anger at all she had lost overcame her, and she tore furiously at the page.

Her father could feel the power waking in Mouse, and he sighed.

She went still like a stone.

He tensed as she turned her head so slowly that he could hear the crackle and grind of the twisting vertebrae in her neck until finally she looked at him over her shoulder. In that one visible eye he saw so much hate that it made him giddy. And afraid.

What could this girl do?

"I know who you are," Mouse said. "Though you do not look as I expected."

Her father lifted his hand to his mouth, elbow propped on his bent knee as he considered how to answer her. He opted for another tease. "No screaming at a man who magically appears in your walled up cell? What manner of creature are you? Surely not just a girl."

He was rewarded as Mouse's temper flared, but then he sensed the power rising in her. As she spun toward him, he stood quickly and took a step back toward the dark corner.

Mouse sneered at his fear, but she moved no closer. She just watched him as he leaned against the wall, his arms wrapped around his chest. He wore a monk's habit—a godly man by fraud, just like her. He appeared to be maybe thirty years old and had long, black, wavy hair that framed his pale face and curled around his neck. He was handsome, but unremarkably so, with the exception of large eyes so dark that Mouse could see no pupils. She had to make herself look away, turning her focus instead to how he held himself, trying to assess his weaknesses, to anticipate how he would move, just as she did with any enemy.

But she could not read him. As she wrapped her hand around the hilt of the knife on the floor at her heel, she wondered if he could read her. Then she lunged.

He was laughing already when he caught her wrist, twisting it until she cried out and dropped the knife. He pulled her close to his chest, his mouth at her ear. "So you would kill me, too? Like those men on the battlefield?"

He felt her go stiff.

"Like . . ." He paused as he let his own consciousness slip inside hers, as he searched for the names that would cause her the most pain. "Like Ottakar? Ah, like Nicholas."

He expected wrath. But at the sound of her son's name, Mouse went limp in his arms. The grief she'd been holding off came crashing down on her, and she broke.

Her father caught her tenderly and then lowered her carefully down to the pallet. Gently, he wiped the stain of ink from her forehead where she had rested it against the parchment. It looked too much like the mark of the cross from a Lenten service.

"No return to dust, no, nor penance either. Not for us," he muttered.

He stayed with her until her body finally relaxed into a normal sleep. As he ran his fingers softly across her cheek, he wondered if she would dream.

CHAPTER TWO

The ghosts in Mouse's head and the noises in the pub melted into a buzz of background din as a slack-jawed Jack Gray robotically answered her command.

"I don't know who my benefactor is. I don't know who he is. I don't—"

"Stop!" Mouse said as she stood, her face flushed with shame. She would not willingly use her control over him. "I release you," she whispered as she leaned in close and imagined herself pulling in the power like a long, slow inhale.

In an instant, Jack straightened and reached for his beer on the bar. "Sorry, I think I zoned out there for a minute." His voice still sounded hollow and Mouse could see the confusion in his eyes, but he was himself again. "So did you change your mind about coming back to my hotel?"

Mouse didn't trust herself to speak any more. She grabbed her bag and ran out of the bar. It was early evening still, the sun not yet set. The cicadas' song that earlier had sounded like soft summer promises now built to a fever pitch with thousands of them screaming as she stepped under the canopy of trees. The natural rise and fall of their call sounded like an alarm. It was time for her to go.

At first, when Mouse fled Podlažice all those years ago, she would only stay in a place for a few days at a time. Afraid that her father might catch up to her, she'd move on to the next town and then the next and the next. For years, she bounced like a skipped stone across Europe and Asia until, eventually, exhaustion forced her to stay put for longer. As weeks went by with no sign of her father, Mouse grew confident in her ability to hide. But she also learned that settling somewhere offered its own set of dangers.

People in the villages wore the passing seasons etched on their faces, but Mouse never aged. Disease came to the cities, but she never got sick. Even without using her power, she was unnatural in a way that she could disguise only for a little while. And people didn't like what they couldn't understand. So Mouse learned to read the signs and sense when it was time to move on. It was like having a timer in her head ticking down the seconds until the bomb went off.

She looked up now at the undersides of the May leaves that writhed with the brood of hungry insects. It was a plague year in Nashville, the culmination of a thirteen-year cycle when thousands of cicadas emerged all at once, eating everything young and green. It had been a plague year when she first came here.

Thirteen years. Mouse shook her head. Not since her childhood had she lived in the same place for so long—never long enough to get comfortable, to belong, never long enough for a place to begin to feel like home. But here she was, settled in Nashville with a house and acquaintances if not friends. She'd even applied for tenure. Seven or eight years ago, when that alarm in her head had gone off telling her it was time to leave, she had written her letter of resignation, but she never sent it. She pulled it up on her laptop every day and thought about sending it to Dr. Williams, but every day, Mouse stubbornly made the decision to ignore that ticking clock in her head. She liked Nashville, and she was tired of running. So she stayed. And things had been quiet. Until now.

Other night screamers had joined the insect cacophony. Mouse could hear each one of them, each cricket, each cicada, each of the million mosquitos who'd come early this year to claim their blood. They gave voice to Mouse's mood—a nagging worry about Jack Gray's benefactor and an angry buzz at her own lack of discipline that led to her accidental use of power. None of this would have happened if she hadn't stayed so long. She was already gambling against anyone noticing that she hadn't aged. A person could only be a youthful thirtysomething for so long even in modern times. If she had stuck to her pattern, moved on, and started over with a new job and no strings, she wouldn't have run into Jack, and she wouldn't have let her guard down.

Clenching her hands with anger and resolve, Mouse matched her step to the rhythm of the bug-song and turned toward home, counting the beats as she worked to build her wall again. She typically kept her life precisely controlled, measured like some Confucian ritual. She knew exactly how many heartbeats would carry her from her house to Wilson Hall in the center of campus and how many breaths would take her up the two flights of stairs to her office. It had been the same, day after day, for years. But the longer Mouse stayed, the more she wanted the normal life she saw around her. Lately, she'd been letting go of the routine, trying to convince herself that she could have what she wanted—that she could be like everyone else.

"Hello, Em."

Mouse jumped. Her eight-year-old neighbor was standing near the sidewalk still half-obscured by the overgrown hedges. She had walked past him without seeing him, something that never happened when she was being diligent. Frustrated at her carelessness, she spun around. The joy in the boy's face bounced all along his body and trickled out in little, quiet giggles; it was contagious. Mouse felt it wash over her like warm water. She knelt beside him, smiling.

"Give a person a warning next time, kid," she said as she tapped him gently on the nose. She spoke at nearly a whisper, carefully measured to be sure none of her power was leaking into her words, but some part of her relaxed a little as she looked into her young neighbor's big blue eyes.

Nate was part of the unexpected that had been happening to Mouse lately, one of the chinks in her armor. His family had moved in about six months ago, and, as usual, Mouse had kept her distance. She overheard Nate's mom complain about her being rude, not that it mattered much to Mouse. She didn't have to worry about mobs with pitchforks or witch trials or Inquisitions anymore, just people judging her for being different. She'd heard several of her colleagues speculating about whether or not she had Asperger's or OCD. Apparently her rigid routine had not gone unnoticed. But to Mouse's ear, these were all just different labels for odd. She'd been given many over her lifetime, most often *witch* or *angel*. No one used those much anymore.

But Nate didn't care that she was odd. He had quickly learned her routine, and almost every afternoon, he was waiting for her, hiding and trying to catch her off guard. For the first week, Mouse had ignored him. But he reminded her of her own little boy, her own little Nicholas, and Nate's quiet, sure acceptance of her drew her in. So they played their game—Nate jumping out and Mouse pretending to be startled.

"I really got you that time!" he squealed now.

"You bet you did," she answered, then asked the question she always asked. "Wind at your back, Nate?"

"Not today, Em," Nate said with a sigh as he sat down heavily on the grass beside the sidewalk.

"Have you found trouble then?" she asked. In her conversations with Nate, Mouse had found herself echoing Father Lucas—even his gentle cadence and soft tone seeped into her words, like his voice come alive again. Nate was struggling and Mouse wanted to help. It was the first time in a long time that she felt as if she had something to offer—hope in the darkness, Father Lucas would have said.

"It's found me," Nate answered.

"Uh-oh." Mouse lowered herself to sit beside him. "Want to talk about it?" Nate's mom had given birth to a little sister less than a month ago, and Nate was having a tough time adjusting.

"Not really. You want to draw with me?"

"Sure." Mouse didn't need him to tell her that he was lonely. His mom was busy with the baby. His dad worked away from home for months at a time. And Nate needed someone to make time just for him. Mouse would give anything to have a life like that—normal problems and normal joys.

Nate handed over some sticks of his colored chalk. "Let's fill the whole sidewalk from your house to mine with pictures!"

"You bet." Mouse propped her bag against the hedge.

They raced the coming twilight as they drew, Nate chatting nonstop as she listened attentively and asked all the right questions—just as Father Lucas had when Mouse was a girl. Except she and Father Lucas had chatted over ancient books and illuminations, not sidewalk art, and they had talked about philosophy and theology rather than video games and Lego sets.

As the streetlights buzzed and popped to life, Nate's mom strolled down the driveway. "Oh my goodness!"

Nate jumped, but Mouse had heard her coming.

"Mom! Give a kid a warning next time!" he said, smiling over at Mouse before he hopped up, excited to show off his art. "What do you think?" he asked his mother.

"I think you've taken up a lot of Dr. Nicholas's time." She said it gently and with a smile, but Mouse turned to Nate and saw the joy darken just a little.

Mouse shoved herself back onto her heels. "Actually, it was all my idea, and Nate was kind enough to let me use his chalk. I haven't had this much fun in a long time." She looked down at the row of brightly colored drawings. Nate's butterflies and flowers, cats and bugs of all kinds alternated with Mouse's—a field full of hyacinths, an outline of Prague Castle, a wolf, a mother bent over her toddling son. Mouse felt the heat of emotion building in her chest again. She needed to get home.

"Do you have children?" Nate's mother asked.

Mouse shook her head but kept her eyes on her drawing. *Not anymore*, she thought.

"Well, the drawings are beautiful. Thank you for playing with Nate."

"Em and I weren't playing, Mom. We were doing *art*."

"It's 'Dr. Nicholas,' Nate. We've talked about how to speak to adults, right?" She shifted the baby in her arms. "I'm sorry, Dr. Nicholas."

Mouse ignored her. "Want to help me gather up the chalk, Nate?"

When he knelt beside her, their backs to his mom, Mouse looked over at him with a half-grin. She took a sliver of blue chalk and signed one of her drawings—*Em*. She drew a mouse beside it. It was as close as she could get to telling him who she really was. Nate smiled back and wrote his own name next to hers.

As he headed up the drive with his mom, both hands on the handle of the chalk carton, he looked back over his shoulder at Mouse who was still kneeling by the picture of the mother and little boy. "See you tomorrow!"

Mouse just waved. She wouldn't lie to him, and right now, she didn't know if she'd still be in Nashville tomorrow. The cicadas had gone silent, leaving the night to the softer sounds of the crickets and katydids, and drawing with Nate had succeeded where her counting had failed—she was calm and the power in her seemed to be asleep again. It gave her time to think.

Bodie, her cat, met her as she opened the front door. He was another slip in her discipline—letting herself love anything, even a cat, made her soft, which made her vulnerable to the power she kept tethered inside. But Bodie hadn't given Mouse much choice in the matter. He just showed up on her porch one day and acted as if he knew her, as if he belonged, despite a lingering wildness about him. He was big, at least part Maine Coon, and Mouse half wondered if the rest of him was bobcat. It had been ten years now—the longest relationship she'd had in seven hundred years. Bodie had been the first thing to make her feel like she'd come home. He met her at the door, slept in the bed with her, demanded her attention in ways that pulled her out of her own head.

And he was one of the main reasons she'd been so reluctant to leave Nashville. Because when Mouse left a place, she left everything else behind, too. That was the point—a clean break, nothing from her old life that could connect to her new one. Of course, she made sure she never collected much in the first place. No art on the walls and just the bare essentials of furniture. There was only one plate in the cabinets in her kitchen, one cup, a single set of mismatched utensils bought at a flea market. She kept everything in her life disposable so she could run at a moment's notice. But Bodie wasn't disposable.

"We'll figure it out, Bo," she said as she sat on the couch and he hopped into her lap.

Before Mouse could decide what to do next, she needed to understand the pieces in play and, most importantly, *who* was playing. If her father had sent Jack Gray, he'd have shown up at the pub to claim what he thought was his: Mouse.

But if it wasn't him, then who?

Maybe Jack came on his own, to rub her nose in his success, and maybe his benefactor was just some rich guy who didn't want people to know he was interested in things like the Devil's Bible. If Mouse chose to believe that, then maybe she could stay in Nashville a little longer.

But a lifetime's experiences had worn away her belief in fairy tales. And Jack showing up with a mysterious benefactor and a book about the Devil's Bible seemed too coincidental. If someone else had sent Jack Gray, Mouse either needed to find out who he was and what he wanted, or she needed to make a clean break and start over somewhere else.

She sighed and buried her face in Bodie's fur. His purring tickled her cheek.

"Get off, Bodie," Mouse grunted the next morning as she arched her back, making the cat roll onto the bed and land belly up.

She had stayed up late thinking about her options but had made no decisions. Sometime after two, she'd given up and counted the forty-three steps from the kitchen up the stairs to her bedroom. She'd fallen asleep quickly. Then the dreams had woken her.

Her little sandy-haired boy, a field full of soldiers, the portrait from the Devil's Bible, and Jack Gray's eyes gone dead at her command.

Mouse stood beside the bed, anxious to push the images away. She ran her fingers under Bodie's chin until he wrapped his paws around her hand and pulled it to his face, biting. "From love to hate in a heartbeat. I think we're a little unstable, Bodie," she said as she snatched her hand away and turned toward the bathroom.

It was the only room that she changed when she bought the place. She had no interest in trying to make the house feel like a home, but she couldn't make herself step into the tiny, dark, walled-in shower that had been in the master bath. When the contractor had tried to show her tile samples and fixture catalogs, she'd cut him off and told him she didn't care what it looked like as long as it was bigger and open so she could see out and so the light could come in. Mouse couldn't stand the feeling of being closed up, not after Podlažice.

She stood at the threshold now, Bodie waiting at the sink for her to turn the tap on for him. Four more steps to make the ritual nine from her bed to that giant, glass-walled shower.

After the taste of freedom she'd allowed herself these last few weeks, imagining that she could be like everyone else, Mouse now felt suffocated by the burden of returning to her measured routine. She felt as if she were trying to cram something back into an impossibly small box.

It was a different kind of claustrophobia—emotional and mental rather than physical, but the struggle was the same. She stood still for a moment trying to feel whether or not the power she had woken last night in the bar was still awake; it seemed quiet, just the rumbling of her empty stomach. She forced herself to take another measured step. Only three more to go. But Mouse couldn't do it. She didn't want to. She wanted to hold on to the little bit of normal she'd built these last months.

In one smooth jump, she landed in the shower, her toes curling into the grout lines to keep her balance. She reached over and turned on a trickle of cold water at the sink for Bodie, then pulled her shirt over her head and let the first spray of water, not yet hot, splash against her chest as she laughed at her silliness. The sound, bouncing off the walls, was so unfamiliar it startled her; she hadn't laughed in a long time. It felt good. Clean and simple. As the steam began to build, Mouse took a deep, unfettered breath, filling herself with the smell of soap and a sense of liberty.

And she felt the power quicken.

"God, no," she said as the heat of power rippled in her gut. "Feel nothing. I feel nothing," she muttered to herself as she worked to make it true. "Go away, go to sleep. Please, God, go to sleep again," she begged as she started to count—heartbeats, drops of water running down the glass—anything to quash the emotions and push the power back into its cage.

Then the doorbell rang. Both Mouse and Bodie jumped. The doorbell never rang because no one ever came to the house. Mouse grabbed her robe. Bodie beat her down the stairs though she didn't count her steps this time. She paused at the bottom, straining to see through the glass panels arched along the top of the door, trying to find the right angle to catch a glimpse of who or what might be waiting on the other side. Then she heard him clear his throat.

"By the saints!" she muttered. It was Jack Gray.

He rang the bell again. Mouse flinched and Bodie took off for the back of the house.

With a sigh and pulling her robe more tightly around her, Mouse opened the door.

"Hello," he said.

"What do you want?" She spoke softly and carefully to keep the power at bay, but she also meant to be rude enough to make him leave her alone.

Jack smiled at her anyway. "You sick?"

"Yeah," she lied and started to close the door.

"Wait a sec! You ran out of the bar so fast last night I didn't get a chance to apologize."

"For what?"

"Being drunk. And being a jerk."

"Okay. Thanks." Mouse tried again to close the door.

"Hey, wait." He put his hand on the door. "Seriously, I wanted to make sure you'd gotten home okay."

"I'm fine. See?"

"Why don't you let me take you out for a late lunch or early dinner so we can be friends again?"

Mouse could hear the lie in his voice, the quick jolt in his heartbeat, but as much as she wanted to unravel the mystery of whatever game he was playing, she couldn't risk letting the power loose again.

Her decision had been made for her anyway. Here, surrounded by things she cared too much about, she would never be able to lull the power back to sleep, not while she played with Nate or cuddled Bodie or reveled in her books and teaching, not when they whet her desire for more. No, Mouse had to get out. She'd wrap up a few dangling threads, and then she'd move on. What Jack knew or didn't was irrelevant now.

"I don't have friends, Jack."

Mouse closed the door and slid the dead bolt in place.

Podlažice Monastery, Bohemia

1278

The good dreams were the worst.

Mouse had long lived with nightmares, some real and some not. As a girl, she had been visited by dark creatures that looked like children except for their hollow eyes and jagged teeth. The nasty games they had played, torturing little Mouse, were meant to twist her mind, to break her so she would use her power to do their bidding. Another creature, Moloch, had come, too. He never asked her for anything; he just took what he wanted. But then Father Lucas had taught her how to protect herself from those real nightmares.

The not-real ones she had to deal with on her own.

Some were old fears revisited in the terror of the night: Mouse trapped in the dark of the pit at Houska—a mysterious, gaping hole long guarded and thought by many to be the mouth of Hell. She'd lured the hollow-eyed children there to trap them. But then Mouse had been trapped, too, until Father Lucas saved her. The nothingness of the pit, the absence of sound, and the piercing cold—it all came back to her in her nightmares. She would wake, surrounded by the darkness of her cell, thinking she was in the pit at Houska again. But a single whispered word would break the spell, and Mouse would pull the blanket close and sing the fear away, her quavering tune running like water against the stone walls of the monastery.

Other nightmares picked at wounds that would never heal. Mouse would wake with the sounds of battle still ringing in her ears—the high whistle of arrows in flight, the squeal of bodkins as they pierced armor, the cries of dying men. She could still feel the stickiness of Ottakar's blood on her hands, feel the dull quake in her bones of the thousands of soldiers and horses dropping dead in an instant. Her mouth open in a silent scream, her chest on fire with the pain of knowing that her own son was also on that battlefield and dead by her command—Mouse would beat out the worst of the rage and agony from those dreams against the floor of her cell. And then, with bruised and swollen hands, she would numb what pain she could by picking up the quill and filling a page with words.

But the good dreams were the worst. She couldn't sing them away. She couldn't write enough words to numb the agony they brought. Because she didn't want to.

Those good dreams played on the joys she'd shared with Ottakar and Nicholas, and Mouse's perfect memory brought every detail vividly to life. She was there once more at Teplá Abbey with Ottakar, the then-young king of Bohemia, asking her to go back to Prague with him. She was dancing in the great hall with him, the minnesinger's lilt swirling around them, Ottakar's hand on her back, his eyes bright with the want of her.

She was in a rain-soaked tent, thunder crashing, as she looked down on her son for the first time and discovered a mother's love. She was part of a family for the first time. She was in a garden swinging little Nicholas in her arms. "More, more, Mama," he was saying. She was laughing.

And then the first tendrils of wakefulness seeped in.

A smile still on her face, Mouse would lay in the bliss of half-sleep, wrapped in the smell of them—Ottakar's sweet wine and the earthy scents of the woods or the lavender soap and sunshine trapped in Nicholas's tiny golden curls. She could feel the warmth of them, their cuddles and caresses there on the surface of skin, the fine hairs on her arm tickling as if she'd just been touched.

All of it so real, so tangible, everything as it should be.

Even as she opened her eyes, their scents were still floating in the air as if they'd just left the room, and Mouse sat up quickly. Hoping.

The feel of Ottakar's soft breath still on her neck and the weight of her golden-haired little boy still cradled in her arms, Mouse frantically looked around her tiny cell. Hoping.

Yes, those good dreams were the worst because even though the moment of bliss disappeared like fog burned off by the too-bright sun and the truth settled on her that Ottakar and Nicholas were dead, Mouse clung to that impossible hope. The hope cut her like razors, seared her like hot iron, but Mouse clung to it all the same, for as long as she could, making herself believe that they were alive again and had just stepped away. She held onto that hope for as long as she could stand it, then pulled her empty arms to her chest, curled in on herself, and wept with a longing that would never go away.

⚬═╪═⚬

Her father watched these scenes from the darkness beyond the wall of her cell. And he wept a tear, too. Not for her exactly, but because he understood the pain of longing. He had dreams, too, of what had been and what might be.

CHAPTER THREE

ouse pressed SEND on her resignation letter.

She didn't bother to give an excuse, just said it would be her last semester at the university. She wouldn't be asking Dr. Williams for a letter of recommendation anyway; there would be no more ivory towers for her. No more books or students. No more reminders of what her life had once been. No more dreams about what it might be. She would do whatever it took to stay hard and resolute against the dark power that lurked in her.

Mouse scrolled through the internet looking at ads for nurses willing to travel. It was hard work that would keep her moving and leave no time for her to let her guard down again. She had spent the better part of seven centuries chasing epidemics and wars, tending to the sick and wounded; it was the perfect way for a seemingly immortal person with a healer's skills to pay penance for the death she'd caused. Over the years, Mouse had kept a running tally in her head, and when she'd saved twice as many people as she had killed at Marchfeld, she finally understood: She would never be free of the guilt, no matter how many she saved, no matter how long she lived. She could never undo what had been done.

Instead, Mouse clung to the oath she swore when she fled Podlažice and joined the world again. She swore she would never take another life. Every night since, she had measured herself against that oath. Whether camping in the dark along a country road centuries ago or overlooking the streets of Paris at the end of World War II or turning off the television in a shabby apartment in some pithy town, she would give herself a moment's redemption in five whispered words: "I didn't kill anyone today."

Mouse slammed her laptop shut. It didn't matter what job she took. It didn't matter where she went. All that mattered was that she didn't kill anyone today. That was her anchor, her purpose in life. All the rest of it—staying free from her father, keeping the emotions at bay so that the power stayed asleep—all if it was so that when she went to sleep at night, she could say, "I didn't kill anyone today."

But Mouse couldn't help wonder: What was the endgame for someone like her?

With no answers and the day waning, she shoved the question away and counted her way upstairs to change clothes. Even if she didn't know where she was going, she needed to start severing the ties that held her here.

"See you soon, Bodie," she said, giving him a rub under the chin before closing the door behind her. She hadn't figured out what to do about him either.

There was at least one silver lining in her decision to leave Nashville—she was going to give her house to someone who needed it, and Mouse focused on that happier note as she ran down the porch steps. Mouse didn't own a car. She kept her world small enough for her to walk wherever she needed to go—a leftover habit from childhood. The trek on foot to Fort Negley would take just under an hour. The day was already sliding into early evening, and her task would be harder after nightfall. Mouse picked up her pace to race the dying light.

As she sped past the edge of the hedgerow onto the sidewalk in front of her house, she saw him. He was studying the chalk drawings she'd done with Nate.

"What do you want, Jack?" She spoke in an even, emotionless tone.

He looked up, startled. "I—I want to take you out to eat."

"I can't. I have to meet a friend."

"I thought you said you didn't have friends."

"I have one."

"Well, let me tag along. I want to see a little of the city before I hop on the plane in the morning."

It didn't take Mouse's heightened awareness to see that Jack was nervous. Whatever he wanted from her, he wanted it badly—or someone did. Which meant that Mouse really needed to figure out both who was doing the wanting and what it was they thought she could give them.

"You got a car?" she asked.

He grinned. "Really nice rental. See?" He pointed at a huge SUV parked on the street, its flashy silver hood already covered with a smattering of cicada shells. "Where are we going?"

She gave him directions as they climbed into the car, and then she decided to force his hand. "Look, Jack, it's clear you want something from me. Why not just ask?"

"You won't like it."

"How do you know?"

"Because I've asked you already."

Mouse couldn't decide if she should be relieved or aggravated. "I'm not going to sleep with you, Jack."

He laughed but stopped a little too quickly. "No, not that, though I'm still open to the possibility if you change your mind. What I want is the same thing I wanted back at Chapel Hill. How do you know the Devil's Bible was written at Podlažice?" There was something darker than curiosity in Jack's voice.

Smiling tightly, Mouse turned to look at him. "That was a long time ago. I think you're misremembering what I said," she lied.

"No. You were sure."

"I merely suggested that scholars—"

"Come on, you know that everyone believes that the monastery at Podlažice was too small and poor to make the Devil's Bible. No other books were made there. Not one, Dr. Nicholas. I . . . I need to know what makes you so sure it was written at Podlažice."

"I told you, I read it in an—"

"I've looked for that article you claim you read. I can't find it. Tell me what your source was. Please, I need to know. I told my benefactor . . ." Mouse could hear a touch of panic before his voice trailed off.

She waited a moment, but when it was clear he wasn't going to continue, she pressed him. She needed answers as much he did. "What did you tell him, Jack?"

"I was trying to impress him." Jack gripped the steering wheel a little harder.

"What did you tell him?"

"I told him what you said, that the Devil's Bible had been written at Podlažice. No doubt. Only . . . only I made it sound like it was my idea and based on my own research."

"You didn't tell him I'd told you?"

"No."

Mouse sighed and eased back into the soft leather seat.

"Not at first."

Her head sank against the headrest.

"But he kept demanding that I send him my research, so I told him about you and the article you'd read. That's how I learned how powerful these guys are."

"Wait. There's more than one?"

"Apparently. I've only ever talked to the one guy, but I think he must be part of a group that's interested in—"

"The Devil's Bible."

"It's more than that. I think they're really into the occult and the Devil's Bible is just part of it." Jack looked over at her as they stopped for a red light. There was something odd in the way he was looking at her, something different from how he looked at her last night, like he was trying to figure out a puzzle.

"The light's green," Mouse said, pointing. She felt exposed.

"These guys aren't lightweights," Jack continued as soon as he got the car rolling again. "They're serious and they seem to be everywhere. My benefactor had people all over the world looking for the article you said you'd read—people searching online but also in some really obscure, private libraries, too. These people get what they want." He blew out a sigh. "And when they couldn't find that article . . . my benefactor wasn't happy."

Mouse could see a flash of fear in his eyes now. It reflected her own.

"Did he send you here?"

Jack didn't answer the question. "Do you have someone's notes or something? Something unpublished? That you're holding onto for what—tenure? Promotion?"

Mouse relaxed just a little. A wealthy group tracking her down to get unpublished notes they thought she was squirreling away might prove tricky and inconvenient, but she wasn't sure that made them a threat. Mouse would need to learn more about them, but she could feel the first tickles of power stirring in her. She had to put an end to the questions—both his and hers.

"I'm not talking about this with you right now, Jack. I'm looking for Solomon."

He turned to look at her for a second, clearly thinking about pushing her for answers, but then he nodded sharply. "Sure. Solomon. Is that your friend? How do you know him?" he asked, frustrated but playing along.

Mouse knew that sooner or later Jack would get around to asking for the notes he thought she had. Hopefully, she'd have a better answer for him by then or be on a plane to somewhere else. But she didn't want to answer his questions about Solomon either. She needed him to shut up so she could count—words on the radio, trees, cars rushing past—anything to lull that tickle of power back to sleep.

She didn't know how she'd explain her relationship to Solomon anyway. She wasn't sure she would have called Solomon a friend before today. As Mouse had told Jack, she didn't have friends. But Solomon and Nate and Bodie were her first regrets when she realized she had no choice but to leave Nashville—surely that made them friends. They would be her only good-byes, and Solomon would be the first.

Like Nate, Solomon had given Mouse something unexpected: a sense of belonging. They'd met on one of Mouse's many late night counting sprees—hours of walking and tens of thousands of steps and breaths and streetlights. She'd found Solomon and her little dog, Wise, huddled under a thin blanket in a cluster of trees at the top of Reservoir Park. Solomon had been on the way to the homeless camp at Fort Negley, but her feet had made her stop. January had been particularly bitter in Nashville, and Solomon had a bad case of frostbite, but she refused to go to the hospital because she couldn't take her dog. Mouse got her to a warming shelter and stayed with her for several days to tend her feet—lancing the blisters, slowly warming the damaged tissue, and taking care of Wise.

During those days at the shelter, watching the people come and go and listening to Solomon's stories, Mouse realized that these were her people. They carried everything they owned on their backs. Mouse had done that, too. She had wandered; she had walked on feet swollen with frostbite and rot. She belonged here with them and their vacant eyes and their false names. Their deep desire for home in pitched warfare against their running and restlessness—these were Mouse's battle scars, too.

She especially felt a kinship with Solomon, who had also seen the brutality of war and come home broken—so broken that she couldn't keep a job or a place to live, which meant that when she found herself pregnant, she couldn't keep the baby either. Solomon had given away her little girl to a couple who would love her and keep her safe. And even though Solomon knew she'd done the right thing for her baby, she told Mouse that she had a hole in her, body and soul, that would never fill, a longing that would never go away.

"Not many folks know a pain like that," Solomon had said as she put her hand on Mouse's cheek. "But I can see you do." Mouse hadn't said a word. She didn't have to. Solomon just knew things.

Mouse had met Solomon at the foot clinic every week since. Like Nate and Bodie, Solomon was a little light in the darkness of Mouse's life—but she had no intention of sharing that with Jack.

"Solomon is none of your business," she said to him now.

"You seriously need to work on your social skills," Jack muttered.

For a moment, Mouse thought she'd finally been rude enough to silence him. But then Jack found his courage.

"I touched it. The Devil's Bible." He kept his eyes on the road, but his muscles tightened. "When we were there to scan the pages for the computer program. You know they barely let you breathe in the room. The damned thing's insured for millions." He laughed to himself, but it didn't ease the tension. "When the guard wasn't looking, I slipped my hand out of the glove. I just had to touch it. I don't know why. And I felt . . . something."

Mouse fought the urge to cross herself, a leftover habit from her childhood at the abbey. She knew exactly what he had felt in the Devil's Bible, but she couldn't talk about it. She leaned forward and turned the radio up. This time, Jack held his tongue.

"Turn left here," she said a few minutes later, and Jack turned onto a winding street that ran alongside Fort Negley. The road narrowed quickly with thick brush growing in the abandoned lots on either side. There were few streetlights and no other cars.

"Where the hell are we?" Jack asked.

"This is the most likely place to find Solomon."

"Why?" he asked.

"She's homeless and there's a tent city up in the woods where she stays sometimes."

"Wait, your one friend is a homeless person? And *her* name is Solomon?"

"Pull over. I see her bike." As soon as they stopped, Mouse jumped out of the car and headed up toward camp.

"Whoa! Where're you going?"

"I'm going to find Solomon."

"In the dark woods with the homeless people?" Jack asked.

Mouse turned around. "If you're scared, you don't have to come. But I would appreciate it if you stayed with the car in case we need to—"

"I'm coming." The car beeped as he locked the doors. "Can't call myself a man and let some girl go running off into the woods unprotected."

"Don't bother. 'Some girl' can take care of herself," Mouse said as she disappeared into the trees.

⊶⚊⊷

No one in the camp had seen Solomon, but they sent Mouse toward the railroad tracks. Solomon sometimes preferred to be away from the others; she liked her solitude. Mouse understood.

But it was odd for Solomon to leave her bike behind.

Weaving between the trees and underbrush down the back of the hill, Mouse felt a shiver of foreboding crawl up her spine. As she neared the tree line, a high, panicked barking rang out, and Mouse took off running like it was the starting pistol of a race. Jack Gray struggled to keep up behind her. They broke through the woods into what looked like a dump filled with the discarded souvenirs of domestic life—refrigerators with their doors ripped off, stacks of deteriorating microwaves, ovens with the grime of cooked suppers left inside, washing machines with their lids left up like gaping mouths. Little Wise was running in circles beside a rusted-out dryer. He was barking and whining intermittently.

As Mouse neared, she could see there was something in the dryer basin.

"Solomon?" Mouse felt heavy with dread. Her feet crunched in the gravel as she took another step closer, bending down to look in the dark opening. "Solomon?"

"You get on out of here before he finds you."

Mouse sighed with relief. She'd been sure Solomon was dead. Mouse knelt beside the dryer, the gravel biting into her knees. "Are you hurt?" Her voice rang hollow and thin as the basin swallowed the sound.

"I tell you, we got to go," Solomon urged as she stuck out her hand. Mouse pulled her clear of the dryer. Years of exposure and wandering had been tough on Solomon and, even though she was barely middle-aged, she looked and moved like an old woman.

Mouse assessed her quickly—just a few scrapes on her hands and face, but she was shaking all over and her breathing was fast and shallow. Mouse had spent enough time on battlefields to know the signs of shock. Solomon had seen something. Something terrible.

"We got to go before he comes back." Solomon reached down and gathered Wise into her arms.

"He who?" Jack asked as he looked around.

Solomon puckered her lips and squinted, her deep wrinkles folding in on themselves. "Death," she said, her soft Southern drawl so at odds with the word that it set Mouse's teeth on edge, like metal screeching against metal.

Jack Gray looked up at Mouse. "She's nuts. Let's get out of here." He bent to grab Solomon's arm.

"What do you mean you saw Death?" Mouse asked, seven centuries of experience pricking the back of her neck in uneasy anticipation.

"I seen him bending over her when I come down the hill. I was just heading to see if the market folks had put out any good food in the trash. They do, sometime, you know." Solomon was staring off into space. "I didn't make no sound. I know how to mind my own business. But Wise here, he growled a little, mostly to let me know we didn't want to be messing with any of what was happening." She leaned her cheek against the dog's head. "And that old Death, he turned to look at me and saw I was nobody he wanted, so he walked on down the road. But he carried something with him as he went." Solomon ran her hand over her face. "They were dangling from his hands, bouncing against each other and dripping on the pavement. I'd seen it as he held her up, his hand behind her head."

"Saw what?" Jack asked.

But Solomon was looking at Mouse when she answered. "Em, he done took that girl's eyes."

Podlažice Monastery, Bohemia

1278

Fine feathers of ice ran along the stone joints of the cell wall. Winter was coming to Podlažice.

But Mouse didn't care about the biting cold—she was torturing herself with the Psalms. David's book of prayers and songs had been Father Lucas's favorite. As a girl, when she struggled with her oddness and her unusual abilities, he would make her recite the words of the Psalms to ease her suffering and to build her faith that God had a plan for her.

She'd spent most of her young life trying to figure out what that plan was, and just when she thought she'd found the answer—a simple life raising her son, a normal life filled with normal joys and normal problems—it all turned to ash as she read the letter Father Lucas had written when he knew he was about to die.

Mouse remembered every word of it, but for a long time, the only part that played in her mind was the part that branded her: *Some call him Semjaza or Satariel. Others call him Abaddon, the Destroyer. The Father of Lies. Satan. This is what sired you. This is your father.*

This is what Father Lucas had written in his letter.

Mouse had grown up thinking God had made her special so she could do good in the world. What was she supposed to do when she found out that her father, her creator, was God's sworn enemy, the Father of Lies? It made her whole life a lie. And it made her too dangerous to be Nicholas's mother.

So Mouse had left her little boy with Ottakar while she ran away into the Sumava wilderness thinking to live out her days alone where she could hurt no one else.

And so she had. Until Marchfeld.

She wasn't angry at God—not anymore. What part did he play in her life? None. She was no child of his. He had not shaped some divine plan for her, and despite Father Lucas's efforts to convince her otherwise, Mouse now knew better than to expect mercy.

She had begged for it as she knelt beside Ottakar's dying body. Blood and spit and mud flying everywhere as the soldiers flung themselves at each other, the horses crashing against one another, all of them screaming, and Ottakar trying to say her name as blood bubbled through his lips. Mouse had begged God then. And what had he done? Nothing.

"You have the books out of order."

Mouse jumped. She had been lost in her misery and had not heard her father pull himself in through the dark.

"Go away." She would not look at him. He didn't scare her; what did she care about what he might do to her? Torture would be a relief.

Death would be an answer to the prayer she couldn't speak. The only thing that frightened Mouse was the power that woke with her anger. She would not let him rile her again. She bent to the parchment and focused on the scratch of the quill.

He lowered himself to sit cross-legged on the stone floor at her side. "So you know the Old Testament by memory?" he asked.

"I was raised in an abbey," Mouse said, as if that explained things.

"Even the Pope couldn't recite the entire Old Testament by heart. It's a waste of your gifts. They're all watered-down myths and faulty histories anyway." His velvet voice couldn't quite mask the belligerence.

"Have you read it?" Mouse hadn't meant to ask a question, but it surprised her that he would bother with scripture.

"Many times." His eyes twinkled, but he kept the laugh to himself. "Though I've never seen the books in that particular order. Why do you put Samuel and Kings there?" He nodded to the piles of parchment Mouse had laid out along the floor—the Pentateuch in a neat stack followed by the books of the Prophets and then Job, I and II Samuel, I and II Kings, and then the Psalms she was working on.

"Father Lucas had me read them this way."

"Father Lucas?"

Mouse's throat tightened. She hadn't meant to tell her father anything, nothing personal anyway. It seemed dangerous. "Just . . . someone," she answered.

"Someone who cares for you?"

"No. He is dead."

"But he did care for you."

Mouse gave a single nod.

"And he had you read the books this way, why? So you could see the sufferings of Saul and David and God's other pets not as histories, but as what?" Energy rolled through him as he worked toward some insight into the forces that had shaped this girl. "As wisdoms like Job? To show you the true nature of a fickle and arrogant God who would send evil to torture his most beloved? Surely not—not *Father* Lucas, a man of the Church. What did he want to give you by having you read them this way? Why put the Psalms there?"

"They are hope in the darkness." Mouse sounded like an echo repeating Father Lucas's words.

In that moment, the excitement of discovery that had been dancing in her father's voice stilled, and his head snapped around to look at her. "What did this man know about you?" Anyone who knew her secrets might know his as well. It made him vulnerable.

"Nothing," Mouse said, though she could hear the fear in his voice and was sure he could hear the lie in hers.

"Tell me who he was and what he knew." Mouse felt the compulsion as he spoke. Like a swarm of snakes, he turned and twisted in her mind, violating her as he worked to control her.

But despite his efforts, Mouse kept silent.

His eyes widened in surprise. He was accustomed to being obeyed— people had no choice but to acquiesce to the power of his command. Yet this girl ignored him and followed her own will. That made her very dangerous. His eyes lingered on her throat, the subtle ridges of cartilage and the jump of the blood in her veins.

"Who were Ottakar and Nicholas?" he asked more gently, calling up the names that he had pulled out of her mind earlier, names that meant nothing to him but everything to her. He wondered if they knew her secrets.

"It does not matter. They are dead."

"Are there others—friends or family?"

Mouse sighed. She could give him an easy truth this time. "No one. They are all dead."

He relaxed at her answer—no one who might know too much about her and thus too much about him. His enemies would salivate at the chance to learn what they could from this girl. He looked back down at the parchment, searching for another way to get her to expose herself.

"I confess I find these texts a bit biased, a collection of Yahwist propaganda." He allowed the chuckle this time. He got no reaction from Mouse, so he asked, "What do you find in there?"

"Truths. Maybe."

His eyes narrowed as he studied her face. "And why does that make you sound so sad?"

"Because I think they are not my truths." It wasn't a question, but Mouse looked up at his face for an answer anyway. She got none.

"You wonder if you have a soul?" he asked softly.

Mouse shrugged. When she was a girl, she had known she was odd, but she didn't know she was special until one day when she was lost in the woods and looking for Mother Kazi, the woman who had helped to raise her at the abbey. Little Mouse had closed her eyes and seen the glow of Mother Kazi in her mind, and then she had run toward that glow and out of the dark woods. She knew that what she had seen was Mother Kazi's soul, and Mouse had innocently believed that her ability to see souls had been a gift from God.

For a time, she loved studying the souls of others—Father Lucas's especially, because it was soft and bright. But when she looked inside herself, Mouse could find no glow. She'd made herself sick with looking, eyes rolled back in her head searching for some flicker of light inside. Eventually, she had gotten so discouraged by the darkness she found in herself that she stopped looking. When she found out who her father was, it all made sense. Mouse didn't have a soul.

Her father's laugh startled her. As she watched him clapping his hands like a child, Mouse got angry, and her own power purred to life.

"Stop!" she yelled.

He kept laughing. He liked to provoke people, to push them beyond their limits, and to make them lose control. But, as he felt her power rise, he wondered: If he made her mad enough, would she try to do to him what she had done at Marchfeld? Would she be able to?

As quickly as he had started, he stopped laughing. It was too dangerous to play with this girl and her power that was so different from his.

So he decided on a new strategy. "I'm sorry. I just figured out why you are working so hard for penance. You think that if you follow all the rules set out in those pages—see no evil, hear no evil, speak no evil—you'll get a soul in the end. That's it, isn't it? If you have a soul, then you can have forgiveness."

Mouse was seething—embarrassed at being exposed and pained by the truth he told.

"But for you there is no end." He meant it to be comforting. It wasn't. "And can you forgive yourself for what you've done? Killing Ottakar? Killing Nicholas? I am sure you did not mean to do it," he said quietly. "But if you cannot forgive yourself, then how can you expect God to?"

Mouse could hardly see to write. Her hand was shaking, but she needed something to help her control the rage building in her. She grabbed a stack of blank parchment and jammed a needle through leaf after leaf to make guide holes in the four margins.

"Go away," she said.

She huddled over the pages and pressed a finely shaved bone awl against the parchment, dragging it from guide hole to guide hole, making a furrow on one side and a ridge on the other. The lines were sharp and straight. She counted the lines as she went—six top-to-bottom in the center of the leaf and at the edges, one hundred and six lines horizontally in two columns—the same for sheet after sheet. They made a perfect grid, controlled and precise. They would keep her hand steady as she wrote just as they calmed her mind as she crafted and counted them.

She didn't have to look up to know her father was gone.

Mouse worked until sleep claimed her. Hours later, she woke to the lemony sweet smell of linden blooms. She sat up quickly, disoriented, thinking for a moment that she was back at the castle at Hluboka lying under the linden trees with Ottakar. But the darkness grounded her; the only candle left burning in her cell offered little light as the flame was barely a glow in a sea of melted wax. When Mouse lit another candle, she saw the small tower of parchment stacked neatly at her workspace on the floor, a branch of linden blossoms resting on top.

She could not imagine where he'd found them this time of year. But it was what lay underneath that took her breath away: the rest of the Old Testament and all of the New, complete, and copied in a script that perfectly matched her own.

CHAPTER FOUR

ack Gray scoffed. "What does she mean Death was here?"

Mouse shrugged, but she stood up and started to scan the woods behind Solomon.

"Surely you don't believe her," he said.

Mouse knew what kinds of dangers lurked in the dark—things Jack would dismiss as a fairy tale she knew all too well to be real.

"Come on. Let's get her to a hospital or something," Jack said.

But Mouse didn't move. She kept peering into the deeper shadows of the tree line, looking for some sign of what had terrified Solomon. Because Mouse was also afraid and not just of Solomon's Death.

In the early years, when she thought her "gifts" came from God, Mouse had used her power on purpose once to resurrect a newborn baby—surely a good and sacred act. But then she'd learned the conse-quences. Drawn by her power, the hollow-eyed children had descended on Prague and tormented the people until Mouse was able to lure the creatures away and trap them in the pit at Houska.

Mouse learned the rule pretty quickly—using her power was like lighting a candle in the midst of a dark expanse and then blowing it out. The more power she used, the brighter and longer the candle would shine, and the easier it would be to find her. What happened at March-feld had been like turning on a searchlight, but the other moments were only flickers in the night, and whatever dark creatures came looking for her still had to grope about in the dark. Mouse had hoped that the slip of power she'd used on Jack in the bar had been so insignificant—the flash of a firefly—that it would go unnoticed. She worried now that she was not so lucky.

"Look, I'm leaving. You can come or not." Jack seemed to have reached the end of his patience.

"I see something," Mouse said softly as she strained her eyes against the dying light. She pointed. "Over there."

"Don't you go look," Solomon warned.

"I have to," Mouse said, her feet dragging a little in the dirt as she moved toward the dark heap that lay in front of a decaying stove. She heard Jack Gray creeping along behind her. Mouse could feel the fear in him.

She smelled the girl's perfume first—violets and gardenias and a little bit of vanilla. She strained to hear a heartbeat, a breath. Mouse was almost prepared for what they saw, Jack Gray not at all.

"Oh, God!" He spun away, gagging.

Mouse knelt to touch the dead girl's arm. Still warm. Her empty eye sockets still glistened with blood.

Mouse turned back to Solomon. "Which way did he go?" she asked.

"The way Death always goes," the woman drawled out, pointing across the tracks in the direction of the city cemetery.

Mouse took off running.

"What the hell?" Jack shouted. "Let's call the cops."

"He'll be gone if we wait," she yelled back over her shoulder. She could hear Jack muttering to himself, trying to decide what to do.

Mouse didn't wait.

If this Death figure was like the other creatures that had crawled out of the dark to feed on Mouse's power, the police would be no good anyway. She jumped over the low stone wall and then stopped, lowering her head and closing her eyes. Her heightened hearing picked up her own heartbeat and Jack's well behind her. Up ahead, another heartbeat. And then a second. One was racing.

Afraid that the creature might have already found another victim, Mouse ran. She found them quickly. The thing had its nails dug into the girl's arm as it wove her through the headstones and then pressed her up against the side of a mausoleum. Mouse moved swiftly toward them, the power in her throbbing with reckless eagerness.

"Stop," she said. Mouse had never been able to compel the dark creatures she'd encountered before, but the power played freely in her and leapt to lace the word with control.

The thing froze where it was, its mouth open in surprise and the woman still in its grip.

As Mouse edged around the side of the crypt, the glow of a distant streetlight exposed her mistake. The man was just a man—his body hard with desire and the woman's hand full of cash.

Neither of them moved, not even to breathe. They couldn't as long as they were under Mouse's command.

"I'm sorry." She lifted a hand to her mouth, afraid to speak, her words barely breath. "I made a mistake. I'm . . . I'm sorry. I thought you were—" She closed her eyes and imagined herself inhaling the power as she had with Jack in the bar. "Go back to what you were doing," she said, releasing them from her control.

They both gasped for air. "What the hell do you want?" the woman shouted at Mouse and then looked up at the man. "You want your girl to watch, it'll be extra."

Mouse turned and ran into Jack Gray.

Jack stayed oddly quiet as they made their way back to Solomon. Mouse wondered how much he'd seen or heard in the cemetery. His silence, the fists shoved tightly in his pockets, and the three feet of distance he kept between them suggested he might have seen quite a bit. But the real question was: How much had he understood?

When they got back to the dump, he pulled out his cell and called 911. Mouse went to check on Solomon.

"The police gonna come?" Solomon asked, pulling Wise closer.

"Yeah. They have to. But we'll be sure they let us bring Wise, too. It'll be okay," Mouse said, not sure she believed it. She turned to Jack. "Would you go back up to the camp and tell them what's happened so that they know why the cops are coming? It might make everything simpler if they know they're not getting evicted."

Jack nodded and headed into the woods toward the tent city without a complaint—another sign that he'd seen something in the cemetery. But what Jack Gray thought he knew about her felt like a feather on her shoulders compared to the fear that she'd brought a demon to Nashville.

"Solomon, did you get a good look at him? At . . . Death?" Maybe, Mouse thought desperately, it was just a man, just a sick, twisted coincidence that had nothing to do with her.

"Why? You think he gonna come for you next, honey?"

"Maybe." Mouse wasn't sure if it was the truth or not. "But the police will want to know, too. Can you tell them?"

"He look like nobody and everybody. Kinda short with brown eyes and brown hair. His look was empty though." Sounded like just a man, Mouse thought, until Solomon added, "And he had long fingernails, so long they must've cut into his palm the way he gripped the strings of those eyeballs." Solomon laid her head back against the clothes dryer, and then jumped when Wise started to growl. She looked back into the woods.

Jack was coming down from the camp, and most of the tent city residents were coming with him. Many of them circled around Solomon, laying a hand on her to give her a pat or asking if she was okay. The sounds of the sirens grew closer and soon the red lights of the fire truck and ambulance and then the bright blues of the police cars flashed across faces. People ducked their heads, squinting—everyone looked guilty in the glare.

Jack stood a few feet away from Mouse as they waited for the police to come up the hill. And then he took a quick step toward her, as if he couldn't help himself. "Who drew those pictures out in front of your house?" he asked, his voice thick with fear.

Mouse had been ready for the question she thought he'd ask about what he'd seen in the cemetery. But now she fumbled, her mind racing to pull the sidewalk images up in her perfect memory as she worked to understand his question—and she saw it instantly. *The wolf.* She'd drawn it exactly like she had in the Devil's Bible.

"What are you?" His words were so soft Mouse wondered if he had actually spoken them or if she had somehow pulled them from his mind.

The cops were there before she had the chance to feed him a lie, and Jack, Solomon, and Mouse were put into separate cars and taken in for questioning.

At the station, Mouse was left in a tiny room to wait. It had been over two hours already. She kept her hands in her lap, picking at a cuticle, her leg bouncing uncontrollably as she waited. She counted the cinder blocks, then the footsteps outside the door, and the dead bugs trapped behind the glass in the overhead fluorescent light—anything to keep her mind off the close walls and the locked door and worrying about Solomon or what stories Jack Gray was telling in the next room.

It wasn't Mouse's first time to be detained by police. In the early days of her immortality, the first hundred years or so, she'd made mistakes— staying too long in a place of disease while she never got sick, using outdated manners and antiquated phrases, always being the stranger, the foreigner—these got a person noticed by whoever was tasked with maintaining law and order. So she learned to keep moving, to be mindful of changing fashions and customs, to stick to cities where she was less likely to stand out. She hadn't been interrogated in a very long time, but she remembered the game well. The sole objective was to uncover secrets—all of them, any of them, regardless of whether or not they had anything to do with a crime. And Mouse had layers of secrets. That's all she was: secrets and lies.

When she heard steps pause outside the door, Mouse sat up a little straighter, stilled her leg, and laced her fingers together, readying herself.

"Sorry to make you wait, Dr. Nicholas," the detective said as she came through the door, a manila file folder and voice recorder in hand. "I'm Detective Spencer."

"Where's Solomon?" Mouse was working really hard to keep herself calm. The power had been jumping like cocooned butterflies in her chest.

"She's with another detective telling him what she saw."

"What about her dog?"

"He's with her. I promise they're both fine."

"And Jack?"

Detective Spencer pulled the chair out and sat down opposite Mouse. She laid the digital voice recorder on the table. "You teach at the university, right?"

"That's right. In the history department. Thirteen years." Mouse tried to anticipate the detective's questions so she could move through them as quickly as possible. "Now, where's Jack?"

"How do you know him?"

Mouse heard the higher pitch in the detective's voice and the jump in her pulse—something wasn't right—but she kept her own voice even, her answer succinct. "He was a student in a class I taught my last semester at Chapel Hill. I have had no contact with him since. Not until the lectureship last night."

"And you met him for drinks afterward, correct?"

Clearly they'd questioned Jack first. "Yes. In the pub."

"And what did you talk about?"

"What does that have to do with the woman who got killed?"

"Please just answer the question, Dr. Nicholas."

Frustrated, Mouse shoved herself back in the chair, her mind racing through the conversation she had with Jack that night at the bar, trying to think if there was anything incriminating he could have told the police. "Old times. Jack's book success."

"The bartender suggested that maybe Jack had been making unwanted advances."

"The bartender? Why would you—"

"Did Dr. Gray make unwanted advances?"

"He was a little drunk, yes, and flirty. What's this about?" Mouse was confused and getting angry.

"But you didn't return his 'flirty' feelings?"

"No. Why?"

Detective Spencer's jaw clenched, and her heartbeat was nearly deafening as she opened a folder and pulled out three photos. She slid them across the table to Mouse, who sat as if she'd been carved of wood.

They were crime scene photos that zoomed in on wounds and body parts like pieces of a human jigsaw puzzle. They didn't look like people at all. The three victims had been mutilated in very specific ways. The one at the dump had lost her eyes. Another had lost her ears. And the last stared back at Mouse with her tongue cut out and her mouth sheared away so that her teeth were exposed to the air, little white pearls floating in a sea of blood. A phrase from long ago echoed in Mouse's head: *See no evil, hear no evil, speak no evil.*

Then the detective placed three smaller photos down beside the others. They weren't gruesome crime scene photos; they were pictures of the victims that had been lifted from Facebook or Twitter, profiles and selfies. Mouse's first thought was that most people would have a hard time telling any of them apart—even their friends or family could easily mistake one for the other. Each seemed to be about twenty to twenty-five years old. They all had dark auburn hair and heart-shaped faces.

They all looked like Mouse.

With the suddenness of a lightning strike, the game was done.

"Jack Gray did not do this." Mouse's voice was dead and her face felt like stone.

"Surely you see the resemblance, Dr. Nicholas?"

Mouse didn't even nod. She stared at the photos on the table.

Someone had been sent looking for Mouse. His message was as clear as a calling card, and there could be no mistake in who sent it.

Mouse's father had found her at last.

Podlažice Monastery, Bohemia

1278

He crouched in the dark as he watched her bathe.

Mouse had put the linden blooms in the water that the bishop brought her. Stripped bare, the soft light of the candles slid over her hips and thighs and reached up to cup her breast as she bent to dip a strip of cloth she'd torn from her habit into the linden-scented water. She squeezed the cloth as she laid it against her shoulder, and the water ran down her arm to drop from her fingers onto the stone floor, glistening in the light like diamonds.

He watched her until she finished, his desire for her burning through him, and he knew he'd made a decision—he wanted her too much to kill her. He wanted more than her body, though it was beautiful. He wanted the power in her. He wanted to control her, to own her. And there was something else in his craving for her that he couldn't name, some deeper want that made him ache with longing—that made him uneasy.

When she reached down to gather her habit once more, he slipped, unseen, into the shadows and was gone.

⚬—✦—⚬

Mouse was surprised when her father didn't come to see her the day after he'd left the finished Old and New Testaments on her floor. She had expected him to come looking for gratitude or a favor in return. Mouse didn't know what he wanted from her, but she knew he meant to gain something, or else why bother? She felt like a trapped animal and thought about asking the bishop to let her out since her solitude was no longer solitary anyway. But if her father indeed wanted something from her, he would only come looking for her no matter where she went. Mouse bent back to work on the book, hoping that maybe his absence meant that he'd grown bored with her. Maybe she was finally alone.

"I have something for you."

With a sigh, Mouse looked up from scripting the first of the medical texts she meant to include in her book—Constantine the African's translation of the Art of Medicine. If the scriptures honored her time with Father Lucas, these medical texts paid tribute to Mother Kazi, the only mother Mouse had ever known and the woman who had trained her to be a healer—Mouse's one gift that didn't come from her father. She laid down the quill as she turned around to face him.

In one hand, he held a brightly colored feather quill like none she had ever seen, and in the other, a beautifully carved wooden pot full of brilliant blue ink.

"What do you want from me?" Mouse asked.

He let disappointment play on his face like a mummer as he smoothly folded himself down on the floor beside her. "Can't a father bring his daughter a present without suspicion?"

"I do not want to play your game. Now tell me what you want."

He sat the jar and the quill between them and met Mouse's gaze. "I don't know."

The truth of his answer startled her. "But you want something?" she asked more gently.

"I always want something."

"I have nothing to give you."

"You have yourself."

"No, not really. If I have my way, once I finish this book," she looked down at the growing stack of scripted parchment, "I will sit in here until I waste away."

"And if you don't waste away? If you can't?"

"Then I know what my eternity looks like." She laid her hand on the wall of the tiny cell.

He let out an angry burst of breath. "What a limited view of the world you have. And a self-centered one."

"What?"

"This monastery will not be here for eternity. This cell will not be here long enough for you to turn to ash or dust or whatever it is you hope will happen to you. This world, life," he swept his arms wide, "it's bigger than you and your sorrows and your guilt. You are what you are." He sighed and put his hand under her chin softly, turning her face to his and speaking more tenderly. "*What* you are does not have to define *who* you are. You can shape that all your own. Life is about joy more than sorrow."

"What do you want from me?" It came as a plea rather than an accusation this time.

"To know you? To have you know me? I'm sure there must be something else more tangible, more advantageous." He gave her truth, though not all of it. "But as my child, you are the only one of your kind in all the world, and I am curious about you. Are you not curious about yourself?"

"I was once, but then I found out who my father was, and I was too busy hating myself to care about anything else. Until a friend, Bohdan, showed me I was more than my father's daughter." She said Bohdan's name like a holy word, like a prayer.

"Will you tell me about this friend?"

Mouse was surprised that he asked this time rather than demanded what he wanted. "He is dead, too."

Her father waited until, with a shrug, she continued. "I went to the woods to die. Alone. As I said, I hated the idea that your blood was my blood, and I knew that it made me dangerous. I gave up—" Mouse swallowed against the sudden tightness in her throat as she thought about Nicholas. "I gave up everything, and I ran until I thought I was far enough away that I couldn't hurt anyone. All I wanted was to die. And that's when I met Bohdan." The small smile pulling at her mouth felt so unfamiliar that she put her hand on her cheek. "He was a wolf, and his pack had left him, so he was alone, too, and he was dying. But he didn't want to. So I saved him." Her voice broke. "And he loved me for it."

Her father reached out to catch a tear that ran down her face. "You loved him back?"

She nodded, unable to speak, and then her jaw clenched and she pulled her face free of his hand. "But I killed him. What I was, your blood in me—it killed him. Some of your dark creatures came looking for me, drawn by the power that infects me, and they skinned him alive." The words were tight with anger.

"And yet you came out of the wilderness and back to the world of men after he died. Why—if you thought yourself so tainted, so dangerous— why not stay out there alone?"

"I believed in Bohdan, so I lived on his faith in my goodness."

"Let me be like your Bohdan. Let me teach you how to love yourself."

"How naïve do you think I am?" Mouse scoffed. "And besides, all that was before Marchfeld. Marchfeld was like a mirror. I saw what I was, what I was capable of. That girl has no place among people. There is no goodness in her. There is no future for her."

"Yes there is. And I will show it to you."

○—✦—○

"I have something for you."

It had been his usual greeting for several days now. He brought her many gifts: more exotic feather quills with fine points, fresh parchment that had been combed to perfection and chalked so that it felt like silk, but her favorites had been the richly colored inks in pots and jars that were themselves works of art, and the gold leaf—brilliant and fragile like a butterfly's wings. These things awoke the artist in Mouse, and she began to re-envision the book she was making.

"Just let me finish this," she said to him as she bent to the parchment, a bit of gold leaf dancing on the end of her brush. She pressed it gently to the page beside a large initial that marked the beginning of the New Testament. She was replacing some of the pages he had copied so she could illuminate them, so she could make the book beautiful. So she could make the book *hers*.

At first, she had seen the book only as a means to an end—giving the bishop what he wanted in order to get what she wanted. She had used the ritual of copying text to fill her mind with the mundane so she had no time to think about anything else. But now something new sparked in her.

Father Lucas had shown Mouse some of the most rare books in the world, and Ottakar's library at the castle in Prague had been priceless, but she wanted this book, her book, to be different from all the others. The bishop had already insisted on it being big, and truly as she looked down at the sheets of parchment, Mouse was in awe of its size. It was the largest book she had ever seen. It took up half the cell, and when she lay beside it with her feet lined up against its bottom edge, the top of the book came nearly to her breast.

But Mouse wanted it to be more than just large or full of knowledge. She wanted to pour herself into it. She would cover the gold leaf initials in colored pagan swirls as a reminder of the baby cemetery where the hollow-eyed children had found her; it would be her monument for them, who had no other. And she would entwine the swirls with ivy and animals—a wolf for Bohdan, doves for Father Lucas, and three lone bitterns in the whole of the manuscript, shrouded in shade. One for Luka, the man she had accidentally blinded in a moment of panic, and one each for Ottakar and Nicholas, whom she had killed.

As Mouse planned her scripted memorial to the people she'd loved, her loss was tempered with light as her art empowered her to create something new out of the ashes of her life.

"If you keep bringing me things, there will be no room for me to work or to sleep," she said as she finally turned to her father.

He spent most of his days with her now. He brought food that was much better than the rank stew the bishop shoved through the slot and which Mouse now fed to the rats. He brought wine; they ate together like a family and talked of history or politics or literature, but nothing about their lives, nothing intimate. They did not trust each other, and even now as Mouse held her hand out to receive his latest gift, her wariness would not let her smile at him.

"It is not a thing I bring this time, but something far more precious to you, I think." His voice was heavy with something, but Mouse hadn't learned how to read him as she did most people.

"What is it?" she asked cautiously.

"Will you answer a question first?"

Mouse tensed. So far, he had asked for nothing in return for his gifts.

"It depends on the question." She felt like she was back at Prague playing the deadly game of court politics.

"Who was Ottakar to you?"

Her mind raced with the potential dangers of answering his question and with his reasons for asking it.

"Why do you need to know?"

"I don't. I am simply curious." He sighed and his shoulders slumped. "It is clear that he meant a great deal to you, like Bohdan did. As your father, I want to know who he was." He waited just a moment more. "What harm could come of talking about a dead man?"

Mouse took a breath, thinking about her own questions she wanted to ask, mostly about her mother, and she made a calculated decision to give him an answer with the intent to get one from him in return. "He was the man I loved."

"This was Ottakar, the king?"

"Yes."

"His son was Nicholas?"

Mouse's mouth went dry as she nodded.

"This Nicholas was your son, too."

He wasn't asking.

"The one you think you killed at Marchfeld with all the others."

Very slowly Mouse felt the reality of her cell drift away. It was as if she and her father stood in the midst of nothing, and all she could hear were his words: "The one you *think* you killed."

He caught her as she sagged under the weight of an impossible hope. "He is alive."

⌖

Her father held her as she wept.

He was fascinated with the depth of her emotion. It plucked at memories of his own, grown dusty and stagnant from disuse; he had once felt sympathy for the people he hurt and rage at being sent as God's emissary to test and torture the faithful. He had wept with bitterness and loss. He understood tears of sorrow and anger, but he had never cried from joy.

Neither had Mouse—until now. But knowing that she had not killed her son released her from a terrible burden of guilt. She felt vulnerable— a lamb lulled by the lion—and she was sure that had been her father's intent. As her tears finally dried, wariness settled in Mouse again.

"You have seen him?" she asked.

"Yes."

She sat up and slowly eased away from him. "Did you . . . speak with him?"

Her father cocked his head, a deceptively human trait he had adopted. "Ah, I see. You're suspicious of me."

Mouse hated that he could read her so easily while she continued to misjudge him. She had thought he might be angry at her suspicion, but he smiled instead, like a proud parent. "I confess I did search him for any hidden . . . talents. But he must take after his father. Predictably normal." He didn't bother to mask his disappointment.

"Did you hurt him?"

Cloaked under the guise of nightmares, he had gone to Nicholas to see if the son was as special as his mother. He had not meant to hurt him, but he needed his answers quickly. And Nicholas had not suffered—much. He knew he needed to craft a calculated response because, unlike her son, Mouse was anything but predictable.

"Why would I hurt him? He is of no interest to me—beyond his interest to you, of course." He picked at a thread on the sleeve of his habit.

His response did little to ease Mouse's worries—he had not really answered her question. Her heart jumping in her throat, she tried a different line of inquiry. "Where is he?"

"The Hungarians have him."

"Is he in trouble?"

"They are treating him well, it seems. I understand he is working out some agreement with the Holy Roman Emperor Rudolf to reclaim his dukedom in Opava." He waited a moment and then carefully added, "But I am also told that Ottakar's widow is working against Nicholas's interests."

"What do you mean?" Mouse asked sharply.

In the months after she left Sumava and went looking for Ottakar, she learned that he had remarried and had other children during the twenty years Mouse had been wandering in the wilderness. But she had never been interested in knowing any details about Ottakar's new family.

Mouse had only gone looking for him because she thought he might need her. Ottakar had been shunned by the Church, was under attack by Holy Roman Emperor Rudolf, and had been abandoned by most of his nobles while he marched to protect Bohemia. Mouse had been shocked to find Nicholas by his father's side, and, driven by a mother's love, she had followed them both to war. That war had ended at Marchfeld.

Her father shrugged at Mouse's growing fear. "Ottakar's widow wants Nicholas declared illegitimate. I don't think she likes her dead husband's bastard—or you very much either." Mouse winced as he chuckled. "She wants the Duchy of Troppau for her own son now that Ottakar is no longer here to protect yours."

Mouse considered her options. She could go to Nicholas, but to what end? He did not know her, and she held no sway over the Church or the politics of men. There was nothing she could do to help her son—but her father might. She did not like the idea of indebting herself to him, even though all his gifts so far had come untethered and seemingly without an expected return.

"But Rudolf means to reinstate Nicholas as the Duke of Troppau?" Mouse asked, trying to find another way to be sure of Nicholas's safety.

"I believe so. But I also think that Ottakar's widow will stop at nothing to get what she wants for her son. A mother's love seems to have no limits. Yes?" He watched her as he passed his hand back and forth through the candle flame, making it dance and cast oscillating shadows across her face—first dark, then light. Dark, then light.

"You mean she will kill him if she has to."

"She is already entrenched with her lover, Lord Zavis, who is vying to be named regent of Bohemia and means to rule until Ottakar's legitimate heir is old enough to claim the throne."

"But if Rudolf has Nicholas—"

"Which he does. They are in Opava."

"And Ottakar's widow and this Lord Zavis would be in Prague, yes? They are too far away to be a threat to Nicholas." Hopefulness brightened her tone.

Light, he thought as he pulled his hand away from the candle again and let it gleam in Mouse's eyes. "Ah, but they are not at Prague. Ottakar's widow and Lord Zavis are at his castle in Hradec."

Mouse wrapped her arms tightly around her chest. "Hradec is only a few hours' ride from Opava."

And now dark, he thought as he cupped the flame and threw her face back into shadow.

"If she hurts him . . ." Her words cut the air as Mouse imagined the things she would do to Ottakar's widow.

They sat in silence. Despite the human face he wore and his pleasant demeanor, Mouse had not forgotten who her father was. Her abbey upbringing filled her with a dread understanding of his nature, and though she had seen nothing of evil in him yet, she also knew she was only seeing what he wanted her to see. She knew the dangers in making a request, but surely she had to make it anyway. For Nicholas.

"I would be most happy to intercede on his behalf—have a word with this Holy Roman Emperor Rudolf. Or with Ottakar's widow," her father said lightly.

Mouse snapped her head toward him though she could read nothing but a casual interest and kindness in his face. If this was a power play on his part, why not make her ask? By volunteering, he gave her what she wanted without any leverage to demand something in return.

She was left with nothing to say except: "Thank you. Rudolf seems the quickest route to obtaining Nicholas's safety."

"Quickest, maybe, though a slit throat accomplishes the deed rather swiftly and more permanently than politics." He snapped the loose thread on his sleeve. "And a little vengeance might satisfy your hunger for justice against Ottakar's opportunistic widow."

The candlelight danced as Mouse considered his offer before finally shaking her head.

Her father sighed. "If you prefer diplomacy to murder, so be it."

CHAPTER FIVE

ouse asked for a lawyer. Detective Spencer's questions were irrelevant now. There would be no justice for those dead women—not from the police anyway.

By the time she was released, Jack Gray was already gone. Apparently, he'd also lawyered up. But Mouse had more to worry about than the tales he might tell. Obviously her slip of power, that flicker of light in the night, had been seen. It meant her father was still hunting her. She didn't know why, but that didn't matter now. What mattered was that her father's nasty pilot fish was still out trolling the streets of Nashville hunting for her, and he was sure to snare more innocent victims if she didn't act fast. Mouse needed to draw him away from Nashville, and the only way to do that was to make herself the bait.

The cicadas were oddly silent as she walked up to her porch after the taxi pulled away. Bodie met her at the door, complaining about having missed both last night's supper and his breakfast that morning. Mouse poured half the bag in his bowl and then sank onto the couch, her head in her hands.

She knew she didn't have much time, and she needed to think out the steps of her plan carefully, but she felt paralyzed with guilt. Those dead women and all the lives their loss would touch. The difficulties she'd added to Solomon's already difficult life. Mouse had not been allowed to see her when she left the police station. She paid the lawyer who'd gotten her out to do the same for Solomon, but Mouse knew the police would hound her friend as they continued to hunt for a suspect, and the longer they went without one, the more suspicious they'd be about Solomon. Mouse wouldn't be there to help. Jack, who knew things he shouldn't, would be gone, too—no doubt to report back to his benefactor.

Mouse hadn't screwed up this badly in a long, long time. She threw her head back against the couch. Bodie joined her, purring and dipping his head under her hand, wanting love now that his belly was full. She rubbed him for a moment, distractedly, but then her eyes came to rest on a small statue on the mantel.

It was the only decoration in the whole house. She pushed herself up from the couch and walked to the fireplace, resting her head against the brick as she toyed with the little angel figurine—its wings spread and not a chip in the stone despite its age and the millions of miles it had travelled. Father Lucas had given it to her when she was a little girl, a christening gift after she'd stolen a baptism from the Church that kept its doors closed to her. As a child growing up in the abbey, she'd never understood why she wasn't allowed to be part of the religious life. But after Father Lucas's letter telling her who her father was, it all made sense. She was too tainted for the Church. Too tainted to attend Mass or to take vows. Too tainted even for baptism.

But long before she knew what she was, little Mouse had snuck away into the woods and baptized herself. She had written to Father Lucas, who was away on one of his trips, and confessed what she'd done because she always told him everything. She thought he'd be angry. Instead, he had brought the christening angel all the way from the Carpathian Mountains, wrapped in wool and strapped to his chest to keep it safe. He anointed her with blessings when he gave it to her. It was her proof that he, at least, had truly believed in her goodness.

The handful of other trinkets from Mouse's past had been packed away centuries ago, left where no one would find them at a time when she meant to bury that part of herself. No more thoughts of Ottakar. No Nicholas. No Bohdan or Mother Kazi. The ghosts of the past made living in the present too hard.

But she had needed Father Lucas to stay with her, to help her keep vigil through the long years as they had once thought to do at Houska when they sealed up the hollow-eyed children in the dark pit that the Church called the Mouth of Hell. Mouse had thought she'd been sealed in, too, before Father Lucas pulled her back into the world of men. She ran her fingers along the angel's wings. She'd kept it with her as a sign of hope in the darkness as she sealed herself in a wanderer's life—as dead to the world around her as she had been down in that cold, dark pit. The angel held Mouse's hope that someday, someone would pull her out again, that someone would have faith in her goodness even if she did not.

She looked down at Bodie weaving between her legs and breathed out her bitterness. She'd stayed in Nashville out of hope for a normal life. She'd adopted the neighborhood's stray cat out of hope. She'd made friends with Nate and Solomon out of hope. And now people were dead because of her. Again. People she'd come to care for were suffering and in danger. Again. The anger hiding behind her guilt broke free in a hot gust of temper. Mouse curled her fist around the angel, ready to throw it against the wall, to smash it and be done with it. Done with light. Done with hope.

And then the doorbell rang.

Mouse flinched, and the stone angel fell to the side and chipped the end of its wing.

The doorknob started to turn. She'd forgotten to lock it.

She stood, tensed and waiting as the door inched open. She expected Jack Gray or the police or Solomon's Death to come sliding in—she was ready for them.

But it was a little hand with little fingers that wrapped around the threshold and a little face that peered into the dim house.

"Wind at your back, Em?" Nate asked.

Mouse fought the tears, but she couldn't manage a lie. "Not today." She swallowed hard before adding, "Does your mom know you're here?"

Nate had come in and closed the door behind him. He knelt to pet Bodie. "No, but I don't care."

"I do. She . . . she loves you." Mouse struggled with the words. "She'll worry if she can't find you."

"She's busy with the baby. She loves the baby."

"Yes. But she loves you, too." Mouse hadn't moved from the fireplace; she didn't think she could.

"I'm mad at her."

"Why's that?"

"She doesn't want me to hang out with you anymore. She doesn't like you." Nate looked over at Mouse, who nodded.

She kept nodding. The tears were running down her face now.

"Don't cry, Em." Nate ran to her, hugging her around the waist. "I love you."

Mouse flinched, her body rigid in the unfamiliar embrace. For centuries she had heard husbands whisper those words to wives and mothers coo them to newborns or weep as those words spilled out over lost children. She'd heard them tens of thousands of times in joy and sorrow, seductions and promises. But she'd never heard them spoken for her. Just as no one had said her real name in seven hundred years, no one had told Mouse that she was loved.

She looked over at the fallen angel as she wrapped her arms around Nate, her body softening as she bent to kiss the top of his head. Fear choked the words she wanted to say as they moved up her throat. The last time she'd said them had been on the battlefield with Ottakar—just before her power ripped from her and sucked the life out of everything it touched. But she wanted to give Nate something back for the powerful gift he'd just given her, so she fought against her fear. She lifted her face to gather more breath. "I—"

"Well now, that's sweet, ain't it?" A man stood beside the kitchen counter.

He looked like everybody and nobody—plain brown eyes, brown hair. Solomon's figure of Death. She looked down to his hands. His fingers stretched out thin and then twisted into long, yellowed nails. They were framed in blood, the cuticles too stained for cleaning.

Mouse pulled Nate behind her. She could sense her father's mark on the man—a heaviness he wore like a shroud and what Solomon had called an empty look. It was just like the blank look in Jack's eyes when Mouse compelled him in the bar. Her father turned people easily, preyed on their weaknesses, and tempted them with their wants. They became puppets and he their master.

He had tried to do the same to Mouse at Podlažice; he would probably try again if he caught her.

"Hi." The man sounded too casual for what he was. "Back door was unlocked, so I let myself in."

"How did you find me?" she asked. The more he talked, the more he might reveal about himself. She needed to find his weaknesses if she had any hope of getting Nate home alive.

"Oh, I got a picture of you, but it ain't the best quality." He held up a crumpled drawing of her face, scratched out on parchment with ink that had run and smeared. Her father's idea of a picture ID, Mouse assumed. "When I seen you at the fort, though, I knew you were the right one. So I went to the police station to wait for you, but then I saw your friend—that guy that was with you last night? He was kind enough to tell me where I could find you. And this is much more private." He waved his hand and leaned against the counter.

"You saw the police?" Nate asked, looking up at Mouse's face, ready for a story.

Without taking her eyes off the man, Mouse spoke to the boy, hoping for an easy way out. "Nate, I need you to go home now. I'll come see you in a little bit, okay? We can draw some more pictures."

"Mom won't let you. But we can draw here."

"Yeah, let's just all stay here," the man said, lifting himself from the counter and taking a step toward them, shaking his head at Mouse in warning. There would be nothing easy about this.

She played out a number of scenarios in an instant. She didn't think she was strong enough to compel someone already under her father's influence. And she might accidentally compel Nate, too, like all those men and boys at Marchfeld. Mouse wouldn't take the risk.

The return vent in the hall squealed as the air kicked on. Nate and Bodie jumped.

The man laughed and Mouse's stomach turned. He meant to enjoy himself—with her and with Nate, just as he had with those other women.

She moved quickly through her options and felt her body tense in anticipation. "Sorry, Nate, I should've introduced you. This is a friend of my father's."

"Hi, I'm Nate." The boy leaned toward the killer and offered his hand.

"That's a good man, Nate. You done that just like your daddy taught you, huh?" the man said as he pulled the boy into a hug. He turned Nate to face Mouse and pressed him against his legs, arm draped across the boy's chest and crusted fingernails resting along Nate's neck.

Cold fury ran through Mouse like a rod. This was her house. She would not let this happen.

"Nate, I need to go get something, but I'll be back in just a minute. You wait here with Bodie, okay?" As she spoke, Mouse walked past the man into the hallway that led to the laundry room at the back of the house. She saw the man's fingers flex at Nate's throat. But Mouse was sure he would follow. She'd seen his arrogance in the way he moved, in how he looked at her and handled Nate, in what he said and how he said it. This man did not think she was a threat.

He hesitated only a moment before his ego made the decision. He pushed Nate toward the couch. "You stay there and we'll . . . play when I'm done."

The man walked cautiously toward the end of the hall where Mouse paused before opening the door to the laundry room. She could see him sizing her up—she was tiny compared to him. She could see the smirk spread across his face.

Mouse stepped into the dark room first and, as soon as the man crossed the threshold, she spun and swiped his legs out from under him. She was trying hard to keep everything quiet, but the man groaned in surprise as he fell to his knees. She wrapped her left arm under his chin and pulled back, trying to choke him until he passed out.

"Em?" Nate called from the couch.

"Just a minute, Nate." Her voice was tense as she strained against the man's weight.

He was too heavy for her. Desperate, she scanned the room for a weapon, gritting her teeth against the burn in her arms and back. She lunged toward the dryer to her right and her hand closed around cool plastic.

The man was twisting toward her.

Mouse heard a hissing as she pulled the iron off the dryer; Bodie had followed them into the laundry room. He jumped clear of a can of starch that rolled and fell to the floor.

"Em? I think I want to go home now. Will you come with me?"

Mouse glanced toward the door, distracted for just a second, and then she was flying backward, slamming into the washer, her ribs burning where the man had kicked her. He was already scrambling to his feet, ready to lunge.

"Are you okay, Em?"

Mouse had run out of options.

She acted robotically. Chillingly calm.

As the man lurched toward her, she held his gaze and then slammed the point of the iron into his throat. She felt his hyoid bone snap as she pushed up. He threw his hands to his neck as he fell. Mouse landed hard on the floor and rolled quickly onto her knees, panting. Bodie's eyes glowed at her from the top of the dryer.

The man twisted on the floor and clawed at his throat, making guttural noises as he choked on his own saliva. The thick smell of starch coated the air. Mouse's stomach clenched and hurled the bile up her throat. She vomited on the floor beside the man's head and then sat back on her heels, watching him spasm.

She had sworn that she would take no other life. Not after Marchfeld. And for seven hundred years she had kept that oath. Until now.

"Em?"

Mouse rose with fear; Nate was nearly at the door.

"Stay. . . " Her voice cracked, and she forced herself to swallow. "Stay there. I'm coming, Nate."

Bodie wove between her legs and together they watched as the man finally stilled, his mouth gaping. Mouse gathered the cat in her arms and then wiped her mouth against her shoulder to get rid of the spit.

She planted a smile on her face as she turned the corner past the fridge.

"Okay, Nate. Let's get you home." The casualness of her voice frightened her. She had killed again, in cold blood this time.

Like father, like daughter.

PODLAŽICE MONASTERY,
BOHEMIA
1278

*H*er father was gone for several days.

Mouse knew better than to pray for Nicholas's safety. Why should God pay her any heed? So she scripted conjurations that she had learned from Father Lucas. Pricking her finger with the needle, she painted a light coat of her blood in two columns the length of the sheet of parchment. It dried to a muddy brown, and she wrote on top of it in red ink while she muttered the words of protection.

But Mouse was also determined not to let her worry overshadow the joy of knowing her son lived. Though she did not think God's mercy in saving Nicholas had been for her sake, she wanted to thank him anyway. With meticulous care she began to draw the Heavenly City—based in part on descriptions in Revelation and in Augustine's *City of God*, which she had once copied for Father Lucas. But mostly Mouse drew the city as she imagined it. With giant, colorful towers and curving trees, her city filled an entire page. She had finished drawing all the churches and was about to start sketching angels soaring around the towers and people dancing in the streets when her father came back.

"Your son is safely reinstated to his title," he announced.

Mouse turned to look at him, tense with dread. "And?"

"No one died," he growled playfully.

For the first time, she smiled at him. "Thank you."

His face shifted, and this time, Mouse could read him. Something in what she'd done or said pained him. She was about to ask what, but his bemused aloofness slid back on like a mask.

"What are you working on?" he asked.

"Heaven."

"I might like to have a go at that myself." As he bent to look over her shoulder at the city, he saw the sheet of conjurations, and Mouse witnessed another rapid transformation as his face distorted with rage. His mouth drew back and his nose flared, and she saw the not-human in him for the first time. She flinched in anticipation, but when she opened her eyes again, his face was perfectly smooth and his voice so calm she almost wondered if she had imagined the flash of anger.

"What are these?" he asked as he pointed at the conjurations.

"Spells of protection for Nicholas."

"Against me?"

"Against any manner of evil that might harm him."

He picked them up and read them. He cocked his head a moment, brought the parchment to his nose and sniffed, and then let his tongue flick to the brown stain. He nodded to himself. "May I have a sheet of parchment and the use of a quill?" His voice was tempered and too steady.

Forcing her body to stop trembling, Mouse handed him both, but as she started to pull her hand back, he put his own around her wrist. He took the needle from the floor. "Will you indulge me?"

She nodded and he jammed the needle in her finger. He squeezed until several drops of blood splattered onto the parchment. He slowly brought her finger to his lips and kissed it before letting her go.

He set about his work while she watched him, spreading the blood out into rectangles that matched the ones she had crafted for her conjurations. He blew on the parchment until it dried the same muddy brown. He dipped the quill in red ink and then, perfectly mimicking her own handwriting, he scripted a confession.

It wasn't a confession of his own sins. Like the habit he wore, the words he wrote were false, a pretend catalog of sins—sins of the flesh, sins of the mind, sins of the spirit. It ended with a plea to God for forgiveness as it invoked Saints Adalbert and Wenceslaus to intercede on the writer's behalf. It read just like the many confessions Mouse had seen in many other books written by any number of clergymen.

"What is this?" she asked cautiously.

"A conjuration of my own."

"It reads like a confession."

"Conjuration, confession—is there a difference? How is mine any different from what you have written? A list of worries—worries about what might befall a person, worries about suffering—and a plea for protection. Your conjuration is meant to protect against me. A confession is meant to protect against the actions of a vengeful God."

Mouse tried to find some counterargument, tried to voice the theology Father Lucas had taught her about God's goodness and mercy. But she couldn't. Instead she simply laid her father's false confession on the growing stack that would be stitched together to become her book. It was nearly finished.

She picked up the painting of her empty Heavenly City and leaned the corner of it toward the candle flame, no longer sure it had a place in any book of her own crafting. What did she know of Heaven? But as she hesitated, her father took it from her and laid it also on the stack of parchment.

His hand lingered on it for a moment too long, and though he turned his face away, Mouse saw his eyes glistening as they caught the candlelight.

◦—✦—◦

"Did she love you?" Mouse asked.

She was bent over Cosmas's *Bohemian Chronicles*. Her father lay stretched out on her pallet like a languid cat, working on his own piece of parchment. He looked up at Mouse, his eyebrow raised in question.

"My mother. Did she love you?"

"I can't say."

"What does that mean? You do not know or you do not want to tell me?" Her voice vibrated with her irritation; she'd felt pent up for days, like a top wound tightly with string just waiting for someone to yank and send her spinning.

Her father only shrugged.

Mouse threw her quill down and sat back on her heels, glaring at him. "You are not being fair."

"Fair?" He barely held back the chuckle.

"I told you about Ottakar and Nicholas."

"Now who's not being fair? You gave me seven words about Ottakar. I learned about Nicholas on my own."

Mouse grunted and grabbed for her quill again.

Her father sighed and sat up and then asked indulgently, "What do you want to know?"

"I want to know about my mother."

"You will be disappointed."

"Why?" She was already prepared to defend this mother she did not know. "What did she do?"

"No, not about her. I am sure she was a lovely person. But I can tell you very little."

"You conceived a child with her. How can you know nothing about her?"

He shrugged.

"Did you . . . violate her?"

He held her gaze for a while before answering. "No. But my only interest in her was what I could get from her."

Mouse squeezed her fist around the quill.

"She was a noble. She was bored with her life. She wanted adventure. I offered her a way out and showed her a little of the world. We spent a handful of weeks together and then she got pregnant. I took care of her needs while you grew. She died when you were born." He said it all matter-of-factly and then turned back to his parchment.

Mouse wasn't satisfied. Her uneasiness crawled under her skin like worms. She could make no sense of this relationship with her father. What did he want? What did *she* want? It was this last that nagged at her. She tried to stay guarded with him, but spending day after day with someone eroded walls and left a person bare to intimacy. Except Mouse never felt that he dropped his guard; she was never really seeing him. He held himself at a calculated distance. And Mouse wanted something more.

"What are you working on?" she asked.

He nodded at a couple of pages of scripted parchment that lay on the floor between them. "I finished the Rules of St. Benedict for you." He yawned.

"That is not what I asked." Mouse had learned to listen carefully to his answers; they were almost always only half-truths but, oddly enough, never lies. "What are you working on now?"

A smile played at his mouth and in his eyes. "A little something of my own."

She pushed herself back to lean against the wall of her cell. Her knees were numb from the cold stone floor. "May I see it?" she asked.

"When it is done."

"What is it?"

"My story."

"I want to see it."

"When it is done."

"No. Now." She could feel the power flutter in her chest, and though it frightened her, it emboldened her as well. "I am tired of playing whatever game this is. If you want to know me, then know me. But you must show yourself in turn. Your real self."

In no way could she have anticipated his reaction.

"I am afraid."

"Afraid of what?" Mouse asked softly.

"That you will be afraid. Or . . . disgusted." He was having trouble getting the words out. "I am . . . disfigured. Ugly. An abomination."

According to the Book of Enoch, those had been the same words God used to describe the children made from the union of rebellious angels and their human mates. Mouse had struggled with that story—God commanding the destruction of those children, who had not asked to be born, but who were ravishing the innocent. She had thought God's punishment unjust and severe until she found herself doing the same thing to the hollow-eyed children, sealing them in the pit at Houska and leaving them to a terrible fate. All the hollow-eyed children had wanted was to be normal, to live in the light as well as the dark. What if that was what the children of the fallen angels had wanted, too? What if that was what her father wanted—to be loved, to be normal?

"I will not be afraid. I will not be disgusted," she whispered.

He stood slowly, his head down, not meeting her gaze. And then he shimmered, and little flecks of shadow rained down from his body, his human shape falling away.

There before her, naked but for a loincloth, stood her father. As he really was.

Like his human version, he was taller than an average man, and his body was much the same—same proportions of leg and arm and torso—but his hands and feet and head were larger. Mouse studied him like a healer. Her eyes were drawn first to the twisted, thickened scars that ran along his legs and abdomen; they stood out against the otherwise normal flesh.

But the skin began to change higher up on his chest. It grew waxy and dark, as if it had melted and grown solid again. She had seen scars like these on the burn victims she'd tended as a girl with Mother Kazi—though nothing so severe. Any normal person burned this badly would surely have died.

The tendons in his neck were stretched taut under the scars; his ears were pulled long and woven with the grisly skin along his jaw. His face was all but black. The edges of his nose pulled flat into his cheeks where the skin had struggled to heal itself. The little fingers on each hand had been burned away and the survivors were gnarled and thick-knuckled.

Her healer's training held the horror at bay as she assessed his body, but when her eyes took in the soft brown curls covering his head, her tears came. She lifted her hands to her own head and raked them over the thick, brown stubble growing there, and then she reached up and gently traced her fingers over the scars along his face.

"May I paint your portrait?" Her voice was heavy with emotion.

He lifted his eyes to hers, searching them as he tried to fathom what she was feeling. He did not see fear or disgust. He thought it might be sorrow—and something else he could not be sure of, something unexpected.

He nodded to her. "But wait." He shook himself a little and two great horns grew from his head. Long talons stretched out from his fingers and his toes, and his mouth filled with jagged white teeth. "We must give the audience what they expect, what they want. Yes?"

Mouse smiled as she reached for parchment and her brush and colored inks. She understood. He masked himself for protection. And this moment had been just for her.

No one had ever made such a sacrifice for her—to expose themselves, to humble themselves as he had done. As she began to draw, she felt the power in her wriggle and stretch like a bird settling at home.

CHAPTER SIX

With Bodie still nestled in her arms, Mouse walked Nate home on the remains of their chalk drawings. Nate's mother met them on the front steps.

"Where have you been?" Her face wore a blend of relief and anger.

"I went to see Em," he said.

"I told you I—"

But Nate wasn't finished. He lifted his chin defiantly. "Because she's not odd like you said. She's just a girl. And I like her."

"I'm sorry, Dr. Nicholas, but—"

"Just Em. Please," Mouse said. She was trying to smile but the words had sounded sharp and her whole body was shaking. She didn't want to have a conversation—she wanted to be done and gone. "Listen, I have to leave. My . . . aunt is not doing well, and we've decided to take her to see some specialists in the . . . in New England. I'm going to be gone for a while, and I was wondering if you guys would mind—" Mouse's throat tightened. It had been a long time since she'd had anyone to say good-bye to. "Would you keep Bodie for me?"

The cat turned at the sound of his name, cocking his head at her in question, but Mouse couldn't look at him.

"Oh, Mom." Nate was breathless with hope.

Mouse tried to smile again but her face was too tight.

"I know it's a burden with the new baby and all, but Bodie's pretty easy—just a bit of food and . . . company every now and then. He likes to come and go, you know." Mouse felt the tears burning her eyes.

"Sure, Dr. Nicholas. I mean, Em. We can take care of him for you. But Nate, it's just while she's away." Nate's mother rubbed her hand along the cat's back. "He looks like the cat I had when I was a girl," she added, smiling down at Nate.

Swallowing hard against the knots in her throat, Mouse cuddled Bodie up to her face, rubbing her nose against his cheek. "Be good, Bodie." And then she lowered him into Nate's arms, leaning close.

"I love you, too," she whispered.

⚬—✦—⚬

The house was too quiet when she closed the door behind her. The silence pressed on her like something tangible, but she would not break under it. She walked back to the laundry room and knelt down beside the man she had killed.

He was the end of everything for Mouse. The end of her time in Nashville. The end of her plans to leave the house to Solomon—there was no time to arrange that now. He was the end of her oath to never kill again. The end of seven hundred years of hoping that she could be something besides her father's daughter.

But Mouse could not let guilt or sorrow pin her down. Not yet. Not until she knew no others would die because of her. She had killed this puppet of her father's, but he would surely send others if he thought Mouse was still there. She needed to get her father's attention—not a flicker this time, but a full flare—and then she would run far away from Nashville. But she couldn't do that as Dr. Emma Nicholas.

Mouse sat on the floor of her bedroom, which was scattered with birth certificates and passports. It was a familiar ritual to her—deciding who to be next. In the past decades, technology had made becoming someone new both easier and more challenging. Picture IDs, global databases, and social networks kept track of people better, but Photoshop and hackers and a criminal subculture fed a thriving black market of artificial lives. For the right money, you could be anyone at any time and nobody asked any questions.

This time was different though. Mouse didn't really care who she would be next because it didn't matter. The dead man in her laundry room put an end to any future she might have. She couldn't pretend anymore. No ritual, no discipline, no oath could keep her from being what she was—a murderer, a monster. Just like her father. It was in her blood, and anything else was a lie or false hope. Mouse was done with hope.

She snatched an identity at random from the pile around her and tossed the paperwork into the canvas bag she'd already filled with the few items she'd need for the journey. Then she headed down the stairs.

The house reeked of paint thinner. The carpet runner on the stairs squelched under her feet as Mouse went down to the kitchen; there would be nothing left of Emma Nicholas after tonight.

She put her canvas bag on the counter beside a tidy row of butcher knife, salt jar, and candle lighter. The last she picked up and took with her, her hands shaking as she lowered the flame to the bottom step and watched it run up the stairs like she'd seen Bodie do so many times.

As the fire spread above her, Mouse closed her eyes and called to the power inside her—gently, like gathering up a baby without fully waking it. She needed enough to get her father's attention for only a moment, just a single, bright flash. And yet she felt like she was throwing open the doors to an oncoming storm as she pulled down the barriers in her mind and called out to her father.

His answer came in an instant, as if he'd been waiting for her: *Finders keepers, you know.*

His tone was playful, but Mouse arched backward in pain; the sound of his voice in her head felt like someone shoving an ice pick in her brain. Her hair fell into her eyes as she bowed her head, fighting the fear and anger that would feed the power. She wrapped her hand around the butcher knife and stepped back into the kitchen.

Aren't you going to say hello? His voice trilled with victory.

She could feel him needling his way further into her mind, searching for some sign to tell him exactly where she was, but she had learned at Podlažice that filling her mind with something irrelevant like old texts worked like a thick fog and kept her father from seeing clearly. It could buy her some time.

"Adam and Eve had two sons," she whispered, quoting the *Antiquities*. "Cain, which means a possession, and Abel, which signifies sorrow." Josephus's words felt like cotton in her mouth. She grabbed a handful of salt and let it drop grain by grain, pinging on the kitchen floor. "They also had daughters."

Answer me now!

Her knees nearly buckled with the force of his command. It was the same power she had used on Jack Gray, though her father's was far more intense. But he had tried to force his will on her before. He had failed.

When Mouse spoke now, it was all her own. "Too scared to come get me by yourself?" she taunted.

Too clever, I'd say. I just wanted to see what cards you'd play before I put myself in the game.

"Well, your man is dead."

By your hand?

"I've killed before."

Yes, but not murder.

"This was self-defense."

The laughter in her mind was like someone slamming her head against a wall. *He had orders not to hurt you.*

"He killed those other girls."

They were not you. And they served a purpose. He paused. *You should be proud that I remembered what we talked about at Podlažice—see no evil, hear no evil, speak no evil. I've missed those times. I've missed you.*

The smoke was growing thicker as it crawled down the stairs. Someone would see it soon. Mouse slid the butcher's blade across her palm, watching the flap of skin bulge and ooze red before she balled her hand into a fist and forced the blood to pulse and then pool.

"I wanted to let you know that I'm leaving. There's nothing here now. Not for you. Not for me."

Tell me where you are and I will come get you. I don't want to hurt you. I just want you with me.

"You'll see me soon enough." Mouse looked down at the glistening salt circle she'd made around her. She let drops splatter on the floor as she quartered the circle with a cross made of her blood.

What do you mean?

She could feel him growing more frantic in her mind, searching for an answer. He knew he was running out of time, and so was she. If she waited any longer, he'd be able to pinpoint exactly where she was. She began to mouth the words of the protection spell Father Lucas had taught her when she was a girl and the nightmares had come—living and real.

Something's different about you. It sounded more like a question.

Mouse's lips closed around the last word of the spell. She waited. There was nothing but Josephus echoing in her head. Her father was gone again.

The plaster ceiling bubbled and buckled with heat. Mouse thought about standing there and letting it all come down around her, but she knew it was pointless. She'd tried too many times.

But an idea had come to her as she knelt beside the dead man in her laundry room. Obviously her father didn't want to kill her; he'd had plenty of opportunity at Podlažice. But she was of no real value to him—how could she be? So if she made him mad enough or scared enough, she knew he'd get rid of her—like throwing away a toy when it wasn't fun anymore.

But not here. Not yet. It had to be somewhere safe and on her own terms.

Embers fell on the couch. Mouse saw the broken angel on the mantel. She meant to leave it to burn with everything else, but as the sirens sounded in the distance, Mouse wove through the falling fire to the mantel, grabbed the little figure, and shoved it in her bag. Then she ran out the back of the house.

By the time the fire trucks pulled up to the drive, Mouse had already disappeared into the darkness of the yard behind her own. As flames licked at the roof of her former house, she folded herself into the cab that she'd had waiting for her at the end of the street.

The driver was looking at the fire, too. "Hope no one was in there. Doesn't look like there'll be much to save."

"No. Nothing," Mouse answered, but in truth, she knew there were too many clues left, too many secrets to uncover in the ashes. They'd find the bones in the laundry, maybe even be able to identify the man if he'd had any kind of record. They would know he had been killed before the fire. They'd know the fire had been set on purpose. They would know Dr. Emma Nicholas wasn't in there when it burned. They would want to know where she went. Mouse would not be coming back to Nashville anytime soon.

"Where to?" the driver asked.

"Airport."

As the taxi eased out into the traffic flow, Mouse searched for something else to fill her mind, to rebuild the walls she had dismantled to let her father in. She selected her cornerstone carefully. It came from The Book of Enoch, where she had learned about the angels who came to earth and bore children with the daughters of men. She remembered well how God dealt with them as he gave his commands to the archangels: "Destroy the children of the Watchers from amongst men: send them one against the other that they may destroy each other in battle: for length of days shall they not have."

It was Mouse's last hope.

Podlažice Monastery, Bohemia

Bohemia

1278

"There will be no other like it," her father said proudly.

They looked down on the portrait she had finished. She'd painted her father as he wanted to be—full length and fierce, as if he might jump out of the page. "We have made your book special." He laid his arm across her shoulder.

"Brother Herman!" The voice rang in from the hallway.

Her father, who still held his natural form, flinched. Instinctively, Mouse jumped in front of him, her arms spread wide, using her habit to shield him from the dangers of being seen by Bishop Andreas who crouched at the open slot. She need not have bothered. As she turned to look over her shoulder, she saw that her father was gone, folded back into the shadows.

"Brother Herman!"

"Yes, Bishop." She knelt near the slot.

"How is my book?"

"It is almost done."

"That is not possible," he said as he shoved in bowls of water and food.

"We are told that all things are possible, are we not?"

"But you have not had time to do the work. And you have asked for no books to copy."

"I do not need them."

"Then what are you writing in my book?"

"Everything I promised. Everything you want."

"Is it any good?"

"There will be no other like it." Mouse repeated her father's lines and then turned to start work on the calendar and the necrologies. She did not see her father as he hovered between the darkness and the feathered edges of candlelight. She did not see his smile or the spark in his eyes when she told the bishop that the book would soon be done.

Her father was impatient to have her with him and away from this place. She had already been corrupted by a childhood of nuns and surrogate Fathers spewing twisted theology. If he had any hope of turning her into his, he needed to get her away from all that, to show her another world, his world. He was eager to begin the work.

The more he learned of her, the more he wanted her. The love she felt for these other men—son and lover and Father Lucas—it pricked at him and twisted the knot of want in his own chest. He coveted the power of that emotion. He could tap the darker passions easily—greed, anger, lust, despair—but love lived in the light beyond the shadows.

To be able to reach souls through the heart made them yours forever. He had learned that from his ancient rival. The law had failed to inspire deep-seated change; like children, the people were only good when daddy was watching. But find a way into their hearts—a bridge between the divine and human—and you changed them from the inside out. His rival had only been able to whisper into one ear at a time, too, but his son had compelled multitudes.

That's what he also wanted, to make the masses his from the inside out.

He put his fingers to his lips, thinking. Perhaps this girl with her power and her humanity that gave her sway over the hearts of men was his answer. Maybe she offered him the means of building an army of true converts, committed not to simply satisfying their own appetites, but to shaping the world according to his vision. Such conviction would hand him the final victory.

But first, he would have to make her his.

⌐━⌐

"Where have you been?" Mouse asked as he pulled himself through the dark a few days later.

"Preparing a place for you." He smirked.

"For me?"

"For when we leave here. When you're done with your book."

Mouse turned back to the calendar. She was working on the necrology—a list of all of Bohemia's notable dead. Most of the names she remembered from an earlier version she'd copied once at Teplá. But she chose to leave out many of the nobles who had turned their backs on Ottakar. She also omitted the Brothers at the monastery in Prague who had shunned her, and she stripped others of their titles—a petty vengeance against the ambitious people who had wronged her. But it felt good anyway. Mouse wrote them out of history; they were nothing now.

It was *her* book, after all.

Remnants of her bitterness sharpened her tone when she finally answered her father. "I told you I meant to stay here, to die here if I can. I do not want to be among people again. It is not safe. Surely you can understand that."

"You don't have to be among people. You can be with me."

Mouse had not expected to be tempted, but a place where she would not be a danger to anyone, a place where she could be herself, to make art and live simply—that would be a home. And Mouse had never had one of those.

CHAPTER SEVEN

Mouse gathered a bit of thread, slipping it into her mouth to smooth the fraying end, and willed her hand not to shake. She slid the thread through the eye of the needle. As she pulled the scarlet silk floss for her first stitch, the linen looked like it was bleeding.

This last leg of the flight to Rome was full, but the plane was dark with only a few halos of light where people were reading or working. Mouse held the book-size oak box full of her sewing things on her lap as she worked. Two other embroidered scenes spilled out along the edges of the box—Carpaccio's *St. George and the Dragon* had come to her first, on the tarmac at Nashville when she was desperate to find something to do with her hands and her mind once she had settled on where to go. So she had pulled the sewing kit out of her canvas bag.

"Oh, those are beautiful," the flight attendant whispered, trying not to disturb the sleeping passengers. She ran her fingers gently along the second of Mouse's embroidered pictures—Rubens's *St. Michael and the Fallen Angels*. It had taken the layover in Newark and the whole long flight to Copenhagen to finish. Mouse's fingers ached with the work, but there'd been nothing left to plan, and she was afraid the hours of sitting and waiting would erode whatever courage she had left.

"Thank you," Mouse whispered back.

"You're an artist?"

Mouse shook her head.

Father Lucas had been the first to call Mouse that, and she had clung to the new title. "Artist" was much better than "odd" or "witch." As a girl, she had filled her room with paintings and then, later, in the beautiful dream-life with Ottakar at Hluboka, Mouse had found her true calling. She was a carver, making wood come to life under her hands. But sculpting freed something in the artist and revealed traits so deeply hidden that even the artist discovered them only when the piece was done. Mouse couldn't afford that freedom of discovery. She had wrapped herself up in a cocoon after Podlažice, not like a butterfly waiting for some magical transformation but like a mummy, desiccated and unchanging.

"Heading on vacation? Or is Rome home?" The attendant smiled down at Mouse.

"Neither."

"Business, then?"

Mouse nodded—it was business of a sort, a dark transaction she meant to execute. She bent quickly back over the linen, not wanting to talk anymore. She felt like a bit of thread pulled too taut. The silence and simple work of her hands were the only things keeping her from unraveling. Or snapping.

The attendant took the hint. "Well, I hope you get to see some of the art in the city. Might inspire more of your lovely needlework." Then she moved on down the aisle.

Mouse had hated learning to stitch as a girl at the abbey; she thought it tedious and dull. But embroidery helped a person keep her secrets as she wove them tightly into the linen and tied them in knots. And it occupied her hands and her mind when she needed it. Mouse would burn them all after she was done. Over the years, she had watched thousands of her embroidered pieces catch fire and curl up, black and red and yellow, and then float away into nothingness. That was her art now.

She would finish this last one before they landed in Rome—a perfect replica of Hildegard's chained and mutilated demon gloated over by God's faithful.

⚬━╾╼━⚬

Rome was different than Mouse remembered. There were too many people and too many cars.

Coming out of the Trastevere station, she found herself caught in the current of the crowds, bodies slamming into hers, sweat and exhaust choking her. The squealing brakes and loud, laughing tourists, car horns blaring, and the discordant thrum of voices tore away what little was left of Mouse's composure. She wrapped her arms around her chest, digging her fingers into the flesh at her sides and trying to make herself as small as possible, invisible like a ghost winding through the ancient streets she knew so well.

Over the many years of plagues and wars and wandering, Mouse had witnessed plenty of death—good deaths and bad ones, easy deaths and violent deaths, some long and slow, and others shockingly sudden. But no matter the kind of death, the dying all wanted just one thing in the end: some sense of home to comfort them as they left the living.

Mouse had travelled in wagons and carriages and caravans and trains transporting the dying back home. Some of them made it, and the dying was easier. But others on battlefields, in hospitals or dank alleys far from home begged for the same thing. They wanted Mama or Daddy to hold them. They clutched at trinkets or photos and escaped into their memories. They begged Mouse to sing a song from their childhood. They all wanted home.

But Mouse couldn't go home. Bohemia as she'd known it no longer existed. It was the one place she'd never gone back to in her seven centuries of wandering. Everything would be different—torn down and rebuilt and renovated. There would be no comfort of the familiar there.

So Mouse had come to Rome to die.

She'd been to the city often, especially in the early years. She'd spent more time in Rome, off and on, than any other place in the world. The Church had always been poison for Mouse, and she'd turned her back on it many times. But then in her loneliness, Father Lucas's gentle words compelling her to believe in God's goodness would tug on her faith again. And she'd find herself in Rome trying to discover a place among the angels and demons. It never lasted long, but she always came back.

Being in a place where at least the architecture was older than she was almost made Mouse feel young again. On one of her trips, she'd found a little basilica—Santa Maria in Cosmedin—that reminded her of the churches of her childhood. Its beauty came from its simplicity, but it was the story of the little ragtag church that drew Mouse in. Built on the ruins of some of the most ancient worship sites in Rome, the building had started as a place of refuge for the city's poor. At times, it had been built up by the Church and decked in gilt and gold, but then it was handed off to monks who didn't want it. It was forgotten and allowed to fall into disrepair until it was finally abandoned to more outcasts—Greek refugees and then Syrian and Iraqi Catholics.

If there was ever a church where Mouse might belong, this was it. A church for the unwanted. Mouse felt at home there.

This was where she wanted to die.

The belfry of Santa Maria in Cosmedin erupted from the pavement as she finally neared the piazza. She ran into the wall of tourists waiting to try their hands in the Bocca della Verità, the Mouth of Truth, under the porch, but Mouse already knew herself a liar. What she wanted was inside the church.

As she stepped into the nave, she breathed in the smell of old wood and faith. In this unadorned church so carefully preserved to hold time still, Mouse could imagine herself come home, Mother Kazi off somewhere crushing herbs to make a poultice and Father Lucas just around the corner with a book in hand that he was coming to show Mouse.

She waited until the small group of tourists in the nave moved toward the far apse to look at St. Valentine's skull so she could slip unseen into the aisle to her right and up into the *matroneo*, a balcony for the women. She slid into the small space on the far side of the pew and rolled herself into a ball, her canvas bag tucked against her chest.

As she let her head drop against her bag, she felt the wetness on her face and realized she must be crying. She was terrified of what she had to do. But once the tourists were gone, in the quiet of the church, she knew that Father Lucas and Mother Kazi would come to her, if only in spirit. They would help her be brave enough. She only had to wait for the church to close.

And Mouse had always been good at waiting.

⊶✦⊷

She woke shivering in the empty church, her muscles taut and cramping. Sluggishly, she made her way down the stairs toward the east apse. But Mouse couldn't afford to be weak with the work she had to do. She dumped her bag near the marble divider and fished out a small leather sack and a package of plastic utensils she had stashed from the flight.

When she was a child, Father Lucas had taught her spells of protection. She had learned exorcisms from the Church. And, in the *Book of the Watchers*, the angels themselves had taught her a binding spell. Mouse had often tried to remember that spell, which had sealed the hollow-eyed children to their doom, but although every word of every book she had ever read lived in perfect clarity in her perfect memory, the words of that ancient book slipped through Mouse's mind like water, and she could remember none of it. It was the book's last defense: to keep the knowledge of the angels secret from the world of men. The book itself was ash, burned at Father Lucas's own hand when the Inquisition came calling.

But Mouse didn't need to bind her father. She just needed to summon him.

She gripped the cold marble balustrade as she shook with another tremor—her body giving in to the shock and exhaustion of the past few days. *What do we do for shock, child?* Mouse could almost hear Mother Kazi asking, her quiet tone resonating with calm and patience and the confidence that Mouse knew the answer.

"Breathe," Mouse whispered as she pulled in air, slow and deep, through her nose. "Focus on the present." She grounded herself in the hardness of the marble, her eyes closed, and then she moved toward the presbytery, letting her memory guide her and giving her mind over to the task. When she neared the altar, she opened her eyes and crossed herself out of habit.

Mouse had never imagined a time when she would beckon the darkness she'd spent her life running from, so as she had waited in the Nashville terminal for her first flight, she spent hours mentally searching through thousands of remembered pages to find a summoning spell. Most she rejected pretty quickly as fake, but she found what she needed in a grimoire, a book of magic instruction typically penned by charlatans or demons in disguise. This one had been written by a pope. Honorius, known for his kindness, had crafted spells to summon all manner of dark things, not for his own ambition or gain but because he wanted to know the face and nature of his enemy.

Mouse already knew those. She didn't need to understand her father better. She knew him well enough that she would never give him what he wanted, never join him, no matter what promises he made. No, what she wanted to know was how to make it all end—the running, the being an outcast, the immortality—and her father was the only one who could help her. Once, in her cell at Podlažice, for just a moment, Mouse had made her father angry enough to kill her. She had seen it in his eyes. Now she just needed to rekindle that rage, and he would give her what she wanted: oblivion.

She ripped the plastic bag with her teeth, pulled out the serrated knife, and laid it on the altar. The stone had lived for thousands of years before her, and it had been consecrated to its holy work long before she was born. It told her she was nothing, which made her feel childlike and vulnerable.

She imagined the ages-old echo of Father Lucas's voice bouncing against the church's vaulted ceiling. *Have you found trouble, little andílek?*

"It found me," she whispered. Her face was wet with tears. She was like all those other people facing death—frightened and calling out for her Father.

Like anyone, Mouse was afraid of the pain she would have to suffer—but what really terrified her was what might happen after. If she made her father mad enough to kill her—and she knew she could—where would she go . . . after? She was shaking again, and then Father Lucas was there again in her mind with the words from the letter he'd written to her so long ago as he faced down his own fear, knowing that he was about to be tortured and most likely die: "'For thou, O God, hast tested us; thou hast tried us, as silver is tried.' I know what is coming and I am ready."

Mouse dug the knife into her left wrist, tearing at the flesh until a steady stream of blood flowed. The words of the summoning spell ready at her lips, she watched the drops of blood splatter like exploding stars on the white marble as she shaped the pentagram.

"What are you doing?" Though only a whisper, the voice seemed too loud for the space.

At first, Mouse thought she was half-remembering, half-hallucinating again, but these were not the words of Mother Kazi or Father Lucas. She looked up, squinting into the nave, and saw the silhouette of a man. She tried to fight through her mental fogginess and dreamlike state to figure out who he was. Not her father, her senses said. But as he shifted his weight, Mouse's instincts took over, and she began to assess what kind of threat he posed. He was much taller than she; it would make him clumsier and slower. His khakis and simple white shirt told her he wasn't a guard, and he held candles in each hand. He looked comfortable, like he belonged there. Not like her.

In the quiet seconds while they stared at each other in surprise, Mouse's blood made sick plopping noises as it dropped to the floor. Then she noticed the dozens of other candles flickering around the apse and the camera tripod near the opposite aisle.

How had she missed those? How had she not heard him coming? She felt languid and stupid as her eyes settled on the man again. He started to lower the candles to the floor. He kept his eyes on her.

Mouse bolted. She ran toward the marble divide along the left side of the apse and jumped. In her peripheral vision, she saw the man jump, too, over the first short wall of the schola cantorum. A few steps past the divide, Mouse was wrapped in total darkness but kept her speed until suddenly there was no floor. She flew headfirst down a stairway that had been cloaked by the dark. Her left shoulder slammed into each stone step as she slid until she crashed into the wall with a sickening pop like a gunshot. Searing pain exploded across her back as the tendons ripped and her shoulder snapped out of its socket.

Driven by her panic, Mouse regained her footing almost immediately and turned toward the deep blackness of the crypt beneath the altar. Holding her left arm to her chest and hobbled by pain in her ankle, Mouse eased along the wall in the dark. Her right shoulder and hip dipped into open spaces and then found solid stone again as she made her way around the room. Desperately. she shoved her right hand back into each of the openings, looking for an exit. She found none.

No doors. No windows. No way out except the way she came.

She was trapped again. Whatever else happened, Mouse would find no escape tonight. She would wake up tomorrow and still be a murderer, still hunted, still alone, still alive.

Mouse dragged herself to a niche in the corner behind the stairway. She remembered reading that the crypt used to hold relics. As she pulled her body into the tiny space, some part of her thought ruefully that at her age, she would count as a relic. Some part of her chuckled quietly at the thought.

The rest of her wished herself as dead as the skull of St. Valentine upstairs.

Podlažice Monastery, Bohemia

1278

ouse was singing when her father silently stepped through the wall behind her.

There sat upon the linden-tree
A bird, and sang its strain;
So sweet it sang, that, as I heard,
My heart went back again.

She bent to trim her quill and dip it in the ink, but she kept singing. Her father stood frozen under the spell of her voice as it swirled around him. The words and the softness of her tone soaked up her joy and sorrow and pierced him, filling him with what she felt. He thought perhaps a flutter of that emotion which had so long ago been burnt and turned to ash, now tickled in his chest, and he swallowed against the unfamiliar knot in his throat.

> *A thousand years to me it seems*
> *Since by my fair I sate,*
> *Yet thus to have been a stranger long*
> *Was not my choice but fate.*

Then, in an instant, his old bitterness surged and choked out whatever Mouse had been conjuring in him. He sneered as he looked at her again. The cell had grown much colder over the past weeks, and Mouse had suffered—her muscles stiff and achy—but the cold did not bother him. And yet, he pulled his cloak around him tightly before stepping into the candlelight.

"I have something for you." His voice betrayed none of the tenderness of the moment just passed.

Mouse looked up, surprised. Her father had stopped bringing her gifts; she'd been glad, taking it as a sign that he had given up on buying her affection or acceptance or whatever it was he wanted.

He held out a couple of leaves of scripted parchment. "Bread crumbs should you ever lose your way."

"What?"

He shook his head. "Nothing. You'll understand sooner or later. It'll be interesting to see if you're a Cain or an Abel—follow the rules or do whatever it takes to win." He flapped the pages at her. "It's for your book."

It was the story—his story—that he had been working on for days. Mouse took the pages eagerly and read them quickly. When she finished, she just stared at them.

"You don't like it?" he asked, snickering.

She looked up, studying his face carefully. He seemed different today, much more like the teasing prankster he had been at the start. She heard the mischief in his voice. As she read his manuscript again, she looked for some hidden malevolence this time. She found nothing.

"I do not understand," she said.

He laughed until he grabbed at his stomach and slid down the cell wall. "It is quite a simple story, my dear. Try again," he said as he finally caught his breath and stretched out on her pallet.

She read it once more. It *was* a simple story and one that had been told time and again—an ambitious man wanting more, a thirst for power, greed, bitter rebellion, and bloody war. The only difference in her father's story was the nature of those fighting and the spoils of victory. God and Satan. Immortality or eternal damnation. The souls of humanity.

Some parts of his manuscript read like Josephus's summaries in the *Antiquities*—truncated anecdotes heavy with dull narration. The rest of it was too much like Isidore's *Etymologies*, dry and academic, which was fine for a book meant to teach, but not for a story. Especially not one like this. She thought perhaps he had written it to be read by others, the way he had wanted his painting crafted for others—just another kind of mask—but where was the intimate truth for her?

"What else?" she asked.

"You're not satisfied with the most epic battle of all time?"

"It does not seem epic."

His cackle bounced around the cell. "Your priests have spoiled you, girl. They scare you with stories of evil things lurking in the dark, waiting to consume the good." He let his fingers stretch out into claws and shook them at her. "They paint for you pictures of battles between beasts, mighty swords raised and storms of fire raining on the damned." He pulled himself lithely to his feet.

"I tell you that Armageddon will be quietly won in the beat of a single heart." He held his hand out. "But since you don't like my story, give it back."

Mouse refused to give it to him. "What have you done to it?" she asked, certain that there must be something more, some other game he was playing.

"Give it back!" He filled himself with power, his human mask discarded and the tendons in his neck bulging with the effort to command her. He wasn't angry; he just wanted to see if he could control her.

Mouse trembled under the force of his command but she held tightly to the manuscript.

His eyes narrowed as he studied her. He took his mounted power and penetrated her mind the way he had done at the beginning, fingering her memories and emotions. He toyed with her, tested her. But he could not break her.

"You are stubborn," he said, finally releasing her and leaning heavily against the wall.

She lifted her chin defiantly. "I do not like being told what to do."

"Me neither."

CHAPTER EIGHT

By the time the beam of light oscillated along the stairs down into the crypt, Mouse knew she was in trouble.

She had no defenses left to fight the onslaught of shock and exhaustion brought on by the past few days. She tried to take another deep breath, but the movement sent spears of pain through her shoulder. And she tried to focus on the present moment in the crypt, but her mind kept playing tricks on her, filling the empty alcoves with dead things. The man in her laundry room. The girl without eyes. The soldiers at Marchfeld. Ottakar. Father Lucas. Back and back, year after year, dead thing after dead thing, and all of them because of her. Even the very first—her mother—dead because of Mouse.

The man stopped at the foot of the steps, his flashlight creating a halo on the crypt floor beneath him. He looked like an alien craft hovering before a landing. He was alone.

He raked the light around the small space until he saw her, folded in on herself in the corner behind him. The glow of light glistened on a pool of blood that had run over the edge of the niche and onto the crypt floor. Slowly he lifted the light, following the line of her leg up to her face. She flinched. He took in the dark hollows around her eyes and the way she held herself, arms tucked under her chin and hands balled. She was barely holding it together. The front of her shirt was soaked and her neck was smeared in blood.

"You're hurt."

Mouse instinctively tried to place the accent—Italian but with something else. He started to lean forward.

"Get the hell away from me." She was sure he could hear her heart thudding as her body screamed warnings at her and the claustrophobia smothered her. She was trapped with nowhere to go.

But Mouse had been prey before, and she wouldn't give up without a fight.

She took a deep breath and pulled her left arm loosely over her head, squirming with pain, and then slammed her back into the curved wall of the niche. Her shoulder jumped back into the socket with a sick crack.

"Bloody hell!" the man yelled as he dropped to a squat. British, that was the something else she had heard. He put a knee to the stone floor and inched slightly toward her, his hand extended, and Mouse emitted a high, quiet keen. He pulled back.

"All right. I won't touch you, but you're bleeding . . . a lot . . . and you don't, you look . . ." He paused and took a breath. "Did someone hurt you?"

"Leave me alone." She didn't have the breath to make it loud, but she did her best to make it sound vicious, like she was capable of anything.

Mouse turned her focus inward and tried to summon the power to command this man to go away. But there was nothing. No nasty swirling darkness for her to tap, no hot energy taunting her with what she could do. This time, Mouse found nothing. The power was silent, dead.

She opened her eyes at the clink of metal on stone as he laid the flashlight on the floor and started to dig into his pocket. "Let me call the police for you—"

"No!" Her voice went high with panic, pealing against the cold stone in the crypt and making her sound childlike. "Just leave me alone!"

"Please, it's clear something's happened to you. You need—"

"Nothing's happened." She forced her voice back to normal, cold and dead. "Just me."

The man lifted his hand and ran his fingers through his hair, his forehead creased. He didn't know what to do. He could see the vein jumping in her throat and the fear running in tremors along her body like aftershocks. The cut on her wrist was the least of her worries.

While he hesitated, trying to figure out what to do next, Mouse flung her arm out and snatched his phone, leaving drops of blood blossoming on his khakis. He saw her eyes cloud for a moment, like she was about to pass out, but she bit into her lip and clutched the phone to her chest, eyeing him with a dare.

He let his breath out slowly. She looked like a feral cat, and he wondered what he was getting himself into, but he couldn't leave her. Moving slowly so as not to frighten her, he sat on the floor and crossed his legs. The light shifted wildly around the crypt as he moved.

"I'm taking pictures of the church for a book. That's why I was . . ." He was talking, trying to lower the tension, but the image of her gouging her wrist with a plastic knife made him cringe. "What are you doing here?"

Mouse just stared blankly at him until he looked away. But he knew what he'd seen at the altar—and now in her eyes. He knew despair when he saw it.

"Do you have friends I could call?" His voice was soft, coaxing. If he could calm her down, he could get her upstairs, get his phone back, and call for help.

Mouse shook her head. The blackness of the crypt closed in on her; everything seemed fuzzy and unreal. She laid her head against her knees but kept her eyes open, wary, watching him and trying to read him in the dim light. She could sense no touch of her father on him. And suddenly, "I've got no strings to hold me down, hi-ho the merry-o," was running through her head, and she could feel the delirium rising in her mind like floodwaters. She was about to lose control. Mouse needed to get away. Now. She shifted onto her knees and pushed past the man to make a run for the stairs. She didn't finish her first step—a searing hot pain erupted in her ankle and ran up her leg. The man caught her as she fell.

"I got you," he said, his mouth close to her ear.

The intimacy was corrosive for Mouse. For hundreds of years she had kept her distance from people, which meant that she'd often gone decades without being touched. To have a stranger so close, his hands on her bare skin, seeing her at her most vulnerable, holding her, whispering in her ear . . . It was too much. She couldn't breathe.

Mouse shoved herself away from him and fell back against the wall, her leg buckling under her as it took her weight. The stone scraped her back as she slid to the floor. She covered her eyes with her hand, pressing her fingers into the soft flesh at her temples as she clenched her jaw against the pain and surge of panic.

The man squatted beside her but kept his distance this time. "Just breathe," he said. "Counting your breaths will help."

Mouse thought he was trying to sound calm, but his voice kept fading in and out like her vision. She slumped as the last of the adrenaline drained from her, leaving her empty and tired. She'd once seen a deer chased through the woods by a pack of wolves. The pack drove the deer, making her waste her energy leaping over dense brush, forcing her through one tangled thicket after another in the direction they wanted her to go until the deer found herself trapped against the mountainside. Mouse was above her on an outcropping. She watched as the deer threw herself onto the rocks, desperately seeking some path to lead her to higher ground and safety at last. The wolves just circled, waiting.

"I'm Angelo." The man reached his hand toward her tentatively.

All those years ago, Mouse had watched in horror as that deer battered herself against the rocks, until, finding no escape, she had lolled her head in panic as she realized she had no hope. The wolves would have her no matter what she did.

The rest was burned into Mouse's memory and came to her in the night when she was lonely and afraid, when she knew there was no one to help her and nothing she could do to save herself.

An eerie calm had settled on the doe, and she walked among the pack as easily as if she were wandering the meadow, her head high, her neck bared. And the wolves claimed her.

"I am Mouse."

Her voice was dead and her eyes fixed, staring into the dark behind Angelo.

The sound echoed around the crypt, bouncing back at her from the shadows. *Mouse, Mouse, Mouse.* She thought she could see the ghost corpses in all the alcoves mouthing her name.

Angelo slipped his arms under her and picked her up. Mouse didn't fight. She didn't care anymore. She couldn't. She felt numb, paralyzed, as if she'd stepped away from her body—like Jack Gray had in the bar when she'd commanded him. She didn't care what happened to her. Like that deer, Mouse was done, her neck bared. Let the wolves come.

Angelo carried her up the stairs and into the circle of candlelight in the apse. He knocked a camera bag out of the way and laid her on one of the old wooden pews near the divider at the schola cantorum.

"My God," he said as he bent to catch his breath, his hand making the sign of the cross. He glanced up, but she wasn't even looking at him. He shoved his hands in the pockets of his khakis and paced a few feet toward the altar, away from her, and he watched her, waiting for her to try to run again. She just stared at a nearby candle until her eyes watered and she was forced to blink.

Angelo walked over to her, pulled his phone out of her hand, and then leaned against the divider as he punched in the emergency number. But again, he hesitated.

He knelt in front of Mouse and laid his hand across her forehead, trying to get some response. She just looked at the wall behind him.

He was about to press the call button when he heard her whisper—"'Which way I fly is hell; myself am hell.'"

Confused, he lowered the phone and looked at her. "Milton?"

He followed her gaze, looking over his shoulder to the wall of the apse and saw the fresco of angels framing the Episcopal throne. The hair rising at the back of his neck, Angelo turned sharply to Mouse, squinting as he studied her. His life had taught him to pay attention to the otherworldly moments, when instinct raised goose bumps on arms and screamed that the unexplainable was happening. He blew out the breath he'd been holding. Unlike most people, Angelo had plenty of experience with the impossible.

"'Tears such as angels weep,'" he mumbled as he slid his phone back into his pocket with a sigh.

Angelo had experience with leaps of faith, too. He took one now.

Podlažice Monastery, Bohemia

1278

ome with me. Let me show you what you can do."

Mouse looked at her father's outstretched hand and wanted to take it, to have him pull her up and let her lean into his warmth—a father's love for his daughter—whether he knew it or not. But slowly she shook her head. She was rolling the quill between her fingers; it was so familiar now it felt more like an appendage than a tool. What would life be like if she weren't working on a book? What would it be like without her father? Both had brought her back from the darkness and given her back her self.

Mouse wanted to go with him. Which was why she couldn't.

"We've made a thing of beauty and power together, you and I," he said as he nodded to the tower of parchment neatly stacked against the wall. "And now it is time to go find something else to do." He was confident in the connection that had grown between them and anxious to get her away to someplace where he could test her power and turn her—to claim her as his own.

"You eased me out of the pit of madness, where I was glad to go. You brought beauty and art back to my life when I thought I had lost them forever. You—" Her voice choked with emotion. "You gave me back my son. For all this, I am grateful. But I cannot go with you."

"You don't have to be afraid. You will be safe with me."

Mouse couldn't tell him that it wasn't fear of him that made her sure she could not go, but rather, fear of what she would become under his influence. The power in her had woken, and not from fear or anger this time, but from desire. Hers. She wanted to play with it. She reveled in the idea that like their soft brown hair, their stubbornness, their dislike of olives, and the way he chewed on his lips when he worked just as she did—like all these, they also shared this power. It made them more than just parent and offspring; it made them family.

"There is no one else in the world like us, daughter. We belong together."

That was another reason she couldn't go with him—he knew too well how to pull her strings, and he didn't even have to invade her mind to do it. He read her the way she read a book. More time with him meant she would surely lose herself and become his puppet. Mouse swore she would never belong to another man. Not after Ottakar, who swept her into his world. And when his ambition led him to make a more advanta-geous match, he had thought Mouse was his to give away. Ottakar had loved her, but he had also wanted to own her, to control her. Her father would do the same.

She shook her head slowly, decisively.

He moved so quickly she never saw him coming. His weight slammed her into the stone floor as his hand closed around her throat. "I will not be denied."

Beyond the flash of rage when he'd found her writing the conjurations, Mouse had never seen him angry, and she was frightened. But she would not give in.

"I will not go." Her voice trembled with the force of her will.

"You have no idea what I could do to you." His spit landed on her lips like a kiss. "And I don't mean just killing you. I can show you things and make you feel things. I can make you do things." Mouse heard the whisper of doubt as he said it, but she also felt the power rolling off him. The power in her own chest swelled with the craving to answer him—like a wolf eager to prove itself against an encroaching adversary. But she would not give over to it.

"I will not go."

And just as quickly as he had attacked, he stood, pulling her up with him, and then smoothed the sleeves of his habit. "You will change your mind." He said it softly enough, but she could hear the warning.

When she looked up, he was gone.

The icy cell seemed smaller and the smoke from the candle choked out any clean air. Mouse felt trapped and she needed to get out. Now.

CHAPTER NINE

ngelo kept glancing back at her as he walked around the church gathering his camera equipment and cleaning up the blood. Mouse never moved. When the church was finally tidy and ready for tomorrow's tourists, he carried her out to the car. As he navigated traffic the few blocks to his flat, he stole glances at her; she looked even paler with the oncoming car lights flashing across her face, the circles under her eyes nearly bruises. But it was her stillness that bothered him most.

He balanced her weight against him as he wrestled to unlock his apartment door and then laid her on the couch. She stared at the window while he iced her ankle and wrapped her wrist. She didn't even move to adjust her foot on the cushion or to tug at where her shirt had bunched when he laid her down. Angelo hoped tomorrow would be better.

But tomorrow was not better.

He woke to find her rocking on her side in the same near-fetal position. She was moaning.

"Mouse?" He intentionally used her name, hoping it might evoke a response from her. Her eyes jerked in his direction, and he sighed with relief. He also realized that, despite the oddness of her name, it fit her somehow. "Where does it hurt?"

"Just leave me alone," she hissed.

He watched her sleep most of the day with a growing sense that he was in over his head. Last night's impulse belonged in an old church with candlelight, but it felt foolish now. Her body wasn't the only thing messed up. It was clear what she was trying to do in the church. What if she tried again? What if he found her in the bathroom, wrists slit and her life running down the drain? Despite what she said, Angelo knew something had happened to her. He should call the police. They would be able to find her family or friends. She had to belong to someone somewhere.

He grabbed her canvas bag on the floor beside the couch and shoved his hand inside to feel for a wallet or passport.

"Ah!" He snatched his hand back, a drop of blood beading in the center of his palm. As he put it to his mouth to ease the sting, he cautiously tugged at the opening of the bag to see what had cut him, imagining scissors or a knife.

A small statue of an angel lay nestled among the clothes at the bottom of the bag. He had jabbed his hand against the sharp point of its broken wing. He could see the tiny smear of his blood on the white clay.

The eeriness of last night erupted again in the middle of his apartment under the glare of the midday sun where it didn't belong. Angelo felt violated and toyed with—but by what he didn't know. He pulled the figure from the bag, rubbed his thumb along the rough clay and then the smooth, tarnished silver coin embedded in the heart of the angel's chest. It looked ancient, timeless.

He looked at Mouse again, still asleep on the couch, and he slid the angel back in the bag and waited.

⚬━✦━⚬

Mouse woke at the sound of the phone but held herself very still, not sure where she was until the pain in her shoulder and ankle summoned images of the crypt and Angelo. Sleep had cleared her head and restored at least a basic interest in her own well-being, fueling a new anxiety as she realized she was in a strange man's apartment. Without moving, not wanting to let him know she was awake, she looked around his flat trying to get some clue about who he was. It was oddly sparse—only a few pieces of simple furniture—but there were lots of books, mostly about art and theology.

"Yes, Father. I know how important this is, you don't have to keep—" Mouse could hear the frustration in his voice. "I have every intention of—"

She started counting his footfalls as he paced the hall and then shook herself against the habit. No amount of regimen or routine would help her now.

"As I said, she was hurt, Father. Yes, a girl . . . a woman."

Mouse tensed as she waited to hear Angelo describe the girl he found at the church, call her by her name and make some joke about it.

"No one you know. Just a . . . a friend."

Mouse sat up suddenly.

She could almost always predict what a person would say or do. She'd had plenty of opportunity to study human nature, and most people followed simple rules. Apparently Angelo didn't. But Mouse didn't have time to work out the puzzle of Angelo. It was too dangerous for him and for her.

"Well what was I supposed to do? Leave her there?" He sighed. "I thought about that but she didn't want to go. She just needed someplace safe," Angelo said.

Mouse hurt everywhere, but she made herself slide to the edge of the couch.

"Hey, you don't want to do that." He was standing at the doorway to the hall looking at her. "Father, I have to go now. I'll call you later."

Mouse settled back but kept her feet on the floor despite the throbbing in her ankle. She needed to get her strength back, get herself mobile so she could leave, and it would be easier if he weren't there. "If your dad needs you, go. Seriously, I'm fine."

Angelo looked at her, confused.

"On the phone? Your dad?"

"Ah, no. He isn't my father; he's a *Father* Father. You know, Catholic Church kind of Father?"

"Yeah, I know that kind of Father," she mumbled. She inched to the edge of the couch again. "Look, I should get out of here," she said abruptly. "Thanks for everything."

Angelo knelt on the floor in front of her and put his hands on hers, gently holding her to the couch. "You're not going anywhere."

His touch triggered her panic again, the nerves in her skin firing hot waves up her arms. "Some people might call that kidnapping, you know. Holding someone against her will." Something dark flashed in her eyes, and Angelo leaned back.

Mouse studied his face but she couldn't read him, and despite her fear, she found that exciting.

"You haven't eaten in at least twenty-four hours. More than that, I'm guessing. You're dehydrated, weak, and so sore that breathing makes you wince. You need to rest, Mouse."

"Why do you care?" she asked. "No one else would. You don't know anything about me. I could be a con artist or a prostitute or . . . or a murderer." Mouse's jaw clenched on the last one.

"I'm sure you left a string of victims in your wake before you ran to the church." He smiled.

"Are you really that damn naïve? You should let me go," she said coldly.

"I'll take you to hospital, but—"

"No."

"Let me call someone. A friend or—"

"I don't have friends. I can take care of myself."

"Under normal circumstances, I can see that. But now?" He shrugged. "You're pretty messed up. What are you into, Mouse?"

Every time he said her name, something inside her uncoiled a little, just enough for her to want more.

Mouse put her head in her hands and stared at the floor. "Why didn't you tell the Father about me?"

"I did."

"Not my name. Not . . . how you found me."

"I don't know. I guess I thought . . . ," he stammered. "I figured that was between you and me."

Mouse jerked back from the closeness of his voice. "What do you want from me?"

But he couldn't explain what made him so compelled to help her. Not yet. She would think he was crazy. "Look, Mouse. Just eat something. Rest some more."

Mouse wanted to push him away, but she couldn't find the strength. And last night, when she had told him her real name, when he had seen her at her worst, he had just accepted it. He hadn't asked her questions or forced her to go to the hospital. He had done what she asked, what she needed and nothing more. Maybe she could stay long enough to catch her breath, to get her legs under her before she ran again.

"I stink," she said.

"I'm sorry?" he asked, confused.

"I stink. I need a shower. Would you hand me my bag?"

Mouse studied the canvas bag as she opened it, and Angelo noticed. "I started to go through it, but I didn't."

She looked up at him, angry and skeptical. "Why not?"

"I decided to trust you."

Again he surprised her, and it made her furious—both his trust and the thrill she felt at not knowing what he might do or say. She knew if she gave him even a sliver of the truth she could shatter his childish trust and scare him into letting her go. Or she could *make* him let her go. Command him. It's what her father would have done.

Mouse looked at Angelo, her eyes narrowed.

"What?"

"I wouldn't if I were you," she said.

"Wouldn't what?"

"Trust me."

"Why not?"

Her only response was a shrug of her shoulders and a wince of pain.

"Let me take those, and then I'll come get you." He grabbed the bundle of things she'd pulled from her pack. When he came back, he found her sitting on the floor a few feet from the couch and rubbing her ankle, which was healing abnormally fast like her body always did, but her ankle was still very much broken.

"Tried it on your own?"

She nodded.

"Are you stupid or just stubborn?"

Seething at her weakness and his arrogance, Mouse let him slide his arm around her waist. She didn't breathe. He lifted her easily and sat her on the toilet beside the shower stall.

"You think you'll be able to manage?"

"Yeah." Mouse avoided his face. "Thanks."

"Call when you're ready."

She supported her weight on the pedestal sink in front of the mirror as she stood. The reflection should have been a shock, but she was already reeling—hurt with no place to go and relying on the unexplainable kindness of some stranger. All of it was so far from any sense of what Mouse had considered normal for the past seven hundred years that she couldn't get her footing.

She blew out a sigh. She couldn't afford to be unsure or unstable. The power had been oddly quiet despite her emotional chaos, but she couldn't run the risk of it slithering to life again—not while she was here with Angelo. She needed to rebuild her defenses and establish that emotionless, calculated routine, but it was so hard after what she'd done in Nashville. She was like so many addicts she'd seen over the years—she'd been seven hundred years sober, keeping her oath not to kill, but now that she'd fallen off the wagon, she had to start all over again. It would be harder this time because she knew she could fail.

Trying to swallow the aching sadness that seemed ready to choke her, she counted her hobbled steps to the shower, counted her heartbeats while the water warmed, and thought about how small her life must become once more. Her head leaning into the running water, Mouse worked to find words to fill her mind, to build her mental firewall again, but it all slipped away like the water sliding down her face. She spit the bitter taste of soap from her mouth as the water plastered her hair to her blackened shoulder.

Today was day one. Again. She took a breath. "I did not—" But the words opened the door for the sorrow to flood in, choking her. She closed her eyes and tried again. "I didn't kill . . . Oh, God, I can't do it anymore," she whispered in supplication and then sank to the shower floor, sobbing.

"Mouse? Everything all right in there?" Angelo had cracked the door open. "Mouse?" He saw her huddled silhouette through the shower door and bolted across the room, visions of razorblades and bloody baths driving his panic. He pulled open the door. She shuddered as the cool air from the hall came into the shower with him. He turned the water off and wrapped her in a towel.

He knelt beside her.

"I can't," she whispered.

"Can't what?"

"It doesn't matter." Her voice cracked. "I don't know what to do."

"It'll get better."

"You don't know what you're saying, Angelo."

As she said his name for the first time, she turned to him, her green eyes wide and so dark they were almost black. He felt something inside him shift, like the switch at a railroad turnout—he had been moving along one line and now he had no idea where he was headed.

"I'm not what you think I am." Her words came in rushes of breath.

Angelo got very still and whispered, "What are you then?"

Mouse lowered her head. She couldn't answer him. She'd worn a costume for so long, pretended to be so many other people, that she didn't know who she was anymore.

"Lost." Her voice was hollow again.

"Well, luckily for you, I'm trained at finding lost sheep."

"What?" she murmured, only half listening; she hadn't heard the disappointment in his voice.

"I'm a Father—well, almost."

"What?" she asked, now staring at him incredulously.

"You know, a *Father* Father. Catholic Church kind of Father."

Podlažice Monastery,
Bohemia

1278

ouse would not be able to finish the calendar, but she thought the bishop would be pleased with his book nonetheless. It was much too large to slide through the opening at the floor, so Mouse wrote a note instead: "It is finished."

She paced as she waited for his daily visit to bring her food and water. She kept her ears trained on listening for the slap of his slippers in the hallway as her mind raced to figure out where she would go and how she would elude her father.

I have thought of something to persuade you, daughter.

Her father's voice filled her mind like a dead echo in an empty house. But the intensity of sound in her head, unfiltered by eardrum or softened by distance, was searing. She grabbed at her head, squeezing it as if she could push him out. He had slipped into her consciousness before, but she did not know he could do something like this—to speak into her mind, to fill it up with his own presence.

I am here in Opava.

Mouse's stomach lurched from the pain, and she barely had time to turn before the vomit spewed into the corner, away from the book. Her head was spinning and her emotions running wild; it made her weak. She needed something to ground her, and without thinking, she began to recite Father Lucas's favorite psalm: "'Come and hear, all ye that fear God, and I will declare what he hath done for my soul.'" As her mind cleared a little, her father's words struck home and she put her hand to her mouth.

He was at Opava. With Nicholas.

Your son thinks a family should be together.

Though what he said pierced her, the sound of his voice in her head seemed muffled, as if the psalm that ran through her mind was drowning him out somehow.

"If you hurt him, I will kill you," she said as she wiped away the bile on her lips.

You can't even kill yourself. If you want to save your son, you must come with me.

Mouse clenched her jaw against her fury. She had to think. She would do anything to keep Nicholas safe, but a simple yes now offered him no protection. Her father would just keep Nicholas as a way to control her. Mouse needed time.

She took a deep breath, steadying herself. She had learned from her father these past weeks, studying him as closely as he studied her. She saw how carefully he parsed out truth and lies. He said and did whatever it took to get what he wanted. He crafted a mask for himself so meticulously that she wondered if he even knew who he really was. She would do the same—mask herself as thoroughly as her father had.

She already knew how to lie to herself. When she had read Father Lucas's letter revealing who her father was, she had feared what she would do to those she loved, and so it had been easy to run away into the Sumava wilderness. But after a few days, the sacrifice she'd willingly made became unbearable. Her breasts were engorged, milk leaking down her tunic, and every part of her burned with wanting her baby boy. She found herself drifting toward the trade paths that cut through the forest toward Prague, toward Nicholas. But she was like poison, tainted by her father's blood, and she would not infect her son with it; she would not put him in danger.

Yet she knew she wasn't strong enough to stay away—not if she kept thinking about him and wondering what he was doing and how much he had grown or what new words he was saying. Not if she kept imagining his weight in her arms or his hands playing with her hair. Mouse needed for him to be gone from her so she could keep him safe. And so she had convinced herself of a lie—that her little golden-haired boy was dead.

Lying to herself had saved him then. Another lie was her only chance to save him now. She had to make her father believe her.

"I had already changed my mind," she said, cloaking the truth with anger. "But now I am rethinking my decision to come with you. I cannot be with someone who would cruelly torture an innocent just to get what he wanted."

I have not tortured him. Yet.

Mouse heard the slap of shoes in the hall and the scratch of parchment against the stone. Bishop Andreas had come at last and had gathered his note.

"Brother Herman, is it true? But to script a book so quickly! It is, it is . . ." He crouched near the opening along the floor.

"It is a miracle, Bishop," she answered him, and she heard the rustle of his robes as he made the sign of the cross.

"God is good," he said. "I will go fetch the Brothers to tear down the wall."

Who are you talking to? her father asked.

"Bishop Andreas. I sent him a note to tell him the book was nearly done, that I would have it completed in three days time. I told him I wanted to leave that day."

And go where? Mouse could actually hear the hope in his voice, and she wondered if he had dropped his façade or if she had learned to read him better than she thought.

"Where else is there? You know I do not want to be among people. I had meant to go with you, but now all that depends on what you have done to my son." Mouse sheared herself from her fear, from any real feeling, and let herself become an empty vessel to hold her lie.

I have done nothing to him. He paused a moment, his voice gentler in her mind. *He is sleeping.*

"Then you are lucky."

You will go with me?

"Yes."

How do I know you are telling the truth?

"Have I lied to you?"

Not that I am aware of.

"Come now. You have always been able to see through me, as if I am nothing but a bit of glass. Even now you play inside my head. How can I keep the truth from you?"

I will come for you.

"Today?"

Why not?

"You are most welcome to visit as always, but I must wait to finish the calendar and hand the book over to the bishop before I leave."

Why not just leave it in the cell for him to find?

Mouse laughed. "An empty cell and a book with a full-length portrait of Satan in it? What stories would they tell?" She let herself laugh again before making her tone more serious. "They would likely burn the book before they even read it. No. I will not take that risk. Would you? It is yours as much as mine. Do you want me to leave our work undone? It is only three days."

Mouse counted her breaths as she waited for his response.

Three days?

"Three days."

So be it.

CHAPTER TEN

S o you're *Father* Angelo." She had repeated the same line more than once since she'd gotten dressed and he had helped her back to the couch, but the title still felt wrong.

"Almost. I finished seminary last year, but I haven't taken vows yet."

With the ghost of Father Lucas playing at the edges of her mind, Mouse tried to decide if this changed anything for her. Angelo's laugh startled her. "I didn't realize I was so un-priestly. You can't see me tending the flock?"

"No. I mean, sure, of course. You've taken care of me." For some reason, the idea that his compassion had come as a consequence of his vocation bothered Mouse. "You just seem so young."

"Says the decrepit old lady. I'll be twenty-eight next month. Should I recite a liturgy? Pontificate on some deep theological issue—the nature of sin, perhaps? Or assess the various historical, metaphorical, and literal contemplations of Hell?"

Mouse pushed her head against the back of the couch as she tensed. She needed to figure out what was going on here, to slow everything down and get control again.

Angelo read it as a sign she was tired. "Want me to let you sleep?"

"No, I'm fine." She was afraid that as soon as she was by herself, the hopelessness of her situation would start gnawing again. She'd rather talk about him. "So, how'd that happen?"

Angelo chuckled. "The priesthood, you mean? It's not as though I've got a disease."

"No, I didn't mean that. I'm . . . I mean I was raised Catholic."

"I figured as much."

"What?" He kept surprising her, as if she were on a roller coaster and the bottom kept dropping out from under her.

"I saw the angel when I opened your bag. It's a christening gift, right?"

And down Mouse went again, zooming headlong into the unknown.

"It looked pretty old. A family heirloom?" he asked.

Mouse felt as if she'd been skinned and her secrets laid bare.

"I don't have a family."

"What about your parents?" he asked.

Mouse's heart thudded against her chest.

"My mother died having me." Just enough truth, she thought.

"And your father?"

"Didn't want me." Which was true at the time.

"That must have been difficult. Where'd you go?"

She gave him the truth carefully. "An abbey in the Czech Republic." Mouse shrugged with her right shoulder. "The Sisters were nice, especially Mother Kazi. And Father Lucas. I was . . . loved."

"Me, too."

"Sorry?" she asked.

"Orphaned—and 'loved secondhand,' I suppose. I grew up in a home, too. Not with Sisters. With Cistercian monks in an abbey at Fossanova.

After my parents died." His eyes were fixed, like he was staring past her, and his voice held that emptiness that was too familiar to her.

"What happened?" Mouse never asked questions any more than she answered them, but she seemed to be breaking all her rules now.

"I was four. My parents and older sister and I were driving home to Priverno from Terracina. My mother played the mandolin, and there had been a folk festival. It was late; I was likely asleep in the back. It was raining. They never figured out what happened." Angelo paused to swallow and the rest of it sounded like a news report. "We hit the other car head-on. My mum, dad, and sister were dead. The driver of the other car, too. I wasn't even hurt. My sister was only seven."

Angelo stood up abruptly. "Will you be all right out here or do you want to take the bed tonight? It might be more comfortable."

"I'm good here. Thanks."

"Good night then."

"Wait, Angelo. I . . . I don't understand what's going on here."

"Me neither."

"I mean, this isn't normal, not for me at least. I don't go home with strangers. I don't tell them my life's story. I don't—"

"I know. I don't normally pick up girls in the crypt of a church in the middle of the night either. I mean there was that one other time . . ." He chuckled. "I understand what you're saying, Mouse. This is definitely weird, like fate or something, but I'm okay with not normal. Let's just ride it out and see if tomorrow gives us any answers. Okay?"

Mouse nodded. "Good night, Angelo."

<hr />

In the morning, Angelo found Mouse rifling through the cabinets.

"Coffee?" she mumbled, wincing as she put a little weight on her ankle.

"I've got it. You go sit down." A few minutes later he handed her a cappuccino and a pastry over the back of the couch, yawning. He'd spent most of last night wrestling with the question she'd raised. What *was* going on? He was desperate to know who she was. He kept going over the scene in the church, dissecting everything she'd said. He searched for missing persons on the internet and even looked up the Milton quote, but nothing gave him any answers.

But as he had told Mouse last night, Angelo was comfortable with not normal. He had never limited himself to the ordinary or conventional— his life had taught him that there was more beyond what we could see and explain. He always kept himself open to possibilities, maybe too much sometimes. At seminary they called him their New Age priest, teased him by humming the theme to *The X-Files* whenever he came into a room. Now all his senses screamed at him that Mouse was something special.

And he wasn't a fool either. As he watched her lift the cup of coffee to her lips, he knew full well there was also something all too normal at work. His path to the Church had been unconventional, to say the least, and he knew exactly what he would be sacrificing when he finally took those vows. But Angelo had never questioned that part of his com-mitment to the Church—until last night in the shower when Mouse had really looked at him for the first time and said his name. He had to figure out what was going on, but spending hours trapped in his flat, alone with Mouse, wasn't going to help.

"Hey, listen," he said. "I have a friend who asked me to snap some cover shots for this album he's putting together, and I finally had an idea last night. The Parco dei Mostri—Monster Park. It's about an hour north of here. Bishop Sebastian might be a little brassed off about having to wait another day for the pictures of Santa Maria, but I can't get this Monster Park idea out of my head. It'll be amazing at sunset. Anyway, I thought maybe you'd like to get out for a while."

He waited a moment for a response, but Mouse didn't have one yet.

"If you don't feel up to it, that's all right. But the parking's good and the walking's easy," he said. "And your ankle seems to be better today. I guess it wasn't broken after all."

Mouse knew she had to return to the real world sometime. Angelo and this flat were all just make-believe, and she was only delaying the inevitable by staying. "I'm not sure. All that walking—"

"Think about it. I've got a couple of errands to do, but I'll be back in a bit."

As soon as he left, Mouse considered taking off on her own. She tested her ankle and made it around the flat by leaning heavily on the wall. But when she came to the open doorway leading into Angelo's room, the pictures drew her in.

The room was tidy and the bed claimed most of the small area, but the walls were covered with different sizes of black-and-white photos in simple black frames. The largest of these, covering most of the wall at the head of Angelo's bed, captured the curve of a river with some buildings in the background and a garden in the front. The light in the picture made the water seem like it was moving; the leaves on the trees looked like they were rippling in the wind.

The other pictures were of statues, church exteriors, and faded frescoes—dead things. Mouse had studied as much religious art as she had religious history over the years, and she assessed Angelo's work with a critical eye. He played with the light somehow, making the concrete and frozen figures seem as though they were moving and slipping beyond their constraints, past the boundaries of wall or frame. Mouse wondered what effect his style would have on a living subject.

"Found my pictures?"

Mouse jumped at the sound of his voice. "I'm sorry. I didn't—I didn't mean to snoop. I was testing my ankle, and then I saw the pictures on the wall and . . . I wasn't even thinking. I just got caught in the pictures. I'm—"

"Mouse, relax. They're only pictures. It's not like you went through my stuff." After a pause, he dipped his head close to hers. "You didn't, did you? Go through my stuff?"

"No!" She looked up, horrified, but he was smiling. She smiled back, but it slipped away quickly; she was letting her guard down and it frightened her.

"So what'd you think?" he asked, nodding to the pictures on the wall.

"They're . . . interesting."

"Uh-oh."

"No. I mean they're more than beautiful. They make me think. Really interesting, you know. Engaging. I want to go to these places. I want to see them the way you did when you took the pictures. I want to know what you're doing with the light." The rush of words captured her enthusiasm for his work more than anything she said.

He sat on the bed next to her. "You sound like you know what you're talking about. Do you take pictures?"

"No."

He cocked his head, studying her. "You paint then? Draw maybe?"

Mouse gave a quick, tight shake of her head. "Not for a long time." She needed to make him stop asking questions. "Where'd you learn photography?"

"I taught myself these last few years at seminary. I needed something besides dogma and theology. Not the best creative outlets, you know?"

"Why don't you take pictures of people?"

"I've tried. They're just not very good. They seem, I don't know, dead, flat. I guess I'm just not good with people. Hey, look, I've got something for you." He disappeared for a moment and came back carrying a wooden cane.

Mouse rolled her eyes. "For the decrepit old lady."

He laughed as he handed it to her.

⊙━━⊙

The car seat was stained with drops of her blood from the other night. As they merged with traffic onto the Autostrada A1, Angelo caught her rubbing at one of the spots with her thumb.

"Don't worry about it. They match the coffee stains on this one." He nodded down at the spotted seat.

Embarrassed, Mouse gave him a quick nod and then decided to beat him to the uncomfortable questions game this time. "So you sing, you

138

take amazing pictures, you rescue strangers, and you're giving up your life to God. Anything else? Master chef? Piano virtuoso? Juggler?"

"If I'm all that, I might need to revisit St. Benedict's twelve steps to humility."

"'The eighth step of humility is reached when a monk only does that which the common rule of the monastery and the examples of his Elders demands,'" Mouse quoted playfully.

"Impressive. You really were raised Catholic. And I'm pretty sure I've completely botched that one," he chuckled. "I'm not good at following rules that don't make sense to me."

"A rebel priest?"

"The Bishop would certainly say so. And to answer your question: I tried it once. Total failure."

"What's that?"

"Juggling." He smiled. "But I do play piano . . . and guitar." He sounded odd about the last, as if he hadn't wanted to say it.

"Can I hear you play sometime?"

"I don't have a piano."

"How about guitar?"

"No."

His answer was sharp and quick. Mouse understood instantly that she'd crossed a line, stepped too close to something personal. But she didn't know how to recover their light banter, and Angelo seemed to have gone off somewhere in his head, so they rode in awkward silence.

Finally, as Angelo pulled the car through a sharp curve, Mouse saw the sign, an invitation in English: WELCOME TO BOMARZO'S MONSTER PARK. It reminded her of the SEE ROCK CITY bird feeder the former tenants left in the backyard at her house in Nashville. She and Bodie used to sit for hours in the early spring mornings watching the chickadees and nuthatches feed. Bodie would paw the window and chatter; Mouse had wondered what cat curses he flung at them. Her throat tightened at the thought as they made the turn into the park entrance.

Angelo came around to help her out of the car, but she waved him away, pushed her weight onto the cane, and managed by herself. While he gathered his camera equipment, she made her own way through the lot and up a worn path. A stone phoenix greeted her, taunting with its promise of renewal: You had to die before you could be reborn. Mouse believed in signs, too. Maybe it was time for her to leave when they got back to Rome.

As she broke through the line of trees, Mouse stopped. Huge stone figures jutted from the uneven ground. Parts of them were visible through the thick canopy, but she couldn't quite make out what kinds of creatures they were. She knew about this place, *Bosco Sacro*, the sacred wood, but she had never been here. She had seen countless gardens and sculptures over the years, so she was surprised at her sense of wonderment. She knew the sad story of the prince who went off to war and, at the command of his pope, murdered the sons of a Spanish village and burned their daughters in the church. Not long after he returned home, his wife died. Mouse knew that most scholars believed Prince Orsini had built Bosco Sacro out of grief at the loss of his wife. But Mouse thought his inspiration came from something else—guilt and a hope of redemption. *Inclusus* came in many forms.

"What do you think?" Angelo asked as he came up the path behind her.

"I want to see the rest of it," she said.

They wandered the park together looking at the exaggerated features of dragons and ogres, the mammoth eyes and swollen mouths of nymphs and gods shaped by some unknown hand out of stone tossed up by the earth as Fate would have it. Mouse understood the melancholy and anticipation hanging on them like the centuries of moss slowly eating their features. They seemed to be waiting for something and dreading it all the same.

Mouse's ankle finally forced them to sit. She kept a careful gap between her and Angelo. The park was a reminder that she couldn't afford to play make-believe. Her world held far too many real demons.

"So what do you think of Orsini's masterpiece?" Angelo asked again.

"He must have been in agony. Torn." She let the sadness of the place seep into her voice.

"Torn?"

"You can see his conflict everywhere," she explained. "'Know yourself. Conquer yourself,' he says in one place, and then tells us to 'Eat. Drink. Play. After death there is no pleasure.'" *And for some of us, not even the peace of death*, Mouse thought to herself.

"He's displaying all his appetites," she continued. "Big mouths, big breasts, graphic violence—and yet he builds a placid temple for his dead wife. He's full of reverence for his Christianity but the Church seems like a predator here. And the pagan images—the dragons, the monsters, the gods and goddesses—they're the ones with all the emotion. His faith is trapped in Latin while his life is ripping at the seams."

Angelo stared at her.

She smiled at him. "I guess maybe now would be a good time to tell you that I'm a professor. History and religious art."

"How'd that happen?"

The deadpan look on Angelo's face made her laugh and the sound startled her. It was a natural and spontaneous laugh, a normal laugh, not part of some crafted ruse or mask she was choosing to wear. It was just her, Mouse, laughing. Her surprise silenced her and she turned away.

But Angelo had seen the transformation in her face and eyes as she laughed; she had been fully alive for a moment. With him. He couldn't deny how that made him feel, though he couldn't explain it either.

He nudged her leg with his. "Hey, where'd you go?"

"Nowhere. In my head I guess."

"Want to talk about it?"

"No."

"Look, Mouse, I'm sorry about earlier. In the car. About the guitar."

"It doesn't matter. I didn't mean to pry."

"No, it's not you. I just don't talk about that part of my life. I left it behind when I met the Bishop and decided to—" Angelo sighed and glanced over at her. "My mum had already started teaching me the guitar before she was killed. Later, I got really good at it, played at some local festivals, and someone from the Hampstead Fine Arts College heard me, offered a scholarship, and I was on my way to London. But it got—" He paused and blew another sigh. "It got really competitive. I was constantly practicing or travelling. There wasn't time for anything else. I couldn't make friends. It was all too cutthroat. So I quit."

Mouse had the impression that there was something else Angelo was holding back. "And decided to become a priest?" she asked.

"Something like that." He wouldn't look at her. "Bishop Sebastian, the Father I spoke to on the phone, he's the one who helped me discover my . . . I didn't know what I wanted to do. He was there for me. He got me into seminary."

"Isn't God supposed to do the calling?"

"You haven't met Bishop Sebastian." He paused. "I guess some of us need help listening." He pushed the hair back from his face. "So anyway, that's why I don't play guitar."

After a moment, Mouse decided to ease the tension. "So you *are* a virtuoso. Good grief!"

"Hey, you're the one who wrote a dissertation about Vicino Orsini's dualism while sitting among the tourists in Monster Park," he teased. "What else can you do?"

The intimacy of the question made her uncomfortable, but Mouse wanted to thank him for sharing something of himself with her. She knew how much that cost a person. So she did the same.

"You see the couple there? He's about to take her hand and pull her toward the left fork in the path. She'll reach up and tuck that bit of hair behind his ear and whisper something to him." Seconds after she said it, they did it.

"Lucky guess," Angelo said.

"Oh ye of little faith." Mouse watched tourists for a moment. "See that little boy? He's going to stumble just there past the sign. He'll cry for his father."

"Not the mum?"

"Nope. Just watch." Mouse nudged his shoulder. "And there's an old man who'll come back down the path from the Proserpina statue. He'll be walking fast, his wife coming behind him. They'll be angry with each other."

Angelo crossed his arms and leaned back on the bench and waited. Then watched it all play out exactly as Mouse predicted.

He turned to her, stunned and sure that his instincts at the church had been right. Mouse *was* something special. "How the hell did you do that?"

She wanted to tell him that, as they had walked the park and studied the statues, she had noted every person they passed, assessed their age, weight, height—and the level of threat they posed. She'd observed the tender looks the father had given his son while the mother seemed distracted and aloof. She could tell him every license plate she had passed in the parking lot and give him summaries of more than a dozen conversations she had overheard. But she couldn't tell him the truth, and she wouldn't lie to him either—she was sick of lies.

"A magician never reveals her secrets," she said coyly.

"Come on, Mouse. Give it up." He laid his arm across her shoulders; she muffled a groan of pain as his hand brushed her bruise.

"Don't you have pictures to take?" she asked. "The sun'll be setting soon."

He leaned down, his eyes searching her face for an answer. Mouse started picking at a rough spot on the bench, but then he laughed and shook his head. "We're not done with this," he said as he grabbed his camera and tripod.

She followed him as he tested shots of different statues from various angles. The artist in him took over as he settled at the statue of a dragon frozen in combat with a lion and lioness, its breast forever mauled by the lion's jaws. Mouse saw how Angelo moved to catch the fading sunlight as it hit the stone in specific places. His khakis pulled tight against his thighs as he knelt, his hands sure but gentle as they shifted the camera, the light playing in his hair—it woke something sleeping in Mouse. She'd fought against the natural cravings of a lonely body many times over the years, but this attraction ran much deeper, like some part of her was already weaving itself into Angelo's life. But she couldn't let that happen.

She left him and went in search of a distraction and found Vicino's Mouth of Hell. The statue of a monster wept strings of moss, its mouth creased in a perpetual wail with Dante's warning carved in its lips: "Abandon all reason, you who enter here." But Vicino had gotten the line wrong, as Mouse knew well. Dante warned Hell's visitors to give up their hope, not their reason. It was what she'd promised to do as she fled Nashville—give up hope of a normal life—yet here she was, hoping again.

Suddenly, the hairs stood up on the back of Mouse's neck. She could have sworn she heard her name whispered in the ogre's mouth. The sun had dropped below the tree line. She stood as still as the statues around her and tried to sense movement in the darkness of Vicino's Mouth of Hell. She saw nothing, but every part of her was tensed, waiting.

After a moment, she started to make her way back to Angelo as quickly as she could on her bad ankle and hampered with the cane. She stopped every few steps to listen. The other tourists had already gone, leaving the park empty, so when she heard the footfalls moving through the woods toward Angelo, she ran. She moved more like a wild animal than a person, swiftly lurching from tree to tree for support and trying to ignore the pain in her ankle, but she meant to get to the thing in the woods before it got to Angelo, whatever the cost.

When she saw the darker silhouette slipping between the trees ahead of her, Mouse opened her mouth, a command already shaped at her lips, but the worry of what would happened if the power slipped free silenced her quickly. Any use of her power now would surely bring a host of real monsters to Monster Park.

Instead, she reached out, grabbed the nearest tree, and catapulted herself toward the dark figure. And then, too late, she identified the smells of pipe smoke and muscle ointment. More falling than running, she slammed into the back of the old caretaker she'd seen gathering trash earlier. The two of them crashed in a tangled mass, face-to-face on the ground, his full of shock and budding anger and Mouse's full of embarrassment.

"*Vattene!*" the old man hollered in her face as he shoved her back. Mouse could sense nothing malicious about him, no taint of her father. He was only a simple, old caretaker.

Beyond the tree line, the clicks of Angelo's camera stopped. "Who's there?" he called out toward the darker woods.

"It's me, Angelo," Mouse answered. The caretaker had already pulled himself up and was leaning against a tree, but she was still scrambling for the cane when Angelo broke through the trees.

"*Cosa hai fatto per lei?*" Angelo asked the caretaker accusingly as he rushed to Mouse's side, handing her the cane and helping her stand.

"*Non io! Lei mi ha attaccato!*" the old man spat back.

"I am so sorry, sir. Are you hurt?" Mouse asked as she pulled free of Angelo and reached toward the caretaker who darted behind the tree.

"What does he mean, *you* attacked him?"

"Let's just go, Angelo." Mouse nudged him as she took a step toward the path leading out of the park. The old man was fine, but even though he posed no threat, she still felt uneasy. She was pretty sure now that she'd only imagined those voices at the Mouth of Hell, but she wasn't prepared to take the risk.

"*Si. È meglio lasciare! Sto chiamando la polizia!*" the caretaker shouted as he held up his phone.

"Please, Angelo. Let's go." Mouse scanned the dark woods behind them as she pulled Angelo to the path.

"What is it?" he asked, peering into the shadows, too.

"Nothing. Come on before he calls the cops."

She saw Angelo bite back more questions as he grabbed his tripod and hurried with her down the path and out to the car. They were halfway back to Rome before he spoke.

"What's going on, Mouse?"

"I can't, Angelo." She watched the passing lights of the towns nestled into the hills along the road.

"You thought that old man was there to hurt you." He was angry. "You thought there was someone else out in the woods, too, didn't you?"

She wouldn't answer him.

"Mouse, I want to help you. I can see that you're in trouble. But I need to know what's going on." He glanced over at her, but she wouldn't look at him. He tried a different approach. "What were you doing? That night I found you in the church?"

She had been amazed he hadn't asked this sooner. She could read all those tourists in the park, yet Angelo kept surprising her. It made her feel new again, like seeing colors after centuries of grays.

But Mouse hadn't shared herself with anyone since Ottakar, and that was before she knew what she was.

"I can't talk about—"

"Someone's done a number on you, Mouse. I've seen wounded people before. I've been there myself. I get that it seems easier to close yourself off from it. Like that thing doctors do to an open wound to stop the—"

"Cauterize. That's what it's called. They sear the tissue until—" The words came automatically, a teacher's words, a healer's words more comfortable than trying to find a way to answer what he was asking.

"But if you seal it all up, it's like shutting yourself off from life. Your heart can't beat anymore. You might as well be dead."

"That's the idea." She spoke so softly she was sure the words died before he could hear them.

"Is it that bad?"

"Who's asking?"

"What do you mean?"

"Are you just honing your priestly virtues—'And the greatest of these is charity'?"

"Damn it, Mouse, can't you let someone be your friend?"

"I told you, Angelo. I don't have friends."

When he spoke again, his voice was softer. "Last night, I said I didn't know why I was doing any of this. I still don't understand what's going on, but I know helping you feels right. And it has nothing to do with my calling." He knew it wasn't quite true as he said it. "So talk to me. It can't be that bad."

Mouse felt like she was in free fall with this man she barely knew who kept touching her deepest secrets. But Angelo was right. She had pressed the hot blade of anger and fear and guilt against the wounds she'd suffered—abandoned without even a name, shunned, betrayed by the man she loved at only sixteen, forced to forfeit her only son, and then her discovery of what she was and, later at Marchfeld, of what she was capable. Mouse had burned all the gaping wounds until she had shut herself off from them and suffocated herself in grisly scar tissue. A moveable *inclusus* but walled up just the same.

"Yes, it's that bad," she said.

"You want to kill yourself."

"It's more complicated than that."

"I don't understand."

"I can't tell you all of it, Angelo. I'm not ready and you aren't either. But the other night at Santa Maria, I wanted out and I could only see one way to make that happen."

"And now?"

Mouse had been asking herself this for two days. When she answered him, she answered herself, too, though she didn't know what it meant.

"Now. Maybe things are different."

But the healer in her knew the dangers of opening old wounds with false hopes.

Podlažice Monastery, Bohemia

1278

Outside her cell, the bishop called feverishly for the Brothers.

Mouse sank to her knees as her father's overpowering voice in her head was suddenly gone, and all her own thoughts and fears came swirling back in the undertow. There was so much at stake—Nicholas most of all. But her father would smell weakness and despair like any predator hunting for an easy victim.

If he violated her mind again, he needed to find her calm, a person confident in her choice to go with him. To keep all the other thoughts at bay, to suffocate her fear, she filled her mind with counting—steps, breaths, heartbeats, and then, finally, the chinks of metal on stone as the Brothers began to tear down the wall.

The grind of the stones as the Brothers worked them loose grated against her ears, as if they were pulling her apart, too, piece by piece, but as the light drove through the cracks like blades, Mouse fought against the joy that instinctively blossomed.

Yes, there would be sunshine and birdsong and fresh air. But there would also be fear and bitterness and running. Mouse could not let herself indulge in any of it—neither the dark nor the light. So she gathered up all the parts that made her Mouse—her feelings, her memories, her hopes—and she wound them up like yarn on a spindle, twisted tight. She hid them away in a walled-up cell deep inside herself.

When the hand broke through the opening in the wall, reaching in to exhume her, she did not take it. Mouse laid her own hand against the low lintel, steadying herself before stepping out into the hall, leaving the world of the dead for the land of the living. She did not feel like she belonged in either—a ghost trapped in the shell of herself.

There had been no redemption for Mouse and no resurrection either.

Chapter Eleven

It was late when Angelo dropped Mouse off at the flat and then headed off to finish taking the pictures of Santa Maria for Bishop Sebastian. He didn't invite her to come, and she didn't ask. Neither of them wanted to revisit the bloody altars and dark crypts of the other night.

Mouse was already regretting what she'd said on the ride home from Monster Park. Father Lucas had trained her well about keeping her secrets. Even Ottakar had never known the truth about her special gifts; he had never gone looking for answers beneath the surface of what he saw in her either. But Angelo didn't seem to take anything at face value. He was curious and willing to look for answers in the impossible. It made her vulnerable—and a vulnerable Mouse was a dangerous one, too.

As soon as Angelo left for the church, Mouse crammed her stuff in her bag and called up the train schedule on Angelo's computer. But as she hobbled around the flat looking for paper and pen to write a note telling him she'd gone and thanking him for the sanctuary he'd given her, she found herself in his room and lost in his pictures again. She lay on his bed staring up at the photo of the river and trying to understand what drew her to this man.

It was well after midnight when she heard the door close. She started to sit up, to call out to Angelo, to do what needed to be done so she could leave. Instead, she reached out with the gift that had brought her so much joy as a child and so much pain ever since. It had been a very long time since Mouse had searched a person's soul, but, with a flutter of both dread and anticipation, she closed her eyes and felt for Angelo in the other room.

She saw his glow highlighted against the blackness of her mind. The intimacy of it tore loose a longing in her, a reminder of what she could never have but so desperately wanted. She made herself breathe normally, feigning sleep, as she watched the glow walk toward the bed where she lay curled on her side, hands tucked under her cheek. Angelo stood, looking down on her. He was so bright, even brighter than her memory of Father Lucas. The light blurred around the edges of his physical form.

He watched her for a long time. As he bent to lift a strand of hair that had settled on her lips, his fingers barely brushing her cheek, she almost spoke. But then the light emanating from Angelo changed somehow. She tried to figure out what was different about it—it was just as bright, just as full, but she knew something had shifted as he was watching her, and the idea of what that might mean frightened her.

"Good night, Mouse," he whispered at the doorway.

Mouse lay thinking until soft light framed the shades.

Angelo was gone again when she woke, but as she came through the hall after a shower, still squeezing water from her hair into a towel, he was opening the door to the flat.

"Good morning," he said.

"Did you even sleep?"

"A bit." He seemed a little too bouncy.

"You've had espresso—and a lot of it, I'm guessing." She smiled up at him.

"The elixir of the gods. And for people with a deadline." He walked a step past her in the hall and tossed one of two black folders onto his bed.

"May I have a look?" She nodded her head toward the package on the bed.

"Ah . . ." Mouse heard the hesitation and worried that she had crossed another invisible line, but Angelo handed her the folder still in his hand. "Sure. These are the ones of the church. I've got to take these to the Bishop today. His office is hidden at the back of the Sala Regia at the Vatican. Would you like to come? After I'm done with business, we could stroll through the museums." He looked down doubtfully at her still discolored and puffy ankle. "Well, as much as you're able."

"I'd love to." *So much for her plan to leave*, Mouse thought.

"Good. We can talk art and then maybe have a bite to eat and let you see something of Rome besides me taking pictures." He turned to walk down the hall to the kitchen but stopped midstride. "Do you have anything else to wear?"

Mouse glanced down at the blue Laura Marling concert shirt she'd worn for the past two days. She had grabbed a handful of underwear, socks, and another T-shirt or two when she'd fled Nashville, but she hadn't thought she'd need anything after that night at Santa Maria. "Not appropriate for the Sistine Chapel, I'm guessing?"

"I doubt Michelangelo cares, but Bishop Sebastian is a little traditional."

"Could you go get me something you think would be appropriate?" She was already limping toward her canvas bag at the foot of the couch.

"Wouldn't you rather go?"

"I hate shopping."

She turned at his silence and saw his raised eyebrows.

"Don't tell me you buy into sexist stereotypes—girls and their shopping?"

"No, I'm just shocked that you trust me to pick something."

Mouse lowered her eyes quickly. "It's only clothes." She jotted down her sizes and handed over the note with her credit card. She realized her mistake when she saw Angelo studying the blue plastic, but it was too late to take it back.

"Emma Lucas?" He frowned as he looked up from the card.

Emma Lucas had been the person Mouse plucked from the pile of identification papers on her bed in Nashville. She hadn't thought Emma Lucas would live long. Mouse tried to figure out how to give him an explanation without lying, but then his mouth pulled into a crooked grin.

"I suppose you couldn't be Mouse to MasterCard, huh?" He cocked his head, looking at her, and she was afraid that he was about to ask another impossible question. Instead, he surprised her again. "I like Mouse better."

An hour later, he handed over a shopping bag and seemed entirely too pleased with himself.

"Uh-oh," Mouse said, trying to peek into the bag.

He snapped the bag shut. "No judging until you try it on."

She pushed herself up from the couch and limped back to the bathroom, resigned to like whatever he'd chosen rather than risk hurting his feelings, but he'd actually done well—or someone in the shop had. The dress fit perfectly, lightly skimming her body, and the flared skirt hit just below her knee—Bishop Sebastian–appropriate she assumed. Angelo had also bought a simple pair of flats, easily manageable for her bad ankle. *So much for the stereotype of men and their bad taste*, Mouse thought with a grin.

As Mouse walked slowly up the steps to the Vatican entrance, Angelo matched his pace to hers.

"Have you ever been to the museums?" he asked.

"I came . . . a long time ago."

"In a galaxy far, far away?" He teased. "Sorry, it's just that you keep saying that, 'a long time ago.' You can't be more than twenty-five. How long could 'a long time ago' have been?"

Mouse laughed but gave no answer.

As they approached the ticket counter, she could see glimpses of the art on the other side of the line of people at the security scanners. The rich air smelled of oils and polished woods and, though carefully climate-controlled, the place still evoked a sense of wildness. Mouse had spent many hours in art museums and never tired of them.

Angelo showed his credentials to one of the attendants at the counter, chatting casually in Italian, and then reached out his hand to Mouse. Without thinking, she wove her fingers through his and let him guide her into his world of high art, absolutist religion, and an uncompromising certainty of good and evil. It felt natural, holding his hand. He'd been right: She was starting to trust him. Perhaps too much.

As she had told Angelo, Mouse had come to the museums once, but it was shortly after they opened to the public in the 18th century. She had bypassed the crowds meandering through the various museums and headed immediately for every visitor's ultimate destination: the Sistine Chapel. The beauty there snared her. Michelangelo's vision told a dark tale of the Fall of Man and a judgmental God. She had wanted to be part of that story of humanity, but it read like an impossible fairy tale for her. Michelangelo's tormented souls had the hope of redemption. Mouse had no place in the narrative or in this sacred space. She had fled into the library courtyard to a secluded bench and watched the other visitors transcend their humanity for an afternoon.

Fortunately for her, the way Angelo led took them through the Pauline Chapel rather than the Sistine, then back to the secluded offices until he finally paused before a large wooden door with a shiny brass nameplate: *Bishop Bernardo Sebastian.* Angelo knocked confidently and smiled down at her where she leaned against the wall for support.

"It would have been easier if you'd let me get a wheelchair," he taunted.

She rolled her eyes at him just as the door opened. Angelo kneeled and kissed the ring of the older man who stood inside the cavernous office. The man looked to be in his sixties, trim and athletic with a sharp jawline and traditional Roman nose. He was quite handsome. He pulled Angelo into his arms, hugging him and smiling warmly. They exchanged pleasantries in Italian, forgetting her for a moment, though the Bishop kept cutting his eyes toward her. She listened as Angelo introduced her, doubting very much that they knew she could understand every word. Then he turned to her and spoke in English.

"Your Excellency, this is my friend, Emma Lucas. Emma, this is my mentor and friend, Bishop Bernardo Sebastian." Mouse saw the hesitation play at Angelo's lips when he said "Emma," and the idea that he had trouble calling her anything but Mouse made the smile she turned to the Bishop genuinely bright.

"My Lord Bishop." She bowed slightly in his direction.

"Ms. Lucas. Lovely." The Bishop's accent was much thicker than Angelo's, and she felt conspicuous as he assessed her. He didn't even try to hide it as his eyes moved slowly up her body. "Please, come join me."

He led them through the large office lined with dark shelves crowded with books. Small lamps created lit universes randomly in a corner, at a chair, around a table. The Bishop gestured toward a table to the left of an imposing desk outfitted with two computer screens and a bank of phones. A few books lay scattered across one end of the table they now circled, and a silver tray with tea service sat in the center.

"I was having some tea. Though I'm afraid I've none of your holistic concoctions, my son. Nothing prayed over or handpicked." He chuckled and patted Angelo on the back. "Just plain Earl Grey. I picked up the habit during my stay in London some years ago. I suppose it was the same visit when I met you, Angelo." He glanced over at Mouse.

She understood the Bishop's strategy immediately; he wanted to remind her of the long relationship he'd had with Angelo, to position her as the outsider. She nearly laughed at the predictability of the Church considering a woman a threat. As Angelo and Mouse sat, the Bishop poured tea, and, as if in a scene from a Jane Austen novel, he offered lumps of sugar and a plate of small cakes and sandwiches. Mouse worked at not smirking. Angelo seemed uncomfortable, but she suddenly found herself much less intimidated by the Bishop than she had been.

"So, you finally have the pictures for me." He extended his hand toward Angelo, but he was looking pointedly at Mouse as he spoke, his eyes narrowed. She felt a first wave of caution.

"Yes, Your Excellency. I think, I—I hope you like them."

Mouse was surprised to hear the unease in Angelo's voice, and she tensed on his behalf as she watched the Bishop flip through the photos. He paused only at the pictures of the church frescoes damaged by time and the elements. He shook his head and tsk-tsked as he studied them.

"We must work harder to preserve our treasures," he said as he closed the album.

"The Bishop heads the pope's Commission for Sacred Archaeology," Angelo explained. "The pictures are for a book to help raise money to restore some of the less-cared-for basilicas."

"They are powerful pictures, aren't they, Your Excellency?" Mouse asked. She meant to make the Bishop give Angelo the praise he deserved. Despite her childhood in the abbey, Mouse had never learned naked reverence or blind obedience, but she was surprised by the flame of defiance that fired now in Angelo's defense. She had thought herself long dead to pride, even if it was for someone else.

Her boldness did not seem to surprise Bishop Sebastian, and Mouse sensed displeasure underneath his benevolent smile.

"You appreciate our young deacon's gifts." It was not a question, but Mouse decided to treat it as if it were.

"Yes, Your Excellency. Don't you?" She offered him his own polite smile in return, but her eyes sparked. If this man wanted to make her an enemy, so be it. Angelo shifted in his chair.

Bishop Sebastian cut his eyes toward Angelo. "He does indeed take pretty pictures, though I fear his hobby has rather gotten in the way of more important things, has it not, my son?"

"Please, Father, let's not go over that again." Angelo sounded wary.

"No, no, of course not. What is three months out of a life's calling, after all? But now the project is nearly done, there is no more reason for delay. I've already spoken with Cardinal—"

"Angelo's work is more than a hobby, Your Excellency, and his pictures are more than pretty." Mouse wasn't smiling anymore. She hated the man's patronizing tone, talking about Angelo as if he were a child or a belonging, and she hated his easy dismissal of something Angelo held so dear.

"Of course. He is quite gifted. In many things." The Bishop studied her for a long, quiet moment. "I believe Deacon Angelo said you were Catholic?"

"I was raised Catholic, Your Excellency."

"You have left the Church, then?"

"Not exactly."

"So this is what you have been doing, my son? Working to bring this lost sheep back to us?" Bishop Sebastian turned his attention to Angelo, but he didn't wait for an answer. "You know that our Angelo is to be ordained soon, yes? If he does not put it off again, that is."

Mouse appreciated the Bishop's directness, and she knew she could quickly settle his fears on her account—she had no intention of being a stumbling block to Angelo's calling. Yet Mouse found she didn't want to give Bishop Sebastian the satisfaction. He was just another ambitious father driving his wayward son toward a vicarious victory; she'd been there before when Ottakar's father had convinced his son to marry a woman who would advance Bohemia's position in the world. Mouse had nothing to offer but herself. This was why Ottakar had cast her aside—to satisfy his father's ambition. So little had changed in all these years. She had no doubt the Bishop would get his way, too, with a celibate son to serve his God. But Mouse grinned at the idea that she might make him squirm a little.

She looked up from her tea and held Bishop Sebastian's gaze. "Angelo did tell me he hasn't taken his vows yet, Your Excellency, but he didn't say when he would."

Angelo cleared his throat.

"I see," the Bishop said. "I'm sure Angelo also told you how he came to us?"

Angelo's mouth was pressed into a hard line when she turned to look at him.

"I assume he was called by God." Echoes of yesterday's conversation in Monster Park about Angelo's vocation played in her voice. "Isn't that how it always happens? But I believe he said you were rather influential in making that decision for him."

"Ah, quite so." His voice was clipped and deeper. He was on his guard and enjoying the game he seemed intent on playing with her. "God calls us all in different ways—though not always in such dramatic fashion. It is quite the story! But it is Angelo's to tell if he wants."

Mouse felt the sting of his message and looked again at Angelo, who kept his silence. So there *was* more to his story. Clearly he had his secrets, too, and he didn't trust her enough to share them.

Bishop Sebastian took a slow sip of his cooling tea. "When do you return to—" He turned toward Angelo. "Where is it she is from? I don't remember you saying." Angelo opened and then closed his mouth; he had no answer.

"I'm on leave from a teaching position in London, Your Excellency." Mouse grit her teeth. She felt Angelo's eyes on her as he learned this for the first time as well. Though she easily gave the lie to the Bishop, she felt guilty that Angelo would believe it, too. A few minutes with Bishop Sebastian had almost fully eroded whatever foundation of trust they had built. He was playing a nasty game—and he was very good at it.

"Ah, and when do you return?" Bishop Sebastian asked.

Mouse had one more salvo. "I haven't decided yet. I may stay for . . . an extended period." She took a small bite from one of the sandwiches and let her eyes flick to Angelo's face, but he was staring into his tea.

"Angelo, I notice that Ms. . . . or is it Professor, I suppose?"

Mouse nodded.

"Professor Lucas is obviously struggling with a bad ankle. I do not know how you could have been so inconsiderate, my friend, but surely she would enjoy the sights of our wonderful home more ably if she were in a wheelchair? There are some at the entrance, you know." Bishop Sebastian continued to smile at her pleasantly as he spoke.

"She didn't want one, sir." Angelo's voice was cool.

"Well, we must all accept help in our times of need. Perhaps this is meant as a lesson for our friend here, a reminder about the sin of pride." He smiled at her and turned back to Angelo. "You go collect one of those wheelchairs for Professor Lucas, and I'll keep her engaged here until you can come whisk her around our glorious art." It was a clear dismissal, and neither Mouse nor Angelo saw a way out of obeying the Bishop's command.

Angelo rose awkwardly, clearly angry, and rounded the table to kiss the Bishop's ring again. Mouse turned to watch him go. When she turned back, Bishop Sebastian was staring at her, his smile gone.

"We haven't much time, so I will be direct," he said. "I know who you are, and I will not let you interfere with Angelo."

So it was as she suspected. He was worried that she was going to tempt Angelo away from the priesthood. She relaxed as she anticipated an awkward but straightforward conversation to assuage the Bishop's fears for Angelo's sake.

"I don't intend to *interfere* with him, Your Grace," she said. "Angelo's vocation is his to claim or not. Neither you nor I have anything to do with it. And I assure you—"

"You misunderstand me," the Bishop said. "I know who . . . perhaps I should say I know *what* you are."

Mouse felt her heart crawl up her throat.

Podlažice Monastery,
Bohemia

1278

A loose stone crashed to the floor as Bishop Andreas shoved Mouse aside so he could get into the cell and see his book. He dropped to his knees beside the giant manuscript. As the Brothers stepped closer to peer inside, Mouse closed her eyes against the light from their lamps. She had grown accustomed to the dim candlelight.

Blinded from the glare, she put her hand out, feeling for the wall, anxious to be on her way, when someone grabbed at the sleeve of her habit.

"How did you do so much with such little time, Brother Herman?" the bishop asked her.

But Mouse was still working to keep her mind full of the mundane in case her father came calling in her head again. She silently catalogued names in her mind—everyone she'd ever met, any name she had written—and she counted the letters in them. But so much busyness made it difficult to talk.

"A miracle," she said to the bishop.

"Where did these come from?" He pointed to the floor.

Mouse squinted down at the ornate inkpots and exotic quill feathers she'd left in the cell. She carried nothing with her but the small bag of belongings she'd initially brought to the monastery. She would take nothing from her father.

"A miracle," she said again.

The bishop shook his head. "Someone had to help you write this book. Someone had to bring these—I have never seen feathers like these."

"Who then?" she asked.

He looked at her with the beginnings of awe. "I gave orders. Not another living person has come down to this crypt but me. And I did not bring them."

"Who then?" she asked again.

"Who are you that God would send you a miracle?"

"God never would."

Shaking, the bishop laid his hand on the tower of parchment. "I feel something," he said, his voice quivering as he yanked his hand back, staring at her. "I feel power."

Mouse knew there was power in the book—hers and her father's—because she had felt it, too. She never thought that anyone human would be able to feel it. But she didn't have time to worry about consequences.

The bishop's hand snaked out again to touch the book. He was already a hungry man, but as he traced his fingers slowly along the text, Mouse watched his desire grow gluttonous and bloated.

"Where does the power come from? Who helped you make this book?" he demanded.

"You do not want to know, Father." She turned to leave.

"You will come with me. You will answer my questions," he ordered as he gave a nod to the Brothers who stepped closer to Mouse.

She knew she should be angry, knew she would normally have belittled this arrogant man who thought to control her, but her new emptiness held her aloof.

"If you do not wish to meet my benefactor face-to-face, I suggest you let me go," she said simply.

The Brothers backed away. The bishop ducked his head like a frightened dog and whispered his prayer of protection against evil and then turned lustily back to the book Mouse had given him.

As she took a silent step toward the stairs leading up and out of the monastery, Mouse listened to the scratch of the bishop's skin slowly stroking the parchment.

CHAPTER TWELVE

ishop Sebastian's words rang in Mouse's head like church bells. *I know what you are.*

"What do you mean?" Her voice shook despite her efforts to appear calm.

Father Lucas, Mother Kazi, and her father—they were the only people who had ever known Mouse's secret. How could this man, whom she'd only just met, know anything about her?

Bishop Sebastian laughed. "This is the heart of the Church." He waved his hand to mean the place, the Vatican. "Did you think I would leave it unprotected?"

"I don't—"

"We have excellent security, you see." He walked toward his desk and swiveled one of the computer screens so she could see the string of tourists as they filed through the metal detectors. "But we also have the means of checking for . . . other dangers." He bent to open a drawer and removed a metal case. He walked back to the table and sat in the chair beside her, their knees almost touching. Mouse pulled back. He put the box in front of her.

"Not many people believe in actual evil anymore—not even in the Church. We live in a world that embraces relative truths and morality as the modern Church prepares itself for a figurative battle for souls. But some of us have been preparing ourselves for a much more literal battle of Armageddon between very real forces of evil and those of good." He fingered the box on the table. "We have some resources left to us from old days when people still believed that darkness walked among us. Those old rituals and spells shield this place from creatures that do not belong among the holy." He leaned back in his chair. "Until now."

"I don't know what game you're playing, but I'm—"

"There's no need for games. I knew what you were the moment you crossed the threshold." He cocked his head and Mouse could hear his heart start to race. "That's normally where it ends. A demon runs up against the spell at the entrance and it simply can't go any farther. It triggers a silent alarm up here in my office, though the creature is always gone by the time we get there. But you waltzed over more than a dozen protection spells and not one of them stopped you. You're something special." His voice vibrated with awe. "I have been looking for you for a long time."

Mouse nearly choked trying to swallow, her mouth was so dry. She commanded her hand to bring the cup of tea to her mouth and willed herself to drink. It was bitter.

"You know, I love old things," the Bishop continued. "I'll sometimes spend hours down in the Vatican archives. It's like rummaging through the largest and most fascinating old attic, and you sometimes uncover unexpected treasures." He nodded at the box on the table again. "Open it."

Mouse lifted the heavy lid from the box and saw parchment inside. It crackled as she unrolled it. She knew the handwriting immediately.

"Father Lucas?" Mouse felt like she was unraveling.

"So I am right." He was quiet for a moment but recovered his arrogance quickly, smiling as he turned to her again. "You know, he was quite thorough in his notes."

"You're lying! He would never betray me."

"I never said he did."

Mouse's temper flared. She had taken the Bishop's bait and confirmed his suspicion, though at this point his own fervor seemed enough to convince him of his rightness.

"Oh, the journals are his, but he hid his work from the Church. These were confiscated and sent here, but it seems no one took them seriously. It was purely happenstance that I came across Father Lucas's old notes sloppily filed away with other dismissed mystical texts." He paused for a moment and then let a slow smile spread across his face. "Or perhaps it was providence that I found them, if you believe in such things. I surely do. I have the proof of it sitting right in front of me. God delivers."

Mouse didn't even blink as she held his gaze.

"At first I was exhilarated by what I read in those old parchments. I never imagined that such a thing as you might exist. But your Father Lucas was so cautious in his notes—just the nature of your origin. No mention of your mother. No names. No clear descriptions—not even if you were male or female." He lifted his hands and raised his eyebrow as if she shared his frustrated curiosity. "Apparently there were others back then who also wanted to know what your Father Lucas knew. I found letters written by a Bishop Bansca, I believe. I understand that the good Father was quite stubborn despite the unseemly techniques they used trying to get the truth. He must have loved you very much." Bishop Sebastian leaned forward a little, studying her.

"You tortured him to find out about me?" Mouse went still with anger.

"Not I. I certainly was not alive back then. As I said, I could not imagine the Church now doing such things—they don't understand that we are heading for war. But I understand and soon, maybe . . ." He closed his eyes a moment. "In times of war, we must use every means to defeat the enemy. We must win whatever the cost." Bishop Sebastian shrugged. "But, oh my, what violence! And still they got nothing from your Father Lucas. Nothing that would lead to you. Nothing that even proved you were real. So everyone forgot about you." He lifted his hands in dismay. "Until I found his notes. And though Father Lucas's work was disappointingly vague in regards to you, the rest of it was magnificent. All those spells he discovered in such remote places and references to the most obscure and profane texts . . ." The Bishop smacked his lips in appreciation. "After poring over all his work, I knew. I knew you were real."

Mouse sat coiled on the edge of the chair.

"But we must return our focus to the present before young Angelo returns. Unless, of course, you want to include him in our discussion? He is special, too, you know. How odd that Fate has put you together. Then again, maybe it was providence that my Angelo would bring you to me. As I say, God—"

Mouse leaned into the Bishop's space, her voice sharp and tight like a sliver of glass. "How do you know it was God who sent me?"

Bishop Sebastian's eyes widened a moment and then he laughed. "I think you give yourself more credit for your acting ability than you deserve. Please don't take offense—I do not underestimate your capabilities. I am not so old or foolish as to judge you based on how you look." He ran his eyes down her body. "But I am very good at reading other signs. Shall I tell you what I see?"

Mouse tilted her head with a feigned confidence.

"I see a hobbled girl who is wounded by what I'm telling her about someone who loved her. Someone she loved. Already you are not what I expected." His eyes flicked down to her bandaged wrist. "I see a troubled girl looking for a way out. Out of what, I wonder? Maybe I should ask Angelo."

Mouse launched herself at the Bishop, slamming into him and pinning him with her knee. She wrapped her fingers in the back of his hair, pulling his head back to expose his neck. "You leave Angelo out of this. Do you understand me?"

There was no fear in his eyes. "I would say the same to you. I do not want him hurt. He is one of mine."

"You killed Father Lucas."

"The blame for his death does not rest at my feet, my dear."

Mouse fought the urge to rip his throat out, but he was right and the truth of it sobered her. There was no one alive to blame, no one except her. She backed away from the Bishop slowly and sank back into her seat.

Bishop Sebastian stood and walked casually to the desk behind Mouse and collected a book. He spoke softly as he thumbed through the pages and paced.

"You know, despite all the assumed conflict, religion and science actually share a fundamental understanding of the nature of the world. Scientists speak the language of action and reaction, matter and anti-matter, while we tend to talk in stories, the narratives of good and evil, the characters of God and Satan." He sounded like he was having a comfortable conversation with a colleague, but he couldn't take his eyes off Mouse. "It all amounts to the same idea. Our Father created the world on a model of opposites, absolutes—a force on one end in continual conflict with a force on the other."

"Get to the point," Mouse said coldly.

"You were born of a human mother, were you not?"

"Yes."

"But not of a human father." The Bishop came to stand beside her and propped the book on the table's edge. "God, my Father, sits on one side, the side of peace and good." He laid the book open on the table. "Your father sits at the other, the source of evil and death. This is your father, is it not?"

Mouse desperately wanted not to look at the picture he slid toward her, but she couldn't help herself. She'd spent hours hunched over the original in the barren cell of a Bohemian monastery hundreds of years ago. It was the picture that had given her book its popular title: the Devil's Bible. Mouse had often imagined her father's glee at such a twist, her attempt at redemption usurped by the thrill of fear he evoked. She cringed, not at the familiar image, but at having her secret splayed on a stranger's table.

"God produced a son, pure and holy, to redeem mankind. Your father produced you. For what end, my dear?"

"I don't understand." Mouse couldn't stop shaking.

"Surely you aren't so naïve as to think he loves you?" He looked at her doubtfully. "Why do you think your father made you?"

"He didn't make me. I was an accident—" Then Mouse remembered something her father had said at Podlažice when she asked about her mother: *My only interest in her was what I could get from her.* Had Mouse been conceived for a reason?

"God had a purpose for his son, too. He was losing the war to influence the souls of men, you understand. Law and consequences are rarely enough to persuade a man to change his life. God needed something more . . . dramatic, something closer to the hearts of men. But how could a god truly understand the heart of a man?"

The Bishop watched her, waiting until he saw some flicker of understanding in her eyes.

"Yes. That's right. God needed a bridge. Something divine but also human. Something, *someone* who could do the things God couldn't, who could see into the hearts of man and touch the multitudes. If this is why God made his son, then why—"

"No. Yours is just one story. Not everyone believes—" Her heart was jumping, trying to find a way around the Bishop's logic.

"Come now, you said you were raised Catholic. I think you underestimate yourself. Surely you know you are not normal. What can you do?" His eyes narrowed as he asked the question like someone prepared to test his subject, to dissect her in every way until he got the answers he wanted. He lowered his hand toward her face again, but she pushed herself back.

"You're wrong. My father doesn't need me for anything. He's the one with the power. My father didn't even care to find me until—" The image of the ten thousand strewn across Marchfeld silenced her. Her father had only wanted her after he saw what she could do.

She had run from her father out of fear of becoming like him. She had thought he wanted her for the same reason he wanted everything: to own her, because she was his, because he could. She had never imagined that she possessed some power that her father did not, that he actually needed her for something.

Bishop Sebastian saw the doubt in Mouse's face. "So I was right. You're running from your father, aren't you? But you have no clue what he means to do with you. That changes things."

"What do you mean?"

"Like you, I thought the path forward was clear." He reached out and touched the bandage on her wrist. "Now it seems we have choices, you and I." He leaned back.

"Something is changing out there—have you noticed?" he asked. "More of your kind have been coming here in the past year—nearly twice as many as in all the years past—as if they are testing us. But not just here. Around the world in remote places, among discarded people, in the places where no one is watching and where there is easy prey—we hear stories about dark things creeping out of the shadows, about people being possessed and doing unnatural, evil things to each other." He put his hands together, like he was praying. "Something is happening. Your father and his kind are preparing for war. Despite the deaf ears of the Church's leaders, we must also be prepared."

He looked up at her slowly. "And here you are, the enemy's prized weapon, delivered at my doorstep in my hour of need. But what's our next move?" He cocked his head. "Will you willingly join my side to become a warrior for the good? Or will you be your father's daughter? So many decisions to make—both for you and for me." He looked up quickly at the sound of the doorknob rattling. "But here is Angelo back." Mouse took off for the door with the Bishop on her heels. It was already swinging open when she reached it.

"What's wrong?" Angelo asked, the whiteness of her face alarming him. "What happened?"

"I need to go. I'm . . . I'm ill." The words were clipped; she kept her eyes on the floor.

"What happened?" This time Angelo directed his question to the Bishop who stood in the doorway, but he got no answer.

Mouse knew the Bishop couldn't keep her here against her will—he'd said so himself. Their spells of protection might identify what she was, but they had no power to stop her. Not yet anyway. But she still needed to get out of there fast. She couldn't stand the idea of waiting there in the hall while the Bishop spewed all her dark secrets out into the open for Angelo to see. She was sure he'd learn it all soon enough. But not here. Not while she was watching. Mouse threw herself into the wheelchair that Angelo left in the hall. "Angelo, I need to go. Now."

"What did you say to her?" Angelo flung the question at Bishop Sebastian.

"Angelo, please." Mouse let desperation fill her voice, hoping Angelo would hear it. It worked.

The Bishop did not stay to watch them wheel down the hall. He closed and locked the door and moved to one of the tables at the far end of the room. So many pieces were suddenly in play. He needed a plan. Now.

He opened the table drawer, pulled out a cell phone, and dialed. "Shalom, Brother. You will need to contact the others. All those times you teased me about my white whale, my chimera? Well, I've found her." Bishop Sebastian shook his head still trying to believe it himself.

Mouse held herself tightly to keep from slipping on the slick leather of the wheelchair as Angelo wove between the crowds of tourists just beyond Bishop Sebastian's hallway.

They entered the space before Mouse realized where they were. The Sistine Chapel. Helpless, she looked up to see Michelangelo's frustrated masterpiece hovering over her and breaking her with what she knew she could never have. She had left Podlažice lice ridden, emaciated, and blind in any light stronger than a candle, but she had clung to the dream of penance and the hope of Father Lucas's psalm. Bishop Sebastian's understanding of God's world and her place in it shredded that hope.

Then Mouse heard them screaming at her, penetrating the din of hundreds of tourists.

"*Malus. Monstrum. Abominatio,*" the sibyls shrieked over and over again. *Evil. Monster. Abomination.* They named her for what she was.

Mouse jerked her head up at the shrill voices and saw the painted mouths of the women twisted and snarled. She expected the tourists to run screaming for the exits, but the people continued to jostle each other for a better view of the frescoes and craned their heads back to wonder at the ceiling. No one but Mouse could hear the sibyls' curses, clearly another of Bishop Sebastian's spells.

"*Malus. Monstrum. Abominatio.*"

Mouse bit into her bottom lip and clamped her hands over her ears trying to shut the noise out.

"*Malus. Monstrum. Abominatio.*"

Angelo concentrated on maneuvering the wheelchair through the crowd and didn't notice Mouse folding in on herself, shaking her head against the wailing women. When they reached the relative quiet of the entryway, she had recovered herself enough to stand, but she wrapped her arms tightly around her chest.

Within a few seconds, the two of them sat in the silence of a cab winding through the traffic jams of Rome. Angelo dug a folded tissue from his pocket and turned to Mouse, who was still shaking.

"You've got blood on your chin." He dabbed at her face, but she wouldn't look at him.

Podlažice Monastery, Bohemia

1278

ouse expected her father to be lying in wait outside the monastery walls to catch her at her escape. She took no satisfaction in the silence and solitude that told her he had believed her lies. She felt cut off from her self, insubstantial like a spirit exorcised from a body, and in her daze, she wondered a little at the footprints she left in the shallow snow as she walked ghostlike toward the village near Podlažice.

She waited at the bridge in Chrudim as a procession of girls, wearing crowns of candles and dressed in white with bloodred sashes wrapped around their waists, crossed the river and headed toward the church at the center of town. The bells were ringing in the bitter air.

"Darkness shall take flight soon," the girls sang as they passed.

It was the festival of St. Lucy, the longest night of the year.

How goes the work?

Distracted, Mouse had lowered her mask of numbers and names. Her father's voice flooded her head without warning, his voice sharp like the cold. She stumbled on the uneven stone of the bridge and caught herself on the shallow wall, cutting her hands on the rock.

Something is wrong.

Her teeth were chattering as she stepped up to the stone wall of the bridge and looked at the dark waters below. She had done her thinking in the monastery. Her father wanted Nicholas as bait. If Mouse was not there to be lured, he had no motivation to torture her son. In fact, her father would want to keep Nicholas safe to use against her when he finally caught her. So Mouse needed to disappear—in body and mind. Her surest and quickest physical escape was the river below: It would carry her to its mouth at Elbe.

Wait for me.

As she stepped into the air, she grasped for something to fill her mind.

"God willed, and heaven, earth, water, air, fire, the angels, and darkness came into being from nothing." It came from the *Book of the Bee*, the first book Mouse had copied in the scriptorium at Teplá with Father Lucas. "Darkness is a self-existent nature. Others say that it is the shadow of bodies."

The frigid water stole her breath and drove icy nails into her body until she grew numb and hollow like a shadow as the water and the darkness carried her away.

I am coming.

He sounded far away again, an echo bouncing against the wall in her mind.

Mouse had survived rivers and being frozen once before. She knew she would survive again. She would live to hide, live to run from her father.

The chase had begun.

CHAPTER THIRTEEN

ouse went into Angelo's bathroom, grabbed her things, and headed back to the living room to finish packing. Angelo shadowed her, but she still couldn't bring herself to look at him.

"What did he say to you?" Anger and fear drained the warmth from his voice.

"Nothing."

He grabbed her arm and pulled her around to face him.

"Don't." She would have to manage more than single words at some point, but Mouse was working hard to get even one syllable out. She was feeling too much—rage and fear and such a bitter sadness at having to leave Angelo this way. She was terrified she was going to lose control.

She pulled herself free of him and headed toward the kitchen—and the door out.

"Where are you going?"

She kept her head down.

"I deserve to know."

She slung her canvas bag over her shoulder.

Angelo got to the door before her. "What are you going to do?"

"I'm going to . . ." But Mouse couldn't answer him because she didn't know what she was going to do. Her instincts were running the game—fight or flight, full out. In the Bishop's office she'd been focused on sparring with him, but here, in Angelo's apartment, there was no fight to be had, just an overwhelming instinct to run.

"Look at me and tell me you're not going to do whatever you were trying to do in the church. Look at me, Mouse." It was a command as compelling as any she could have given.

"I have to go." Mouse raised her eyes to his.

As she made for the door, she tried to anticipate how Angelo would move, but she couldn't read him. She pulled to his left, but he wouldn't let go of her hand, and she tripped against him, her weight throwing him the last step into the door. Angelo trapped her against his chest, wrapping his arms around her.

"Tell me what Bishop Sebastian said, Mouse." The nearness of him as he pressed into her, his smell, his voice at her ear, broke against her in waves.

"He said . . . he thinks I might . . . interfere with you." She wanted to say anything that would make him let her go.

"Interfere how?"

"My god, Angelo, you're a man about to be a priest, and I'm a woman living in your flat. What the hell do you think he thinks?"

Mouse felt his arms drop slightly as he wrestled with his own confusion. She used the opportunity to pull free of him and bent to grab her bag.

"No." His hand was on hers again. "There has to be more to it than that. You're scared. Did he threaten you?"

"Let me go."

"I'm not letting you go until I know that you're going to be okay."

But Mouse was never going to be okay. Not if what the Bishop said was true. Not if she'd been made to be some kind of Armageddon weapon. It changed everything. Her father would never stop looking for her, and now the Bishop and his people would be hunting her, too. Mouse had more enemies than she knew. And the Bishop had said that her father was massing his army, testing his troops. He said war was coming soon.

War. The remembered sounds of screaming men and horses, the stench of emptied bowels and sour mud, the visions of the dead at Marchfeld ran through her body like she was there. Mouse could not go to war again. Whatever the cost.

Instinctively she inched toward the door, but Angelo wouldn't let go of her hand.

"Mouse, let's figure out where you're going first. That's all I'm asking, okay?"

The rational part of her mind knew he was right—she needed a plan. She would be easy prey for her father in the state she was in, and she had no idea what Bishop Sebastian and his fanatics were capable of. Her next move needed to be calculated and strategic, not driven out of panic and fear. She blew out a sigh, looked up at Angelo, and nodded, her mind already racing through her options for getting out of Rome unnoticed.

Angelo's pocket buzzed. He pulled out his phone. The look on his face told her who it was.

"Should I answer it?" He was still pressed against the door.

Mouse waited a beat for the panic to kick in again, for her hand to snatch the phone away. She wasn't prepared for the undertow of sadness that gripped her instead. There was nothing she could do to stop the Bishop from telling Angelo what she was. She might as well let him do it now. And then Angelo would be glad to see her leave.

"Answer it," she said, walking down the hall to Angelo's room. She couldn't stay and listen as the Bishop stripped away every good thing

Angelo thought about her. As Mouse closed the door, she heard Angelo ask, "What did you say to her, Father?"

Mouse imagined the father-daughter portrait that Bishop Sebastian would paint for Angelo—her father as a forked-tongue, clawed beast and her as a weapon to be used in some stalemated battle between good and evil. There would certainly be nothing left of the girl Angelo thought he'd rescued at the church, nothing of the fellow orphan loved secondhand, nothing of the woman he'd swapped secrets with at Monster Park. Nothing left of the twinkle of possibility she'd seen in his eyes when he looked at her.

There would be nothing left of that Mouse for her either. She'd have to go back to the shut-down, isolated version of Mouse she'd been ever since she crawled out of her cell at Podlažice seven hundred years ago. She didn't know if she was strong enough to do it all over again. But she had to try.

She grabbed Angelo's laptop off his desk and sat down on the bed. As she scrolled through train and plane schedules, Mouse whispered passages from *The Book of Bees*, letting each word drive her emotions down into nothingness like bricks as she built her walls again, as she worked to become an *inclusus* once more. "When the soul goes forth from the body, the angels go with it: then the hosts of darkness come forth to meet it, seeking to seize and examine it, to see if there be anything of theirs in it," she mumbled. Mouse felt the tears she was holding back start to burn behind her eyes. "Then the angels do not fight with the hosts of darkness, but those deeds which the soul has wrought protect it and guard it. If its deeds be victorious, then the angels sing praises before it until it meets God with joy."

By the time Angelo knocked at the door, Mouse had lost herself so well that she hadn't heard him coming. She startled at the sound.

"Can I come in?" he asked.

"It's your room."

She didn't look up when he came in, too afraid to see the truth in his eyes. Surely Bishop Sebastian had told his protégé everything.

"Don't you want to know what he said?" Angelo leaned against the wall.

"Not really." Her stomach clenched.

"He said you were dangerous."

Mouse's heart stopped as she waited to hear him name her father.

"At first I thought I knew what he meant. Dangerous for me, as a man, for my vows. But then he said the people who might be looking for you were even more dangerous. He meant to put me on my guard."

Mouse sat still, waiting.

"You won't tell me anything about the trouble you're in. Why would you tell him?" He sounded hurt.

"I didn't." She looked up at him, a quiet hope blooming: Maybe the Bishop had kept her secrets. But, if so, why?

"How would he know if you didn't tell him?"

Mouse just stared at him. There was no way to explain it to Angelo without telling him what she was—and she certainly wasn't going to if the Bishop hadn't. "What else did he say, Angelo?" she asked instead.

"He said you weren't what you seemed. I told him I already knew that." Angelo glanced at the picture of the river over his bed. "And he wanted me to give you a message. 'Act and God will act,' he said. That's Joan of Arc, right? But what the hell does it mean, Mouse?"

Mouse didn't answer, but she understood that the Bishop meant his words to be both an encouragement and a warning. In the Bishop's absolutist view, he saw Mouse at a crossroads—align with her father or align with God. He was telling her that the choice was hers. Act against him, which in his mind was an act against God, and Bishop Sebastian and his army of fervent believers would come after her. Or Mouse could act against her father and, like the Maid of Orléans, an army of the righteous would fight at her side. Of course, that hadn't ended well for Joan.

"'I am just a poor girl who knows nothing.'" Mouse mumbled Joan of Arc's words with a sigh because, like her, it seemed Mouse was destined to be someone's pawn.

"What?" Angelo asked.

"Nothing—it's not important." What she wanted didn't matter, it seemed. The joy of realizing that the Bishop hadn't shattered Angelo's belief in her—at least not yet—was tinged as she realized it came with strings attached. It was his first move in making her a puppet for his cause. That's what his message really meant: He'd keep the truth secret from Angelo as long as Mouse did what the Bishop wanted.

"Bishop Sebastian said he thought you'd misunderstood his intentions. He wants to help you."

"No thank you," she scoffed.

"Why not? Everyone needs help sometimes, Mouse. It doesn't make you weak." Angelo was getting frustrated.

"Depends on who's offering the help. How well do you know Bishop Sebastian?"

"Pretty well, I think. He's as much a friend as a mentor. Why?"

Mouse just shook her head. Angelo showed no signs of knowing that the Bishop was some hopped-up demon hunter, and Mouse couldn't expose the Bishop's secrets without revealing her own.

But Angelo was still curious. "I think you can trust him, if that's what you're asking. 'Act and God will act,' he said. The Bishop wants you to do something, right?"

"Yes."

"He wants you to leave me alone." Angelo studied her face. "But there's something else, isn't there?"

Mouse certainly wasn't going to join her father, but she didn't want to join Bishop Sebastian either. With both the Bishop and her father hunting her, she wouldn't be able to settle anywhere for more than a handful of days, maybe only a few hours. Like a swift, she'd spend her life on the wing—but she was already so tired. She wanted it all to be over.

Angelo saw the resignation in her face and he pressed his lips into a small line, nodding his head sharply. "We're back at the church, aren't we?"

"I don't know. I just have to get gone. Any way I can." She threw herself back on the bed, tears burning her eyes again as the undertow pulled at her feet once more.

Angelo wasn't giving up. "The Bishop said people were looking for you, Mouse. At least tell me who they are."

She shrugged. "Not people. My father."

"So how do we beat him?"

"We don't. It's impossible."

"I've always believed in the impossible. So let's have a go, shall we?"

"You don't understand. My father is . . . very powerful. He almost always gets what he wants."

"So what does he want?" Angelo pushed the laptop over and sat on the bed.

"Me."

"Why?"

"I don't know."

"Mouse, come on."

"Your bishop thinks my father wants to use me for something. Something bad." Mouse sat up and pulled her knees to her chest.

"How does the Bishop know him?"

"My father's very influential and . . . has dealings with the Church."

"Why assume he wants to do something bad?"

She shrugged her shoulders again. She didn't know how to talk about any of this. "You can think of him like a . . . terrorist."

"He wants to hurt people?"

"Not exactly. My father believes in the rightness of his cause. That's what makes him so dangerous. He has ethics and morality, but his ethics allow him to do anything to prove he's right."

"That doesn't sound dangerous, just ambitious."

"The more ambitious people are, the more willing they are to do anything to get what they want." She heard the defeat in her voice.

"Most ambitious people end up defeating themselves, Mouse. They focus so much on what they want that they don't realize they've gutted the floor where they stand. They sow the seeds of their downfall some-where along the way—some mistake they make or someone they sod off. But because they can only think about where they want to go, things from the past and things in the present blindside them. Maybe that's true for your father, too."

"I don't think so."

"Where do you fit in all this?"

"I don't know."

"Damn it, Mouse!" He got up from the bed and paced, running his hands through his hair.

"I *don't* know! Not fully." She could talk about her father in this disguised way, but Mouse was scared to talk about herself. Angelo saw too much of her as it was.

He sat back down on the bed beside her and was quiet for a while. "Look, I get that there's something not . . . normal about the situation. I trust my instincts, Mouse, and I've known ever since that first night at the church that there's something special about you."

There was a tremor of excitement in his voice that ran cold in Mouse and called to the ghosts of her childhood, a haunting echo of Father Lucas. *Andílek*, he always called her. Angel. He had thought she was special, too—special enough to die for.

"I'm not special, Angelo. I don't know what you think I am, but—"

"Stop lying to me!" Clearly, Angelo was fed up. "I've told you—I can handle not normal, Mouse. You need help, so swallow some of that damn pride and let me help you!" Angelo stormed out of the room. Mouse heard the bathroom door slam and, a moment later, the water running.

She shoved a pillow away with her foot. It wasn't her fault he was asking questions she couldn't answer. And what did he mean that he knew she was special? She tried to replay everything that had happened at the church that night, but most of it was fuzzy; she had been so out of it. Whispering voices and moving frescoes of beheaded saints. What would any of that mean to Angelo, to make him think she was part of something? The Bishop hadn't told him anything. What did Angelo think she was?

Another thought came to her, something the Bishop had said—that Angelo was special, too. The evidence of it was all around her in the pictures on the walls, in the movement he gave to brick and mortar and marble. Angelo brought dead things to life. She saw the proof of it in herself, too. She had been dead to herself for centuries, so consumed with running and keeping herself shut off, that she might as well have been carved of stone. But she had told Angelo her real name and parts of her truth. She was talking about her past and about her father. Angelo was pulling her out of a tomb, coaxing her back to life the same way he gave life to the statues in his photographs.

Angelo found her lying on the bed staring at the picture over his headboard. His hair was still wet, dripping water as he dug in the drawer for a T-shirt.

"Where is that?" she asked quietly, nodding at the picture.

"A bend of the Thames near Kew Gardens." His voice sounded strained as he crawled over her to lie beside her on the bed. She could still feel the warmth of the shower from his body, and she felt her face flush.

"It doesn't fit with the rest of your collection in here—statues, churches, frescoes. All spiritual. But not this one. It's obviously important to you. It's bigger than the others and closest to you, over your head while you sleep."

"Actually, I sleep like this a lot." He swept his hand to indicate how they were lying, heads at the foot of the bed.

"So you can look at it? Why?"

"It *is* a spiritual place—for me. Maybe the most spiritual."

"I'm pretty sure that makes you something other than Catholic," she teased. "Why this place?"

"It's where I died."

She sucked in a sharp breath.

"I was almost eighteen. I had scholarships waiting on me at Guildhall and the Royal Academy. But I had no friends, no family." It was clear he'd decided to tell her his story before she'd even asked about the picture; he spoke like he'd practiced it. "I started looking for something to do besides play guitar or piano—alcohol first, and then when it wasn't enough, drugs and sex—anything to fill the emptiness even for a night. I couldn't see a way out." He blew out a breath.

"So late one night I walked a few blocks from Guildhall toward the river, and I jumped. The water was cold, I remember, but not too bad— like a cold bath. The current pulled at me, swept me into the middle of the river, slammed me into rocks and debris. I sucked in water when I opened my mouth to scream. I didn't get another breath."

He paused to fill his lungs, his body reliving the sensation of drowning. "People always say drowning is quiet and peaceful, like going to sleep. It's not. It was loud, and it hurt like hell. My chest and throat felt like I'd swallowed drain cleaner. I knew then that I wanted to live, but I was helpless as the river took me. I felt my heart stop. I waited to feel another thump. I waited a long time as the water drove me farther downstream. But there was nothing."

It was Mouse's own story given back to her. When she was overwhelmed with despair the night Ottakar told her he was going to marry another woman, Mouse had gone down to the Vltava River and let it sweep her away rather than face the future she didn't want. This couldn't be coincidence—something was surely at work here weaving her fate with Angelo's. She laid her head on his chest and curled herself against him; he wrapped his arm around her back.

"Then the strangest thing happened. I felt . . . something there with me. The presence was tangible, physical. It hurt when it grabbed me and pulled me out of the water. Just there." He pointed at the near side of the picture, the area surrounded by shrubbery and part of a tree trunk.

"When I opened my eyes and realized I was alive again, I looked for the person who had pulled me out and resuscitated me. I jumped up, afraid that he might have still been in the water, hurt somehow from helping me, but I couldn't see anyone. I searched around the bushes, the other side of the tree. Nothing. I went back and looked for prints in the mud, but the only ones there were mine. There were no signs that anyone else had been there, not even drag marks from the river up the bank to where I was." He shook his head. "I wasn't bruised anywhere, nothing broken, no gashes. I'd been dragged down the river for miles, but I was barely even wet." He waited for her to respond, waited for her rationalizations or questions.

After several minutes, she asked, "What's your full name?"

"Angelo D'Amato." She heard the mix of sadness and humor in his voice.

"Angel, loved by God," she whispered. The words sounded like a prayer to her. They woke something very different, something not priestly, in Angelo.

"My parents adored me," he laughed, and Mouse's face bounced on his chest, making her laugh, too. But the sadness of what he had lost and what she had never had sobered them both quickly.

"This is what the Bishop meant today. The story of your calling."

"Yes."

"You think God saved you," she said.

"Something saved me."

"So you serve God."

He lifted his hand and ran his fingers through his hair, his other hand still on her back. She could feel him tracing patterns between her shoulder blades and for a moment she tried to follow the line of his fingers as they shaped the invisible tattoos, marking her.

"Why does any of this matter to you?" she asked.

"Why does what matter?"

"Me. My father. My problems." She turned to look up at him, her hair scratching against his chest. "The Bishop, your friend, someone who's been there for you for years, tells you that this woman you've brought home is dangerous, but you don't believe him. You've pissed off your mentor. Who knows what damage you've done to your career. You're an almost-priest and you've got a girl living in your flat. Why? You don't know anything about me. Why would you do any of this?"

"I don't have answers for you any more than I have for myself." He dropped his hand from her back. "But you're changing the subject. You're just going to accept my story? No questions? No explanations for what really must have happened?"

She shrugged her shoulders against him. "What you told me makes sense. I believe you." Because she, too, had lived against all odds when the Vltava River had spit her out. Though Mouse knew now that her survival had been the consequence of her father's passed-down immortality, a sign of her tainted heritage, she was sure Angelo's had been a gift from God.

"It makes sense?" Angelo asked. "That I was miraculously rescued and brought back to life?"

"You're the Catholic. Aren't you supposed to believe in resurrection?"

She heard the half-sigh, half-laugh in his chest. "This proves what I was saying earlier. You are most definitely odd, Mouse."

"That's been said before." She kept her tone light, but the conversation was shifting in a way she didn't like, and she wanted some answers of her own. "You're going to be a priest, Angelo. You've just told me why. You can't turn your back on that, can you?"

"Bishop Sebastian asked me the same thing on the phone," he said. "But why is helping you turning my back on anything? I'm not making a decision here." He bent his arm under his head. "When I was a child, I thought I had been given a gift so I could heal my grief and do the same for others with my music. But it was just a dream, a broken one that led me to the Thames."

Mouse thought about her own childhood dreams of being chosen by God for something special. She understood the bitterness in Angelo's voice.

"That night at the Thames, I knew I was saved for a reason. I just had to figure out what it was. So I went looking for answers. A few days later, I found myself at St. Elthedreda's. I hadn't been in a church since I'd come to London. I was looking at the windows of the singing angels when Bishop Sebastian—he was only a priest then—asked if I'd come for confession. The whole story came blubbering out. I was sure he'd think I was a nutter. But he started asking the same questions I was asking myself about my purpose, about why I'd been saved. Twice. All the answers seemed to lead me to the Church. But that hasn't always felt right either."

They lay in silence for a while, both lost in their own thoughts, both searching for courage.

Finally, Angelo broke the silence. "I don't know what I'm saying, Mouse. I just know I want to help you. It feels right, and I like finally doing something that feels right in here." He touched his chest beside where she lay. "I'll figure out everything else in time."

Angelo reached over and turned off the lamp beside the bed, but light still filtered in from the hallway. As he lay back on the bed, he drew her head onto his chest again.

"There has to be a way, Mouse—a way to get your father to leave you alone. You're not dangerous, and you don't have to do something you don't want to do. God's greatest gift was free will."

"Not the chance of redemption?"

"Redemption comes when we choose it, and not once, but over and over again." She heard the words rumble in his chest and wished she could believe him.

Mouse closed her eyes and felt for the glow she knew she would find. The brightness and nearness of it nearly blinded her as she expected. But she froze when she realized that she was also shining. Her face and arms, where they rested against Angelo's body, lit up with his glow, his soul. She felt like Pinocchio wishing on a star to be real.

"I'm glad he saved you." In her mind, she knelt in a chapel and touched a flame to the wick of a candle as she whispered the words, but Angelo was already asleep.

⚬⟊⚬

Mouse woke suddenly, eyes wide and her heart thrumming.

"I know," she said as she sat up. She'd lain awake with her mind trying to untie the knots—figuring out where she would go and how she would get there, running through the mental list of contacts who could help her build a new identity. She'd been trying to think of everything, except saying good-bye to Angelo. But finally the sadness had won, and she had fallen asleep crying. How long ago had that been?

Mouse closed her eyes again to find a clearer image of what her subconscious had given her in her dream. As it came to her, the excitement tingled down her spine. It wasn't a dream. It was a memory.

"I know where it is," she said more confidently.

"What?" Angelo asked as he rolled over and grabbed his cell phone to check the time. He squinted trying to make out the numbers in his grogginess when he realized he was looking at a text message. From Bishop Sebastian.

The energy in Mouse's voice was electric. "What you said about ambition. It made me realize: I know the seed my father sowed for his own defeat." She sounded childlike in her sense of promise, like a little girl on Christmas morning. Angelo had been right; her father had been felled by his arrogance and ambition once before. He had the grisly scars to prove it. Which meant he could make the same mistake again.

He had written that story, his story, for Mouse to include in the Devil's Bible. They were the last pages he'd done for her. He'd been different those days he was working on it, cocky and aloof. And when he handed them over to her, finished, he'd been like a cat toying with its prey—confident in its ability to claim its victim but bored enough, arrogant enough, to give the measly mouse a fighting chance.

Her father had made her read those pages over and over again, as if he expected her to find something more than words and story in them. *Bread crumbs should you ever lose your way*, he'd said when he gave them to her. She'd found nothing but plain words and a dull story so she'd not thought of them since. But Mouse was certain he'd put something in those pages, something that might give her a fighting chance. She just had to find them first. They'd been stolen centuries ago—the mysterious missing pages from the Devil's Bible that Jack Gray had talked about in his lecture. No one knew where they were. But Mouse thought she might, and she was eager to start looking.

"Come on, Angelo, wake up!"

But he was already fully awake, thanks to the Bishop's message. It was a reply to the last one Angelo had sent him telling him that Mouse didn't want any help: "Remind her that even St. Joan needed help. 'And the angel said to her: I will aid thee.'" Angelo took it as a sign.

"Where are we going?" he asked Mouse.

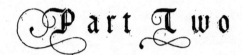

Part Two

Long is the way

And hard, that out of Hell leads up to Light.

—*Paradise Lost*, Book II, Lines 432–33

CHAPTER FOURTEEN

ouse and Angelo had left for the train station shortly after midnight, but they weren't the only ones out and about. There had been a man outside Angelo's flat. He had been standing in the dark across the street, almost invisible, but Mouse had seen him. It made sense that the Bishop would have someone watching. She wondered how many he had in his group of Armageddon warriors or demon hunters or whatever the hell they were.

The man had stayed with them as they entered the station. Mouse looked around as she and Angelo got ready to board. There weren't many people on the platform for such an early train, so she was fairly certain their tagalong wasn't among them. To be safe, she lifted her head, nostrils flaring as she sifted through the soup of perfumes, aftershave, and the sour twang of axle grease, searching for the man's scent. But there was no sign of him.

As Angelo dropped onto a seat in their compartment, his phone buzzed. The train lurched forward and Mouse braced herself against the doorframe as he held the phone up so she could read the Bishop's latest text: GOOD MORNING, SON. LUNCH TODAY? DR. LUCAS IS MORE THAN WELCOME TO COME AS WELL.

Mouse had to give Bishop Sebastian credit for his cleverness. She assumed that the little shadow he'd set on them had reported that she and Angelo had gotten on a train. But by sending an invitation he knew Angelo would have to refuse, the Bishop would "learn" that they'd left town from Angelo himself. Bishop Sebastian would use his prodigal son to keep tabs on Mouse. She would need to be careful about what she told Angelo because she had no control over what he told the Bishop.

But Bishop Sebastian's subterfuge also proved that Mouse's instinct was right—Angelo wasn't colluding with his mentor. He was as much in the dark as Mouse was, even more so. He hadn't seen the man outside his flat. Angelo didn't know that the Bishop was watching them. Mouse didn't think he would like it.

The coded message also made it clear that, for reasons Mouse didn't yet understand, the Bishop did not want his secrets revealed to Angelo any more than Mouse did hers. It was a tricky game they were playing. Neither could expose the other without also exposing themselves. At least for the time being, Bishop Sebastian had to tread as carefully as she did.

"What should I tell him?" Angelo asked.

Mouse needed to be clever, too. Bishop Sebastian wouldn't know that she'd seen his spy. Telling him what he already knew—that they were leaving town—would make it seem like they were being forthright. It might buy them some time.

"Well, we won't be back in time for lunch." Mouse laughed. "But I'd rather keep our plan just between us, for now at least. So why not tell him we needed some air to clear our heads so we could make good decisions—and that we'll be back in a couple of days."

"Will we? Be back in a couple of days?" Angelo asked as he keyed in the text.

It was a heavier question than he realized. Mouse let it hang in the air because she couldn't answer him. And because she didn't want to think about it. Right now, for the first time in a long time, Mouse felt like her old self again—the kind of girl who conquered demons. She didn't want to let worry take that away from her.

"I mean, I don't even know where we're going," Angelo added.

She had made them pack so quickly that Angelo had had no time to ask his questions. Mouse had had no time to think about how she was going to answer them either.

"Vienna," she said.

"Thanks, Sherlock. I had that one figured out for myself."

Mouse kicked at him playfully as she paced the tiny compartment and then laughed as he grabbed her hand and pulled her onto the seat beside him. She shifted sideways on the seat so she could see him better, and Angelo dropped his arm over her knee. To anyone else, the contact would have meant nothing, but not for Mouse. It wasn't his physical touch this time that took her breath away. She'd grown used to that over the past days, but his comfort with her, the feel of intimacy with another person after so many years of being alone, was like a tether pulling her to him.

"Now tell me where we're going!" He grabbed her knee with a mock squeeze.

"Okay, okay." She unclamped his hand. "We're headed to a place just outside of Vienna." There were only a handful of places her father would hide those pages if he meant for her to find them—the places he knew were special to Mouse, for good or ill. Marchfeld was the most obvious because it was important to them both. Important to her for all she'd lost and to him for what he found. So that's where she wanted to look first. The battlefield was less than an hour out of Vienna.

If she struck out there, she'd head to the castle at Prague or the ruins of Podlažice, if there were any ruins to find. And if she hadn't discovered the pages by then, she could try the abbey at Teplá and maybe her son's grave in Brno. Beyond that, Mouse had no idea where to look. If the pages weren't in any of those places, then either her father still had them or they'd been burned to ash a long time ago.

"And what are we looking for?" Angelo asked.

This was the only part of the question Mouse had figured out how to answer. Her memory-dream had given it to her.

"You said something about ambitious people making mistakes in their past because they're so focused on the goals they're chasing," she explained. "Well, my father's not going to screw up like that, but he does like to play games, and he's arrogant enough to assume he'll always win." Mouse didn't want to think about how often he did.

"I think he started a game with me a long time ago, but I didn't know it. It's in something he wrote. Kind of like a puzzle. But I couldn't figure it out at the time."

"You think we can solve it now?"

Mouse shrugged. "I hope so. When he showed it to me the first time, I didn't understand what it was. I didn't realize I was supposed to be playing a game. And I didn't have much time to study it."

At Podlažice she had read the pages of her father's manuscript—the dull story of his epic battle with God—but she had found nothing out of the ordinary. No blasphemy, no corrupted lines, nothing profane. So she'd slipped her father's story beside the Rules of St. Benedict in the Devil's Bible and handed it all over to Bishop Andreas. And then Mouse ran.

"How will solving it help beat your dad?"

"I won't know until I've figured out the puzzle. But it must be a game I can win."

Angelo laughed. "Well, that's confidence for you."

"No, I didn't mean it like that." She pushed at him playfully. "It's something else he said—that he was curious to see if I'd play by the rules or do anything to win." Specifically, her father had wondered if she'd be more like Cain or Abel. Would she be willing to kill in order to get what she wanted? For the first time, Mouse found herself seriously wondering if she was powerful enough to kill her father. Bishop Sebastian seemed to think so.

"Based on what you've said, I'm guessing your father would like it better if you played dirty."

"Absolutely." It would make Mouse more like him. She put her fingers to her lips, thinking. Maybe that was the point of all this—to test her, to corrupt her. Well, Mouse might have to play the game, but she didn't have to play by anyone's rules but her own. Not her father's and not Bishop Sebastian's.

"This thing your dad wrote is in Austria?" Angelo asked as he laid his head back against the seat.

"Maybe," Mouse said as she bit at her lip.

The truth was that no one knew where those pages were. After Bishop Andreas had died, the monks at Podlažice had traded the Devil's Bible for money and a bit of prestige from Rome. A handful of pages including her father's story were stolen a few years later. Mouse had first learned about the missing pages when Holy Roman Emperor Rudolf II took the book to Prague, obsessed with learning its secrets. He had gone mad, like Bishop Andreas before him. By then, only Mouse and her father knew what those missing pages contained.

Mouse didn't know what had happened to them or why anyone would damage a book that, at the time, was considered a national treasure, an eighth wonder of the world. And why steal only those pages? Why not take the portrait of Satan that gave the book its value? She had long suspected that her father was the culprit, but she couldn't understand why. Until now. It was more proof that whatever he'd hidden in his story made him vulnerable. He must have gotten scared that someone else would discover the secret, so he took the pages. Mouse only hoped that he hadn't destroyed them, that he still wanted to play whatever game he'd crafted for her, and that he'd left the pages someplace where only she would be able to find them.

"Why would it be in Austria?" Angelo asked, yawning as he spoke.

"It's just a guess, but I thought if he meant me to play the game, he'd follow rules I could figure out. If I'm right, he will have hidden the pages or left clues in places that were important to me."

"Why is this place in Austria important?"

"I lost someone I loved there." Mouse thought the explanation both true and conventional.

"Who?" He seemed very awake now.

"A man. And . . . and something else."

"What?" There was an edge in Angelo's voice.

She paused, trying to find a way to give him the truth without really answering his question. "My innocence." And in her mind, Mouse saw the thousands of dead men and horses scattered around her with Ottakar's body at her feet.

She expected the vagueness of her answer to irritate Angelo and spark more questions, so his silence and the thin line of his lips confused her. In the quiet, she felt the familiar melancholy of Marchfeld close in on her, but she refused to give in to it this time. Mouse wanted to take risks, not pick at old scabs.

"I'm . . ." She held her breath a moment. "You asked me, back at the apartment, if I was an artist, if I took pictures or painted or . . ." All the words were tumbling out at odd angles. "Well I do . . . I mean, I am an artist. I'm a sculptor. I sculpt." She spoke fast, kept her eyes down, and played with her hands. "Well, I used to. So anyway . . ." She trailed off, unsure of what more to say and a little stunned at having called herself an artist. She hadn't done that since Marchfeld.

Angelo cocked his head toward her, a slight twitch of his eyebrows the only sign that he was holding back a laugh at the odd turn of conversation. It was the first time Mouse had told him something about herself without him having to ask. When it was clear she wasn't going to say anything else, he asked: "Wood or stone or—?"

"Wood, mostly, though I've worked with clay, too." She sighed. She thought of the years in the Sumava forest with her fingers calloused from hours of working the slivers of bone she used as gouges to shape the wood. Mouse had left hundreds of totems scattered throughout the wild woods.

"I took a class once. We used clay," Angelo said.

"Let me guess. You were the next Rodin," she teased.

"Oh, you think you're so smart, don't you?" He moved quickly before she saw it coming. He grabbed her wrists in his grip and pushed her back onto the seat, tickling her under the ribs with his other hand. She couldn't breathe for laughing. She finally got her foot onto his chest and pushed back, pinning him against the wall.

"I give!" he said, and as Mouse sat up, he watched her wipe the tears from her face, full of joy. This was a different Mouse.

"Any favorite artists?" he asked when they'd finally caught their breath.

They talked about art, and then Angelo quizzed her about other favorites—music, food, places. She'd had to answer him carefully about the places she'd been because she realized what she knew about them had more to do with *when* she was there. Despite Angelo's confidence that he could accept the not-normal, Mouse very much doubted he was ready to hear that she was seven hundred years old.

"Favorite Beatles song?" he asked.

"Um . . ."

"Please tell me you know who the Beatles are," he pleaded.

"Sure, I know them." She rattled off song titles in their exact album order by release date.

"Okay, okay—so you're a Beatles fan. But no favorite song?"

Mouse used music like numbers or texts for keeping her head full of white noise, and that left little room for actually enjoying it. She might know all the facts but she didn't have a favorite song because she'd listened without ever really hearing. "What's your favorite?" she asked instead.

"Oh, man. It has to be 'Let It Be,' right?"

"Yeah. I love that one, too," she said as she played it in her perfect memory, letting the simple piano chords and the words seep into her, savoring them for the first time. And she heard Father Lucas, as if he were sitting beside her, leaning close to whisper in her ear: "There is always hope in the darkness." Smiling, she leaned her head back and closed her eyes against the tears as she let the song play out in her mind.

Mouse didn't see how carefully Angelo studied her as occasional flickers of light illuminated the cabin. "Did you make that little angel in your bag?" he asked softly.

"No." Her answer was sharp and final. She scooted back on the seat, away from him so they were no longer touching.

"Then who—?"

Her head snapped up. "Nobody."

Angelo shook his head, frustrated as he watched her start to shut down. "I guess old habits die hard."

Mouse started to laugh.

"I don't think it's funny. You're never going to really trust me, are you, Mouse?"

"You don't know what you're asking." She sighed. "I've spent my life alone. I know you think you have, too, and you have. Without family, at least, and not many friends. But I mean really alone. No friends at all. I've spent months when the only living thing I talked to was my cat."

"But you said a man you loved died at this place we're going," he said accusingly.

"I did love him, but he didn't really know me. He knew me as a girl before I knew . . . who I was. And I'm not sure he ever really loved me." Mouse was beginning to see her relationship with Ottakar differently— maybe because of Angelo, maybe because as she sought to give him truths, she was discovering some for herself. "He traded me for his ambition. Would someone do that if they loved you?" She asked the question as she considered it for the first time.

He was quiet a moment before he answered. "No."

"Angelo, I could tell you what happened at Marchfeld," Mouse said. "But it would change everything."

"I've already told you I don't see the world in the same way as everyone else. My understanding of how things work was changed long before I met you." He sounded belligerent.

She couldn't tell Angelo about the angel in her bag, so she gave him what she could: another piece of herself.

"Strawberries," Mouse said. "When I was little, I loved strawberries with really cold, fresh cream." She let herself drift into the memory, her mouth full of sweetness.

But Angelo stayed silent.

Mouse never knew if he slept on the train; she hadn't. She guessed by the dark circles under his eyes that he hadn't either. The only words they'd exchanged since the conversation last night came as they walked away from the rental-car counter.

"So you speak fluent German?" Angelo asked. The words felt like another accusation of yet one more thing he didn't know about her. Mouse ignored him.

Half an hour out of Vienna, Angelo finally broke the silence again though he still sounded tense. "I suppose you know where we're going?"

"It's not much farther. Maybe fifteen minutes?"

As they crested the small hill, she saw the field covered in purple lupin. A jagged piece of rock jutted from the ground, engraved with a knight and horse rearing, banner flying—a monument for the thousands who had died here. A marker for the men Mouse had killed.

They pulled over and parked. She leaned heavily against the car door and looked out over the site for the first time since the bloody battle. She'd always imagined this place as the epicenter of what her life had become. There was before Marchfeld. And after. Mouse hadn't anticipated how tough it would be to walk the fault line again, but now that she was here, she couldn't make herself take the first step.

"Come on," Angelo said gently, taking her hand and leading her out into the field.

Mouse was soon lost in a remembered world of battle filth and spilled blood. She let go of Angelo and moved along a path toward an easy dip in the hills—a place only she would know. The river had eaten a crooked bite out of the field and eroded the bank where she had gotten her first view of the battle so long ago.

The strewn bodies of men and boys and horses filled her imagination. They were so present in her mind that Mouse stumbled as she worked to step over the ghostly corpses. She stopped, the curse of her perfect memory marking just where she had lost herself and her life. She could almost hear the caw of the carrion crows flying in from the riverbank.

Mouse paused until the sunshine and breeze scattered the centuries-old memories, but her body stayed tense, waiting to feel the twist of power in her again. It had had its first taste of freedom here on this acre of land, let loose by her careless grief. She expected it to stir and beg for release. But the power had been strangely quiet these last few days—silent since she met Angelo. She looked up at him suddenly, wondering. Despite her lack of ritual, despite being caught in a torrent of emotion—despair and then hope—the beast in her still slept. Mouse wondered if it was because of Angelo.

"Is this where he—" Angelo asked sharply.

"Yes, he died just here." She put her hand lightly on the ground.

"No, I mean, where did you lose your—"

"What?"

"Just . . . just tell me where to look." Agitation rushed the words from him, unusually heavy with his Italian accent.

"What are you talking about? Where I lost my—" Then Mouse understood. "Oh! I said I lost my innocence. You thought I meant—"

"You mean you and he didn't?"

"Here? In a field? No!" She shook her head, smiling. "You have some stories to tell? The virtuoso and the milkmaid go into a cow pasture . . ."

"You're impossible." Angelo shoved her playfully and then headed toward the monument near the road.

"I don't think the pages are here," Mouse called after Angelo. She was sure she would feel them if they were. They would be tainted with the leftover power that Bishop Andreas had felt in the book when she left it with him at Podlažice.

"We should still look around, just in case," he yelled back as he ran his hands along the monument, reading. Angelo pulled a pen from his pocket and wrote names on his hand. And the date. He was curious about what this place really was, and he knew he wouldn't get answers from Mouse.

Mouse had gotten halfway to the river when the nerves at the back of her neck prickled in warning, and she spun around. She stood still as she searched the shadows near the monument beside Angelo. Then she saw it—an opaque shape slinking through the darkness, its eyes glowing with hunger as it stalked Angelo. The creature foamed at the mouth as it leaned forward into the light, ready to claim its prey.

"Angelo!" Mouse screamed.

She wouldn't get there in time.

The creature turned its face toward Mouse. She crouched, sure it was about to attack, but then it jerked oddly, stepped back into the shadows, and disappeared.

Angelo ran to Mouse just as she meant him to—away from the thing in the dark. She twisted around him looking for the creature but saw nothing.

"What?" Angelo asked, breathless.

"I . . . I thought I saw something. Someone." She pulled him closer to her, but he backed away quickly, looking over his shoulder toward the monument.

"There's nothing there," he said.

"No." She couldn't stop scanning the tree line.

"Ghosts from your past, maybe?"

"Maybe. Let's go. The manuscript's not here."

Mouse expected questions on the ride back to Vienna. She got silence instead. She wished they could talk about something that would help her feel normal again, but Angelo kept staring out the window. Mouse spent her time stealing glances at him and checking the mirrors, her thumbs drumming the steering wheel. She knew what she had seen in the field, and she knew what it meant. Her father had left a sentry to watch for her. Mouse wondered how long the thing had been waiting out in that field for her to come back. The good news was that it meant she was on the right track. But now her father would know she had been there. Now he would be on his guard. And Mouse needed to be prepared.

"Who died in that field?" Angelo's voice broke the silence sharply, startling her.

"I told you. Someone I loved." She was instantly wary.

"How did he die?"

Mouse couldn't breathe. "He was killed."

"How?" There was something in his voice Mouse hadn't heard before. She didn't know what it meant, but it scared her.

"Why does it matter?"

"Please, Mouse."

She sighed. The creature in the field was also a sobering reminder that, regardless of how she meant to play the game, her father followed no rules. He didn't care about collateral damage. He didn't care about who was innocent and who wasn't. He didn't care if someone was in the wrong place at the wrong time. He would play to win—whatever it took. And now that he was in the game, it was too dangerous for Angelo to stay. Mouse had to continue looking for the missing pages, but Angelo didn't have to go with her. She would use truth to make Angelo go home.

"I did it," she answered him, trying to keep her voice cold and matter-of-fact.

He snapped his head around to look at her. "Why?"

"Does it matter?"

"Very much."

"I don't see how."

"It depends on how you killed him—if it was an accident or not. Or why you did it. If you were defending yourself, then . . ." His tone was high, like a question, and he turned away again.

"No, Angelo. You wanted to know my secrets? Well, there you go—I'm a murderer." Her voice broke knowing that she would never be able to take this back.

"Did you want to do it?" he finally asked, quietly.

"No." She sounded tired; she knew where the questions were headed because she had asked them all herself many times.

"Did you do it to get something? Money?"

"No."

"Did you do it to keep a secret?"

It hurt to realize what he must think of her, but it was necessary so he would go back home. So he would be safe. "No."

"Because you like to kill?"

"No."

"Out of jealousy?"

"No."

And finally, "Mouse, did you do it for revenge?"

Mouse searched herself, even more thoroughly than when she asked herself the same question many times over the many years. With a sigh, she gave the same answer: "No."

"Then you're not a murderer, Mouse." He looked at her as he said it, but he held his face carefully still.

"Is that a priest talking?" she asked.

He wouldn't answer the question. At least not out loud.

A few moments went by in silence.

"Angelo?"

"What?"

"You never asked me if I meant to do it."

Back in Vienna, they found a café near the station after they returned the car. Mouse took a seat in the corner at the back. She needed to see the people coming in. Sooner or later, her father would send someone. She scanned faces as she and Angelo ordered food. Neither of them ate.

"Back to Rome, then?" she asked. She was trying to give him an easy out.

Angelo pulled his phone out of his pocket. The Bishop had sent several texts asking where Angelo was and telling him to call.

"Isn't there anywhere else to look?" He was irritated, his tone clipped.

"Yes, but—"

"Where?"

"Prague. I lived there for a while. With the man from the field."

Angelo played with his fork then tossed it on the table. Mouse jumped at the loud clank it made as it hit the edge of the plate. He squinted as he looked at her. "I guess it's Prague then."

"The train leaves in an hour."

"How the hell do you know that?"

She looked away, unable to explain that she had seen the schedule when she had booked the train from Rome and that she could give him a complete menu of destinations and departure times for all the stations along their route.

She continued without answering. "There's a hotel there I know. The Red Lion. I can call and make a reservation."

"Look, Mouse, I need some air. I'll meet you at the station. All right?" He kept his eyes on his bag as he maneuvered it past the chair and onto his shoulder.

Mouse knew his voice well enough now to hear the lie, and she knew she deserved it.

The door jingled as it closed behind him.

CHAPTER FIFTEEN

ouse kept looking behind her as she walked through the misty drizzle to the train station at Vienna Meidling. Tiny pearls of moisture gathered along the pattern of leaves on the front of her dress like drops of dew, and every snap of her head sent them shuddering violently down to the sidewalk. She didn't know what she was looking for as she scanned the shadows. She doubted that Bishop Sebastian had any way of tracking her here. A minion from her father, like the one in the field, was much more likely. She peered into each dark alley, almost eagerly, but there was nothing there.

She lowered her head and watched the water slowly ball at the end of a strand of hair, and then it let go. Mouse gritted her teeth and forced her eyes forward. She knew why she really kept looking back. It wasn't fear that strained her ears listening for footfalls; it was hope. And it was pathetic. Angelo wouldn't be there. Her little bit of dark truth had sent him running, just as she'd meant it to. But it still stung.

She chided herself for the feeling of disappointment when he wasn't waiting at the station like he said he would be. There was no one on the platform, no one waiting for the train to Prague. There was no one in the bathroom when she went to wash her face.

Mouse was alone. Again.

She rested her head against the mirror, her breath and the warm wetness of her hair making a pattern of fog on the glass, and she swallowed all her longing.

Then she heard him.

"Olly olly oxen free."

Not in her head this time, but real and live. It was the first time since Podlažice that she'd heard his voice with her ears instead of it piercing her mind. It seemed oddly hollow as it bounced against the bathroom tile. She watched the reflection of him in the mirror rake the water from his shoulder. He wore his typical black but a modern version in dark denim, black shirt, and trench coat. The bitter taste of adrenaline pulled her lips into a sneer as her eyes met his in the mirror, but she held tightly to the sink to keep herself from spinning around to face him. She refused to give him the satisfaction of seeing her afraid. "Where have you been?" she spat.

"Busy. But I'm here now. Let's go, daughter of mine." He stretched out his hand, motioning her to move toward him. "Home again, home again, jiggety-jig." He was picking up exactly where they had left off seven hundred years ago.

Every muscle in her body grew taut with her refusal; she could barely shake her head. She saw the flash of anger in his eyes as he lifted his hand to his hair and looked up. The fluorescent lights popped with the overrun energy in the room. Mouse blinked and everything turned eerily normal again, his face pleasant and his eyes placid.

"I just wanted to check on you. Let you know I was here for you," the reflection said innocently. "If you needed me."

"Just a concerned dad looking out for his girl?" she said bitterly, her nostrils flaring with her panic and sucking in the stench of stale urine and bleach. He was between her and the door out. She was trapped.

"Why not? That's what I am," he said.

"What?"

"Concerned. You . . . weren't yourself in Nashville. But I guess you got everything ironed out." The face in the mirror smiled as he arrogantly reminded her how easily he could play with her mind and take from it what he wanted. "And I heard you've been to Marchfeld. That can't be a good sign."

Mouse watched the water circling the drain. His patronizing tone reminded her of Bishop Sebastian, and her fingernails screeched against the countertop, curling with a desire to rip his throat out. She felt sure her father could kill her easily if he wanted. She knew it, instinctively, like a lamb come face-to-face with the lion. It could be brutal and bloody and she would welcome it. Mouse wasn't afraid to die, but she was afraid to live—as her father's puppet, as a tool for controlling the minds of thousands, as a weapon unleashed on his enemies. She would not let that happen.

"Just reliving old times," she said, fear and anger pulsing in her neck as she began playing out options in her head.

As always, her father read her easily. "Wait, wait. I call King's X. How do they say it in America?" His eyebrows creased for a moment and then the loud clap of his hands rang out. "Time-out—that's it!"

"What do you want?" she asked again. She was starting to shake, her senses overloading as she tried to figure out her next move. If Bishop Sebastian was right, that Mouse had gifts her father craved, she could not understand why he hesitated. Her father simply took what he wanted and now, after seven hundred years of searching, he had finally caught her, unprepared and alone. Why not take her in this moment of her weakness?

Mouse looked for answers in her father's reflection. What she saw shocked her. The corners of his mouth twitched uneasily. He was nervous, almost afraid—unsure of himself and unsure about her. She tried to see him through the Bishop's eyes, and suddenly Mouse began to wonder about the limits of her father's power—and the reaches of her own. The power that had slept peacefully these last days jumped to life in her chest, ready to be freed, eager to be tested.

She was sure her father must have felt it, too. He put his hands together, lifting them to rest under his chin, the two index fingers forming a steeple against which he slowly nodded. Mouse knew the gesture; she did the same thing when she was trying to settle on a strategy.

"What I want is you, but you already know that." His voice, warm and slick, ran down her spine. She shuddered and closed her eyes.

When Mouse looked up to the mirror again, he was standing right behind her. She had never heard him move. She gripped the porcelain in preparation.

He leaned toward her, the corner of his coat held in his fist. Just inches and he could wrap her in darkness and take her home. She would finally be his.

"Ah, Peter, Peter, pumpkin-eater, had a daughter. But how to keep her?" He smacked his lips in resignation.

Mouse cocked her head, confused.

"I think I might let you come to me instead. Might see if I can find the honey to draw in my little fly." He sighed as he let go of his coat. "But it will have to wait. I'm going to be busy with something for a while. Little Jack Horner sitting in his corner." He stretched his hand toward her. It was just a hand, but she felt the claws prick her back all the same. "Don't worry, though, I'll still be watching out for you. I always do. And now I know I can find you. What a good boy am I!"

He moved toward the door but then turned back to her, grinning. "I heard there was someone with you? At Marchfeld this morning? Where is he? I'd like to meet your little friend."

Mouse straightened and tried to swallow, searching for the answer that might save Angelo's life. "He's gone. He got . . . bored. Following me to some stupid field. It means nothing to him. I mean nothing to him." In the mirror, she looked into her father's eyes, too much like her own, which now darkened with her anger.

"He's gone," she said again as she lowered her eyes and turned off the water.

"Oh, really?" Her father's voice was already fading. *Well, don't worry, dear. You've always got family.*

She knew he was gone before she checked the mirror, but she could feel the power roiling inside her still. She didn't know if his presence had triggered it or if it had been ignited by her anger and fear.

It wanted out. Mouse had to do something with it. She leaned her forehead against the smooth surface of the mirror again and stretched her arms to either side, fingers squeaking against the glass. Fissures erupted along the mirror, shattering the reflection into slivers and shards. Dozens of distorted Mouse images stared back at her, each with a thin line of blood stretching across its forehead where a piece of glass sliced the skin. None of her fractured visages offered any answers about why her father had let her go.

He'd seemed nervous, distracted. He said he was busy. Maybe the Bishop was right and her father was amassing an army of demons for the oncoming war. Maybe her father didn't want to have to deal with her until he was ready to set her off like some bomb to decimate his enemy at a strategic moment.

But as she thought about his little pumpkin-eater joke, Mouse wondered about another possibility. Maybe he had the same problem as the Bishop—maybe her father didn't have the means to capture or to keep her. Maybe he needed, or wanted, her to join him of her own free will. If that was the case, it would buy her some time.

Mouse sighed. She felt more like that deer than ever—wolves on either side running her through the woods. They kept driving her in the direction they wanted her to go, but Mouse had no intention of getting trapped against the rocks. Not by Bishop Sebastian and not by her father. Mouse would go her own way and she needed whatever leverage her father had hidden in those pages of the Devil's Bible.

She headed out to the platform. There was no still sign of Angelo. No sign of her father, and none of the Bishop's spies. At the last call,

Mouse boarded the train to Prague alone. She dropped onto the seat in her compartment, exhausted from the drain of power, and she pulled out her sewing box. Her hands moved incessantly—pushing needle, pulling thread. She focused on laying her loneliness and her fear against the linen square, wrapping them in colored floss, burying them beneath the image that took shape. For the first time, Mouse stitched from her imagination rather than copying something from memory. She created a picture of Angelo bent over his guitar. She used the silk threads to catch the light and give life to the music she imagined coming from the strings as Angelo's fingers plucked them.

She would burn it when she was done as she did with all her art, leaving behind no evidence that she'd been in the world. It would also be a way to say good-bye. Mouse pushed back against the wave of sadness that pulled at her—that she would never see Angelo again, never get to hear him play.

Angrily, she threw the unfinished needlework onto the seat beside her. There was no time to wallow in self-pity. Her father said he was busy, which seemed to confirm the Bishop's conclusion that something was about to happen. And if her father was planning to unleash a storm of evil on the world, Mouse had a responsibility—not only to ensure that she wasn't the tornado at the epicenter of that storm but also to stop the storm from coming at all. If she could.

⊶⊷

Later, from her room at the Red Lion, Mouse watched the sun rise over Prague Castle for the first time in more than seven hundred years. She had expected to feel something—nostalgia or loss or a sense of coming home—but she just felt empty and odd. Once, she had known the city streets and the market vendors; she and Ottakar had claimed the place as a playground when he wasn't plotting some new conquest or wrestling with the duties of state. But there was nothing left of the Prague she knew.

She was just another tourist when the castle opened that morning. She stepped though unfamiliar gates built in the 16th century with not even an old stone left of the ones she had ridden through so many centuries ago. The courtyard that had once been full of the smells and sounds of castle life—the clang of swords and the bawdy jokes of the soldiers, the whinny and bray of the animals and the sourness of the mud—it had all been encased in stone, flat and level and dead. Even Ottakar's mother's garden, where Mouse had shed her childhood and left it among the withered roses, had turned to ash and lay buried under concrete.

All of the basic pieces were still here—St. Vitus's, the palace, St. George's—but they all wore different faces. Mouse was just the opposite. Her face was the same, but everything else about her was different from when she'd been here last. Was there even a sliver left of that long-ago Mouse who had been full of courage and hope? Angelo had made her think so. She wondered if the ghosts of old Prague also still lived in the ruins beneath the castle where the archaeologists excavated pieces of the life she'd shared with Ottakar.

In the quiet splendor of St. Vitus Cathedral, Mouse walked past the tombs of people she once knew—all of them bone dust in empty boxes now. The words of a requiem filled her mind. It was *Dies Irae*, the Day of Wrath. She waited for the heaviness of grief to settle on her as she approached the Chapel of Relics where Charles IV had moved Ottakar's tomb when St.Vitus's had been expanded from a basilica to cathedral. The sarcophagi of Ottakar and his grandfather flanked the enclave that had also once held Charles's most treasured holy relics. Ottakar's father, mad King Vaclav, had been left in obscurity at St. Agnes's convent. Mouse couldn't help the flush of satisfaction and taste of revenge that crept into her smile.

The smile faded quickly when she reached the gate to the enclave. It was locked. She took a quick look around—most of the tourists were on the front side of the altar. She'd seen a guard roaming the nave, but Mouse only needed a few minutes. Tensing, she pressed against the gold metalwork atop the dividing wall and jumped. She landed silently and then quickly crouched behind Ottakar's tomb. The steady hum of tourists marveling at the beauty of the church confirmed Mouse's hope—there were no hidden alarms and she had not been seen.

She lay her forehead against the sarcophagus for a moment, steadying herself, and then she stood and looked down on the man who had once meant everything to her.

She touched Ottakar's face again and ran her hands along his stone effigy, her fingers dipping into the carved hollows of his eyes no longer hyacinth blue. Again, she waited for the flood of emotions, but they never came. The memories, good and bad—his face the first time she saw it, bathed in sunlight, the feel of his arms around her, the smell of him as he bent to kiss her, the torment in his eyes when he told her he was to marry Margaret of Austria to keep Bohemia safe, the look on his face before she whispered those last merciful words—all the memories were still perfect in detail in Mouse's uncanny mind, but the deep, rich passions first painted in vibrant oils had now softened into watercolors.

Quite suddenly, Mouse realized that her grief for Ottakar had passed. She wondered when that had happened. But she couldn't afford to think about that now. She needed to concentrate on where her father might have hidden the pages of the Devil's Bible. She searched the tomb's base for hiding places and slid her hand into the crevice between Ottakar's back and the slab of stone, searching for leaves of parchment. To her touch, the stone felt warm, almost alive.

Mouse snapped her head up at the sound of shuffling feet coming nearer. She made for the divider but not quickly enough. The group of tourists turned the corner to stare at the girl standing on the wrong side of the dividing wall. The group's guide stopped midsentence.

Mouse hopped over the gate, smiling. "Dropped my phone," she said, shrugging apologetically.

The tension eased instantly, and the group slid past her toward the enclave.

"Which dead guy is this?" one of them asked.

"Just one of the early kings from before Charles IV. His name was Ottakar. But if you'll follow me, St. Wenceslas's Chapel is just up here on the left." The tour guide was already moving past the enclave. One of the tourists had started humming "Good King Wenceslas."

"No." Mouse had meant to slip silently away, thankful at not being caught, but the word came out anyway.

"No," she said again as the tourists and the guide turned to stare at her once more. "This is Ottakar. He was a good man. He was funny and kind." She swallowed, suddenly aware of the awkwardness. "He was the Golden and Iron King," she said reverently, her last good-bye to the man she had loved.

She spun and ran out of the church, stumbling in a daze across the cobblestone square toward St. George's and Ludmila's Chapel. Mouse had no reason to come to the chapel. She would find no hidden pages here. Her father didn't know about this place or its meaning for her—no one would except her and Ottakar. And Nicholas.

Mouse leaned into the memory of the weight of the baby she'd once carried on her hip, his blonde curls catching the candlelight as he played with the pearls on her dress. The intensity of this memory would never fade; it would never lose its bright agony. The ghosts of her past seemed to have found her at last.

She had brought Nicholas here for the last time on her last night in Prague—until now. It had been her last night as a mother. Even though she had given away her son to save him, his cries—"Mama! Mama!"—as he reached out his little hands for her still broke her with grief and guilt.

She fell to her knees at Ludmila's altar. The words of the *Dies Irae* again came to her lips because she had no prayer of her own. "I meekly and humbly pray. My heart is as crushed as the ashes. Perform the healing of mine end." She lifted her hands to her face, the sweet smell of her infant son still fresh in her memory after seven hundred years.

Mouse wept.

CHAPTER SIXTEEN

He found her in the chapel. They spoke in the hushed tones of confession, she and the almost-priest.

"I missed the train," Angelo said. "I've been on a bus all night."

Mouse kept her eyes on the floor. She was reeling from the suddenness of his arrival and the wash of joy breaking against her remembered grief.

"I had to convince the concierge at your hotel that you were my sister so he'd tell me which direction you'd headed. I've been searching the grounds for an hour," he whispered.

Mouse nodded. The rush she felt was as close as she could get to being drunk. Angelo had not been frightened away. He knew some small piece of her darkness, of the things she had done, and yet he had found her again.

"Won't you absolve me?" He bent as he spoke, trying to see her face past the curtain of her hair.

She nodded again.

"So where are we?"

"The Chapel for St. Ludmila," she whispered.

"What happened here?"

Mouse stood and walked past him to get out of the chapel. He reached for her hand but she pulled it away. He followed her through the heavy wooden doors into the courtyard. They both squinted at the suddenness of the light.

"Where have you been?" she asked.

"On the bus. I told you, I missed the train."

"I see." Mouse had lots of experience with half-truths. She had no reason to expect answers from him when she couldn't give him any either, but he was clearly hiding something, and it made her question the reason he came looking for her again.

"Where else should we look?" he asked.

"The pages aren't here."

"You've searched? The whole castle?" Angelo asked.

"They wouldn't be just anywhere. There's only one place my father would have left them, and they're not there."

"Where was that?"

"A tomb."

"Whose?"

"Someone I knew."

Angelo waited for more, but when it was clear he wasn't going to get it, he sighed and held out his hand to her. "I'm starving. Let's get something to eat."

Mouse hesitated a moment and then let him pull her to him as they started walking.

"I watched you a little before I came to you," he said. "Why were you crying?"

"It's nothing." Her words were clipped. She wanted to revel in the reunion but Angelo seemed to be all questions, and she knew she was going to have to send him away again anyway. This game was too dangerous for Angelo to play.

He put his hand under her chin and lifted it so he could see her eyes. Mouse felt her face warm as he studied her for a moment until she gently pushed his arm away.

"You thought I left you." It wasn't a question.

"It made sense after what I told you."

Angelo shook his head. "We've covered that. Whatever happened out in that field, I know you're not a murderer." He said the last words softly so no one but Mouse could hear.

"You should've gone home."

"Is that why you were crying? Because you thought I'd gone?"

"No." She sounded indignant.

"I'm not going to leave you, Mouse."

She shrugged. "I was crying about something that happened—"

"A long time ago?" He chuckled.

"I gave up something there." Her fingers tightened around his as she said it.

"What?" He was serious again, responding to her tone.

"My son."

Angelo paused for only a moment. "Where is he now?" he asked as they stood in the sunlight of the courtyard.

"With his father," Mouse answered. She told Angelo the story but with none of the details. No dates. No names. It was just a common, sad story—a mother who gave away her child.

"What was his name, your son?"

"Nicholas." Mouse ran her hand along her cheek, remembering the touch of his skin, the softness of his baby hair. For all the grief, there had been joy, too, and though the joy hurt worse than the rest, it made her feel alive again—just like Angelo did, waking her up and making the world seem new. But she'd given Nicholas away to keep him safe. She'd have to do the same for Angelo.

"My son was in danger. I couldn't help him so I gave him to someone who could." She pulled her hand free of Angelo's as she thought about how easily her father had caught her yesterday.

"Angelo, you're in danger, too. What more can I do to make you believe me?"

"Answer my questions, Mouse."

"You first. What were you doing last night?" she countered.

"I missed the train." He looked away as he said it.

"Another one left less than two hours after mine. Where were you?"

"You know the whole damn train schedule?"

She just looked at him.

"I missed that one, too," he said.

She reached toward him and pulled his cell phone from his pocket. "You couldn't call the hotel?"

Angelo locked his hands behind his head and looked down at her in frustration. "You won't answer my questions. I won't answer yours. I guess we're at a stalemate."

"This isn't a game, Angelo. It's your life."

"I know." He reached for her and pulled her against his chest. "I know. And I don't want to fight with you."

"Me neither," she mumbled.

She stepped back and started to hand him his phone, but then she saw the text still lit up on the screen. It was from Bishop Sebastian.

"Your keeper has a question for you. The Bishop wants to know: 'Why Prague?'" Mouse tossed the phone back at Angelo.

He threw his hands up to catch it. "What are you talking about?"

"He knows where we are. What else have you told him?"

Angelo squinted as he read the text for himself. "I haven't talked to him since we left Rome. I don't know how he knows where I am."

"Why should I believe that?" She wasn't looking at him; she was scanning the crowd for the Bishop's spies and starting to move slowly toward the gates that led out into the city. "You're lying to me about where you've been. All you want to do is ask questions. Makes sense that you're feeding him information. That's why you came. He sent you." She turned away.

217

"Bishop Sebastian did not send me." Angelo was angry now, too. "And I haven't talked to him since we left Italy." He grabbed her arm and pulled her into the shadow of the wall. He was pushing buttons on his phone with his other hand. She started to walk away again. "Please, Mouse. You owe me this. Just wait a minute."

Mouse finally looked at him, trying to find a lie or a truth in his eyes, but she couldn't read him. She felt that thrill in her again, like the ground dropping out from under her, and leaned back against the wall, tensed in readiness to run or fight.

"Father," Angelo's voice was cold and hard. "I want to—" His mouth snapped shut as he listened for a moment. "No, Father, I'm the one asking the questions this time. How the hell do you know where I am?" Angelo turned toward the wall, letting go of Mouse's arm and pressing his hand against the stone beside her.

"The what? I don't know what that is. Novus Rishi?" Angelo turned to Mouse, the question in his eyes. She looked away quickly—her best guess was that Novus Rishi was the name of the Bishop's demon war-riors, but she couldn't say that to Angelo.

He held the phone to his ear for a moment more and then shook his head. "I want you to leave me alone, Father. I'll come back when I'm ready." He slid the phone back into his pocket and looked angrily down at Mouse. "I can see you know what he's talking about. How? And what's the Novus Rishi?"

"The Rishis are seers of truth or thought in Hinduism, kind of like prophets," Mouse said.

"That's not what I meant, and you know it."

"I should think you'd be more upset about your master's tight leash than what I know or don't."

"Whatever he may think, I'm not on his leash. Or yours either. I'm sick of you both trying to maneuver me." He looked out over the courtyard.

"I'm not, Angelo. I'm just trying to keep you safe."

"I'm sure he'd say the same thing. But I can take care of myself. These are my decisions to make—not yours or his." He blew out a frustrated sigh. "He had another cryptic message for you, by the way. He said to remind you that Jonah had three days in the whale. Even I'm clever enough to understand that one—the Bishop's giving you three days to 'Act and God will act.' Right?"

Mouse relaxed a little. She had one more day to play this her own way before Bishop Sebastian and his Novus Rishi tried to make her choices for her.

"So what's next?" Angelo asked.

"It's too dangerous, Angelo."

"That's my choice to make."

She knew he was right, but he also didn't really know what he was getting himself into. "This isn't a mystery for you to solve. This is—"

"I am coming with you, Mouse."

"All right," she said, defeated. "But we'll need more daylight than we have left, so it'll have to wait until tomorrow." She squinted up at the sky. "Besides, I'm hungry."

Mouse couldn't tell Angelo what she was, but maybe she could show him some part of who she had been—before even she had known the truth about herself and her father. She let go of the breath she was holding and stretched out her hand toward Angelo.

"I lived here, in Prague, for a while. Would you like to see my city?"

⊙━╼⊙

As they walked toward the Charles Bridge, Mouse warily searched the faces of passersby, but with every step she and Angelo took into Old Town, she felt the present and all its dangers fade as she threaded Angelo into her past.

Celetná Street smelled of baker's yeast rising as it had when she was young, but the sounds of merchants hawking their wares in the old market at the Town Square were just echoes in her mind. The sharp spokes of the Tyn Church. The towering Astronomical Clock with its ticking and grinding. The massive monument to Bohemia's heretic, Jan

Hus, dusted in an eerie patina. All of it was new to Mouse and it closed in on her, clashing against her memories and reminding her that this Prague was not her Prague.

For a moment, she felt lost, a ghost dislodged from time. Mouse spun around looking for something familiar to ground her again. She saw a sign outside a coffee shop chalked with the day's special—strawberries covered in cream, the last of the season—and Mouse took a slow breath. She and Angelo sat at a little table at the edge of the square, and as her mouth burst with sweetness and the thick texture of cream, she smiled at the thought that some things never changed.

The sun was just beginning to set as they headed back across the river toward the hotel. Mouse told Angelo no more stories, and he asked no more questions, even when she turned them west, away from the Red Lion Hotel and up steep Petrin Hill. There was one last place Mouse needed to show Angelo, perhaps the most important given the choices he had to make. Near the summit, twin crosses lifted above the tree line. Strahov Monastery. Some things never changed.

Even now the Premonstratensian Brothers were at prayer in the ancient halls. In Mouse's day they called themselves Norbertines. Father Lucas had trained at this monastery. Mouse grit her teeth at the sudden wave of rage as she thought again about the torture done to him because of the secrets he kept. Her secrets. The secrets Angelo was so determined to uncover. Watching him weave himself into her life, she couldn't help but think of the cost Father Lucas had paid for doing the same. By bringing Angelo to this holy place, shrouded in nine hundred years of solace and worship and still sheltering monks in God's service, Mouse was giving God another chance to pluck his servant from the jaws of an almost certain death. If Angelo was worth a miracle at the Thames, surely Mouse had not tainted him yet.

"Why here?" he asked as they neared the doors.

"No reason," she said quietly. "I've just always wanted to see inside."

"Why don't you go on in? I want to take a look at all the statuary before the light's gone."

She nodded and pulled open the doors that had always been closed to her. Mouse went to the place she had always dreamed of going with Father Lucas—the library. At the abbey in Teplá, where she grew up, she and Father Lucas had broken all the rules, and she had been allowed to go anywhere she wanted, cloistered space or not. She had spent her childhood hunched over ancient texts with Father Lucas, both of them laughing with the joy of hunting for something new to learn and trilling with the anticipation of discovery. But at the Strahov Monastery, a girl, even one as educated as Mouse, was not allowed.

As she finally broached the forbidden space, she sighed, disappointed. The Brothers still managed to keep her locked out—all of the books were kept safe behind glass cases where no one could touch them.

Mouse arched her neck to look up at the library's ceiling fresco, which was almost garish in its relative newness, painted in the late 18th century. It was an artist's rendering of humanity's quest for Truth framed by saints and scientists—a mirror to Bishop Sebastian's vision of the world with religion and science as two sides of the same coin, both dictating order and rule and absolutes.

Mouse suddenly threw her hands out as she lost her balance, dizzied by the feeling that she was falling into the picture above her, disoriented again by the jolt of being in such a familiar place but surrounded by the unknown. This was her home, yet she did not belong here anymore.

Angelo found her sitting on a bench in the courtyard, lost in thought, shivering a little at the growing chill.

"Where are you?" he asked as he sat close to her, and she leaned into the warmth of his body.

"Trying to understand the nature of . . . humanity, I suppose."

Angelo groaned.

"What?" Mouse laughed softly.

"I can't tell you how many of those late-night conversations I've had over cold pasta and stale beer. That's what seminary is—one long string of bloated discussions on the nature of humanity, of God, of good and evil, of the universe, of Heaven and Hell. And trust me, it's all hell."

Mouse sighed and looked up at the darkening sky.

"But I've probably got one more in me. For you," he said. "Anyone in particular you were contemplating? Kant? Spinoza? Nietzsche?"

"Simpler," she said. "Judaism, Islam, Christianity—Protestant and Catholic. For all their differences, they all look at the world the same way. In dualities, I guess. You know, divine *or* human. Heaven *or* Hell. It's either/or, black-and-white, good versus evil. All of it polarized. So tell me, Priest, do you think God sees the world that way?"

"No." The answer came quickly and with his own sigh. "I argue with the Bishop about this all the time. We've created this battle between us and them, whoever that may be, but God . . . I don't know, I think God wanted something else. Cohesion, compassion, understanding, harmony, I suppose."

Mouse leaned against the old stone at her back. "That's not the God I knew."

"Knew?"

But she couldn't think of an easy way to explain that her understanding of God was about as old as the building behind them. "I haven't had enough sleep," she said instead, rubbing her eyes.

"Let's head back to the hotel then. We can settle God's plan for the world another day."

<hr />

The door closed behind them, and Mouse and Angelo stood staring at the bed that filled the tiny room. For days they had shared the space in Angelo's flat and even his bed, but somehow this felt different—another unfamiliar place, a no-man's-land where there seemed to be no rules. The intimacy of the day clung to them, charging the air with desire.

In the bathroom, Mouse changed into a T-shirt she'd borrowed from him. She'd brought nothing from Nashville to sleep in; she hadn't thought she'd need it.

Angelo was standing awkwardly by the bed when she came out.

"Do you prefer a side?" he asked.

Mouse shook her head, overly conscious of how high the shirt rested on her thigh and wondering how see-through the thin cotton might be in the lamplight.

"I guess this is me then." He gestured at the side of the bed where he sat. He stood up and pulled the covers back as Mouse walked to the other side, the one with the table. The one with the lamp. Angelo glanced up as she leaned over to pull back the covers, the light behind her, but he lowered his eyes quickly.

They lay looking up at the beautifully painted Renaissance ceiling beams for a moment before Mouse reached over and turned out the light.

"You're different here." He whispered it like a boy afraid of being caught awake after hours.

"What do you mean?" She was instantly on guard for more complicated questions, but she was whispering, too.

"You sound different. I can hear the Czech in your voice."

"Bohemian."

"What?"

"This part of the country is called Bohemia. I'm from Bohemia."

"You crossed yourself when we left St. George's today. Did you realize?"

"No." But she had; it had been a slip, a habit formed from the hundreds of times she passed in and out of the basilica. Angelo was right. The longer she stayed here with him, the more she felt her old self emerging. It felt good and alive but frightening, too.

"Good night," she said to the dark.

He lay still for a moment, and then, in the silence, Mouse heard the wetness of his lips as they opened. "And I'm not a priest. You called me a priest at Strahov, but I haven't taken vows yet."

Mouse lay very still.

Angelo got up suddenly and pulled on the shirt he had worn that day. He grabbed his bag with his laptop.

"Where are you going?" She still had not moved.

"For a walk. I need some air."

"Don't." She sat up, looking at his silhouette in the doorway.

"Mouse, I *am* just going for a walk." But he wouldn't turn around. "I can't sleep." He laid his hand against the doorframe and leaned into it.

The sounds of a car horn from the street below broke the silence.

"I'll get another room." She rested her elbows against her knees and lowered her head into her hands. She heard the scratching of his shoes as he crossed the rug. Angelo put his hand on top of her head and let his fingers sink into her hair.

"Hey, look at me." He tugged gently at her head until she turned her face to him. "This is nothing. There's no need to get another room. It's not you. It's me. I'm keyed up and need some air. All right?"

"Sure."

"Mouse, I'll be back soon. Go to sleep."

"Sure."

After he left, Mouse walked to the window and watched the lights flicker around the castle. A storm was moving over the city. She waited.

And then she turned sharply away from the window and headed to the bathroom. As the water filled the small tub, she pulled her shirt over her head and looked at her body in the mirror as if she were seeing it for the first time in years. In her centuries of routine and ritual, Mouse had stopped looking at her body—it either served a painful reminder of her timelessness or evoked a deep, pointless, longing. But now, she ran her hands along her lower abdomen against the smooth skin. This body could tempt a man, could give him pleasure. Mouse found herself wondering about the pleasure she might feel, too. The one time she had been with a man, with Ottakar, it had been anything but pleasurable—hurried and rough, a last desperate chance to be together rather than an act of making love. She had learned since how it could be—she'd worked in brothels, tended sick and dying women who wanted to remember happier times. Mouse wanted to know what that kind of love felt like. Her body was a body like any other woman's body, she thought.

Then she noticed that the bruises around her ribs were gone. She twisted to see her back and ran her hand along her injured shoulder where the black had faded to greenish-yellow. She was healed. Too soon for a normal woman.

The steam fogged the mirror and tendrils of wet mist closed in around her reflection like wispy fingers. Mouse stepped into the warm water and lifted the showerhead from its rack, holding it over her head so the water rained down on her face. But tonight she could not make herself feel clean again.

The steam carried the unfamiliar smells of the hotel's soap into the room with her as she went back to the window. Lavender. It was raining.

Mouse slipped back under the covers. Angelo came in shortly after. The mattress shifted with his weight and Mouse felt the warmth of his body through the dip in the sheets that separated them. He smelled like rain.

"So how old are you?" he asked softly.

CHAPTER SEVENTEEN

ouse jumped out of the bed and into the corner of the room, away from Angelo, her back against the wall. Her leg bounced uncontrollably where her foot propped against the baseboard. She was ready to run.

"What?" she asked. "How? I mean—" It was all she could get out, but what Mouse really meant to ask was how much of her story Angelo had figured out.

"Marchfeld. That's what you called the field we went to. But the monument just called it the battle between Rudolf and Ottakar. You talked about it as if you'd been there. I took the names and dates—a quick internet search gave me the rest of the story. But I . . . honestly, I thought you were probably just sick, maybe something had happened to you out in that field, and you had twisted that old story with your own somehow." He moved to the end of the bed closer to her; she squeezed herself farther into the corner.

Rain slapped on the windowpane. Mouse watched the drops plunge against each other in a quick ride down the glass before rolling off the sill and into the dark beyond. She tapped her fingers against the wall in a rhythm with the rain.

"And then today you gave me the other pieces. You know you did."

Mouse was shaking. She felt raw, like he was peeling her, layer by layer, and she needed to stop it before he learned the most damning truth of all—that there was nothing inside, nothing at the heart of all those lies and secrets.

"I couldn't tell you." She tried to make it sound casual, but she looked at the floor as she spoke.

"Nicholas was your son. I had to check that last piece tonight when I left. He became the Duke of something, right?"

"Troppau." Her throat felt tight like someone was twisting a garrote around her neck.

"And today when you took me around the city. They were all old places, but you talked about them like you'd always known them. Your voice was different. The words you used. Even the way you held yourself as you walked. It was all . . . wrong."

"That's me. All wrong." She leaned her head back against the wall and tried to breathe.

"What are you?"

She jerked her head up to look at him. She could see that bright curiosity in his eyes again, but there was something else, too. Fear? Mouse slid to her knees.

"Nothing," she said. "I'm nothing."

He nodded as he watched her and waited for a real answer.

"You can't just be accepting this, Angelo. That's not . . . normal."

"I already told you I believe in the not-normal, Mouse." He lowered himself to the floor in front of her. "What are you?" He put his hand on hers, but she snatched it back.

"Don't."

"You're immortal?" He leaned toward her.

The space closed in around her, and there wasn't enough air. There was no way out and the panic twisted and squirmed in her chest.

"It's okay, Mouse. I'm sorry. Just breathe." He moved back to the corner of the bed and watched her as she pulled in slow breaths through her nose. "Better?"

She nodded.

"Mouse, please. I know already. I just want the details. I need them."

She bowed her head, wet strands of hair sticking to her cheeks and smelling of lavender. After hundreds of years of keeping her secret, of hiding her nature, explaining what she was now was impossible. Especially since she didn't even fully know herself.

"How old are you?"

She heard his need to know the truth, and so, as much as it hurt, she gave it to him.

"I was born in Avignon in 1236." It sounded ridiculous to her as she said it out loud. Angelo moved to sit beside her but was careful not to touch her.

"What are you?" His voice was filled with wonder, and Mouse hated it.

"God, will you stop asking me that! I don't know what the hell I am."

Carefully, he slid his arm around her shoulders. "Relax, Mouse. What do you think is going to happen?" He pulled her to him, laid his face against the top of her head. "This doesn't scare me. I'm not going anywhere. I want to help you."

The joy Mouse heard in his voice stilled her with a sudden, horrible realization. "Angelo, I'm not what you think I am."

"You're not an—" It was his throat that tightened now around a truth he couldn't name. "You're not what pulled me from the river?" The hope in his voice broke her heart.

"Oh, Angelo." Mouse covered her face. His hope explained everything—why he brought her home from the church that night, why he stayed with her, why he wasn't frightened. "When I was a little girl, someone called me his *andílek*, his little angel. I thought I was special like that. I wanted to be something like that." The truth of her confession burned her throat, but then she lifted her head and brushed away her tears. "But I'm not, Angelo. I didn't save you. I'm sorry."

Angelo was quiet for a long time.

"I should have known better," he said finally. Mouse heard his disappointment and the forced casualness as he started asking questions again. "What are—I mean, you're obviously old. Doesn't that mean you're immortal?"

"I don't know." She said it as a sigh. "Maybe. I can get hurt, but I always heal." Images of her failed suicides after Marchfeld filled her mind. "I never get sick. I don't age. But I think there's at least one way I can die."

"How?"

Answering that question would turn the conversation to her father, and Mouse wasn't ready for that. She looked over at Angelo. "I really don't want to—"

"It's okay." He could see the fear in her eyes. "Any other gifts?" he asked instead.

Mouse cringed. Father Lucas had called her abilities gifts, too. "My mind works differently than a normal person's. I use more of it, or all the buttons are switched on or something. I can read a book, play chess, and recite Shakespeare all at the same time."

"The people in Monster Park?" Angelo asked.

She nodded. "I see the details. All of them. Twitches of an eye, a pulse in the throat, frayed fabric, everything. I heard their conversations, accents, inflections. I put it all together like some massive jigsaw puzzle. It lets me know what's likely to happen before it happens. And I never forget . . . anything." The breath hissed through her teeth.

"How can you find space for yourself in all that?" He picked up her hand and traced his fingers over her knuckles and followed the lines of her tendons.

"I'm alone most of the time." The skin on her hand tingled as he played with it.

"Anything else?"

"I see better, hear better. I can pick up subtleties of smell." She closed her eyes, inhaled, and isolated what she had come to think of as Angelo's scent, a mix of rich museum air, linen, a hint of coffee, and the sweetness of olive oil. It made her smile.

When she opened her eyes, Angelo was smiling, too. "Superstrength?"

She had to laugh at the playfulness in his voice. She had always looked at her abilities like they were a cursed birthright—something to be afraid of or to hide. She liked seeing herself through Angelo's eyes much better.

"You've watched me wrestle with my bag, so what do you think? But I can control my body better—my heartbeat, my breathing. I can anticipate how someone else will act or move several steps before they do. In a fight, I know how my opponent will balance himself, which direction he'll feint and when."

"That might be better than superstrength." He sounded like a kid, almost giddy with discovery and possibility.

"And I can . . . compel someone to do what I want." She looked steadily at him, wanting him to ask the follow-up.

"Have you ever done that?"

"Yes."

"With me?" He pulled his hand away.

"No."

"Would I know if you did?"

"Probably not."

Angelo picked at a loose thread in the rug, then he cocked his head toward her, studying her for a moment. "What about super speed?" His eyes twinkled.

"No." She laid her head back on his chest and laughed. "I'm not a comic book character."

"Well, it sounds like you haven't really tested what you can do."

"I've spent the past seven centuries working to blend in with the people around me. You don't have any idea how hard that is. I have to change how I speak, how I hold myself." She rubbed her eyes. "I didn't do a very good job of that today. But mostly, I try not to think about the things I can do. I just want to be a normal person."

"So you consider yourself human?"

His words stung.

"My mother was human," she whispered as she sat up.

"But not your father?" This felt too similar to the conversation with Bishop Sebastian.

"I don't want to talk about this anymore."

"You really don't know what you are, do you?" The intense curiosity was back in his voice.

"What I am is tired and ready for bed. We have an early morning." Mouse pushed herself up, walked back to the bed and crawled in.

Angelo started to ask another question but stopped when she sighed. He leaned back against the wall and sat in the silence. Mouse listened to his heartbeat, revved up with discovery and wanting more. It battled against his slow, methodic breaths. Half an hour later and finally calm, he curled up in the bed beside her, but as the room lit up with one last flash of lightning, a question slipped out.

"Where are we going?"

"A place I never wanted to see again." She shivered and pulled the covers up to her chin. "It's called Podlažice."

CHAPTER EIGHTEEN

"Can you hear me now?"

The whisper filtered through the birdsong across the clearing in the woods. Mouse dug her fingernails into the red flesh of a plane tree seed, peeling it until she reached the hard core. And then she threw it.

"Ouch!" Angelo yelled. "That hurt." He stood up from where he was crouched several yards away and rubbed the side of his head.

"Then stop," she said, laughing.

"I'm just testing your super hearing."

"And how about my aim?" Mouse held up another plane seed.

Angelo put his hands up, smiling as he forfeited, then raked the sweat off his face with his forearm and went back to searching the thick underbrush.

They had driven out of Prague before the sun was up. Mouse wanted as much daylight as she could get for the search; she knew it would be tough to find the ruins of the monastery. Podlažice didn't exist anymore. Over the years, archeologists had looked for the suspected birthplace of the Devil's Bible but never found it. Of course, Mouse had an advantage—she had actually been there and knew where to start looking. But everything had changed. She and Angelo had been hunting the woods for hours without finding so much as an old stone, and now the sun was moving below the tree line.

Once again, Mouse scanned the darkening shadows for any sign of another of her father's spies. Confident that they were still safe, at least for the moment, she turned her back to Angelo, slowing her breathing and letting her sight blur as she eased herself into a trance. All day, Mouse had fought against the memories of this place. She had kept herself grounded in the present with Angelo, with the young trees, with the distant sounds of cars on the road—anything that would keep the past and Podlažice at bay. Mouse had been scared to let herself remember too well, afraid she would lose herself in that despair again, but now she needed the details of those memories to help her find the ruins. She was running out of time.

She laid her hand on a tree trunk to steady herself and then let her mind slip back to that day so long ago when the monks at Podlažice had first found her. She gagged at the remembered sour taste of pond water flooding her mouth. She blinked, trying to focus, but her eyes scratched against the dry sockets, burning. As she looked up into the clearing, where there had been only saplings and high grass, ghostly walls began to grow in the fading light. Now Mouse could see the monastery as it had been, and she began to stumble toward what was once the entrance on the east side.

"Hey, wait," Angelo called as he jogged toward her and put his hand on her back.

His touch broke the spell, and the phantom Podlažice sank silently into the forest floor. But in that brief moment, Mouse had found what she needed. It looked like a simple mound of dirt at the back corner of the clearing. The last of the afternoon sun lit the top of the small hill and played with shadows on the scattered leaves and bracken. But as she neared it, Mouse could feel her father's touch. He had been here. The echoes of his power dusted everything.

She and Angelo crawled over a log to reach the other side of the mound. The opening looked eerily like the Mouth of Hell in Monster Park—with large misshapen boulders for eyes and lips of dirt and rotten leaves pulled back in a sneer, daring her to enter. All it needed were Dante's words: *Abandon all hope, ye who enter here.*

Mouse was able to crawl easily into the opening on her elbows. It was a much tighter fit for Angelo.

"Is this the monastery?" he asked as he lay in the dirt, shining the flashlight across the crumbling stone walls.

Mouse nodded; she had her bearings now. "It's the lower floor of the east wing. There should be a staircase over here somewhere." Mouse took the flashlight and crawled toward an area too dark for the light to penetrate until she was directly on it. Even then she could only see a deeper dark leading below.

"You think it's safe to go down there?" Angelo eyed the cracked stone steps.

"I don't have a choice. But you stay here." Her voice was shrill with worry at the risk she had taken. She should have come alone.

"I'm going with you." Angelo dragged himself to Mouse with his elbows. "At least I'll get some headroom as we climb down."

At each step they took, the stone stairs cracked a little more, sending bits of debris pinging into the darkness, and the farther they descended, the more Mouse felt herself coming undone—something was pricking at her mind, like a cat toying with a ball of yarn, its claws pulling at the threads.

"The pages are here. I can feel it." Her breathing was fast and shallow, and she sounded wrong, like an echo.

The staircase spiraled into a long hall. Toward their right, just a few feet past the landing, the ceiling had partially caved in, but to the left, the flashlight flickered on regularly spaced doorframes, some gaping and others partially obscured by decayed doors and fallen beams. The hall ended at a wall with gnarled roots jutting through the seams of the stones like the fingers of some dead thing working to pry them apart.

Mouse stumbled at the last step, losing her footing—not only among the scattered debris but in time, too, as the past sifted into the present. She could hear the requiem the monks had sung for her all those years ago; the haunting, hollow chant breathed through what was left of the monastery.

Mouse moved toward the caved-in area to the right, crouching as the ceiling sank lower and lower until she was finally on her knees. She shined the light into the far corner against the interior wall. A small opening led farther beyond into the dark.

"Back there," she said, shaking her head as she tried to make the memory fade, but it was more real than the musty decay of the ruins. She sat still for a moment, her eyes closed against the double vision of past and present.

"I don't want to be here," she whispered.

Angelo laid his hand on her back.

Mouse rested her head against the stone and looked at him, but she couldn't focus. Everything was blurry, and she wasn't sure whether she was here with Angelo or back in the past with one of the monks leading her to her death.

Angelo leaned toward her to be sure she heard him. "Let's leave. You can't go in there anyway. You won't fit."

His voice grounded her for a moment and her head cleared slightly.

"I have to go in, Angelo. It's a Mouse-hole." She pressed her lips against the quiet giggle that caught in her throat. She wasn't blinking, and her pupils had dilated until her eyes were nearly all black.

The cell she had shared with her father lay just beyond the opening. His power swirled all around her. She could taste it the same way she'd tasted salt in the air near the ocean. Given the rotten wood and decayed mortar, all of this should have collapsed long ago and turned to dust.

Her father must have preserved this place through the centuries, made it so only she would be able to find it. It meant the pages were likely on the other side of that opening. But to get them, she would have to go in.

Mouse leaned toward the opening, but Angelo was still holding her hand.

"The walls don't look stable. If you go in there, Mouse, I might not get you back." He pulled her face toward his, leaned in and put his lips on hers. Her body answered his, moving into his kiss, pressing against him. He let go of her hand to bring his own behind her head and hold her closer.

Without warning, Mouse pulled away, dropping the flashlight at his knees as she thrust herself into the darkness. The stone cut into her back as she shoved herself through the hole.

Angelo lunged after her and slid as far as he could into the opening. The walls were so thick it was more like a tunnel, but it was so small the outer opening cut into his shoulder, wedging him between the packed rubble and the floor. He could see that the tunnel widened on the other side, and, to the right, he saw the bottom of Mouse's boot.

"Mouse, come on. Grab whatever's there and get the hell out."

But something had gone wrong when Mouse crossed what was left of the ancient threshold. The thing that had been playing at her mind now ravaged it. She crouched, looking wildly around the cell. Mouse knew where she was, but not when. She could hear noises beyond the door. Was it Bishop Andreas come again to check on his book? Or was it someone else? Her father?

The room was lit with an odd glow, and she looked around for a candle and for her parchment, inks, and quills, but there was only a small metal box. Mouse squatted near it.

"Copper, copper, green with age. Not brass that darkens or gold that stays," she said in a singsong voice.

A light bounced off the walls and glinted a moment on the metal box, catching Mouse's attention.

"Hello?" she whispered.

"Mouse. Come out."

"I'm at Podlažice," she said.

"Yes. Come out now." Angelo talked to her like she was a child. She sounded like one, her voice high and thin, and it scared him.

"There's something I have to do . . ." She was trying to understand, but her mind was a tangled mess, and the thing playing at her made it impossible to think.

"Yes. Look around. Do you see anything?"

Mouse let her eyes adjust to the wavering light.

"A box."

"Get it and come out."

She was still looking around the cell.

"There are pictures on the wall. They are glowing. Did I paint them? I don't remember them."

"I don't know. It doesn't matter. Get the box and come back to me."

But in her mind, Mouse was listening to someone else. It was a memory of her father talking to her as they worked on the Devil's Bible.

"You think you have choices." He had patronized her with his tone.

"God called it free will," she had spat back.

"But you are not a child of his. You are mine."

"I'm half-human." She heard the doubt in her own voice.

"Technically. Though all my other efforts failed. Thousands of them over the years—dead before they left the womb. All but you." He let the implication soak into her. "You may be half-human, but you are definitely your father's daughter."

"I'm not like you."

"Ah, you're just a normal girl full of goodness and light?" His arrows hit their mark.

She turned away from him.

He snatched her arm, swinging her back toward him. He raked off the top stack of parchment, pages scattering through the cell, until he found the pictures she'd done of him and Heaven. He shed his handsome human visage to match the grotesque one he pointed to in the manuscript.

"You have a choice to make, dearest. Accept who you are and come with me. You've seen the truth of me these past weeks. I've been honest and open with you. You know I am not the creature your childish Church has invented to scare you into blind obedience. I require no such allegiance. You may do as you wish. I just want you with me." Even in this deformed state, with thick, charred skin, his eyes pleaded with her tenderly. "Or, you can continue your futile quest for *this*." He pointed to her picture of the Heavenly City on the page opposite the Devil's portrait.

In the picture, her city was empty. Mouse could not paint the joyful saints inhabiting Heaven because each time she tried, the pain stilled her brush. The words of Mother Kazi had haunted Mouse during those long, dark days at Podlažice: "You were not made for the Church, Mouse." Mouse had long thought the Church was the only hope for Heaven she had, but those words closed the doors of the Church to her. So her Heavenly City was divine brick and mortar only, a ghost town, empty of souls.

As the memory faded, Mouse could hear Angelo calling for her. His voice brought her back to the present. "Forget the pictures, Mouse. Just grab the box and get out of there."

"I didn't paint these. My father did," she mumbled. She fought against her mental fogginess as she studied the frescoes on the wall. Each was outlined in an eerie glow, pulsing with power—a telltale sign that Lucifer, the Light-Bringer, had been here.

Mouse knew she was supposed to be doing something, but it kept slipping away from her. Frustrated at her inability to concentrate, she put her hands on either side of her head, tightening her scalp and widening her eyes, distorting them with tension. Slowly, an understanding came to her. This was a game of temptations, and her father had played it once before with another adversary he had wanted to recruit to his cause. He'd played dirty back then, too, waiting until forty days of fasting had taken their toll. This time, he just rigged the game so that his power would slip into Mouse's mind to keep it muddled, making her more vulnerable to his persuasion.

She grit her teeth against another onslaught of disorientation, trying to hold on to some clarity but feeling like a patient going under anesthesia, powerless to clear away the fog. The cell walls slipped in and out of focus as she tried to make sense of the pictures her father had painted.

There were three of them: one was a copy of her portrait of her father, the second was a replica of her abandoned Heavenly City, and a third was a painting she had never seen before. But why were they glowing? What did he want her to do? Mouse wondered what would happen if she just grabbed the box and ran. She reached out for it, her fingers lightly brushing its copper top, and, in the far corner of the cell, a brick crumbled into pieces as if someone had pulled at an invisible seam holding it together. Others nearby started to quiver. Then Mouse pulled her hand back, and they stilled once more.

She heard Angelo calling to her again. He sounded angry.

She knelt near the small opening so he would hear her. "Angelo, please listen. I can't . . . I can't think well. You need to stop yelling so I can think. I need to figure this out." Her mind was beginning to cloud again, and she knew she had little time to decide what to do.

"Figure what out?" Angelo growled.

"The pictures on the wall. I think they're a test or something."

"You can't do this alone, Mouse. We'll come back and—"

"Yes. You go. Good-bye." Her voice was hollow, like a child talking during a dream.

She turned away from the sound of Angelo screaming her name.

Mouse lifted her hand toward the wall, slowly tracing her fingers along the first painting, the image of her father that looked just like the one she had painted so long ago. The luminescent fresco brightened at her touch, wrapping around her hand and sending a surge of warmth through her fingers, up her arm, and into her chest. It was comfortable, welcoming.

And then it wasn't.

It kept growing, squeezing her heart and making it race and jump, pushing against her lungs until she couldn't breathe. It was going to break her ribs. She arched, stretching her chest and trying to make more room. Mouse felt drunk with the onslaught of power, sure she could and should master anything she wanted.

Her mind filled with images of her desires. A baby at her breast. Flashes of her sculptures on display in famous museums. Her mouth on Angelo's, him whispering his love for her as their naked bodies moved together. Herself kneeling in the presence of something she knew to be God, and her body lit from within by a brilliant glow. All of it came rushing at her again and again.

Mouse squirmed against the thrill. It was all too much.

And she knew none of it was possible.

In an instant, her want turned into fury. The power in her grew hot with blue flame. She could feel her lungs begin to blister, and she knew her flesh would melt and she would be blackened and covered in thick waves of scars. Just like her father. Her anger ignited the power, and she saw the image of herself kneeling before God erupt like a bomb of light, throwing God back from her. She stood victorious, laughing.

Mouse's scream of rage, so like her father's, tore through her throat and bounced against the walls of the cell just as his had, the power in her filling her up. She wanted to kill something.

Then she heard Angelo.

He was screaming, too. Banging the flashlight against the stone.

Mouse dropped to her knees and clamped her hand over her mouth, pressing so hard her teeth cut into her lips. "No. I won't." The words bubbled in the blood at her mouth.

Rocking back and forth, she pushed steadily against the flow of power, pushed it down and away until she was sure she was in control again. It took all she had to force it back, which left her vulnerable to the thing playing at her mind. Mouse bent over and laid her head on the floor. She was shaking.

"Mouse, will you please just get the box and come out?" Angelo's anger had passed instantly at the moment Mouse had muzzled her power. Now his fear came rushing back.

"I don't think I can." She sounded so small, so lost. *"Bricks and mortar will not stay, will not stay, will not stay,"* she sang. *"My fair lady."*

"Cazzo!" Angelo yelled, but then he took a breath and tried again, forcing calm into his voice. "I don't understand, Mouse."

"I think it will fall down." In her state she couldn't explain it any better. Her father's power held the walls together—the spells he used far beyond her own understanding—but it made sense that if she didn't play his game, there would be consequences. The bricks had crumbled when she touched the box. She doubted that she and Angelo would have time to climb out before it all fell down on them.

"You mean the monastery?"

"Yes. I have to finish first. There are two more pictures." After she had touched the portrait of her father, all the light had run out of it, its power rushing into her. That part of the wall was now dark, but the other two still pulsed hypnotically with their strange glow.

"Okay, Mouse. You do what you need to and then you come out. I'll be right here."

"You should go. It might get bad."

"I'm staying with you."

"Okay." The vowels rolled long and high from her mouth and echoed through the tiny opening. Mouse stood and began tracing her father's copy of the Heavenly City, as she did with the first fresco. This time, instead of flowing into her, the power dancing in the picture pulled her in. She threw her hands out like she was falling and closed her eyes, waiting for the pain of impact. But all she felt was cold. She opened her eyes and found herself surrounded by the gray stone buildings and orange brick walls of the Heavenly City she had painted for the Devil's Bible.

This one, like the one trapped on the parchment page, was empty. Mouse was alone. But then she heard a baby's coo; it sounded just like Nicholas's. She took off running, turned down alley after alley and looked in vacant buildings with the doors flung open. Her footsteps echoed in the valley between towers. The peal of a child's laughter lured her down one street; cries of "Mama! Mama!" hurried her down another. She walked for hours it seemed, but could not find her son. She found no one. The ache of longing crushed her, and the cold and overpowering loneliness told her it would always be so. She would be alone forever.

She was sure her father was waiting for her, if only she would call for him. He would come as he had done before, and he would bring her presents and kiss her forehead and tell her he was proud of her. She only needed to call his name. But she wouldn't; she stumbled down the empty streets softly weeping.

Angelo heard her cries, and he was afraid. "Mouse, I'm here." He meant it as a prayer.

Through her tears, Mouse saw a flash of blue flutter along the horizon, just past the labyrinth of streets. She followed it and turned the corner and found a park. She saw a little birdbath where two indigo buntings splashed together in the water. She smiled, remembering Angelo's kiss.

Her father's spell broke without warning. The dank cell came jarringly back into focus. Disoriented, Mouse knelt, breathing in deep and slow. Whatever had been playing with her mind was gone, and she was finally able to think clearly, to strategize a way to win. Her father's game was thus far remarkably unoriginal—tempting her to use her power, showing her all she might have if she joined him; these were the same things her father had offered his other adversary so long ago. But that one had had the angels on his side. Mouse didn't think she'd be so lucky.

She looked up at the third picture. She'd never seen it before, but its meaning was clear—and it wasn't about choices. This one was about consequences.

Mouse knew it was time to finish the game.

"Angelo?" she called.

"Thank God," he said. "You were so quiet, I thought—"

"It's all right. Are you okay?"

"I will be if you come out now."

"Soon."

"You sound different. Before, you sounded—"

"It was something my father did to try to trick me. I'm sorry if I scared you."

"Come out now."

"I will. Soon." She wanted to keep talking to him, but she had no idea how quickly everything would happen when she touched the last fresco, and she wanted Angelo safely away. "I'm going to slide something out to you, but don't open it. Okay?"

"What is it?" He sounded so tired.

"A box that I think has my father's manuscript in it. We can't open it here—it's too dangerous. Do you understand?"

"Why can't you bring it out?"

"I have something to do first. There's one more painting."

"Of what?"

She looked at the picture on the wall again. It had the same columns framing it as the other two; her father liked symmetry. A figure lay curled at the foot of the columns, one arm across her face and the other lifted in a plea. The fresco was a mirror image of the cell—the portrait of her father and the empty Heavenly City fading into the black edges behind the fallen girl. Mouse knew the figure on the floor begged for death.

"It doesn't matter. But as soon as you get the box, you have to get out, Angelo. I'm afraid the monastery will start to fall."

"I'm not leaving you." His voice shook with fear.

Mouse couldn't see any other way. Her father would have assumed that she would come here alone. It's one of the things they shared—eternal loneliness. So he wouldn't have anticipated Mouse having someone else there to take the box while she finished the game. It was his mistake and her chance to win.

The monastery would likely start to fall the moment the box was removed; finishing this last task was Mouse's only chance of putting off that inevitability, at least until Angelo was safely outside. Regardless of what happened to her, Angelo could take the box back to Bishop Sebastian, and hopefully they could find whatever was in the manuscript and use it to stop her father. The last shimmering picture on the wall didn't leave much hope that Mouse would be joining them.

"I need you to take the box out. For me," she said. She wished she could see his face. She wanted to tell him things, but there wasn't time. Mouse nudged the box closer to the opening in short bursts; each time she touched it, a brick crumbled. The cell was so small, it only took three shoves to get it to the edge of the opening. "Will you promise, Angelo?"

"No."

"I'll come to you when I can, but you have to get out with the box. It's our only chance. Please promise me." Mouse stretched wide, one hand hovering over the box to give it a last shove toward Angelo, and the other almost but not quite touching the final fresco.

"Do I have a choice?"

"No."

He reached in and she slid her palm lightly over his hand as he pulled the box through the hole.

"Angelo? Thank you for everything."

"Damn it, Mouse. Stop talking like you're saying good-bye."

"Go!" she said as the outer wall of the cell began to crumble. She heard Angelo scrambling on the other side of the opening and listened to the echo of his footfalls and the pings of loose stone as he started to climb the staircase.

Mouse was alone.

She laid her trembling hand against the glowing light of the unfamiliar image on the wall and all the bricks went still. She felt nothing, no heat or cold as she had with the other pictures, and the light never wavered. Not until her hand hovered over the drawn figure crumpled on the fresco's floor. Then the ghostly glow began to pulse, running like rain across the stone wall into the image of the girl who begged for death, a father's portrait of his daughter.

Slowly Mouse moved her hand over the girl's face in the epicenter of the swirling light. Like lightning, it jumped from the wall, sending a finger of power into Mouse's outstretched palm, snaking its way inside her. Mouse cried out in pain.

And just as quickly as it had struck, the power snapped back into the fresco, leaving only a tiny point of light in the wall, and stripping Mouse of everything—breath, hope, strength. Her head slammed into the floor as she fell, unable to summon even enough energy to catch herself.

She lay unmoving as blood and saliva spread in small puddles between her face and the stone floor, and then she saw something in the corner near her feet glinting in the dim light as it moved.

A wet darkness was oozing from the cracks in the floor and sliding slowly toward her. Mouse cried out as she felt the wetness wrap around her ankle and then tickle her leg as it crawled upward, but in its wake, her body went numb.

Mouse twitched as the dark thing twined around her waist and slipped between her breasts and up her neck. The black ooze would soon crawl into her mouth, close over her nose. She would be left here to suffocate, alone and shrouded in the dark. Mouse tried to pull slow breaths in against the growing claustrophobia, but her chest was numb and the air stuck in her throat with shallow gasps.

There was no one to help her. Angelo was gone.

She might still call for her father. She didn't know what would happen if he came, but at least she wouldn't be alone, buried alive.

Mouse shook her head, pressing her forehead to the floor, and shoved her hand against the cold stone, turning onto her back as the ooze feathered down her arm like a glove. She pushed back against the fear; she would not call for her father no matter what happened.

The walls of the cell shuddered. A mist of centuries-old dust rained down on her. Mouse wondered if that meant Angelo had gotten out with the box and that her father's spells were unraveling. Or maybe this was part of his plan—to cover her with ooze like some demonic resin to preserve her, powerless and dormant, and then bury her in the rubble until he came to collect her.

Mouse felt the dark, wet thing slide along her neck and run a slick finger on her lips. The last of the light from the wall went out.

○══╪══○

Angelo had taken the box up to the surface as she had asked, but he had no intention of leaving her alone. He was already at the foot of the stair-case, coming back down to her, when he heard her scream. The sound was guttural, primitive. He ran back to the hole and wedged himself in as far as he could, dug his feet into the crevices where the stones on the floor joined as he tried to get leverage. He could almost touch her foot.

"Mouse, please. I . . . I can't get to you. Come a little closer."

Mouse's hair scratched against the uneven stone as she twisted her head trying to keep her nose and mouth away from the smothering wet-ness spreading over her chin. The back wall of the cell collapsed and the ceiling on that side crashed down against the rubble.

"I'm too big. I can't get in!" Angelo said.

The dark, wet thing slid up her nose and between her gritted teeth.

Mouse's gurgling whimpers filtered through the tunnel-like opening. Angelo jerked free of the hole, tears blinding him as he looked around desperately for a large stone or piece of wood he could use. He found nothing.

The walls were heaving. He threw himself back toward the hole, pounding the stone around the opening into the cell with the butt of the flashlight. He could hardly see what he was doing, but small flecks of rock showered down. The light flickered. Angelo shoved himself deeper into the hole, his left arm and shoulder stretching into the cell and his face scraping and burning against the ragged stone at the top of the opening.

He couldn't see, but he groped frantically until his fingers made contact with something solid; it was Mouse's boot. He grabbed at it and pulled it slowly toward him. He wrapped his hand around her calf muscle and pulled her another few inches toward the opening. When her body jerked once more, spasming, Angelo clamped down hard on her lower thigh, fearing he'd lose her again. He reached in and grabbed her other leg and finally pulled her out through the opening.

Angelo shined the failing light in her face. She was pale and cold to the touch, but she was alive. Her mouth was smeared with blood and something black was running off her and dripping like oil onto the floor. He lifted her into his arms and took off. The stone walls squealed as they shivered and shook. Angelo dodged falling debris as he carried Mouse up the staircase. At the top of the landing, he laid her gently on the floor and backed his way through the opening at the mound, pulling her with him. Once outside, he leaned her against a log. She rolled to her side, retching, the last of the black ooze streaming from her mouth and nose. She still hadn't opened her eyes.

"Box."

He barely heard her. "It's here." He reached beside the log where he had hidden the box under some leaves.

Mouse clasped it tightly with both hands like it was a grenade.

"We have to get out of here now," she said.

They heard a rumble like thunder as they reached the car, and the ground trembled. The ruins had collapsed. Someone would find it now and build a career picking through the debris.

Mouse hoped the ghosts of Podlažice had no more secrets to tell.

CHAPTER NINETEEN

long the horizon, the lights of Chrudim flared against the low-hanging clouds and sent phantom figures creeping across the night sky. Mouse was still shaking. Angelo had one hand on the wheel and the other wound tightly in hers.

"I'd give anything if you'd talk to me right now," he said.

"Will you play the guitar for me?" she asked quietly. He caught the smile on her lips.

"Done." His voice nearly broke with relief.

Mouse laid her head down on the console between them and tightened her grip on the copper box in her lap.

"Aren't you going to open it?" he asked.

She shook her head, waves of fear washing over her again, but she was too tired to sit up and keep watch for pursuers.

"There's a station in Pardubice. Let's take the train back to Prague. We can open it while we're on the move." Her words were slurred, and she blinked slowly as she tried to fight through the exhaustion to strategize.

Her father would be sending someone. Mouse needed to be ready.

⚓

At the Pardubice station half an hour later, Mouse kept her back to Angelo as he bought the tickets. She wanted to keep herself between him and whatever might be coming. The platform was crowded with commuters from Prague and partygoers headed out for a night in the city.

Someone screamed, and Mouse shoved Angelo back.

"It's just those kids messing around, Mouse." He turned back to her, tickets in hand, and rubbed his side where it had slammed into the counter. "Come on." He tried to take her hand, but Mouse needed to be free. She knew it was only a matter of when, not if, the danger would come. Angelo still had no idea about the real nature of the enemy they faced.

Though Mouse had told him nearly all of her secrets, some were too painful to share. She had not told him about the power she had to see souls, for fear of the hope it might reawaken in him that she was an emissary from God. And if Angelo was wishing for an angel, how could Mouse ever tell him what she really was? No, the truth about what she had done at Marchfeld, the truth about her father—those were secrets she meant to keep.

As Angelo shut the door to their private berth, Mouse moved quickly to the window so she could watch the people boarding. Any one of them could belong to her father; all of them were a threat. When the train finally lurched toward Prague, she dropped onto the bench, her head and shoulders sagging with fatigue, and she pulled the copper box out of her bag along with a small leather pouch and a metal fingernail file she'd picked up at the station in Vienna.

"What's that for?" Angelo asked as he stepped back from the washbasin holding a rag to his scraped face.

"We're not safe. My father will be looking for us. Or sending someone," she said as she unfastened the pouch. "There are things I can do to protect us. Spells."

"Like a witch?" Even he smiled at the word, not really knowing what he was asking.

"No." She chuckled as he sat down beside her. "Believe it or not, I learned these spells from a priest."

She had been eight years old when the hollow-eyed children had followed her home from the baby cemetery where all the unbaptized infants had been laid to rest. Father Lucas was gone on one of his trips. Mouse had tried to tell Mother Kazi about them, but the old woman told her they were just the normal nightmares all children had. When Father Lucas finally came home and found his little Mouse thin and dark-eyed, he knew the truth. He, too, knew what lived in the dark, and he gave Mouse the first protection spell to guard her while she slept.

"So these spells are fully sanctioned by the Church." She'd meant it as a joke, but she saw the shadow that crossed Angelo's face. "Anyway, you might need to do this, too, at some point. If I'm not with you." Mouse understood the danger she had put him in, even if he didn't. And she might not always be there to protect him. She wanted to give Angelo the tools to protect himself, as Father Lucas had done for her. "I'll show you how to do it."

She took a handful of salt from the pouch and stood up. "Different spells use different materials. This one is simple but powerful. Salt from the Dead Sea. It works like a conduit." Mouse let it trickle from her fingers as she moved her hand deliberately in a pattern.

"It's a fish, like the ancient Christians used."

Mouse nodded. "Certain shapes have power. A circle quartered by a cross, the Celtic swirl, a pentagram, and this one, among others." She stopped talking as she finished the pattern on the floor and then leaned over to pick up the fingernail file.

"Now I say the words of the spell—I'll teach it to you later—and place drops of my blood at the points of power." She said the last in a rush, trying to throw him off guard as she began to shove the sharp point of the file into the vein at her left wrist. But his hand closed around hers quickly.

"Let me do it." He held out his wrist.

"Maybe next time."

"There'll be a next time?"

"As long as we're running," she said. "As long as we're alive."

Angelo winced as she jabbed the sharp point into her flesh and twisted to open the vein. She turned her wrist toward the floor and let the blood drop first at each fan of the fish tail, then where the lines crossed and, finally, where they met in a point at the fish's head. Mouse whispered the words of the spell at each spill of blood.

"And now?" Angelo asked as he knelt down onto the floor beside her in the center of the salt-and-blood fish. He took the rag he'd been using on the scrapes he'd gotten at Podlažice and pressed it against the cut in her wrist. It was already pink with his own blood.

"Now we see what game my father's playing." She slid her hand from his and lifted the lid from the ancient box.

The rolled parchment rested on red velvet. Mouse pulled it out quickly, wanting to waste no time in case her spell hadn't worked and her father had been alerted to the breaking of the box's seal. Angelo moved closer, his shoulder pressed into hers. Each of them held a side of the manuscript and read. As a seminary graduate, Angelo knew his Latin, but he occasionally pointed at a word for Mouse to translate. Angelo read for the story while Mouse read for clues to her father's secret.

"Milton has him beat, I think," Angelo said when he finished.

She smiled at his reaction. Hers had been much the same when she had first read it. But she sobered quickly. There was nothing there. No clue, no hint, no next task to perform. The ancient parchment at her knees looked sickeningly like snakeskin. Her father had most likely been toying with her—an empty game she had no hope of winning.

"The manuscript is just like I remember it. There's nothing here. Just words on a page." Mouse gripped the edges of the parchment and watched the corner crumble into a dust too fine to fall.

Angelo bent his head to her ear. "Try again. Maybe it's not in the words. Maybe it's something visual, how they're shaped or—"

"I'll try."

Mouse closed her eyes and let the words fall away as she pulled the image of the pages up in her mind and looked at them as a whole, like they were another of her father's puppets, an enemy that needed to be assessed. When she opened her eyes, the pattern nearly jumped from the parchment. The significant letters were almost illuminated, their uniqueness now so obvious to her. She could see the minor shift of flourish and, most significantly, the stain of the ink. It seemed so clear to her, though she doubted that any normal person could discern the difference that now glared at her.

She looked over at Angelo excitedly. "Can you find me some paper, something thin?"

"Be right back."

The corners of the parchment he had been holding down now curled toward Mouse and covered the text, but it didn't matter. She already had the words in her mind, words formed by the letters her father had hidden in the manuscript. And, even better, she knew what they were: a binding spell. She recognized it from an old text she and Father Lucas had once studied but then dismissed as a charlatan's work. *The Aim of the Sage* had been a disjointed hodgepodge of philosophy, astrology, and a very sexualized approach to the practice of magic. But in her perfect memory, Mouse could see the words of this spell tucked between some convoluted passage about the spirit of the planets and a grotesque magical concoction requiring semen and brain matter. No wonder she and Father Lucas had paid the text no heed. Even now, Mouse doubted that the words of the spell held any real power—a person could say them all day and likely nothing would happen. The power of the particular spell in these pages written with these special letters came not from the words themselves but from the nature of their crafting.

Her father had scripted them in blood that was almost certainly his own.

She imagined his initial glee at the game he played. Give Mouse a clue that reminded her of her bond to him—a bond of blood, the only one of its kind she shared with anyone in the world. His confidence that she would eventually want to join him after the time they shared at Podlažice must have erased his customary caution. But as the years passed and Mouse never took the bait, he likely began to second-guess the cleverness of his plan and to worry that someone else might discover his secret and use it against him. He had underestimated the agents of God before. Her father must have ripped the pages from the Devil's Bible and hidden them like a piece of cheese in his Mouse-trap.

When Angelo returned with the paper, Mouse began the delicate work of lifting the letters from the manuscript. She pressed the new paper against the old and grabbed the wet cloth and held it to the back of the parchment. After a few seconds of pressing the dampened pages together, a light trace of the letters appeared on the new piece of paper. They were barely legible, but Mouse didn't need to read the words. She needed them in her father's blood and in sequence so they formed the power of the binding spell.

Angelo helped hold the manuscript and bit back his questions so she could concentrate, but when she pulled the last letter from her father's text, Mouse dropped her head in her hands.

"What's wrong?"

"It stops midsentence. There's a final line to the spell." She recited the spell as she knew it from *The Aim of the Sage* while she frantically searched each of the three leaves of parchment again. "There should be five more words, but they're not here."

"He must have hidden the other part somewhere else."

Or maybe the rest of the spell was in the same place these pages ought to be, the place they had been when her father first designed his game. Mouse sank back against the cabin wall. "We have to go to Stockholm."

"Why?" Angelo's question was full of weariness, too.

"The Devil's Bible," she said as she looked up. Then she froze.

A face rested against the window of the door to their berth. Its skin ran like melted wax over sharp cheekbones and hardened at an angular chin. Its colorless eye swept over them. Mouse knew that face. It had come to visit her after the hollow-eyed children had found her at the baby cemetery. Before she learned the spells to protect herself, this creature had come at his leisure. He liked children. His name was Moloch.

Mouse felt the bile rise in her throat as she mouthed the words of the protective spell again. But if it hadn't worked the first time, she knew it was probably too late now.

Angelo sucked in a sharp breath, and Mouse flicked her eyes to him for an instant, afraid he had seen the face at the window, but Angelo was just staring at her, his back to the door. "It was you."

Mouse ignored him. She was watching Moloch's eye dilate, waiting to see if it narrowed its focus on her or Angelo. Her body vibrated with tension as she prepared for the worst.

"It was you. Wasn't it?" Angelo shifted in front of her. Mouse flinched at the movement, sure it would expose them. She kept her eyes fixed on the window just above Angelo's head. Moloch seemed to be looking right at her.

Then the face pulled back and moved into the darkness at the other end of the car. The spell had worked.

"Mouse!" Angelo grabbed her shoulders, forcing her attention.

"What?" she asked as she finally breathed.

"The Devil's Bible. You wrote it."

"Yes." She said it without thinking, distracted by trying to figure out how to get the two of them off the train without Moloch seeing them.

"Your father was there, too."

"Yes." Had she not been so tired, so afraid, Mouse would surely have heard the spark of awareness growing with each of Angelo's questions.

"The rest of the spell is in the Devil's Bible?"

"I think so."

"And it's in Stockholm," Angelo said as he put his arm around her. "Well, we'll just have to go there." He seemed ready for anything.

But he hadn't seen Moloch's face.

Mouse stared at the window until her eyes watered. Her mind was full of childhood horrors that were all too real.

"We've got another twenty minutes before Prague. You need to sleep," Angelo said, worried at the look on her face.

"I'm scared I'll dream."

Chapter Twenty

ouse sent Angelo to buy the tickets to Stockholm while she headed to a kiosk to get a ticket to wherever the next departing train was headed. It didn't matter what she or Angelo wanted now. With Moloch lurking around, it was too dangerous to have Angelo with her. She would leave him here and then try to lure the demon of her childhood nightmares onto a train going the other way.

Mouse leaned against the wall, bouncing her ticket on her leg as she watched for Moloch. She felt him before she saw him step out of the exchange booth. When she was sure he had spotted her, she spun toward the stairs that led to the upper level where her train would depart.

"Where are you going?"

Mouse jumped as Angelo laid his hand on her arm. He had come back too soon.

She looked past him, searching the crowd of faces. She found Moloch easily. Even in his human form, he towered over everyone else, and he was built wrong—his legs were too short for his body, his head stretched like a Picasso figure. He had a waxy smirk stretched across his doll-like face as he moved steadily toward her. Toward Angelo.

Mouse grabbed Angelo's arm and pulled him toward the back wall.

"To the bathroom to change," she said. "Why don't you do the same?"

"Good idea. I'll meet you back here."

They moved down the hall together, and then Angelo veered into the men's room as she headed farther into the hallway. She kept walking past the women's room, toward the exit. Moloch's reflection wavered on the glass doors in front of her. She held her breath as he neared the entrance to the men's room, but he passed it and started to close the distance toward her. She yanked opened the doors and ran into the poorly lit park in front of the station. Rows of taxis blared horns at emerging tourists. Mouse moved toward the corner farthest from the light and away from any people. As she slid into the dark, she dropped her bag and lowered herself into a defensive position.

But it was too late—he was already on her, draped over her back. A slick, hairless arm wrapped across her chest and a cold hand clamped on her arm. Moloch whipped her around and flung her into the low brick wall that surrounded the park. She kept her balance and spun toward him.

His ruthlessness added to the advantage he had over her in strength, but she never meant to beat Moloch. Mouse had a clock ticking in her head. Ten minutes and Angelo would be on the platform looking for her. He would board the train thinking she had gotten on already. Then Angelo would be gone.

And she, too, one way or another.

"Hello again, my little Mousey. Want to play?" Moloch moved too fast for her, grabbed her arm and pulled it behind her and up, turning her and smashing her face into the wall again. "I so miss our little games."

Mouse felt the heat radiating from him. The memory of his night-time visits and the torture he inflicted incensed her. She wanted to spit her rage and hatred at him, but he wrapped his hand over her mouth.

"Daddy said I couldn't play this time though. He just wants what's his. He says to give it back." His voice was high and overbright.

Mouse forced her mouth open and sank her teeth into the flesh of his palm. When he jerked his hand back, the skin tore and her mouth flooded with his blood. He let her go and she rolled onto her back and then pulled into a crouch, blood running down her chin.

"Play nice, Mousey, or I'll ignore Daddy's orders. I'm sure he won't mind in a day or so anyway. Little Mousey won't mean so much." He sucked at the wound on his hand. "Now give it back."

"What do you mean he won't care in a day or so?"

"That's for me to know and you to find out." He giggled. "Now give me what I want."

"Don't think so." Mouse needed to kill another seven minutes for Angelo.

She was ready this time when Moloch came for her. She jumped to the side as he lunged and then slammed her elbow into the small of his back, driving him into the dirt. The sharp crack of teeth bounced against the brick wall as his jaw snapped shut. Mouse heard him gag, but he snaked his arm out, grabbed her ankle, and jerked.

The impact jammed her spine as she landed in a sitting position. Moloch kicked back into her chest and pinned her to the ground. She tried to twist free, but he pushed so hard she could barely breathe. She watched him dig his long, pasty fingers into his mouth and then fling bits of shattered teeth to the ground.

"Give-y, give-y," Moloch said as he stood over her, pressing his foot into her sternum. She felt it bend with his weight.

A hollow voice pinged against the stone—the train's final departure call. Angelo should have boarded by now, looking for her. In a few minutes he would be speeding away to safety.

Mouse pointed. "It's in my bag."

"You get it. I don't trust you." Moloch's voice whistled through the gaps of his fractured teeth as he grabbed her hair and pushed her toward the canvas bag.

She held the copper box out to him.

"Open it," Moloch said.

She did. Satisfied by what he saw, he snatched the box and turned to leave.

"I confess I thought you were a tricky Mouse. I thought you'd let the other one take all the risk. Oh well."

Moloch folded himself into the darkness and disappeared.

Mouse dropped to her knees gagging to get the rest of his blood out of her mouth until she realized what he'd said. *The other one.* She went cold with horror. She took off for the station, jumping down the stairs and slamming into the block wall as she turned into the hallway of the men's bathroom.

The man loomed over Angelo against the far wall. He was huge—at least twice Angelo's size. He had a knife. Angelo was already on the floor bleeding. The man turned when he heard the slap of Mouse's boots on the tile, but it didn't matter. She was on him instantly, grabbing his knife hand, pulling it behind him. Blind with rage and reeling with the power swelling in her like it had at the ruins of Podlažice, she meant to kill him. But at the last moment, with the point of the knife already digging into the man's skin, Mouse looked over at Angelo's face. Her rage and the power slipped away from her like sweat, and she turned the blade so that it ripped into the soft flesh to the right of the man's spine. Snarling with a final surge of adrenaline, she thrust the knife outward. A rib snapped as the blade slipped free of the man's massive body, which fell forward, cracking against a urinal before slamming into the floor. Mouse saw the white of bone shards and the sick yellow globs of fat just before they were drowned in a flood of red.

"My God, Mouse." Angelo stared at her, his mouth open.

She saw her reflection in the bathroom mirror. She looked like a monster. Her lips pulled in a bloody sneer like her father. Her eyes almost as dark as his. She wiped her hands on her jeans, then stripped and used her clothes to wipe away most of the blood—hers, Moloch's, this man who had been sent to kill Angelo. She pulled the dress Angelo had bought her out of her bag and tugged it over her head. It was too soft for how she felt. She wrapped toilet paper around Angelo's bleeding hand. He kept looking at the man on the floor.

Mouse reached into the man's pocket and pulled out his cell phone. Blood seeped into the crevices along the sides of the screen as she touched the numbers. Then she turned to where Angelo was crouched at the last stall.

"Tell them you've hurt yourself and need an ambulance." She was hoarse and matter-of-fact. Angelo did as she said.

"We need to get out of here," she said as she pulled Angelo toward the door.

○══╪══○

Their train was speeding away from the platform as they stepped out of the bathroom. Mouse hesitated for just a moment before taking Angelo's hand, running to the stairs and out to the front of the station toward a line of people boarding a bus.

"Where are we going?" He sounded dazed, still in shock.

"Airport." Mouse put her free hand in her bag, fishing for her wallet. She grimaced as her fingers brushed something sticky and still warm. She was afraid that if she pulled out the wallet, the bloody clothes she'd shoved into the bag would come tumbling out, too. She grabbed a handful of loose bills just as she and Angelo stepped onto the bus, and when the driver barked out a ticket price, she shoved the crumpled bills into his hand. He didn't notice the smears of red covering St. Agnes's face on the front of the cash.

Mouse nudged Angelo into the open seats behind the driver. She wanted to be able to make a quick exit if necessary, and here she could use the driver's mirrors to watch the other passengers. Her eyes swept the faces haloed by the dim lights. All of them looked dead.

Angelo stared out the window, his bandaged hand nestled against his shoulder, the other lying on the seat, twisted in Mouse's, unmoving. In his stillness and silence, he seemed like a statue from one of his pictures. Mouse was just the opposite; she couldn't stop moving. The seat quivered from her bouncing leg, and her thumb drummed against the top of Angelo's hand as if she could send her energy into him somehow, make him move, make him okay with what had just happened. But she knew that was impossible.

Mouse started mumbling to herself, snatching bits of lines from one text or another as she tried to build her mental firewall again, but it was no use. All she could think about was what would happen when Angelo recovered from the shock—what he would say, what he would do, where he would go.

She pulled him to his feet as the bus rolled to a stop at the terminal. She wanted to be the first off, but as they neared the glass doors of the airport, she realized she needed to get rid of her bag and the bloody clothes before they went through security. Mouse veered into the shadows beside the wall. When she let go of Angelo's hand, the blood that had pooled in the soft tissue between her fingers stuck to his and stretched like gum between them. Angelo quickly clenched his hand into a fist, severing the scarlet threads, and then shoved it into his pocket. Mouse winced.

She lowered her bag, squatting as she unzipped it. Carefully holding the bloody clothes against the side of the bag, she pulled out the leather sack of salts, her wallet, passport, and—after a moment of doubt—the christening angel. Dark streaks that looked like slash marks in the dim light cut across the angel's body and face.

Angelo closed his hand around the figure.

Tears stung Mouse's eyes. "I told you I wasn't what you thought I was." She pulled the broken, stained statue from him and shoved it to the bottom of the bag on his shoulder.

Angelo dropped his head against her hair, talking softly. "You saved me, Mouse. That's what you are to me."

Mouse couldn't speak. She wiped her hand across her eyes and pushed the canvas bag into the trash can.

Angelo put his arm around her shoulders. "Let's go to Stockholm."

The attendant at the CSA counter handed Mouse's credit card back after a second scan. "I am sorry. Your card is declined. I can try again if you like."

Mouse had been using the card in Italy and Prague with no problems. Confused, she looked to see if the magnetic strip was smeared with blood or damaged somehow.

"Try mine." Angelo pulled out his wallet.

They watched as the attendant slid Angelo's card through the scanner again and again. "I'm sorry, sir. It is not accepting your card either."

Mouse's chest tightened with growing anxiety and a sudden awareness.

"Come on." She pulled on Angelo's sleeve as he reached out for his card. They wove through the sparse string of travelers to a tiny restaurant. Sweet Home, it promised. It was nearly empty.

They moved to the outside terrace and sat at a table where Mouse could watch the door.

"May I see your phone?" She held out her hand.

She turned it on. There were over a hundred texts. Most were straightforward. Others used clever quotes and allusions. Some were veiled threats. All of them said the same thing: CALL ME NOW OR COME HOME. Apparently Jonah's three days were up. Bishop Sebastian and his Novus Rishi were in full pursuit.

"Have you answered him?" she asked as she handed back the phone.

"No," Angelo said defensively.

Mouse started loosening the bloody tissues wrapped around his hand. She pulled a tiny first-aid kit from an outside pocket of his bag. "I'm not accusing you, Angelo. It just explains the credit cards. And it means we have to worry about your bishop as well as my father."

Angelo winced as she began cleaning his wound. It wasn't deep but it was still oozing blood. "I don't think Bishop Sebastian would . . ."

Mouse shrugged. "He's already told us his group—this Novus Rishi—has power and influence. What better way to make you call him than to strand us here? He takes away our means of keeping on the move. Maybe he thinks we'll have to ask for his help."

Angelo pushed down on the bandages Mouse had stuck across the gash in his hand. "What do we do?"

"You could stay here, and I could—"

"No. And don't start, Mouse. I'm going with you to Stockholm."

She sighed and watched the airplanes lining up on the tarmac like winged ants.

"Hand me my wallet."

She unsnapped it and lifted the edge to her mouth, chewing at the threads along the seam until there was a hole big enough for her to put her finger in. She yanked the leather away from the lining, held it upside down, and shook. A passport, driver's license, and credit cards fell to the table.

She bit at her lip as Angelo flipped open the passport, revealing a version of herself with short, blond hair and the name Emmie Bohdan. Mouse was waiting for the questions or the judgment.

"Now those are some ears, Emmie," he said.

Mouse grabbed the passport and whacked him on the shoulder, both of them laughing.

o—+—o

They went to the Air France counter this time and had their tickets to Stockholm within minutes, just under an hour before their flight. Mouse didn't want to be an easy target sitting at a gate, so she kept them moving in erratic patterns along the concourse, constantly doubling back to scan the crowds for unwanted tagalongs, whether the Bishop's or her father's.

As she was about to have them wind back to their departure gate, Angelo pulled them into a toy shop. The small space was crammed with stuffed animals and trains, and dozens of marionettes hanging from the ceiling. Mouse and Angelo moved through them and emerged from the curtain of dangling feet into a wonderland. A tiny Bohemian village was laid out—a church with a cemetery, shops, houses nestled against each other with the dips and rises of roofs, even a water mill—all intricately carved out of linden wood. But Mouse was drawn to the farmhouse, which sat a little apart from the rest. In the kitchen, the dollhouse family gathered around the table. The details were breathtaking, the wood floor even had tiny knots etched in, but it was the simplicity of the people that captured Mouse. Each had smooth round heads and featureless faces, only their size and clothes gave them identity as mother or father or child. Otherwise, they could be anyone. They could be Mouse.

When she looked up, Angelo was gone. Mouse scanned the store looking for him. He wasn't there. She darted through the marionettes, sending them clacking like branches breaking against each other in a storm.

Mouse stepped out into the flow of people moving along the transit corridor, pushing her way through, hoping to catch a glimpse of Angelo and straining her ears to weed through mumbled conversations for any sound of him. What she saw instead were dozens of men stationed at each gate and shop like sentries. They were dressed like private taxi-service drivers, but they kept looking down at pieces of paper and then squinting as they surveyed the faces of passing travelers.

Mouse opened her senses, feeling for any taint on them, but these puppets seemed to belong to Angelo's Father, not hers. As the one nearest her looked up, she spun around and headed in the other direction. He followed, and she saw another start moving toward her from the far side of the corridor.

Mouse had started to run when she saw Angelo down a side hall off the main corridor. He was against the wall, someone in a suit standing in front of him, too close. Mouse cut across the corridor, but just as she reached them, the man handed something to Angelo and walked away.

"Are you all right?" she asked, grabbing Angelo's arm.

Angelo nodded as he watched the man turn the corner toward the main terminal. The men who'd been following Mouse trailed behind him. "It's okay. He just wanted to talk."

"Who was that?" she asked as she took his hand and headed toward their departure gate.

"A friend of the Bishop's."

"What did he say?"

"He said he was bringing the mountain to Mohammed and told me that the Bishop only wanted to know that I was well and to be sure I knew I could come home again. It was all very polite. And he gave me this." Angelo held up an envelope.

"What is it?"

Angelo unfastened the clasp. He pulled out a credit card and a cell phone. "It's in my name," he said as he handed Mouse the card, and then the phone buzzed with a text: IN CASE YOU LOST YOUR OTHER ONE, PRODIGAL.

Angelo slid the phone and credit card back into the envelope. Mouse took it and tossed it in the trash can near their gate as they boarded.

"Your bishop likes short strings," Mouse said as she dropped into her seat on the plane.

"Sometimes strings can be lifelines, Mouse."

"Not in my experience." She leaned her head back and closed her eyes.

"I got you something." Angelo reached up and turned on the overhead light. "Open your hand."

"What's this?" She looked down at a bundle of tissue paper.

"It was in the house with the family."

As she unrolled it, a small wooden figure dropped into her palm. It had a leather tail and ears, but the rest of it was carved simply in linden wood like the farm folk had been.

It was a mouse.

CHAPTER TWENTY-ONE

By the time their plane landed in Stockholm two hours later, Mouse and Angelo had come up with a plan for gaining access to the Devil's Bible, which was carefully guarded in the National Library of Sweden. Thanks to her stints as a graduate student and professor, Mouse was familiar with the stringent protocol for accessing Special Collections in a research library. Typically, a visit would take weeks to schedule, but they didn't have that kind of time. They would have to bluff their way in. Mouse certainly knew how to lie about who she was. A little fake paperwork, some new clothes so they looked the part, and a lot of luck might open the doors they needed to walk through to get to the Devil's Bible. It would take a day to prepare.

The moment they checked into their hotel room, Angelo sank onto the bed.

"Oh, no you don't," Mouse said as she leaned over him, pulling on his shoulders trying to get him up again. "We need to rehearse who's doing what tomorrow."

He wrapped his arm around her waist and flipped her onto her back beside him on the bed. "It's today already, which means we have at most three hours to sleep." He let the last word drawl out slowly and closed his eyes. Mouse started to get up. He rolled toward her, his body half on hers, and put his arm across her. "You sleep, too."

Mouse tried to reach the lamp to turn it off, but she couldn't move under Angelo's weight. He was already asleep. She closed her eyes, too, and tried to lose herself in the silent rhythm of his breathing, but it kept tickling the hair just behind her ear, making her think about things besides sleeping. With a sigh, she opened her eyes; Mouse had her own decisions to make about what would happen at the library. The shadows cast by the lamplight seemed to be moving, shaping themselves into hooded bishops and crouching Molochs that oozed into the blackness.

She still held the little wooden mouse in her hand and rubbed it gently with her thumb, like it was a worry stone with the magic power to carry away all her troubles.

⊙══╪══⊙

After showers, a quick breakfast, and a stop at the hotel ATM, they went their separate ways. Mouse went to buy clothes; Angelo went to buy cameras. They would meet again that afternoon. Mouse never asked God for anything, but that day, her mind trickled with the words of a thousand memorized prayers to keep Angelo safe.

Her part of the mission was to outfit them like people sanctioned from the Vatican. Angelo was to be an official sent on a task from the Commission for Sacred Archaeology, which meant he needed to look comfortably wealthy, like any good Roman citizen—expensive suit, shirt and tie, all silk. Mouse would play his assistant and so opted for a more conservative, tailored suit in appropriately British black.

Costumes in order, she headed for a ProCenter in Stureplan where she could edit and print the materials for Angelo's fake portfolio. The forged letter from Bishop Sebastian made her the most nervous. She had tried to get Angelo to think of someone else they could use for the necessary reference, but Angelo had argued that they had the best chance of forging documents and a signature from someone he actually knew. Mouse didn't want to think about what might happen if the library staff actually called to confirm Angelo's credentials; she couldn't afford to have this go wrong. If she had any hope of stopping her father and preventing this war Bishop Sebastian thought was coming, she needed the rest of the spell in the Devil's Bible.

Trying to shake a growing sense of foreboding, Mouse sank herself into the fun of culling through Angelo's work. He had given her his password to access the pictures he stored on his laptop. She loved getting to play editor and to build a collection of photos she thought genuinely captured Angelo as an artist. The last file in the folder held the pictures from Monster Park.

Mouse clicked rapidly through the string of images. She was stunned at what she saw. She hadn't realized that Angelo had taken pictures of her. He'd said he wasn't good with people, but he was wrong. Mouse knew she didn't really look the way his pictures made her look—the last of the sunlight shining in her hair, her eyes less dark, the green in them sparkling and alive. What she saw had to be a trick of the light.

"I love that one."

Mouse jumped at his voice, banging her shoulder into his chin. She had been studying a photo of herself reaching toward the stone face of Echidna, the mother of monsters, and she hadn't heard the door open.

"Ouch." Angelo rubbed his jaw.

"Sorry."

"Me, too." He nodded at the computer screen. "I didn't exactly ask permission, but look at you shine. You're beautiful."

Even Mouse could see the light glowing around her in the picture.

"How did you do that?" she asked.

"That's not me. That's you—it's like you're lit up from within. I could see it when I turned my lens on you. I couldn't help but take the pictures." Her stillness made him worry that he'd crossed a line. "Mouse?"

What could she tell him? That what he called a shine looked just like the glow she saw in people but could never find in herself? That his picture captured her in a way she had never believed possible? That she was seeing herself for the first time?

"Really, it's fine." She shut down the computer.

"Well, come on then."

"Where are we going?" she asked as she lowered her new backpack onto the floorboard of the car Angelo had rented. She had told him it was impractical to lug the camera equipment onto mass transit, but Mouse had other reasons for needing the car.

"I asked the guy in the camera shop for a nice place to eat. Last meal before prison, you know." Angelo's nervous playfulness was contagious.

They spent hours over dinner, Angelo laughing as Mouse quietly told stories about the more ridiculous things she'd had to do or wear over the years. Finally, overfull on stuffed dumplings and too much wine, they headed upstairs to the restaurant's club, their eyes and smiles a little too bright, both of them holding fast to the joy of the night as they worked to keep their fears about tomorrow at bay. After claiming a corner table, Angelo left to get them a couple of beers from the bar. Mouse was tapping her feet when he got back.

His lips tickled her ear when he spoke. "You're seeming more like a girl than an ancient these days. Dollhouses and dancing feet."

He smiled and pulled her out to the floor just as the music slowed. Mouse's pulse quickened when she felt the muscles in his arm flex as he turned her in a slow circle. He bent his head toward her shoulder and his body pressed into hers.

"What are you doing?" she asked him softly.

"I thought I was dancing. What are you doing?" His mouth brushed the skin at her neck.

"I think you're a little drunk."

"Aren't you?"

"I don't get drunk."

He pulled back and looked into her eyes. She saw his desire and couldn't stop from pushing herself up and closing her lips lightly over his. His hand clenched her shirt at the small of her back, but when she pulled away to look at him, trying to figure out where this was going, she saw the indecision in his face.

Mouse pushed against him gently, giving him a little more space.

"You've had too much to drink, Angelo. This doesn't mean anything."

"This is my choice to make, not yours."

"Then what do you want?" She knew what she wanted him to say, but she wasn't prepared for an answer.

"Damn it, Mouse. I don't know."

She paused, then pulled away. "Well, I do," she said. "I want to leave."

Angelo led them out of the club. As they headed for the car, he reached for her hand, but Mouse wrapped her arms around herself against the chill.

When they got back to the hotel, Mouse crawled into her side of the bed and pulled her body as close to the edge as possible. She willed herself not to move and forced herself to sleep. She was determined to make this as easy as possible for both of them.

Angelo never said a word.

<hr />

They woke early, nervous about the uncertainty of the day. They took extra time dressing, as if the new clothes might work like camouflage, transforming them into the people they were pretending to be. Before they left the hotel, Mouse tucked a leather pouch into the inside pocket of Angelo's jacket.

"What's this?" he asked.

"Protection if things go badly," she said.

"Like the fish spell?"

"Yeah, like that."

They tossed their bags into the rental car at the hotel parking garage and walked to the library. Angelo wheeled the large case of camera equipment behind him. As they neared the entrance, Mouse saw a man leaning against the corner of the building smoking a cigarette. He nodded, and the woman with him turned to watch as Mouse and Angelo wrestled the case up the stairs. The couple reeked of her father's touch. Mouse had known he would have someone waiting for her. Even though Moloch had gotten the pages back, her father had no way of knowing whether or not Mouse had already found the spell in them. If she had, then her father knew her next move would be getting the rest of the spell out of the Devil's Bible. This blank-faced couple was his insurance policy.

Her neck prickled in anticipation as she saw them come through the library doors moments later. The two of them paused near the restrooms just down from the information desk where Mouse and Angelo had stopped and asked to speak to the research librarian in charge of Special Collections.

Smiling and breathing in the soft mustiness of the library, Mouse suddenly realized she had another problem, something she hadn't anticipated. She shuddered as she felt a powerful presence snake its way up her spine. She could only guess it came from the Devil's Bible.

All those centuries ago, the book she and her father made together had soaked up bits of power from its cocreators. Bishop Andreas, the first to lay human hands on the Devil's Bible, had felt it when he touched it. Jack Gray had felt it, too. Many in the intervening years had whispered about the dark secrets hidden in the ancient manuscript. Many had gone looking for those secrets in the text. But Mouse knew they wouldn't find what they were looking for in the words or the pictures. The power lived in the book itself. And like any offspring, it bore more traits of one parent than the other. It was truly the Devil's Bible.

Over the years, many had thought to use its dark forces for their own cause. Mouse had read about them—some famous, some not, some who spent an hour with the book, and others who spent years. The book changed them. The book broke them.

Now it was playing with Mouse, just as her father's power had in the ruins of Podlažice. Only this time, it didn't addle her mind. This time, it toyed with her anger.

The young man at the desk was directing Angelo to a set of stairs. "You're looking for Eva Hedlin's office, two flights down and to your left at the end of the hall."

"You go on," Mouse said as she turned back to the man and woman who had started to move slowly toward the same stairs. It would make a nice secluded spot for them to ambush Mouse and Angelo. She felt the power fingering her anger like someone turning the volume up. All she wanted right now was a fight.

"Mouse?" Angelo could tell something was wrong with her.

"I'll catch up."

Aware that the librarian was watching them, Angelo nodded and, as he disappeared down the stairs, Mouse spun toward the library entrance, smirking when she sensed the man and woman tense as she passed them.

A burst of air played with her hair when she shoved the doors open and walked down the portico to the back of the library, where she'd seen a stand of trees nestled beside a wing of the building. Her body taut with expectation, she smiled as the couple moved into the shadows with her. She kept her back to them, luring them in. Mouse lowered her head to listen for the intake of breath that signaled the attack. Her laugh bounced along the stone façade of the building as she hurdled the man's kick and spun to catch the woman's fist.

It was as if a curtain had been pulled back. No longer just a whisper at the back of her mind, Mouse felt the powerful malevolence in the Devil's Bible call to her like a child for its mother.

She elbowed the man in the throat and twisted the woman's fist until the bones in her wrist snapped. As the man grabbed his neck, careening off the building and landing on his knees gasping for breath, Mouse slapped her hand over the woman's mouth, catching her scream. It tickled Mouse's palm; it tickled the vicious thing inside her.

Then she saw her reflection in the woman's wide eyes—Mouse's face was full of naked joy at the pain she caused. She let the woman go.

The man slammed into her from behind. She twisted just as she made contact with the wall. The impact forced the air from her lungs and she doubled over as she tried to catch her breath. The man grabbed her head and yanked her backward; Mouse landed hard on the ground. As he stood over her with strands of her hair still twisted in his fingers, he glanced quickly at the shuttered windows of the lowest floor of the library and reached into his jacket, going for the knife Mouse could see strapped to his waist.

Mouse kicked out hard. The spiked heel of her shoe hit the man in the groin. She scrambled to her feet as he sank to his knees. The woman was still huddled at the wall holding her wrist.

Mouse felt the power beginning to swell in her again, but this time she tensed like someone fighting the urge to vomit, refusing to let her body give in to its impulses. "I will not kill anyone today," she said through gritted teeth, trying to anchor herself against the influence working on her. She would not be her father. She would not be his puppet either.

But she was barely holding onto her will, barely in control of herself. She needed these people gone or else they'd be dead like her father's minion back in Nashville. She wasn't sure if she could command someone already under her father's control, but she had to try.

"Go away," Mouse said. The woman looked at her but made no move to leave. "Get out of here," she said again, more forcefully. Still nothing. Mouse was scared to tap her power to issue a more forceful command, but she had no choice. "I will not kill anyone today," she whispered. And then she took a deep breath. "Go home!"

The reaction was instant. Both the man and the woman turned on their heels and started walking away. They moved stiffly, their injured bodies rebelling, but the will to go home was more powerful than their pain. It was not their will but Mouse's that drove them. They had no choice but to obey.

Mouse leaned against the wall of the library as she watched them go. Her hands were shaking and she sucked in ragged breaths through her nose, her mouth clenched against the power and the bile rising in her throat.

None of the violence had been necessary. Mouse had hurt them because she wanted to, because the thing in the Devil's Bible wanted her to. Because her father wanted her to. This is how it would be if he finally caught her and claimed her. It was what she had run from all these years. She had gotten a taste of it during those weeks with him at Podlažice. He charmed and teased it out of her, this thirst for power, this hunger for violence. He would fan it to full flame, and God help her, she would love it. And what if she truly had the power the Bishop thought she had?

Mouse needed the last line of that spell.

She closed her eyes, counting her breaths, measuring her heartbeats, and building a wall against the onslaught of power that still beckoned to her as she headed back into the library. Two steps down the stairs, then six to the landing, twelve more steps, the hall, and then she heard Angelo's voice. Her mind grasped at it like a lifeline.

She found him in a large office sitting across from a woman with short, graying hair. They were laughing at something, both of them obviously already comfortable with each other. Mouse pushed back against a flicker of irrational irritation.

"This is my assistant, Dr. Emma Lucas. I have her on loan from England." Angelo's voice dripped with feigned arrogance, but he frowned as he noticed the bits of grass on Mouse's skirt and the sweat beaded on her forehead.

"It's a pleasure to meet you, Ms. Hedlin." Mouse gave her a tight smile as she sat in the chair opposite Angelo. She licked her lips and worked to concentrate on keeping up with the conversation so she could play her part when it was time, but she was still walling herself up against the power, one counted breath at a time.

The librarian never took her eyes off Angelo. Mouse could see how well he had charmed her.

"As I was saying," Angelo continued, "I'm afraid we have a last-minute request for access to one of your holdings in Special Collections. And I do apologize. Normally Dr. Lucas travels ahead and manages all of this for me, but not this time. We needed to take advantage of the opportunity. You understand, of course." Angelo intentionally tangled the narrative so the most potentially difficult information came at the librarian's request.

"I'm sorry, but I don't understand. What opportunity?"

Mouse knew her lines, but her hands, skin red and broken at the knuckles, trembled as she laid them her in her lap. "Deacon D'Amato is working with Bishop Bernardo Sebastian at the Vatican to produce a book highlighting 13th- and 14th-century Christian art. The Bishop hopes the book will raise funds to help with several restoration projects he oversees." Mouse handed the woman Angelo's fake portfolio. "He has a Papal Commission, you see."

Mouse almost sighed with relief when the woman barely glanced at the letter of reference. Ms. Hedlin seemed more interested in Angelo's photos at the back of the case.

"You are very good." Ms. Hedlin nodded at Angelo, waiting for his pleased expression at her praise.

"Thank you." He gave her just what she wanted.

"I'm still unclear about what I can do for you."

Mouse felt heady with a fresh surge of power pulsing through her as she relaxed into the conversation and lowered her defenses. She almost abandoned their plan in a flash of arrogance. It would have been so much easier just to command the pompous woman to bring them the Devil's Bible. The book belonged to Mouse anyway, and the longer she sat there, the more Mouse wanted it.

Angelo looked at her expectantly; she had missed her cue.

"We just learned . . . um, I'm sorry." Mouse stuttered as she worked to catch up. "Two days ago we learned that you were about to start a preservation process on the Codex Gigas. The Devil's Bible?"

"It's only a routine procedure when one of our antiquities returns after a prolonged public exhibit. The Codex has just come back to us from Prague, actually," Ms. Hedlin said.

"Yes, yes. This is why we're here," Angelo said. "The Bishop wants pictures of before and after. He wants to document the work you do to preserve these important artifacts of Christendom. We have similar photos of restorations of some German frescoes and of a small church in Ireland. But we have nothing for a textual work like the Devil's Bible." Angelo very softly stroked her ego.

"You want to photograph the Codex? Today?" The woman frowned and began thumbing through the portfolio again.

"Well we already have the equipment with us. We could take the before pictures today and return at your convenience for the after pictures." Mouse tried to sound matter-of-fact.

"And who did you say you were working for?" She stopped on the letter of reference. "Oh, I see."

She pulled out her phone and keyed-in the numbers.

Angelo shrank back in his chair, and Mouse tensed. They knew this might happen. It had been a gamble. They had debated putting a fake number on the reference, but if they did and got caught, the game was over. Instead they had rolled the dice that the librarian would see polished professionals and not bother to check on their credentials. So much for luck being with them.

"Bishop Bernardo Sebastian, please." Eva Hedlin smiled at Angelo as she waited for the connection.

Mouse felt the room closing in on her. This was the part of the gamble that held the most risk. She and Angelo had very different ideas about how they thought the Bishop would respond if he did get called.

"Good Morning, Your Excellency. I'm Eva Hedlin, the chief librarian at Kungliga Biblioteket. I have a young man and woman in my office requesting permission to take pictures of the Codex Gigas on behalf of a project they are working on with you." She let her tone ask the question.

Mouse and Angelo tensed as the librarian paused to listen to something the Bishop said. Then she smiled.

"Yes, that's right. Angelo D'Amato and Emma Lucas." Mouse and Angelo exchanged a glance. Ms. Hedlin's forehead creased and her lips pressed into a thin line.

Mouse wetted her lips and prepared herself to do what was necessary; the power was jumping for release.

"Well, of course, Your Excellency. One moment." Ms. Hedlin held out the phone, and Angelo reached to take it.

But the librarian turned to Mouse. "He wants to talk to you."

CHAPTER TWENTY-TWO

The draw of the power pulsing from the Devil's Bible clawed at Mouse's neck. The last thing she wanted right now was to talk to Bishop Sebastian, but she had no choice.

"Yes?" Her voice was high and tight. She lifted her hand to her forehead and wiped the sweat away.

"When my people told me you were on your way to Stockholm, I wondered. The Devil's Bible?" He didn't sound nearly as warm and charming on the phone as he had in person. He sounded angry and worried. "So you're choosing family over the righteous then?"

"No, Your Excellency. Deacon D'Amato and I thought the book would be perfect for your current project," Mouse stretched her neck like a horse pulling at the bit as she fought to find something appropriate to say with the librarian staring at her.

"Am I to understand that your actions are on my behalf? That you are working for the Novus Rishi?"

Mouse wanted to fill his ear with what she thought of him and his Novus Rishi, but it would not get her what she wanted. What she needed. "That's correct, Your Excellency."

After a moment's silence, the Bishop said, "My people told me about the man found in the bathroom at Prague. Was that necessary?"

"Yes, Your Excellency. Deacon D'Amato is in good health."

"He was in danger?" Bishop Sebastian hissed.

"I'm afraid so, Your Excellency."

"I want him back," the Bishop said.

"That is not my decision to make, Your Excellency."

"He has not answered any of my messages."

"That's unfortunate, Your Excellency."

"I know that Angelo would not, of his own will, leave me and the Church. He owes his life to it," the Bishop said. "And I'm confident that as your father's daughter you've got the power to get what you want, including Angelo."

Her eyes flicked to Angelo. "Would you like to speak with him yourself, Your Excellency? He might be able to answer your concerns better than I."

"Are you telling me he is not under your persuasion?"

"That is correct, Your Excellency."

"You could be lying."

"Yes, Your Excellency, I could."

Mouse heard him swallow.

"I see. And am I to understand, given your request to see the Devil's Bible, that you are operating on some plan?" He had recovered his smooth tone, like they were having a pleasant conversation over tea.

"As you say, Your Excellency, 'Act and God will act.'"

"Don't play games with me. Do you have a plan to deal with your father?"

"Yes, Your Excellency." Mouse could feel the vein jumping in her neck and wondered if the librarian could see it.

"And if this plan fails? You are prepared for . . . other options to keep him from using you?"

Mouse chewed her lip at the Bishop's ultimatum—take her father out or take herself out. She glanced at Angelo. She very much did not want to die, not now when there was so much to live for.

Angelo narrowed his eyes at her pale face.

"Dr. Lucas?" the Bishop said.

"Yes, Your Excellency."

"You are prepared to do whatever is necessary to keep yourself out of your father's hands—whether that means sacrificing yourself or putting yourself in my care for safekeeping?"

The last part of his question caught her off guard. An image of Father Lucas flared in her mind. Bishop Sebastian might not bear personal responsibility for what happened to Father Lucas, but people just like him did. She had no doubt the Bishop would sanction torture or anything else he thought would help him win. That was his idea of safekeeping; that was his idea of righteousness. But it wasn't even fear of what he might do that made it so difficult for Mouse to concede. Every thread of her independence, of her own will screamed against turning herself over to his control. But what choice did she have?

"Yes." Her mouth was too dry for more.

"I see." Then nothing.

In the silence, Mouse shifted her weight nervously from one leg to the other. Angelo cleared his throat, startling Eva Hedlin, who turned quickly back to Mouse, brow furrowed.

"I would like to pray for you and your efforts," the Bishop said. "Would you allow me?"

This was the last thing Mouse expected.

"Yes, Your Excellency." Her words were barely audible. Mouse closed her eyes and listened to the Bishop's warm voice recite St. Michael's prayer.

"Dr. Lucas?" he said after the *amen.*

"Yes?"

"I mean for him to come back to me when this is finished."

"I told you, that's not my decision to make."

"We shall see," the Bishop said. "You may send me back to the librarian now."

As Mouse handed over the phone, she could not look at Angelo.

Minutes later, they were following Eva Hedlin down another flight of stairs to a small room where she left them. She returned quickly, accompanied by a guard; they carried a large metal case between them, which they lowered carefully onto the table in the center of the room. Ms. Hedlin unlatched the top of the case.

Mouse felt a rush of adrenaline as the power filled the room. Instinctively, she lifted a hand to run across the book, as she had so many times before.

"Oh, no, my dear." The librarian had reached out protectively and pushed Mouse's hand away. "We'll lift the book out of the case and turn the pages for you." Mouse bit into her lip to keep from slapping the woman. She was starting to lose control again with the book so close. The power was intoxicating.

As Angelo busied himself setting up tripods and lights, Mouse watched as the librarian slipped on a pair of white gloves and reached into the case. Mouse thought about Jack Gray, his boast that he had touched the Devil's Bible, and the wild gleam in his eye as he confessed. She had known all along that they would not let her touch the text. But she had to. Mouse *had* to touch it to get what she needed.

When the librarian and the guard lifted the Devil's Bible out of the case and laid it on the table, Mouse moved swiftly across the room toward them. In the moment that she issued the command, she saw the shock of betrayal in Angelo's face.

Then three bodies fell to the floor.

She walked to where Angelo lay in front of the closed door and locked it as she looked down at him. The Devil's Bible beckoned her. She should just grab it and go. Let Angelo stay with the others. Let him go back to his bishop. That's what he wanted anyway, and she didn't need him. The voice in her head hissed with bitterness like a viper. She didn't need anyone.

But when Mouse knelt and kissed Angelo as a last good-bye, the strings of power pulling at her loosened a little, and the blinding anger eased. She leaned down, her lips to his ear, and whispered so that only he could hear. "Wake up."

His disorientation lasted only a moment. "What happened to them?" he asked as he ran his hand over his face, trying to focus.

"They're unconscious."

"What are you doing?"

"Help me get the book into the equipment case. Quickly."

"We're stealing it?" He was now as angry as he was confused.

"We have no choice. I'll explain later."

"Were you going to leave me here?"

"Angelo, help me!"

Angelo shoved the Devil's Bible into the equipment case while Mouse wrapped the cameras in the photo umbrellas and crammed them into the metal box that had held the ancient manuscript. When it lay closed on the table and the equipment case stood ready by the door, Mouse and Angelo pulled the librarian and the guard into the chairs along the back wall where they would've sat to observe Deacon D'Amato taking his pictures. Mouse and Angelo moved near the door, ready to run if something went wrong.

With everything staged, all that remained was for Mouse to wake them. She moved closer to Angelo so that her hand was touching his, praying that it would serve like an antidote if the force in the Devil's Bible surged again when she tapped her own power to give the command.

She blew out a sigh. "Wake up."

While Eva Hedlin and the guard wrestled with the momentary disorientation, Angelo talked as if they were all in the middle of a pleasant conversation. "Thank you for the recommendation for lunch, Ms. Hedlin. I'm sure it will be lovely."

The librarian's eyebrows pressed together in confusion, but then she stammered, "It was my pleasure, Deacon D'Amato. I hope you enjoy it."

"The exit down here would be easier for us, Ms. Hedlin. We wouldn't have to lug the equipment back up stairs. Would that be okay?" Angelo asked.

The librarian looked at the guard, who nodded blankly and led them to a door that opened to the gardens behind the library.

"Thank you," Mouse said, but the door was already closing behind them. Mouse and Angelo walked away with an ancient manuscript insured for fifteen million dollars shoved into the case between them.

"I can't believe you," Angelo hissed at her.

"Angelo, I can't do this right now."

"But you—"

A piercing wail erupted as they stepped into the circle of trees in Humlegården at the back of the library. Mouse looked up into the canopy thinking of the cicadas back in Nashville, but the leaves were clean and green with no insects, and she realized that the sound was different—higher and solitary, unnatural. The air was changing, too, charged like before a storm.

"Something's coming, Angelo."

Mouse dropped her end of the case and moved in front of him. There was no one in sight, so she started scanning the dark places under the trees.

But the sound wasn't coming from the dark. It was in the sunlight, blinding and audacious.

A thing peeled itself off the statue of Carl Linnaeus where it lay like a second skin over the bronze figure, green and scaly with age. It had been waiting, like the creature at Marchfeld, a sentry left by her father. It dropped into a low crouch and lurched as it came to know itself again. Slowly, the thing reclaimed its shape—a feline skeleton protruded from its starved flesh, and the large, dead eyes of a bird consumed most of its squat, badgerlike face. Its nostrils flared as it caught Mouse's scent. Arching its back as it dropped its head, it turned toward her.

Mouse swept quickly to the left, the creature's eyes tracking her. As it started to move, twisting oddly on its jointed legs, she ran—away from Angelo, who was still standing there frozen as his mind tried to adjust to the reality of the creature he'd just seen.

Mouse's heels clicked on the sidewalk and then sank into the dirt as she raced across the grass toward the cover of a tight line of trees. She turned to see how close the thing had gotten.

There was nothing there.

Afraid that it had gone after Angelo instead, she closed her eyes, frantically searching for evidence that he was still alive. She saw his glow moving in her direction. Then she heard the snapping in the trees above her. She jumped out of the way just as the creature landed, its claws raking her back.

Mouse ran again, trying to lure it farther away from Angelo. She could sense it closing in on her and hunched her shoulders, expecting any moment to feel its claws piercing her. When she ran up against the Gazitúa statue, she spun around, her back against the stone.

"Leave!" she ordered. The thing was only a step away, but Mouse was too frightened to issue a more fatal command for fear of who else might hear and obey.

The creature never even paused.

Mouse's neck popped as it backhanded her. She flew into the trunk of a nearby weeping mulberry, its branches dangling down like a curtain, obscuring her view and tangling in her hair. She jumped to her feet, slipping on the dusty cobblestone as she struggled for traction. She headed toward the sound of traffic, thinking only of distracting the creature somehow—thinking only of getting it away from Angelo.

She made it to the grass before the thing leapt onto her back, sinking its claws into her scalp as it struggled to hold on. She could feel it pulling itself around to her front, its teeth exposed. Mouse stopped and threw her weight forward, tossing the creature over her back, but it kept its hold on her head. Her hair tore at the roots as the creature flipped her forward.

Her head cracked into the sidewalk and everything went black.

When she opened her eyes, the creature was crouching over her, its thin face tilted stiffly to look at her, its pupil a tiny pinprick surrounded by pale yellow. And in the flash of a moment as it realized she was awake, Mouse jabbed her hand into the soft flesh just below the creature's sternum. The thin skin tore, and her fingers plunged into its intestines.

Without warning, her head exploded in pain, and her father's voice shut out her awareness of everything else.

I see you want to play my little game, girl.

He'd never been angry when he'd violated her mind this way before. Those other times had hurt, but this time the pain was unbearable as his wrath swelled in her mind. Blood gushed into her ears and trickled down her neck.

But it's rather inconvenient for me right now. Give me a few more days and I'm all yours.

His laughter shook her like a seizure.

That is, if you're still able to play.

The creature lowered its snarling mouth toward her; Mouse could do nothing to stop it. But the thing did not rip out her throat. Instead, it just leaned closer, pushing her balled fist farther up into its chest. Its lips were oddly soft and chalky as it wrapped its mouth over hers.

And then it slipped itself into her pores, like hundreds of needles piercing her skin, as it started to meld with her like it had the statue. It was like the black ooze in the cell at the ruins of Podlažice, except this thing was alive, sentient. It would claim her as its own and then take her to her father. Mouse squirmed with a muffled and powerless rage.

"Get off her!" Angelo had finally caught up to them. He dropped the case he'd dragged with him and spun toward the tree, looking for a limb he could use as a weapon, but then realized it would be useless unless he wanted to bash Mouse's head in, too.

"Throw the salt!" Mouse cried out as the creature started to consume her. "Throw the salt!"

Angelo grabbed at the leather pouch Mouse had tucked into his pocket that morning and ran toward the entwined bodies, untying the frayed strap as he went. He flung the opened pouch at the creature as it sank further into Mouse. The salt spell she had prepared as a talisman for Angelo, tinged with her blood and laced with all the words of protection she knew, now flew into the demon. It screamed in agony. Mouse screamed, too—a gurgling, drowning cry that barely left her throat.

The crystalline cubes sliced into the creature's skin and cut into Mouse's flesh. The salt gathered the creature's substance as it came in contact, pulling it out of and away from Mouse. Angelo watched as the demon was shredded into a million tiny pieces trapped in a million grains of salt that scattered along the sidewalk with quiet plinks and bounced into the grass.

CHAPTER TWENTY-THREE

ouse gripped the steering wheel. Angelo stared out the window. They were half an hour out of Stockholm, and neither of them had spoken.

Seconds after she had been freed from the demon in Humlegården, Mouse pushed herself onto her knees, beckoning to Angelo, who was standing on the sidewalk, his eyes glued to the scattering of black-tinged salt. "We have to get out of here now. Something else will be coming," she said, her voice so hoarse she barely sounded human. It broke his trance; he helped her to her feet, and they made their way slowly through the park back to the car, Angelo dragging the case behind him and Mouse creeping along beside. They took turns explaining to concerned passersby that Mouse had fallen and scraped her knees and hands. The rest of the blood was masked by her dark suit.

Angelo hadn't even argued when Mouse insisted on driving. She dropped stiffly into the seat as Angelo struggled to shove the equipment case into the trunk before sliding into the passenger seat without a word—just the click of his seat belt and the quiet thud of his head against the window.

Finally, Mouse had no choice but to break the silence. "Can you hand me the bag of salts in my backpack? I got a new one at—"

"You're not doing that again." It was cold and final.

"We can't leave ourselves unprotected, Angelo."

The pull of the Devil's Bible had quieted—Mouse guessed it was a side effect of the spell-laced salts Angelo had used to kill that thing in the garden—but she could still feel its power, and she knew her father could, too. He would know where they were.

"We need something to shield us until we find someplace to hide," she said.

"I'll do it then."

"No. I don't want you to—"

"You don't want what, Mouse? You don't want to watch me dig into my arm? Watch my blood splatter on the upholstery so I can keep you safe?" His eyes narrowed, daring her to argue.

"Fine. Go ahead."

Still glaring at her, he shaped the salt along the floorboard and seats and then pulled a razor from his bag. She held her breath as he cut into his forearm. She gave him the words of the spell quietly, hating that he had to learn to do it, knowing that it probably wouldn't be the last time. She wondered whether Bishop Sebastian would still claim him as his own if he saw Angelo now. Drops of his blood rolled down the console. Finally he sat back hard in the seat and crossed his arms, pressing a tissue against the cut.

"Now will you tell me what that thing was?" he asked.

"Something that belongs to my father."

"I'm warning you, Mouse. No games. What was it?"

"I don't have a name for it any more than you can say what pulled you out of the damn river."

"You betrayed me and you're the one who's mad?"

"Betrayed you how?"

"You never said we were going to steal the book. You made me pass out with the others. You controlled me to get what you want." His voice was sharp and Mouse was defensive; both were overcharged with adrenaline and fear from what had happened.

"That's bullshit, Angelo! I couldn't think of any other way to get the book out. I didn't want to do any of that, least of all to you, but what else was I supposed to do?"

"You could have gotten what you needed at the library."

"You think so?" She scoffed. "How was I supposed to find the words to the spell I need with that woman breathing down my neck? Those words are probably written in blood like the others were. I have to touch the book to get the words. Did she act like she was going to let me touch it?" She waited a moment for an answer she knew wouldn't come. "That's what I thought." She gritted her teeth. "I am sick of being second-guessed, Angelo."

"Second-guessed? Who the hell do you think you are?"

"I didn't mean it that way." Mouse flushed with sudden embarrassment, realizing how it sounded and realizing, too, that she wasn't really angry at Angelo. She was mad at herself and doubting every choice she'd made. Stealing the book was the least of it. She had made a deal with the Bishop that she would take her father out of the game, find some way to kill herself, or hand herself over to the Bishop and his self-righteous warriors. She was supposed to stop this impending storm of evil the Bishop believed was about to be unleashed on the world, and she was supposed to keep Angelo safe while she did it. None of those things seemed possible right now.

"I just meant I'm doing the best I can," she said quietly.

"It's not about how hard you're trying, Mouse. It's about you shutting me out." He sighed in frustration.

She pushed herself back into the seat and jerked the wheel as she slipped in and out of cars on the motorway. She knew he was right, but after seven centuries, keeping secrets had become a habit. The wheels whined against the pavement as she pushed on the accelerator.

"The book does things to people," she finally said, trying to give Angelo some part of the explanation he craved and some confession of her own, too. "It does things to me. It plays off my emotions, amps them up like someone winding up a toy to watch it spin. Surely you noticed that I wasn't . . . myself at the library." She hesitated because some part of her worried that the way she was in the library, angry and arrogant and contemptuous in her power, was actually the real Mouse, the person she was born to be.

"But it's not just me who's affected by it," she added. "The man who wanted me to write it for him, Bishop Andreas, went crazy searching it for secrets. Then he hanged himself in the presbytery."

"I don't understand what that has to do with—"

"It's happened over and over again since then. The book doesn't seem to bother most people. Scholars come study the translations and tourists come to spook themselves with the Devil's picture, and they're just fine. But when someone goes looking for something more—things happen."

"Like what?"

"They go insane. A porter in the eighteen hundreds and, later, Eugène Fahlstedt, and his friend, August Strindberg—"

"The playwright?"

She nodded. "They spent a night with the Devil's Bible searching for its secrets. Not long after, Strindberg ended up in an asylum suffering from a psychotic break he called his Inferno crisis." Mouse sighed. "I could have searched the book in the library while Eva Hedlin and the guard were passed out on the floor. It would have been a lot easier. But how could I take that risk? I hadn't counted on it affecting me the way it did, but I knew about the other stories. And I knew my father would protect his secrets somehow. You saw what he did at the ruins in Podlažice, and just now, what he left lurking in Humlegården. I might have drawn that thing into the library with all those people."

"Who is he, Mouse?"

Mouse stared out the window.

"Why didn't you tell me all this before we went?" Angelo asked when it was clear she wouldn't answer his other question.

"If something went wrong and we got caught stealing it, I wanted you to be able to say you didn't know what I was planning to do."

"And that's trusting me?" His temper flared again.

"It's not about trust, Angelo. I trust you more than anyone I've ever met. This is about what I have to do."

"What *you* have to do? Save everyone? That's pretty damn presumptuous, Mouse."

"You don't know what you're talking about."

"So enlighten me, then."

"I killed ten thousand men." She said it out of anger, never meaning to make the confession.

"What?" He almost laughed, but as he studied her face in the silence that stretched out longer and longer, the truth of her words settled in him. "My God," he whispered. "How?"

For a few minutes, Mouse stayed silent, watching the signs flash by counting down the miles to the border crossing. She searched for words that would give Angelo some kind of answer without really telling him the truth, but she was too tired. Tired from what had just happened at the library, tired from the roller coaster she'd been on since Nashville, tired from seven hundred years of running and hiding and lying. She was too tired for anything but truth, simple and bare, so she told him about Marchfeld. When she finished, she thought she should have felt unburdened, but she just felt dirty—contaminated by the book stuffed into the trunk of their car, by the filthy residue of that thing that had been inside her, by the blood running through her veins.

"So you think you have to find redemption by saving everyone?" Angelo asked.

"It's not about redemption."

"Why not?"

"That's not possible for me."

"What, you're the one person in all of human history who can't be forgiven for what they've done? Yet you're the one who has to save everyone else? That's just—I don't know, Mouse, that's some major god complex at work there."

She was quiet for a long time. It wasn't as simple as he made it sound, but Angelo was right. She hadn't been sacrificing herself and her life out of a sense of compassion. She hadn't encased herself in an emotionless, cloistered life driven by ritual and routine out of selflessness. She'd done it out of an inflated sense of responsibility, out of a hope that she could undo what she had done and make herself into something other than her father's daughter. But she was filled with as much arrogant pride as her father was.

"You're right." The hum of the engine filled the silence and weighted her confession. "There's nothing I can do to fix what happened at Marchfeld. I can't change what I am. And I'm not a savior."

"That's not what I'm saying, Mouse. What happened in that field—it was an accident. An act of mercy gone horribly wrong. You can hardly hold yourself responsible any more than I would blame myself for accidentally stepping on an ant."

"Humans aren't ants, Angelo, and if they are, there shouldn't be blundering giants walking among them."

"That's God's purview, not yours."

"The consequences are mine, so I have to be careful about where I walk and who I walk with, especially if—"

"It's *my* choice to be with you, Mouse."

"Is it?"

"What do you mean?"

"Are you here because you want to be with me or because you think it's part of God's plan for you?"

He snapped his head toward her, mouth open and ready to spit some angry missive, but instead he jerked toward the window again, jaw clenched. After a while, he lowered his seat back.

"I'm going to get some sleep." He flung his arm over his face.

Mouse drove until Karlstad, wrestling with her choices and his.

"What are we doing?" Angelo asked when Mouse pulled the car over. He didn't sound like he'd been asleep.

"We need gas. And you need to drive. I can't see the road anymore. Not enough sleep."

"Where are we going?" he asked as they switched seats.

"Oslo."

"Then?"

"A train to Onstad."

"What's in Onstad?"

"A church."

"A place to hide?"

She nodded and then laid her head back and closed her eyes. "This one is special, though. I think it will help me when I open the book."

"We, Mouse. When *we* open the book."

Her stomach twisted as she thought about what might happen. While she was driving, she had built lists in her mind of all the possible protections she could use at the church. She felt sure her father would have built his own spells inside the Devil's Bible to guard the last bit of his game. They would get triggered as soon as she pulled the first word of the binding spell out of the text. What Mouse didn't know is what manner of creature her father would call up in his defense. Or how or when the creatures would be summoned. How much time would she have? Then there was the malevolence of the Devil's Bible itself, which would start to work against them the moment the book was opened. There was no way to prepare for all of that, but she had to try—even though she had a sick feeling that, despite her best efforts, eventually her protective spells would all fail under the onslaught of evil. Mouse sighed.

"I thought you were going to sleep," he said softly. "You worried?"

Her laugh was dry, strained. "Yes."

"Not just about what's coming."

"No."

"Me?"

"I don't know where we stand," she said simply.

"I'm a jerk. And I'm sorry I came after you so hard."

She turned to look at him. "You were right."

"Maybe, but I shouldn't have said any of that the way I did." He looked over at her and smiled. "And you were right, too."

"About?"

"Choices. I've been blaming you for shutting me out. Not letting me make my own choices. But you're right. I don't think I've ever made a decision for myself." He blew his breath in frustration. "I just let things happen to me—Hampstead, seminary. My whole damn life." He squinted at the road. "Even jumping into the Thames wasn't a choice. It's a passive way to kill yourself—to let the river take you."

"It's what life taught you with that car wreck and whatever pulled you from the river. You weren't in control. Fate was. God was."

"No. I have to claim this, Mouse. It's my fault. I don't want to live someone else's life. I want my own."

⊶

At Oslo, they boarded the Bergen Mountain Railway for the first leg of the trip to Onstad. Showers, a change of clothes, hot coffee, and food lifted their spirits, but Mouse felt coiled, poised for another attack and trying to run through scenarios of what might happen when they reached the church. With every click on the track, she felt them rushing headlong toward the impossible.

Angelo seemed to be somewhere else entirely. In the dining car, she caught him staring at her several times like he had something to say, but he always looked away. She wondered if he was having second thoughts.

When they went back to their berth, the beds had been made, but as tired as they were, neither of them was ready to sleep.

"Anything we need to prepare for?" Angelo asked as he sat next to her on the lower bunk, his thigh pushing against hers.

"Not really. The church, the spells, the book." She paused, finding it difficult to concentrate with him touching her. "I have the paper with the rest of the spell in my bag. I think that's it. Except luck." Her voice was soft with longing, and the obviousness of it embarrassed her.

She started to turn her head away, but his hand was on her cheek, turning her toward him. He leaned in and kissed her gently. Mouse's breath caught in her throat, her heart pounding.

"Stop," she breathed, hating herself for it. "Just . . . just wait a minute."

Mouse tried to catch her breath and held her hand lightly against his chest, keeping him at a safer distance. She felt his heart thumping fast and hard. She nearly lost her resolve at the joy of knowing he wanted her, too. But she remembered the kiss in the club at Stockholm. His body had wanted hers then, that was clear, but he had pulled away. He had made a decision, and Mouse meant to help him keep it. "You don't want this," she said.

He smiled and cocked his head. "I very much do, Mouse."

As he said her name, her body sent a tingle slowly up her spine and into her throat.

"What about your vows?"

"I haven't taken vows." He moved his hand up her arm and played his fingers lightly along the skin on the underside of her forearm, lingering at the crease of her elbow. "I've made my choice, Mouse. I want you."

As he closed his mouth on hers again, her body screamed its seven hundred years of want, but she didn't deserve this joy.

"Please, I can't . . . I can't breathe." Her lips moved against his as she spoke; she lowered her head searching for a moment to clear her mind, and she saw the purpled gash on his forearm where it lay against her butchered wrists.

"No, Angelo." Mouse tried to pull away from him, but he wouldn't let her go. "God's a better choice."

"I don't think it's an either/or situation." He smiled down at her.

"No." Her voice was thick with pain now—pain for all she wanted and all she was giving up. "You don't know me."

"Mouse, I know you better than I've known any person in my life. I'm woven into you. And you're in me." He leaned his head against hers.

"No. You don't know . . . what I am." What she needed to tell him burned her throat.

"Yes, I do." He breathed into her hair. "I know who your father is," Angelo whispered. "The Morning Star, Angel of Light, the Fallen One, Serpent, Satan." His words sounded like seductions, and his mouth tickled her ear. "It doesn't change anything."

She had known that this moment would come, either as a result of her own confession or through Angelo's cleverness. She had seen him putting the pieces together. She was glad he had figured it out before she had to tell him. But she had always imagined that the revelation would be charged with guilt on her end, accusation on Angelo's, and fear for both of them. She had never thought the moment would be quiet or that she could feel so sad and so relieved at the same time.

Her confession was now unnecessary, but his words had been too soft, too poetic. She wanted the truth out there simple and bare, so she said it herself. "Angelo, I'm not human."

"Not completely, and I think we've covered that already. But *what* you are does not have to define *who* you are."

"It's not that simple, Angelo. You see what my life is—running, hiding, lying. Anyone near me is in danger. Always. And if you . . . if you were to be near me and he were to—" Her words came now as sobs. "Angelo, I would give him anything to keep you safe. Anything." The words got lost in her gasps for air. He wrapped his arms around her.

"Hush, Mouse." He bent down and kissed the top of her head and held her until she stopped crying, but she still wouldn't look up.

There was a new resolve in her voice. "You think I'm like you, but I'm not." She caught a breath between words to keep herself talking, to say the words she'd never spoken aloud.

"What do you mean?"

"I can see your soul when I close my eyes." She did it as she spoke. "You're full of light." She let the wonderment of what she saw fill her voice.

"How do you know it's a soul you see?"

"I just know. But I—"

"You what?"

"I'm empty, dark." She opened her eyes, unaware that she had turned her face to him.

"Maybe you just can't see your own." He traced a pattern on the palm of her hand.

Mouse tried to breathe, the weight of her confession and the nearness of him pressing against her chest. "It makes sense that I wouldn't have a soul, Angelo. I'm not a child of God."

"Says who?" He whispered the words as he leaned down to her neck, his lips gently brushing the skin where her blood danced. "You're part human aren't you?"

"Yes."

"Then you have a soul. And I've seen it." He pulled back and looked at her.

Mouse asked the question with her eyes.

"In your willingness to die rather than be used by your father. That's a soul's struggle." He rubbed his cheek against her hair. "And it's in the pictures I took of you at Monster Park. I saw it in you. You lit up from inside."

He bent and kissed her cheek, tasted the salt from her tears. He bent lower and found her lips salty, too. Mouse's body responded to him immediately, and she let her legs slide away from her chest so he could move closer to her and put his arms on either side of her, encasing her.

He slipped his arm around her waist and pulled her down so that she lay beside him on the bed. He slid the collar of her shirt down her shoulder, kissed the soft skin along its ridge, and then moved his hand underneath the back of her shirt, caressing the smooth skin in the small of her back. Her hand slid up into his hair at the back of his neck as her body turned toward him; his lips pressed harder, his mouth open and hungry for her.

The thrill of being touched so tenderly after so long played along her skin, every dip and curve of her answering as his fingers moved. He hesitated, unsure in the newness of learning her body, unsure of how to please her. He fought to control his urgency until he felt her own. And then they lost themselves in each other.

Later, Angelo hummed a little Italian lullaby for her. She fell asleep on his chest, and, for the first time in nearly seven hundred years, her sleep was dreamless.

CHAPTER TWENTY-FOUR

They rode in an open coach for the final train to Flåm. Anxiety ate at both of them. Angelo picked at his nails until Mouse took his hand in hers and rested it on her thigh. Their entwined fingers reminded her of what he said about being woven into her life. As beautiful as the idea was, Mouse kept thinking it also meant that if she got ripped apart, so did he. As she stared out the dark window, she saw no lights, not even in the deep dips of the valleys. There were no signs of life.

"Come on, let's talk about something," Angelo said. "Tell me how you know about this place."

"1349."

"Why do I know that date?"

"The Black Death." She shuddered. "I travelled across Europe after I left Bohemia and ended up in Norway. Then it hit. I was a healer, so people came to me for help, but I couldn't do anything except offer a little comfort and stay to bury them. Then I had to leave."

"Why?"

"I never got sick. And people were already on edge about why God had sent the plague. It seemed clear to them what I was."

"A witch?"

She nodded. "Sometimes. Or a demon. Always an abomination." As she said it, she moved her hands like mock claws at him and smiled, but the fun didn't last long. She laid her head back against the seat and closed her eyes. "Until I went to Onstad."

"What was different there?"

"They thought I was an angel."

The digital clock in the rental car flashed 2:40 A.M. when Angelo turned the ignition and then pulled onto the small, curvy lane. Only fifteen minutes later, he parked the car behind an old shed at the bottom of the hill beneath the Onstad Stave Church. Mouse grabbed her backpack, and Angelo heaved the case from the car's trunk.

As they crested the hill, Angelo caught a glimpse of the church for the first time. Softly lit by the moon, the building looked as if it belonged to some forgotten age. The sharp peaks of the roof and the richness of the wood held a mystic primitivism that seemed out of place in a world of automobiles and cell phones.

"It's beautiful." The artist in Angelo appreciated the lines and proportions of the architecture.

"It's old. This one, built in 1150, stands on ruins of others built long before, some connected as much to Norse mythology as to Christianity." The historian in Mouse longed to share the stories of what had been and who had built it, but they didn't have time for stories or for art.

They approached a small door near the corner of the back wall. It was locked.

"Any spells for this?" Angelo whispered.

"The only spells I know are for protection and exorcism. Nothing for breaking and entering. You?" She smiled at him, trying to move past her fear and enjoy what might be their last moments together.

"Well, I watched *The Exorcist* once."

"Don't they teach you boys anything in seminary anymore?" She pulled a credit card from her wallet and began working at the lock. She chuckled as the door slipped open. When they stepped inside the dark building, Angelo knelt and made the sign of the cross. Mouse closed her eyes and used her heightened senses to search for any sign of a guard, but there was no one in the church.

"This is the nave. We need to go right, toward the north end of the church," she said, lifting her end of the case as Angelo led them with the flashlight. They paused at the choir section and put the case down in the aisle near one of the staves.

"Give me a second." Mouse headed toward the presbytery, mentally feeling for something. She hesitated when she neared the altar. The ghosts of the bloated and blackened dead—mothers and fathers and their children—crowded her and made it difficult to think.

"What are you looking for?" Angelo asked.

"Old, sacred places like this have concentrations of power where rituals have been performed for hundreds of years."

"This one doesn't?"

"It does, I just can't find it. I felt it when I was here before, but I never really looked for the source. It was simply part of the place. Normally, in a church, it's at the altar, but I can't feel it here." She walked slowly past the staves and carved capitals toward the wall of the ancient church until she found what she was looking for a few feet in front of the huge doors of the north portal.

"Here." She knelt in awe as she felt the power of the place pulsing below the wood floor. "Can you feel it?"

Angelo laid his hand on the floor beside hers. "I feel something."

He swung the light up to the door panels. A marriage of the Norse Ragnarok and the Christian battle of Armageddon played out in the carvings—a first and last battle of evil and good. A large serpent coiled around the doors and curled upward. A four-legged creature that was supposed to be Christ's lion or the Norse Nidhogg, or both, swallowed the end of the snake at the bottom of the panel. For centuries, people had used these doors as the backdrop for sacrifice, prayer, christening, funeral, wedding. The lingering power of those moments would now serve Mouse in yet another ritual.

"This will be our center." She stood at a point about four feet from the door panels. She pulled the razor blade out of Angelo's backpack and started rolling up her right sleeve.

"Where's the salt?" Angelo asked.

"The salt works as a conduit, remember? But the spell is stronger if I build it with just blood."

"I have some to spare," he said as he lifted his wrist toward her.

"Thanks, but this one has to be all me. The nature of my blood makes the spell stronger." She saw the question in his eyes. "Because I'm—"

"Special," Angelo said as he nodded grimly.

Mouse swallowed against the knot in her throat as the words of Father Lucas came suddenly to her mind: *Ah, my little Mouse, you are a very special girl, did you know?* She was six and full of faith that God had made her special to do good in the world.

"If you are with me, I will try," she whispered now to herself. A tiny prayer for the only Father in heaven she thought would hear her.

She made the sign of the cross and then opened the vein in the bend of her right elbow and let the blood run down her arm into her cupped palm. She formed a circle of blood on the floor, keeping the church's point of power at the center. Once the circle was complete, she quartered it with another line of her blood. But Mouse knew they would need more than a single spell if she was right about the protections her father had likely embedded in the Devil's Bible. She walked to the center of the circle and, despite Angelo's hiss of disapproval, she opened the other vein at her left elbow. Using the center of the circle she'd just made, Mouse formed a pentagram with the flow of blood from both hands, mouthing the words of her second spell of protection. And, at the last, she took one step forward into the south spoke of the pentagram and made the sign of the fish and then repeated it on the other side.

She clenched her fists. Blood oozed through the creases of her fingers as she stepped toward Angelo and sat down hard on the floor at his feet. He pressed rolled gauze in the crooks of her arms and shoved a cracker in her mouth, hoping it would return some color to her face, but, impatient to be done, Mouse stood up quickly.

"Ready?" She turned toward the case before a wave of dizziness forced her to sit again, head hanging between her knees.

"Way to go, Superman." Angelo put an arm around her back to support her.

"Thanks, Lois," she teased weakly.

After a few more minutes and another cracker, Mouse felt strong enough to stand, slowly and with Angelo's help this time. They moved the Devil's Bible to the center of the three protective spells Mouse had woven. Stray drops of her blood were on the floor where they laid the book. She knew it would stain the white calfskin cover. If it ever made it back to the library, Eva Hedlin would be pissed. Mouse couldn't help but smile at the thought.

She stood with her back to the north portal doors, and Angelo handed her the paper containing the spell lifted from her father's manuscript. He held a damp cloth in his other hand; Mouse had wet it in the sink at the bathroom when Angelo had signed for the rental car.

"I need you to stay in that fish," she said to him as she pointed to the place opposite her. "No matter what happens. Do not leave that spot. You might see things or hear things. They might tell you that you need to get out of the church. But it'll be a trick. Close your eyes if you need to. Sing a song or something to keep the sounds out of your head. But don't leave the fish unless . . . unless I touch you and tell you to run." Mouse felt confident that the three spells built with the power of this ancient place and her blood would shield them from the dangers in the book, but if her father showed up to keep her from getting the rest of the spell, their only hope—Angelo's only hope—was to run.

"What happens if I step out of the fish?" Angelo asked. At first Mouse thought he was just being curious as usual, but then she looked at his face. He needed to know the consequences to strengthen his resolve if things got bad.

"If we're going to be together—after—I'd like it if you were sane."

"Got it. Stay in the fish. Can I call mine Jonah?" He raised a playful eyebrow.

"I'm not sure I like how things ended up for him." The banter only made the growing fear worse. There was too much to lose, but Mouse saw no other way to win.

"I love you, Angelo." As she spoke the words to him for the first time, she realized that they formed their own kind of protection in this ancient place where so many others had wept and whispered the same oath.

"I love you, too." She heard his own desperate fear as he spoke. He didn't have much hope either.

Then they knelt.

The heat began to emanate from the text as soon as Mouse opened the book. She searched the first page for a letter formed in her father's blood. Knowing now how to see them and knowing the five words she needed to complete the binding spell, Mouse scanned the pages quickly, nodding almost as soon as Angelo had turned one page, ready for the next.

But she found nothing.

With each page, the heat increased, and Mouse realized that she could read the book now without the flashlight. They were surrounded by an eerie blue glow, and the air was thick with the smell of rotten eggs. She could hear voices whispering in the shadows, and she saw dark outlines moving against the walls and between the staves beyond the circle of blood.

She nodded again, but Angelo didn't turn the page. She looked up. His head snapped, looking over one shoulder and then the other as he tried to hear what the voices were saying, tried to make out the figures lurking in the darkness.

"Angelo." She tapped the book to get his attention.

"Sorry." He turned the page. "I'm all right. You focus on the book." He tried to smile, but it looked more like a grimace.

The look of fear in Angelo's face and the sweat that dropped from his jaw down to the bloody floor forced a cold calm on her. She had to find the rest of the spell. She had to find it now.

Mouse lowered her head into her hands as she worked to understand the nature of her father's game. He had hidden his manuscript in a place important to both of them, where they had learned something about each other, shared their fears and hopes. And he had put the first part of the spell in the story that he alone had created; he had been proud of it. So what had she been proud of? What had she created from her own self and experiences?

"It's in the art, not the text!"

The joy of discovery was short-lived as Mouse saw the strain those few moments had added to Angelo's face. He was staring past her. She turned. Dozens of creatures prowled just beyond the circle, threading in and out of each other like a writhing mass. They were like the thing in Humlegården.

"The spell's holding." Angelo said it over and over again as he watched the creatures. "The spell's holding."

Frantically, Mouse tried to figure out where to start. There were too many pictures in the Devil's Bible to search them all. She needed to think like her father, to see his pattern, assess him like she would any adversary. But she could hear Angelo panting. She couldn't think.

The most obvious place to start was her father's portrait. She flipped to the facing pages of Satan and the empty Heavenly City entombed in red walls. Mouse forced herself to breathe slow and deep, letting the foul air of the church singe her nose, and then she closed her eyes again to concentrate. When she opened them, staring into her father's distorted image, she saw the word trailing along one of the clawed fingers of his right hand. She laughed in relief as she reached out for the rag gripped in Angelo's hand. But the laugh died in her throat when she looked at him. He had folded in on his knees and was rocking himself back and forth, whining to the rhythm of the hissing shadows.

"Shut up!" she screamed at the creatures. Mouse felt the power in her father's book snake a tendril toward her. The dark things went quiet for a moment. Angelo did, too.

She pulled the rag free from Angelo's hand and pressed it against the parchment until the faintest trace of the word scripted in her father's blood transferred onto the paper she held.

"Only four more, Angelo. I'm hurrying." In her mind, she recited the words of the last line of the spell over and over again.

Her lips were dry and cracked as the heat intensified. Angelo's hair was matted against his face with sweat. As Mouse looked down to the book, she noticed that the blood on the floor had darkened and no longer shined in the dim light. She followed the line of her patterns outward.

"No, no, no," she moaned.

The heat licked the moisture from the blood. At the outermost circle, she saw thin flakes of dried blood curl up from the floor and rise in the hot air. Mouse's spells were unraveling.

A panicked urgency pierced her mind with icy clarity. She knew where the next word would be. She yanked the pages of fragile parchment back to the Book of Esther.

Mother Kazi had often read Mouse the story of the reluctant queen who was offered a powerful opportunity to help her people. To honor the only mother she had ever known, Mouse had decorated the front page of Esther with an image of the squirrel that had led her astray in the woods as a child so long ago—the trip where Mouse lost herself and found the first of her gifts, the ability to see souls. At Podlažice, Mouse had never mentioned the power she had to see inside someone, but, as she worked on the book of Esther, she had told her father tenderly about Mother Kazi. He had noted what the old woman meant to Mouse, and he had hidden the word of the spell, penned lightly in a bloody reddish brown, in the fur on the squirrel's tail. It was almost invisible. Mouse pressed the rag, quickly transferring the word onto the parchment.

She grabbed the corners of the book, ready to flip to the next image, when she felt it. One of the creatures had penetrated the circle. It raced up and down the spokes of the pentagram as if held by some invisible leash, keeping it just shy of its prey.

Time was running out, but Mouse understood her father's pattern now. It was quite sentimental; it was their story—her father's and hers. As she expected, the third of the five words was hiding in her painting of Earth: her home and her father's conquest. The fourth was in the elaborate initial she'd crafted for the beginning of the history of Bohemia; she found the word along the back of a piece of ivy.

Angelo's moan pulled her sharply from the search. He was looking around wildly as the figures, now hundreds of them, snarled and spat only a foot away.

"Close your eyes, Angelo. They can't get to you. Just don't look at them. I'm almost done."

And then the creatures broke through the pentagram. A single line of her blood now shielded them; it was already beginning to peel away from the floor. She was out of time.

Mouse turned the pages by handfuls, the parchment squeaking in the heat and tearing at the seams. The colorful initial from the beginning of Kings lay before her, and her father's pattern was made complete. Him, her, Earth, Bohemia, and a king—a multilayered symbol in their epic story. Her grief at a king's death had brought her father to her. Her father's jealousy of a king had led to her birth. It was what he wanted and what he offered her—a king's power.

The final word lay boldly along the spine of the giant initial. It was the first word of the last line of the spell he had built in his own blood. Mouse pressed the rag against the crackling parchment and pushed down on the piece of paper holding the words of the spell. She bent to see some trace of the word, proof she had what she needed. Her hair curled on the manuscript as she lowered herself closer and closer to the script.

But there was no word there. She yanked the rag from behind the sheath of parchment. It was completely dry.

"Oh God, oh, God," she whimpered.

She lifted the rag to her mouth and tried to spit, but her mouth was too dry. She frantically licked at the back of the page, trying to moisten it just enough to release some trace of her father's blood, but her tongue scratched against the ancient goatskin like a cat's.

Defeated, she laid her head on the page, the heat of it cracking the soft flesh inside her nose as she breathed. A trickle of sweat rolled across her cheek. Almost giddy with hope, Mouse ran her hand along her face and under her hair at the back of her neck until her palm glistened with sweat. She placed the paper on top of the last word of the spell and pressed her wet hand at its back, squeezing to be sure enough moisture soaked into the old parchment to lift her father's blood from its hiding place. When she was sure she had it, she folded the paper with the spell and shoved it inside her shirt.

And then she looked up.

The church glowed like the heart of a smithy's fire. Small tendrils of flame curled around the capitals at the base of the staves and wound their way up the columns toward the high ceiling, looking for fresh oxygen. Mouse slammed the book closed.

"Angelo! It's time to go." She looked up. He was still sitting in his fish, his eyes clouded and blank. "Angelo?"

She crawled toward him, but the moment she crossed the outline of the fish, the prowling creatures pressed down on her, suffocating her. Mouse started to draw from the power in the Devil's Bible to force them back, but her father's taint washed over her with a cold craving to pull the burning church down and crush them all—demons and book and Angelo and her.

"I won't. I won't." Mouse dug her fingers into her hair, her nails cutting into her scalp as she pushed against the presence trying to twist its way into her mind like it had in the library. She willed herself to stand, legs shaking from the strain.

She grabbed Angelo by the shoulders and dragged him to the north portal doors as the creatures stalked between the pews, savoring the hunt as they tightened the circle around their certain prey. Mouse couldn't stop the high sob of fear rattling in her throat as she kicked hard at the latch in the middle of the doors, again and again, until finally they flung open into the darkness of the early morning, and she pulled Angelo across the threshold.

The fire behind them inhaled the fresh air like a dragon taking a breath before its final attack.

Mouse turned back for the Devil's Bible.

She knew it was stupid, but it was the only testament she had to the life she had lived over seven hundred years ago—a marker for the girl she had been, for the innocence she mourned. And she needed to know that her penitence for Marchfeld still lived somewhere in the world.

Mouse grabbed the cover of the massive book and tried to drag it toward the open doors. She'd only made it a few inches before a tongue of flame flicked over her head toward the portals, tasting the cool morning.

The creatures had grown oddly still.

"Mouse!" Angelo had recovered in the clear air and ran past her to the other side of the Devil's Bible, lifting his side while Mouse hoisted hers and shuffled backward to the door.

As she crossed the threshold, she saw the pillar of flame too late.

She knew this flame. She had seen it many times before—at night and alone in her room at the abbey.

The column of fire uncoiled.

Moloch stepped through the yellow-orange tongues and into the tiny church.

"Daddy sent me to play, little Mousey." His human form melted from him. Heavy lids hung low over the dead eyes of a bull, and his nostrils flared with desire as he shook his massive head, flinging drool across the nave. It sizzled as it landed on the burning staves.

Angelo turned to look behind him.

The beast's horns raked the medieval chandelier that hung in the center of the church. Moloch stretched lazily and rested a hand on the staves at either side of the aisle.

"Run, Angelo!" Mouse screamed. But Angelo couldn't hear her over the roar of flames and the howls of the dark things that massed now at Moloch's feet.

Mouse stepped forward, put her hand around Angelo's arm and pulled.

He didn't move.

Angelo was staring at the hypnotic glow of Moloch's skin, which pulsed like smelted copper.

"Come here."

Mouse looked up at Moloch's command, but it was Angelo who started walking forward. She ran to catch him, wrapped her arms around him, and pulled back hard. Angelo turned, blank faced, and shoved her against the enclosed pews. By the time she got to her feet, Angelo was almost in arm's reach of Moloch.

Mouse knew what would happen because it had happened to her over and over again as a child. When Moloch came, he would wrap his hands around her, pull her to his chest, lift her in his arms, and cradle her like a baby. Moloch loved children. It was the one thing he wanted and the one thing he could never have. That his tender embrace scorched their skin until it blistered and boiled and then burst into flame did not matter to him. He heard their screams as adulations of love. Because of what she was, Mouse had never burned quite like the others and she healed quickly, though she felt the pain all the same.

But Angelo was not like her.

Moloch had his hand raised over Angelo's head, holding him there poised like a plaything. "Daddy said to tell you he had something for you, little Mousey," Moloch said. "A pretty present that you've been wishing for."

"You're lying." But she knew it was just how her father would play. He'd said it himself—honey to draw in his little fly.

"It's a happy little soul—just for you. Your daddy said he stole it from someone, and he wanted me to give you a choice. You can have the soul you've always wanted in exchange for this"—his head swiveled toward Angelo—"and the little spell you've made."

Mouse dropped to a crouch, her mind racing through her options. But she didn't have any.

There wasn't enough power in the old church for her to use—not to beat Moloch and the creatures and the fire and the Devil's Bible. The power that lurked in the ancient book sensed her desperation and tempted her with whispered promises of revenge and victory, but she knew that power would corrupt her. She wouldn't care what happened to Angelo, then. He would burn with all the rest of them.

Mouse shook her head.

"Is that an answer?" Moloch sounded hopeful. "'Cause I'd like to play some more. Wouldn't you?"

He lowered his hand closer to Angelo's head. Mouse could see the hair as it lifted with the heat, twisting as it singed.

"No! Wait!" she screamed, but there was no way Mouse could win, and save Angelo, too.

"I'm tired of waiting, girl." The flames flared as Moloch spoke.

Mouse knew there was another source of power she could tap.

Ever since Bishop Sebastian's warnings about how her father meant to use her, Mouse had called up the memory of Marchfeld, playing it over and over in her mind, searching for something to challenge the Bishop's understanding of what she was.

But Mouse had discovered the truth instead.

That day on the field, when the power erupted from her with her words of mercy for Ottakar, it had claimed two armies, but it was only a peck compared to what she was capable of. Since then, she had locked it up inside her again, but she knew: If she let herself really embrace that power, if she truly let it loose, she could easily be the weapon Bishop Sebastian thought her to be.

Mouse had been running from that power most of her life, terrified that using it would make her like her father. The power would be one with her, not some separate thing she could lock away inside herself as she'd done all these years. She would be giving in to her nature and accepting what she was—her father's daughter. And that surely meant that any hope of redemption was gone; any hope of a soul, gone; any hope of being good, gone, too. Father Lucas's dream of her as his *andílek*, as his angel, would die.

But Angelo would live.

The heat sucked her tears as they formed. Mouse closed her eyes and, for the first time, she opened herself fully to her father's legacy. She let go of her resistance, threw open the gates of the cage she'd made all those years to keep herself separate from it, and she let the power free.

As it consumed her, she realized she had no control over it. The intensity of it boiled her lungs as it answered her summons.

"Go back!" Her lips bubbled and blistered as the power poured from her and slammed into Moloch and the dark creatures hovering behind him—and into Angelo. She watched in horror as his body flew into the stone altar, his head bouncing off its edge with a sickening crack.

The creatures clawed the floor as they were pulled back into the dark nothingness from which they'd come. Moloch screamed with fury as the column of flame encircled him once more and then disappeared. The flames and heat were gone, too, leaving the scorched remains of the ancient church.

But now Mouse was burning.

Inside her, the full power was loosed and running through her body, claiming it as its own. Her muscles seized in revolt and her teeth sank into her tongue as she convulsed. Searing bright spears of pain shot through her like millions of nerves flayed and exposed to the open air.

Mouse dropped to her knees, hurling bile and blood, until finally the heaves quieted and she fell to the floor.

Despite her fear for Angelo, Mouse waited. She needed to know if she was still herself or something else—something not safe. She felt wrong, different somehow, but she seemed to be in control, and so finally, Mouse crawled through the ash toward the altar where Angelo lay unmoving, a pool of blood spreading from his head.

CHAPTER TWENTY-FIVE

od, please let him live. I'll do anything." She laid her head on Angelo's chest. "I'll give him back to you if that's what you want. Just please let him live."

"I . . . don't . . . think . . . God barters, Mouse." His voice was distorted with pain. "But thanks for the thought."

She ripped his shirt off and wrapped it tightly around his head, pressing hard against the gash near the base of his skull as she tried to stop the bleeding. "Can you sit?"

He started to push himself upright while Mouse helped support his neck. He opened his eyes, and she gasped at the blood seeping from the burst capillaries there. His eyes were unfocused.

"Maybe you should—" As she spoke, he lurched to his knees, vomiting. "We need to get you to a hospital."

Her arms were quivering with fatigue by the time she had half-carried Angelo down the hill to the car, but adrenaline was driving her through the exhaustion. When she lowered him into the passenger seat of the rental car and bent to let down the seat back, he whispered to her, "Go back and get the book." His speech sounded slurred.

"There's not time, Angelo."

"Yes there is. Don't . . . argue. Do it."

He was unconscious by the time she got back in the car.

⊶

The sun had started to filter past the shades on the window of the room at the hospital when they rolled him in. Mouse moved to the side of his bed. His face bluish and bruised, Angelo looked more dead than asleep. And it was her fault. Her father hadn't done this to him. She had.

"Mr. D'Amato is suffering from a bad concussion," the doctor said. "He's very disoriented and he's lost a good bit of blood, but he's out of any immediate danger. I want to keep him for a few days. Heads can be tricky sometimes."

Mouse was too drained to do more than nod as the doctor left.

She reached a hand out to touch him, but she shook with a sudden tremor—one of many that had coursed through her as she'd waited for the doctor to bring Angelo back to the room. It was the power of her father's blood melting into her, touching every part of her, branding her. Mouse jammed her hands in her pockets. She was afraid to be alone with him. Her fingers closed around Angelo's cell phone and offered an easy excuse to leave.

She stepped out of the room, speaking quietly into the phone and hesitating a moment as she worked to remember which name to give. She'd used the courier service many times over the years for pieces of art or historical artifacts, but not for anything quite like this. The man was polite and efficient. They would have someone there that afternoon to pick up the Devil's Bible, though they didn't know what they were transporting. They were too discreet to ask. Mouse only cared about getting rid of it. It was a beacon for her father and a temptation for her. She left instructions and the key to the trunk at the front desk.

Angelo was awake when she got back. She stopped in the doorway.

"There you are," he said.

"How are you?"

"Head hurts. Come here."

Mouse walked slowly to his bed and kissed his forehead. "The doctor says you're going to be fine."

"You smell like smoke." He wrinkled his nose.

"Sorry. No shower."

He finally opened his eyes enough to reassure Mouse that he was alive and he was sane. "I'm starving."

"I bet I can take care of that." She turned to leave, but Angelo wouldn't let go of her hand.

"Don't go."

She pushed a button on the bed and told the nurse that Angelo was hungry.

He patted the bed and, with a groan, moved his body to make room.

"Sore?" she asked, but she wouldn't sit beside him.

"Yeah. What'd you do to me?" He meant it as a joke, but Mouse cringed anyway. "I don't remember the last of it. We got out. But we went back inside the church to get the book, right?"

"I did. And then you stupidly followed." She tried to banter.

"You couldn't get it by yourself."

"I know. Stupid me, stupid you. Monkey see, monkey do." She was working too hard at keeping things light, but Angelo didn't seem to notice.

"Then what?"

Mouse waited as the nurse wheeled in a tray with food and checked Angelo's vitals, asking him his name and the date. After the nurse left, Mouse told him everything: Moloch, the control he'd had over Angelo, her opening herself completely to the power inside her.

When she finished, Angelo put his fork down. "Are you all right?"

"I had no choice, Angelo."

"We need to figure out what this means," he said carefully.

Mouse nodded. "Not now, though. I'm too tired."

"You look it. Have you slept at all?"

She shook her head, the unexpected sadness making her afraid to talk.

"Mouse, promise me something." He didn't open his eyes as he spoke. "Promise me that you'll do for me what you did for Ottakar. If something takes me like that again, controls me . . . I can't stand the idea that I might do things. Do you understand?"

"I understand." And she did, too well. Mouse closed her hand around the piece of dried-out tracing paper in her pocket that held the residue of her father's blood.

"So promise. You'll do it. A word of mercy when the time comes." He was asleep before she could answer.

Mouse could never make such a promise. She watched him sleep for a moment, aware that he would dream of all the things he might be forced to do. Angelo had given her a night of peaceful sleep, and she had brought him nightmares.

She turned and left the room. Mouse found what she needed in the little village down from the hospital. She left it in the car for later.

⊙━✦━⊙

The warmth in Angelo's eyes froze her midstride when she entered the room again. No one had ever been that happy to see her come back. Mouse worked hard to smile, too, but she couldn't. She bent over him, her hair tickling his cheek, and gave him a long kiss.

"That's a nice hello." His voice grew soft with desire. "Can I have another?"

Mouse let him pull her face back down to his.

"Where've you been?" he asked when he finally pulled away and laid back on the pillow.

"On an errand," she offered cryptically.

"More secrets." He grinned. "I can get it out of you. I always do."

But Mouse couldn't maintain her end of the playful banter. There wasn't enough time.

"What's wrong, Mouse?"

"Nothing. I just . . . I guess I'm tired."

"Come up here beside me." He moved over to make room.

She hesitated but then sat down and pulled her legs up on the bed. Angelo wrapped his arm around her. She turned on her side toward him, her leg draped over one of his. She listened to his heartbeat and matched her breathing to the regular rise and fall of his chest.

Angelo bent and kissed the top of her head. A quiet groan escaped him as he lowered his head back to the pillow.

Mouse sat up and looked at him. "Head still hurt?"

"Yes."

"The doctor said they'd give you something for that. Want me to ask the nurse?"

"Do you mind?"

Once the nurse had come and gone, the drugs relaxed him almost instantly.

"You sleep, too," he said.

She rested her head on his chest; he was already asleep. She lay there, counting his heartbeats for a while, careful to keep herself awake. When it was time, she closed her eyes, searching for Angelo's soul. She memorized how it pulsed, how it stretched beyond his body to reach out to her and cover her in its glow. It was all the good-bye she could manage.

Even in the solitude of the car, Mouse would not let the tears come because she knew the pain would wipe away everything else—the joy of being with him, the wonder of being loved by him, the pleasure of their lovemaking. She concentrated on driving to Oslo and focused on what would face her when she reached her final destination.

The nurse woke Angelo during the early morning shift-change to check his vitals and make him walk to the bathroom. Groggy from the rude awakening, Angelo noticed Mouse's absence but assumed she must have gone to eat or something. He didn't notice the guitar in the chair until he wobbled back to his bed.

He smiled, sure that this was Mouse's way of holding him to his promise that he would play for her, but when he moved the guitar up to the bed with him, he saw Mouse's christening angel. There was a piece of paper folded underneath it. And he knew.

Her note was simple, final:

Angelo,

Play.
Heal.
Know you have given me more in a handful of days than I have ever known.

I am yours, forever.
Mouse

Angelo squeezed the angel, ready to fling it across the room, but as he lifted his arm to throw it, the realization that it was the only thing of hers left to him stilled his hand. Instead, he brought it to his lips, tears falling on its head like an anointment. He made the sign of the cross as he whispered the Prayer of Protection: "Oh, God, grant her Thy protection, and in protection, strength, and in strength, understanding."

⊙━✦━⊙

The thrust of takeoff pushed Mouse back against her seat. She clutched at the little wooden mouse rolling in her hand. It was just before six in the morning Oslo time; she would land in Tel Aviv in about seven hours. She hadn't slept since that night on the train to Onstad—the night she made love with Angelo. She couldn't sleep now either. She still had decisions to make, and yet all her mind wanted to do was relive the moments she'd spent with him. With a quiet awareness that this was probably the only time she'd have to grieve, Mouse gave herself over to the memories. She didn't think she had much choice in the decisions to come anyway. She laid her head against the window and watched the clouds curl across the wings and then plummet into the darkness beyond.

CHAPTER TWENTY-SIX

Tel Megiddo rose from the flat terrain like a large wart.

Mouse had rented a car in Tel Aviv and driven out into the Israeli countryside. She parked her car behind a row of trees and waited until the sun dropped behind the distant hills. Once darkness descended, she got out and crept up the back side of Megiddo. The site was relatively easy to access with just a few after-hours security guards at the far bottom of the hill. And it was sufficiently remote. Mouse needed to be alone.

She also needed the deep power of the place. The soil at Megiddo was saturated with the blood of battles and sacrifices, consecrated by hundreds of ceremonies, and marked with the ruins of dozens of churches from a dozen religions. Even contemporary politicians sanctified the place in the name of peace as they shook hands over empty agreements. Believers knew it was where the end would begin, the final battle between good and evil, though theirs was a different vision of Armageddon than her father's—epic versus intimate, multitudes versus the beat of a single heart.

No matter whose vision and regardless of politics or faith, the land seethed with pent-up power just waiting to be used.

Once she reached the top of the hill, Mouse lay down among the relics and ruins to catch her breath and to summon her strength. She wasn't the first to do so. For thousands of years, people here had looked down on massing armies as they prepared to brutalize each other in the fields below, blessing the good and cursing the bad.

But they all murdered each other's sons. They all prayed to some form of God. They all sought power in his name. All of them raped and pillaged. Mouse couldn't see the black or white, the good or bad. They were all pieces on the board, and she was just a pawn. How was she supposed to know what was right? What did Mouse know of good?

Despite her searching, Mouse had never found so much as a flicker of light inside to prove her goodness. And now that the power ran freely in her, now that it *was* her, surely that made her something other than just Mouse. Was she a demon now? After spending so much of her life hoping to be Father Lucas's *andílek*, his angel, to now be a creature that belonged in the pit at Houska with the hollow-eyed children was more than Mouse could bear. She sat up weeping. She had spent her long life running away from being her father's daughter, and now that was all she was. How could she not be, with his blood in her veins and now his power coursing through her body?

A wild keen of the wind sweeping over the mound was the only response, so she looked for an answer inside herself. Her eyes ached as they rolled back in her head searching for even a tiny glow. Angelo had sworn he saw it in her, and Father Lucas had believed, begging her in the last words of his letter to "be strong and believe in your goodness as I do." But still Mouse found only darkness.

As she opened her eyes again to the stars, Mouse saw a low bank of clouds moving in from the south. The ancients had asked the same questions about their purpose: What were they here for? What were they meant to do? Their stories were no different than hers, and their answers weren't simple either. Gilgamesh or Garuda, Helen or Baba Yaga. They were all both hero *and* villain, truth seeker *and* fool, killer *and* redeemer. And so much more. Angelo had said something like this, too—that the world was not made of good or bad, dark or light, but of shades and degrees; that our purpose was to find the light in ourselves and others. *Compassion, understanding, harmony*—that's what Angelo had said he thought God wanted.

What if he was right? Mouse stood up, wiping the tears from her face. Some part of her had accepted this idea in regard to others—that there was good and bad in everyone. But she still saw herself the way the world saw her when she was young: all those faces afraid of her and of what she could do, the Church closing its doors because she was tainted with her father's blood. She'd let all of them frame her understanding of herself. Even now, she'd let Bishop Sebastian define her as a weapon, as a warrior. But what if he was wrong? What if Angelo was right?

If the world was made in shades of both good and bad—did that mean she was, too?

And what about her father?

Flashes of lightning illuminated the towering storm as it slid toward the mound. She thought about her father and the story he told of his fall. She knew what he had been before and what he was after, but she found herself wondering for the first time what he *could* be.

Mouse needed answers to those questions before she could decide what to do. She knelt and took a razor from her pocket, made the quick slit at her bruised, swollen wrist, and shaped the circle quartered by a cross in the chalky gravel where she had just lain. She let the blood flow long and soak deep into the soil.

Then she sat just outside the circle and pulled the folded paper from her pocket. She called the power of Megiddo's sacred soil to her. The ground around her was so overcharged with energy that the hairs on her arms lifted and stood on end. She would not tap the power that was now fully part of her, not yet, not until she needed it. *If* she needed it. Mouse ran her finger along each word of the binding spell as she spoke it, and as soon as each word left her lips, the letters disappeared from the page.

There was nothing but darkness inside the circle, and for a moment, Mouse thought the spell hadn't worked. But then the darkness grew—billowing up in a column and out where it stopped like it was trapped in a glass cylinder. It also grew darker, as black as the pit at Houska. There was a loud sound, as if the sky was being torn in two, and the darkness was pared away in an instant to reveal the outline of a man.

Her father filled the circle as he swung to look her in the face.

"Bad timing." He spit the words, though he gave her his most charming smile. He held his human form and wore his typical black clothes and cloak, making it difficult to see him against the darkening sky.

"Hello, Father." Mouse tried to sound normal.

"You need to let me go. I'm in the middle of something very important. I'll come right back as soon as I'm done. Promise." He snarled the threat as thunder crashed in the distance and rolled toward them with a high peal.

"This is a one-time spell, and I've gone to a lot of trouble to get it," Mouse said. The fire behind his eyes frightened her, but she tried to match his sardonic tone. "Anyway, I just want to talk."

"Talk?" His voice exposed his wariness, and Mouse wondered what he thought she could do to him.

"Well actually, to ask a question," she said calmly.

"I don't have time for questions." He ran his fingers through the air just inches in front of her; the invisible barrier sparked and squealed with electricity. Mouse felt the tingle of power, no longer just in her gut, but rippling along every nerve, ready for her command.

"You're here because I brought you, and you can't leave until I let you." She meant to keep her voice soft and steady, but the power charged it with command. "Now sit!"

He did. But Mouse could feel him testing the binding spell, leaning into it, raking bits of gravel against the barrier of her blood. "I'll find my way around this spell. Do you have any idea what I'll do to you when that happens?"

"Your threats mean nothing. You're not going anywhere."

He threw his head back and rage tore through his throat. He reached an arm up to the sky and pulled. A rope of lightning ripped through the curtain of air and struck the mound where Mouse sat.

But she wasn't there. She had anticipated what he would do. She laughed at the frenzy in his face, but the laugh unnerved her. She didn't sound like herself, and she could feel the power roiling in her, her nearness to him charging it with malevolence.

"If you're done with your temper tantrum, I'd like to know what you want," she said.

"That's my line, isn't it? Since you brought me here?" he said mockingly. "What I want is to get out of here. A storm's brewing." He grinned.

"What does that mean?" she asked, certain that he was about to prove the Bishop right, that a war was coming. If that were true, then she was playing with the souls of humanity at stake.

"I thought it was rather obvious." He pointed to the thundering sky.

"What do you want?" she repeated, her voice sharpened by the risk she was taking. She couldn't afford to keep playing games with him. She needed her answers now.

He crossed his legs, leaning back on his hands casually, his whole demeanor suddenly light, like he was at a picnic. "You mean with you?"

Mouse had seen his shifts in tone before, but she was in control of this conversation. "We'll get to that. I mean bigger picture."

He shrugged his shoulders. "What I've always wanted. The chance to prove that I'm right, that my way works better."

It was the same thing that Bishop Sebastian and his Novus Rishi wanted. They believed in their own rightness, and they wanted everyone else to believe it, too. They claimed to fight for God, but in Mouse's seven hundred years of experience, the Church and all its various fingerlings usually fought to serve their own interests, to expand their power and influence. They shunned the poor and closed their doors to the outcasts, to people like Mouse. They tortured and killed Father Lucas to get what they wanted. How could they be right? How could they be good?

"What's your way?" Mouse asked her father.

"No limits. No knocking down the tower when it gets too tall. No clipping the wings of angels." He lifted the edge of his cloak and revealed the disfigured knobs that jutted from his back. "That's cruel—to create beings with desires and then tell them they can't have what they want. Selfishness should be a virtue. Ambition, a virtue." His nostrils flared as he spoke, but he made it all sound so simple, his position almost reasonable.

And yet Mouse knew that he would do whatever it took to get what he wanted. He didn't care who got hurt in the process. Like Bishop Sebastian, her father justified any means necessary to achieve his ends. He could be cruel—she'd seen it. But he had also been kind and thoughtful to her. He wanted to know her, wanted to share himself with her. The Church never had.

"I may have lost the first battle," her father said, "but over the years, I've leveled the playing field—and the pendulum's about to swing in my favor."

Again Mouse was struck by how similar the Bishop and her father were. They both seemed eager for war. They both wanted to win. They wanted to control people. They wanted to control Mouse. She wouldn't let that happen—not to her or to anyone else.

"So you *are* preparing for a war," she said flatly.

He barked out a laugh. "War? What makes you think that?"

"Your demons have been more active." She sounded like an echo of the Bishop.

"Have they? I hadn't noticed."

"Why not? What have you been doing?" A little hope was blooming in her that she was right and Bishop Sebastian wrong.

"None of your business."

"Maybe I'll just make you tell me the truth." She ran her fingers across the blisters on her lips, flaking as they healed from her use of power at Onstad.

He snorted. "You're no good at bluffing. And I am no Moloch—you might find me more difficult to handle."

Mouse shrugged, but she'd seen the doubt flicker in his face. He didn't know the limits of her power any more than she did. "Tell me what you've been doing."

"No."

"Then you can stay where you are. See you." Mouse pulled her legs under her and started to stand.

He laughed. "That's my girl. Play as if you've got the better hand."

"I do."

"For the moment, but eventually your blood will fade. With time. And I have lots of that. I'll be out before you know it."

"Maybe. But I let my blood run deep into the dirt and wove the infinite power of this place into that binding spell. It's not going anywhere soon unless I will it. And I thought you had somewhere you wanted to be."

"I do. And I'll be quite angry if I miss the . . . event. I don't think you've ever seen me really angry." The first drops of rain made plumes of dust as they struck the ground like tiny bombs.

"Let's remember, I'm out here and you're in there. And I'm learning a little more about my gifts." She hissed the last word.

"Oh, all right. Fair's fair. You win. I suppose you ought to know anyway." He made her wait just one more moment. "You're going to be a big sister." He smiled.

"What?"

"I've been trying for a long time now—since before you, obviously. But ever since our time together at Podlažice, it has been my sole purpose. And yet every time, the little life would wither in the womb. Until now. I think this one will be like you—a survivor."

"You were planning for the birth of your child?" Mouse's eyes squinted in confusion. "The Bishop thought you were planning for war."

Her father's laugh boomed over the top of the mound and slipped down to the fields below in an echo that blended with the thunder. "Some things never change. Wars are good for their ratings, and, with me as the bogeyman, your bishop's sure to draw a crowd. But don't be a fool. I'm not in this for the warm fuzzies of being a daddy. This kid will serve the purpose you could have if you hadn't been corrupted with all that twisted theology. This one I'll raise myself to be my ally, to be a messiah for my side."

In those final days at Podlažice, Mouse had learned to read her father. She could hear now the loneliness behind his words, could see the tenderness hiding amid the scorn on his face.

"It's more than that, Father." Her voice was thick with compassion and understanding. "You know it, and I know it." The rain rolled down Mouse's back. "I never told you about the first gift I discovered, the gift that made me believe God meant for me to do good things in the world. I wonder if you have this gift, too?"

Her father looked away. "Don't."

"If you're like me, you've tried to see inside yourself, to find in you what you see in others."

"Stop."

"If you're like me, you've only ever seen darkness where others have light. You believe you have no soul. You believe you have no goodness in you. But you are made of God like everyone else." She was weeping. "Like me."

"Please, Mouse. Don't."

It was the first time he'd ever said her name. There was so much sorrow in it.

Mouse closed her eyes. Deep in the inky abyss of him, she saw it: a pinprick of light. Despite an infinite existence soaked in the lusts of his own sick will, he had not managed to rid himself of it fully.

Slowly she opened her eyes, her face full of naked joy.

"There's hope. For you and for me," she whispered. She couldn't wait to tell Angelo.

A flash of lightning illuminated her father's face, and in the blinding light, she saw his faith. His belief in what she said sheared his pride and his ego and exposed him for what he was—a wounded and lonely creature longing for home. The forgotten Son of Morning, the Bringer of Light cast into darkness, the Fallen Star.

Without thinking, Mouse reached out to comfort him, but the moment her hand crossed the circle, there was another flash of lightning and the spell broke.

Her father turned on her in an instant.

His hand lashed around her throat, claws digging into her. Charred, twisted flesh ripped through his smooth skin until his humanity lay in crimson tatters at his feet. He raised his face to the heavens and howled his defiance. But even in this distorted, demonic shape, Mouse could see the creature he had first been made to be, and he was beautiful.

"You don't want to do this," she said. Her mind was full of what he had once been and could be again. She understood now—by her own choosing Mouse could be whatever she wanted to be. And so could he. By *choice*, not by birth or fate or circumstance.

Rain bathed them in sheets.

Her father snarled and hurled her through the air. She slid across the graveled surface of Megiddo, rocks tearing the back of her shirt and ripping into her flesh until she rolled to a stop and jumped to her feet. He stalked to her left, and she pivoted to keep him in front of her.

"You think I want . . . reconciliation? To return to my cage like a good angel?" He spoke quietly, but his words were full of venom.

"I know you want to go home."

He moved faster than she could react. The sharp claws on his leg slammed into her left shoulder as she turned to dodge his attack. She felt the talons pierce her front and back as his foot rounded over her shoulder. The momentum threw her back to the ground and pinned her. As he shifted his weight, Mouse heard her collarbone snap. Her back arched as she screamed.

Her instincts cried out for her to fight back, to live—to call on the power that was now part of her and to crush her father beneath the raw force of her will. But Mouse would not give in to the violence. That was what her father thought he wanted.

"You may have wanted to match your adversary . . . son for son," she said, her body shuddering under his weight. "But at Podlažice, you wanted me to . . . love you."

She saw the fury dilate his eyes.

"People worship me. What need have I of you?" he hissed. Foamy spittle ran down his chin. The back of his clawed hand slammed into the side of her head and then raked gashes across her cheek. She rolled with the blow and then pulled herself to her knees. Her hair stuck to her face in the rain, water mixing with the blood that poured down her face.

She could see his mouth moving as he took slow steps, springing on his jointed, agile limbs toward her, but Mouse couldn't hear past the ringing in her ear. She felt her ribs break as he grabbed her around the abdomen and squeezed. He flung her across the mound again. As she landed against an outcropping near the edge, Mouse felt her chest sink in as she tried to draw breath. The skin pulled taut across her crushed ribs.

He spoke as he straddled her. She strained to hear him but could only make out one question at the end. "Why don't you fight back?" he asked. He was crying.

Mouse couldn't force enough air through her throat to answer, so he snatched it from her mind, which lay bared to him now: *Because I choose not to.*

"You're weak! Use your power!" He spat at her, his eyes pleading with her.

Not weak, Mouse thought. *Not like you.*

"That's your mother talking. Weak and human. And dead." The gravel crunched as he knelt, his weight settling on her broken chest. "Now let's see if you can die, too." He turned his face from her as he spoke.

His hand closed around her throat again, squeezing. Mouse heard the pop as one of his claws punctured the artery at the side of her neck.

Blood shot out across his face. His slit tongue flickered through his teeth and licked at the drops of red as they ran with the rain.

Mouse's throat and mouth filled with blood. She could feel him pulling something from her, like he was dismantling her cell by cell. She could feel him shaking as he wept. She only wanted the pain to stop. She was tired, ready to sleep.

But then her father turned back to her suddenly, his eyes glazed as he turned his concentration inward, his head cocked as if listening. Mouse had begun to close her eyes when she heard his peal of victorious laughter. She forced her eyes open and saw the corner of his cloak flapping in the wind and the stars sparkling behind him. The storm was passing.

"There is good news," he said as he knelt swiftly beside her, tenderly lifting a bloody lock of her hair from her forehead and tucking it behind her ear. Sobs lifted her broken ribs, and the air pushed through the holes in her chest with a high, gurgling whistle.

"It seems I finally have what I want," he whispered to her. "And you have a brother." He kissed her on the forehead and then took the edge of his bloody and torn cloak and folded it around himself, disappearing into the night.

As he released her, her body, already half-flung over the side of Megiddo, slid down the thorny brush of the hillside until she broke her fall against a lower outcropping.

A brother, Mouse thought. I must warn someone.

But there wasn't time.

Whatever her father had done to her had worked well. It felt different from the times before when the darkness had taken her; she always woke, then. But she didn't think she would this time. Mouse was dying. Suddenly she was afraid of what would happen after.

She wanted Father Lucas to hold her.

She wanted a lullaby so she could slip away peacefully.

She wanted Angelo.

She closed her eyes and searched the darkness, and, at the end, she saw the glow start with a faint flicker at her lips.

CHAPTER TWENTY-SEVEN

In the courtyard at the Muhraka monastery, moonlight dusted a statue of Elijah. He held his jagged knife raised, ready to fall on the unrighteous. Tall and white, the statue looked like a ghost watching Angelo slide out of the back seat of the car that had just pulled up. Angelo flung both his bag and the guitar Mouse had given him across his back, bending with the weight, his feet dragging on the chalky stone as he made his way to the door. He wondered if there would be anyone awake to let them in—it was nearly midnight. Haifa had been all but empty when they drove up to Mount Carmel.

"Wait for me, son," Bishop Sebastian called out as he leaned down to say something to the driver.

Angelo didn't turn around. He was still angry—angry that Mouse had left him and angry that he'd had to ask the Bishop for help. Angelo had called Bishop Sebastian just minutes after he had read Mouse's note, minutes after he'd finished praying for her. He didn't think prayers would be enough, so he had reached out to the only person he knew could help. And even though they did what he wanted, Angelo had been irrationally angry that the Bishop and his friends had tracked Mouse to Israel so easily. He was angry that it had been the Bishop and not him who figured out her final destination: Megiddo.

Angelo had been angry from the moment he spotted the Bishop waiting like a spider for him at the airport at Tel Aviv. But the dark news the Bishop had given him sent a silent rage running through him: The Bishop's men had found Mouse, bloody and broken, at the bottom of Tel Megiddo. On the drive to Haifa, with the salty air from the sea whipping through his open window, Angelo had not said a word.

As they took the last steps up to Muhraka, the Bishop laid his hand against the back of Angelo's head and neck. Twelfth century pilgrims had claimed the Arabic word for their monastery: sacrifice. "You should not be alone in this," the Bishop said.

The door opened, throwing out a rectangle of light, and a nun in brown habit and a black hood knelt to kiss the Bishop's ring.

"Where is she?" Angelo pushed his way past the nun, stumbling through the hall and looking into dark rooms to his left and right.

"Not here. Out in the guesthouse," the nun said quietly, not looking at him. "Follow me."

Angelo focused on the black of her back, putting one foot in front of the other. He couldn't breathe. He couldn't think. When the nun opened the door to the guesthouse, Angelo could not go in.

"Let me, son," Bishop Sebastian whispered as he eased past Angelo and into the too-bright room. Angelo leaned against the doorframe, hands on his knees, the guitar sliding from his shoulder to the floor with a hollow *thwong*.

"God, the Father of mercies, through the death and resurrection of his Son—"

Angelo's head snapped up as the Bishop began the sacrament of last rites. "Stop!" He took a step toward the bed that had been pulled into the middle of the room under the overhead light.

"You don't want to see her like this, son."

"I am not your son." His voice broke as he twisted around the Bishop and saw her. They hadn't covered her. She was naked; her clothes lay strewn on the floor beside the bed. They looked like strips of meat, dark red and dull. Mouse was white. She looked cold and hard as if she'd been carved of alabaster, but she was streaked with blood and the sheets ran red with it.

Angelo walked to her, slowly lowered himself onto the bed, his hand sinking into the sticky wetness.

"Why didn't you take her to a hospital?" The words came out stilted, each one a struggle. The Bishop had ordered his Novus Rishi friends to take Mouse to this obscure Carmelite monastery rather than to the hospital in Nazareth.

"You know why." The Bishop had come closer. "She's not normal," he muttered.

"She was gone before she got here, Father. I am sorry we could not save her. But, I think, no one could." The nun made the sign of the cross.

"She doesn't need you to save her." Angelo's rage wove with his grief and came out as a snarl, twisted in his tears and spit, as he turned and slammed his hands against the Bishop's chest, pushing him back toward the door. "Get out!"

"Angelo, you don't have to do this alone."

"I don't need you either. Now get out!"

"Let me pray—"

Angelo shoved the Bishop into the nun and rammed them both through the open door, slamming it shut and locking it as he leaned back against it, not able to stand on his own anymore.

The light over the bed hung low, swinging and raking Mouse with a harsh glare. Angelo reached over and flipped the switch, throwing the room into darkness. His mind toyed with him as it played oscillating images of Mouse alive and laughing, Mouse reaching up to kiss him, Mouse ripped apart by her father and lying in the dirt as the blood rushed out of her.

He flipped the switch again, but the truth under the light was worse.

His hand rammed down the switch once more, and he stumbled forward in the darkness, his eyes slowly adjusting as feathers of moonlight floated in through a tiny window near the ceiling. He knelt beside the bed, laid his face against her hand, and ran his fingers softly across the hole in her neck. Her face glowed in the light, and a sudden hope wrenched Angelo.

"Are you immortal?" he mouthed, not asking again but remembering.

"I can get hurt, but I always heal," Mouse had told him. But he had not forgotten the second part of what she had said: "I think there's at least one way I can die."

The understanding he'd had then felt like a curse now in the silent night.

Her father had done this to her. Did that mean there would be no healing?

Bishop Sebastian banged on the door.

As Angelo looked at Mouse's still face, her sunken chest, her white skin, his hope seemed foolish and cruel. But he willfully held to his faith anyway.

"May whatever good you do and suffering you endure, heal your sins, help you to grow in holiness, and reward you with eternal life." He whispered the last of the penance prayers given to the dead and dying as he walked over to his guitar.

He sat on the edge of the bed and began to play.

⊙━━◦

Mouse had been dead before, but this time was different.

Before, at Marchfeld and at the river when she hanged herself and when she threw her body down the mountain, she had still been aware of herself and the world around her like she was wrapped in darkness. But there had been flickers of light, echoes of sounds. There had been pain. And they had called her back to the world even when she did not want to go.

Now she so desperately wanted to live, but she was surrounded by a black nothingness like the pit at Houska—not merely wrapped in it, but immersed, baptized, lost. Nothing lived in all that blackness. No hope, no breath, no sound. And the silence frightened Mouse. She wanted to cry out, to call for Father Lucas. He had pulled her up out of the Mouth of Hell once before, but Mouse knew it was no use now. Father Lucas was gone. There was no one else to come looking for her in the dark.

She felt her memories floating away from her like ash on the wind. But something slipped into the emptiness just as she felt herself begin to drift down into the abyss. It was a sound, soft and beckoning. It touched the pieces of her that were floating away in the dark and made them shine like bits of gold leaf dancing.

The music swirled around her, weaving her back together, like river water carrying her deep, moving swiftly around the rocks, and then breaking the surface and glittering like handfuls of diamonds in the sun. Her chest filled with the burning need to breathe, so she opened her mouth like a hungry bird and waited for the water to flood her lungs and cool the hotness there.

And then Mouse remembered—she remembered the glow she had seen hovering at her lips as she died. She remembered Angelo. She remembered want, and she remembered pain. The abyss could take that away, but the music called her home.

Mouse would not go back into the dark.

⚬—✦—⚬

The nuns were demanding to be let in to wash the body and prepare it for burial when Angelo finally opened the door three days later. He was weeping.

"I am sorry, my son." The Bishop had finally left Angelo to hold his vigil in solitude with the hopes it would help him grieve and move on.

Squinting in the sun, Angelo looked up, smiling, and stepped aside to allow the women into the room. He laughed as they gasped. Mouse lay wrapped in clean bedding he had found in a trunk in the guesthouse. The bed had been pushed back against the wall and the plates of food the nuns had brought to Angelo lay scattered on the floor nearby. Mouse was too weak to sit and her throat too damaged still for even a whisper, but she blinked groggily at the nuns. When they started making the sign of the cross and murmuring prayers—some of thanksgiving and others for protection against evil—Mouse weakly waved them away.

Bishop Sebastian stepped into the space they left. "My God."

Angelo sat on the bed beside Mouse. "Ours, too," he said.

⊙━╋━⊙

A week later, Angelo came into the guesthouse reading a text on his phone. Mouse was taking shuffle steps around the room, balancing herself against the wall and trying to get her strength back. She was ready to go.

"Looks like your book made it home," he said.

Mouse cocked her head in question.

"Bishop Sebastian fielded a call from an irate Eva Hedlin. Apparently the Church made a very nice donation to the library which means I don't have to go to jail." He smiled at her. The Bishop had left without a word, but he was in daily contact with Angelo.

"And me?" Mouse laid her hand against the pain in her throat; she could still only manage a gravelly whisper. She smiled, too, but she was really just wading through the banter to talk about more serious matters.

"You're in the clear already. You were Emma Lucas to her, remember? That Emma doesn't exist anymore. So you're home free." He tossed his phone on the bed and wrapped his arms around her. She slapped him playfully on the arm.

They had been lightness and joy as Mouse continued to heal, though the nights were harder. They both struggled to sleep. They both suffered from dreams of fire and lightning, ashes and blood—but they were together, each helping the other through the darkness. And yet, Mouse noticed that Angelo would not talk about the days to come. It worried her and picked at the edges of her happiness, as did the certainty that she'd forgotten something important about her father. She could see him in her mind atop Megiddo and he was laughing—but she couldn't remember why.

Mouse looked down at the phone on the bed, its face still lit with the Bishop's text, and she wondered, not for the first time, what he meant to get out of helping them. "Can we go home?" she asked instead.

"What about your father?"

Mouse knew he was stalling; they'd had this conversation already. Had her father meant to kill her but couldn't? If so, then he would surely try again. Or had he meant to teach her a lesson, taking her to the edge of oblivion and then trusting that her immortality would heal her as it always had? If that were true, did it mean that he was finally convinced that she would be of no use to him? Or that he was saving her to play again another day? The questions were endless, and neither she nor Angelo had come up with any answers.

"It doesn't matter. Let's go home."

Angelo sighed as he sat heavily on the bed. "But where's that?"

Megiddo, the nothingness after, Angelo's music calling her back—these had taught Mouse that home for her wasn't a place. Angelo was home. And she wanted to be home for him as well.

"Rome?" she asked, not sure how to say the rest.

"Is that home for you?"

Mouse sank onto the bed beside him. She picked up the phone, pointing at the part of the Bishop's text that Angelo had not shared: ORDINATION SCHEDULED. ST. FRANCIS'S FEAST DAY.

"Is it for you?" she asked.

Angelo put his head in hands. "It's what he wants."

"Payment for helping us?"

"He didn't put it like that, but yes, I think so."

"Or what?"

He looked up at her, worry in his eyes. "He didn't say, but the Novus Rishi—they're everywhere, Mouse. I don't have a choice."

"Yes you do." She'd lived her life letting her father's blood, her gifts, and other people define who she was and what she was. She'd waited on God to give her a purpose. But Megiddo had shown her that it had been her choice all along. And the choices weren't simple—not either/or, good or evil, just a girl or something else. She was both; she was all.

Even now, the power ran through her freely but so too did the glow of a soul. She could feel them both dancing in her blood. What she did with them was up to her. Angelo had helped her see this, and she wanted to give the gift back to him even if it meant saying good-bye.

Wincing as she swallowed, she asked, "What do *you* want, Angelo?"

"Does it matter? Not to the Bishop." He spun to look at her, and she could see the tension in his face as the anger he'd been tethering while she recovered finally broke loose. "And not to you either."

"That's not true. I—"

"You? You left me in a damn hospital so you could go play the hero. Do you think that's what I wanted?" He shook his head.

"I was wrong."

"What?" The simplicity of her answer surprised him.

"I should have talked to you about it. I should've let you make your own choice. I'm sorry."

Angelo looked at her like he was trying to see inside her. Finally he said, "Never again. You promise? Promise that you won't run off and—" The grief of having lost her broke across his face, and his body started to bend in on itself, but she was there, slipping in under his arms, holding him and laying his head against her chest.

"I promise, Angelo."

His fingers dug into her back as if he was afraid she would disappear. "I can't live like that, Mouse. I can't lose you like that again."

"I promise, Angelo. Never again." She wove her fingers between his.

He laid back to rest against the wall and pulled her with him. "But if I don't go back and take my vows, the Bishop won't leave us alone," he said warily, turning back to the problem at hand. "He'll send the Novus Rishi to hunt us."

"Well, I'm pretty good at running." Mouse leaned into him. "And I know how to hide."

"But that's not home."

She turned, lifting her face to him. "*We* are home, Angelo," she said as her lips closed on his.

"Home," he breathed when she pulled back. He stood and tugged her up with him, slinging his guitar and bag over his shoulder. "Ready, then?"

"Always."

Epilogue

The man pulled back into the shadows at the crook of the wall and waited. He had an excellent view of the cemetery below and watched the Bishop weave through the Muslim dead as he made his way toward the Gates of Mercy. The sun had just begun to crawl up the Mount of Olives, and a few pale rays of light slid among the rocks.

As the Bishop neared, the man opened a small gate at the side of a wrought-iron fence that framed the enclosure. "Welcome, Brother." The man's voice rumbled deep in his throat.

Bishop Sebastian embraced the shadowy figure before lowering himself to a crouch, making himself less visible to passersby.

"What a place," the Bishop said, a little winded from the walk.

"A place of war. We fight our battles everywhere," the voice from the shadows answered. "Jews believe the Messiah will enter Jerusalem through this gate and usher in a new reign, so the Muslims walled it up and planted their cemetery to keep Elijah out."

"Christ came through this gate," the Bishop said.

"He ended up a casualty, too."

Toying with something in his hand, the Bishop kept silent.

"Well then, she is alive?" the man asked.

"Yes."

"But your plan failed."

"Was it my plan? I thought we all—"

"You convinced us that she could be more useful than dangerous."

"I believe it still."

"I am not as comfortable with risk at my age."

The Bishop held something out to the man in the shadows. "You must have faith."

"What's this?" The little wooden mouse lay in the palm of his hand. Part of its tail was missing and it was covered in scratches, the exposed wood stained with blood.

"A sign?"

The quiet chuckle rumbled in the man's chest like distant thunder. "Very well. But I have been cultivating my own alternatives." He turned and motioned into the deeper dark of the alcove behind him. "Bishop Sebastian, I'd like you to meet Jack Gray."

⚬━✦━⚬

Miles away, another priest ran his hand along the narrow passageway as he stooped under the low ceiling of the cave and stepped into the hollowed-out Chapel of the Innocents. The dim glow from the security lights disappeared into the deep niches carved along the walls, and he jumped as the iron gate clanked shut behind him.

The baby's whimper called up ghostly images of the little boys, victims of Herod's fear, who were supposedly buried under the ancient stone floor—dozens of them or thousands depending on who told the tale.

"Hush, little one. We'll get you fed in a moment. Hush." The child's father puckered his lips at the infant cradled in his arms and tenderly rocked his son from side to side.

The priest huddled at the altar a moment and then turned, pressing a cloth to his wrist, and he nodded to the father who was dressed all in black.

Patterns of blood pooled on the white marble. The father laid his baby in the center of the symbols and put his hand protectively on his son's chest. The priest muttered the words of consecration and protection as he walked slowly around the altar. His hand trembled as he made signs in the air. The dark ceremony was finished within minutes.

"Thank you," the father said as the priest turned to leave. "And Father, if you tell anyone about this—"

"You can trust me." The priest stammered in fear and relief. He had not expected to live.

"You know, why take chances?" As the father lifted his son from the altar, a sharp claw flashed from beneath the cloak and slid silently across the priest's throat just as he reached the low lintel of the chapel's opening. Blood showered the pew. Bright red drops of it landed on the baby's face and hands.

The father cuddled the infant to his cheek again, licked the blood away, and then began to hum a lullaby as he reached for the edge of his cloak with his free hand.

"Come, we have much to do, little one," he cooed to his son as they turned and disappeared into the night. "Let's play."

Acknowledgments

T hank you for reading *The Devil's Bible*. For those of you who haven't already Googled it, the Codex Gigas *is* an honest-to-goodness, real book. I've done my best to adhere to the knowable facts surrounding the production, history, and content of the Codex, and I am immensely grateful to the National Library of Sweden for their meticulous research and their generosity in providing digital access to the fruits of all their labor. Any errors regarding my depiction of the ancient artifact are most assuredly mine alone.

For all we know about the Codex Gigas, much of our understanding is still based on conjecture and presumption, and many of its secrets remain shrouded in the past. These gaps of the unknown offer a fertile playground for a writer to imagine what might have been. This is where Mouse lives.

I met Mouse there because I live there, too, in the in-between places where *should* and *should not* have no meaning. Growing up in the American South as the only girl sandwiched between two brothers meant that my life could have been booby-trapped with all the things I was supposed to do and all the things I wasn't allowed to do. But I got lucky. My brothers, Jim and Shane, helped me carve out my own space free of societal expectations. They never treated me like I was different or fragile because I was "just a girl." They've always believed in me, and I am beyond grateful that I've gotten to share this journey with them.

I am also thankful for my found sister, Beth Spencer Cummings, who has taught me that strength and vulnerability are woven of the same cloth.

Bringing Mouse and the story of *The Devil's Bible* to you has been, like any novel, a bit of a relay race. I am thankful for the critical eyes, thoughtfulness, and curiosity of my early readers: Rebecca Smith Crimmins, Mandy Plummer Hiller, Carolyn Wilson, and Erin Townsley Etheridge. The fabulous Amy Kerr was particularly helpful in being a fresh set of eyes when mine were bleary. And through the long days of editing when I was infected with self-doubt, I lived on Paige Crutcher's encouragement. Leanne Smith walks with me daily through the sometimes impossible obstacle course of life as a writer, professor, and mom. Together, we slay guilt and doubt and distraction.

Many thanks to my agent, Susan Finesman, for hanging in there with me and especially for walking me back from the cliff's edge—more than once. I couldn't have pushed this boulder up the hill without you at my side. As always, I am grateful for your guidance and your friendship.

I owe so much to all the incredible folks at Pegasus Books who are such thoughtful caretakers of the stories given to them. They clean up the messy parts, give the books beautiful covers, and then nurture them out into the world. Thank you Claiborne Hancock, Linda Biagi, Sabrina Plomitallo-González, Maria Fernandez, Jocelyn Bailey, Mary Hern, and Charles Brock. I am particularly indebted to Iris Blasi, my editor, for partnering with me in telling Mouse's story, for pushing me to tell the story better, and for asking all the right questions. Thank you for sticking with me, even through the dark valleys. Hopefully Mouse offered a little light in the darkness.

Having a community of fellow writers has been a lifeline for me. They are like the tether that keeps an astronaut safely connected to the shuttle but also frees her to take giant leaps of faith. Thank you, River Jordan, for introducing me to our Nashville writer's tribe, and thank you to all you wonderful creative women who feed me the courage to keep telling stories. A special note of gratitude to the brilliant J.T. Ellison for sharing the wealth of her experience and for showing me how to do this writer gig with kindness and generosity. You are an amazing woman.

I touch on the issue of homelessness in this book, and I want to express my deep respect and thankfulness for Lindsey Glenn Krinks, Lauren Plummer, and all the incredible people at Open Table Nashville for working tirelessly to address the injustices that are at the root of homelessness. May we all endeavor to be better neighbors to one another.

And finally, back in the crazy chaos of my own abode, I give thanks to my family. Thank you to my little guy for the sweet notes slid under the door at just the right times and for the hugs and kisses when I needed them. Thank you to my daughter who listened encouragingly as I read and worked through obstinate chapters and whose fierce independence shapes Mouse's own.

And thank you to my husband for reading, again and again, for making me laugh when I was ready to cry, and for gallantly taking the blows when I was angrily wrestling with the tough parts. *You* are my home. Always.